THE FOUNTAINS
OF SILENCE

THE FOUNTAINS OF SILENCE

RUTA SEPETYS

THORNDIKE PRESS
A part of Gale, a Cengage Company

Farmington Hills, Mich • San Francisco • New York • Waterville, Maine
Meriden, Conn • Mason, Ohio • Chicago

Thorndike Press® Large Print Young Adult.
The text of this Large Print edition is unabridged.
Other aspects of the book may vary from the original edition.
Set in 16 pt. Plantin.

LIBRARY OF CONGRESS CIP DATA ON FILE.
CATALOGUING IN PUBLICATION FOR THIS BOOK
IS AVAILABLE FROM THE LIBRARY OF CONGRESS

ISBN-13: 978-1-4328-7033-1 (hardcover alk. paper)

Published in 2019 by arrangement with Philomel Books, an imprint of Penguin Young Readers Group, a division of Penguin Random House, LLC

Printed in Mexico
1 2 3 4 5 6 7 23 22 21 20 19

For Kristina and John

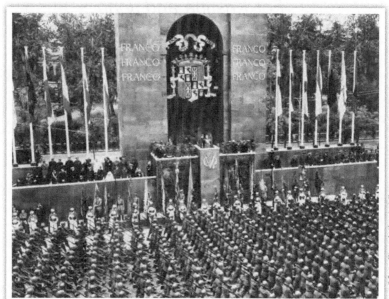

Francisco Franco's victory parade in Madrid celebrating his triumph in the Spanish Civil War. May 1939.

The Spanish Civil War (1936–1939) began as a military revolt against the democratically elected Second Spanish Republic and continued as an armed conflict between the Nationalists and the Republicans. The Nationalists were led by Generalísimo Francisco Franco and aided by Hitler and Mussolini. The Republicans were led by the democratic government at the time and aided by Mexico, the Soviet Union, and volunteers from over fifty countries, with support from academics, creatives, workers, unions, and leftists. Internally divided, the Republicans were not able to stop the Nationalist advance and surrendered in March of 1939.

Franco's dictatorship lasted thirty-six years.

We have only died if you forget us.

— anonymous epitaph
SPANISH CIVIL WAR MASS GRAVE

■ ■ ■ ■

PART ONE

■ ■ ■ ■

1957
Madrid, Spain

I've never been happy about sending an Ambassador to Spain, and I am not happy about it now, and unless Franco changes in his treatment of citizens who do not agree with him religiously I'll be sorely tempted to break off all communication with him in spite of the defense of Europe.

— HARRY S. TRUMAN, 33rd president of the United States August 2, 1951

Memorandum from Truman to Secretary of State Dean Acheson
Acheson Papers — Secretary of State File
Truman Library Archives

1

They stand in line for blood.

June's early sun blooms across a string of women waiting patiently at *el matadero.* Fans snap open and flutter, replying to Madrid's warmth and the scent of open flesh wafting from the slaughterhouse.

The blood will be used for *morcilla,* blood sausage. It must be measured with care. Too much blood and the sausage is not firm. Too little and the sausage crumbles like dry earth.

Rafael wipes the blade on his apron, his mind miles from *morcilla.* He turns slowly from the line of customers and puts his face to the sky.

In his mind it is Sunday. The hands of the clock touch six.

It is time.

The trumpet sounds and the march of the *pasodoble* rolls through the arena.

Rafael steps onto the sand, into the sun.

He is ready to meet Fear.

In the center box of the bullring sits Spain's dictator, Generalísimo Francisco Franco. They call him *El Caudillo* — leader of armies, hero by the grace of God. Franco looks down to the ring. Their eyes meet.

You don't know me, Generalísimo, but I know you.

I am Rafael Torres Moreno, and today, I am not afraid.

"Rafa!"

The supervisor swats the back of Rafael's damp neck. "Are you blind? There's a line. Stop daydreaming. The blood, Rafa. Give them their blood."

Rafa nods, walking toward the patrons. His visions of the bullring quickly disappear.

Give them their blood.

Memories of war tap at his brain. The small, taunting voice returns, choking

16

daydreams into nightmares. *You do re-member, don't you, Rafa?*

He does.

The silhouette is unmistakable.

Patent-leather men with patent-leather souls.

The Guardia Civil. He secretly calls them the Crows. They are servants of Generalísimo Franco and they have appeared on the street.

"Please. Not here," whispers Rafael from his hiding spot beneath the trees.

The wail of a toddler echoes above. He looks up and sees Julia at the open window, holding their youngest sister, Ana.

Their father's voice booms from inside. "Julia, close the window! Lock the door and wait for your mother. Where is Rafa?"

"Here, Papá," whispers Rafael, his small legs folded in hiding.

"I'm right here."

His father appears at the door. The Crows appear at the curb.

The shot rings out. A flash explodes. Julia screams from above.

Rafa's body freezes. No breath. No air.

No.

  No.

    No.

They drag his father's limp corpse by an arm.

"¡Papá!"

It's too late. As the cry leaves his throat, Rafa realizes. He's given himself away.

A pair of eyes dart. "His boy's behind the tree. Grab him."

Rafa blinks, blocking the painful memories, hiding his collapsed heart beneath a smile.

"Buenos días, señora. How may I help you?" he asks the customer.

"Blood."

"Sí, señora."

Give them their blood.

For more than twenty years, Spain has given blood. And sometimes Rafa wonders — what is left to give?

2

It's a lie.

It has to be.

I know what you've done.

Ana Torres Moreno stands two levels belowground, in the second servants' basement. She rips the small note to pieces, shoves them in her mouth, and swallows.

A voice calls from the hall. "Hurry, Ana. They're waiting."

Dashing through the windowless maze of stone walls, Ana wills herself to move faster. Wills herself to smile.

A weak glow from a bare bulb whispers light onto the supply shelf. Ana spots the tiny sewing kit and throws it into her basket. She runs to the stairs and falls in step with Lorenza, who balances an assortment of cigarettes on a tray.

"You look pale," whispers Lorenza. *"¿Estás bien?"*

"I'm fine," replies Ana.

Always say you're fine, especially when you're not, she reminds herself.

The mouth of the stairway appears. Light from a crystal chandelier twinkles and beckons from the glittering hall.

Their steps slow, synchronize, and in perfect unison they emerge onto the marble floor of the hotel lobby, faces full of smile. Ana scrolls her mental list. The man from New York will want a newspaper and matches. The woman from Pennsylvania will need more ice.

Americans love ice. Some claim to have trays of cubed ice in their own kitchens. Maybe it's possible. Ana sees advertisements for appliances in glossy magazines that hotel guests leave behind.

Frigidaire! Rustproof aluminum
shelving, controlled butter-ready.

Whatever that means. Beyond Spain,

all is a mystery.

Ana hears every word, but guests would never know it. She scurries, filling requests quickly so visitors have no time to glance out of their world and into hers.

Julia, the matriarch of their fractured family, issues constant reminders. "You trust too easily, Ana. You reveal too much. Stay silent."

Ana is tired of silence, tired of unanswered questions, and tired of secrets. A girl of patched pieces, she dreams of new beginnings. She dreams of leaving Spain. But her sister is right. Her dreams have proven dangerous.

I know what you've done.

"For once, follow the rules instead of your heart," pleads her sister.

Follow the rules. To be invisible in plain view and paid handsomely for it — five *pesetas* per hour — this is the plan. Her older brother, Rafael, works at both the slaughterhouse and the cemetery. Between two jobs he makes only twelve *pesetas,* twenty cents according to the hotel's exchange desk, for an entire day's work.

Ana hands the sewing kit to the concierge and heads quickly for the staff elevator. The morning is gone, but her task list is growing. Summer season has officially arrived at the hotel, pouring thousands of new visitors into Spain. The elevator doors open to the seventh floor. Ana shifts the basket to her hip and hurries down the long corridor.

"Towels for 760," whispers a supervisor who shuttles past.

"Towels for 760," she confirms.

Four years old, but to Ana, the American hotel smells new. Tucked into her basket is a stack of hotel brochures featuring a handsome bullfighter, a matador, holding a red cape. In fancy script across the cape is written:

Castellana Hilton Madrid. Your Castle in Spain.

Castles. She saw old postcards as a child. The haunting newsreel rolls behind her eyes:

The tree-lined avenue of Paseo de la Castellana — home to Spanish royalty and grand palaces. And then, the bright images fade. 1936. Civil war erupts in Spain. War drains color from the cheeks of Madrid. The grand palaces become gray ghosts. Gardens and fountains disappear. So do Ana's parents. Hunger and isolation cast a filter of darkness over the country. Spain is curtained off from the world.

And now, after twenty years of nationwide atrophy, Generalísimo Franco is finally allowing tourists into Spain. Banks and hotels wrap new exteriors over old palace interiors. The tourists don't know the difference. What lies beneath is now hidden, like the note disintegrating in her stomach.

Ana reads the newspapers and magazines that guests discard. She memorizes the brochure to recite on cue.

Formerly a palace, Castellana is the first Hilton property in Europe. Over three hundred rooms, each with a three-channel radio, and even a telephone.

"If you are assigned to a guest in a suite, you will see to their every request," lectures her supervisor. "Remember, Americans are less formal than Spaniards. They're accustomed to conversation. You will be warm, helpful, and conversational."

"*Ay*, I'm always warm and conversational," Lorenza whispers with a wink.

Ana wants to be conversational, but her sister's call for silence contradicts hotel instruction. The constant tug in opposite directions makes her feel like a rag doll, destined to lose an arm.

A man in a crisp white shirt emerges from a door into the hallway.

Ana stops and gives a small bob. *"Buenos días, señor."*

"Hiya, doll."

Doll. Dame. Kitten. Baby. American men have many terms for women. Just when Ana thinks she has learned them all, a new one appears. In her English class at the hotel, these words are called terms of endearment.

After what happened last year, Ana knows better.

American diplomats, actors, and musicians arrive amidst the swirling dust of

Barajas Airport. They socialize and mingle into the pale hours of morning. Ana secretly notes their preferences. Starlets have favorite suites. Politicians have favorite starlets. Many are unaware of what transpired in Spain decades earlier. They sip cava, romanticizing Hemingway and flamenco. On rare occasion someone asks Ana about Spain's war. She politely changes the subject. It's not only hotel policy, but also the promise she made.

She will look to the future. The past must be forgotten.

Her father executed. Her mother imprisoned. Their crime was not an action, but an ambition — teachers who hoped to develop a Montessori school with methods based on child development rather than religion. But Generalísimo Franco commands that all schools in Spain shall be controlled by the Catholic Church. Republican sympathizers must be eradicated.

Her parents' offense has left Ana rowing dark waters of dead secrets. Born into a long shadow of shame, she must never speak publicly of her parents. She must live in silence. But sometimes, from the hidden corners of her heart, calls the haunting question:

What can be built through silence?

They are calling the Hotel Castellana Hilton here "The Forty-ninth State" and with some justification, because only in America does there seem to be more Americanos. . . .

. . . There are diplomats and generals, admirals and hill jumpers, phony counts and real ones, movie actresses trying to look like movie actresses and non-actresses also trying to look like actresses. Some of the steadies have been here so long now that they have to cut them loose from the bar stools. And there is usually a magnificent assortment of weirdies.

. . . I have seen faces around here that haven't emerged since the old contract-letting days of World War II. They crowd the bar and give cocktail parties and search endlessly for "contacts," for Spain is opening up more and more to outside trade, and there is, of course, big dough to be made in the construction of the military bases here.

— ROBERT C. RUARK

from "Call Hotel Hilton The 49th State"
Defiance Crescent News, *Defiance, Ohio*
March 1, 1955

3

They know he's a tourist.

It's not the camera that draws their stare. It's his clothing. The eyes of the locals pull first to Daniel's mud-dulled boots. Their gaze crawls over his denims, pausing briefly at the belt buckle displaying the silhouette of Texas. A quick survey then continues north over his plaid shirt, but as soon as they see his camera, they quickly turn away.

People look at him, but no one speaks to him.

Two small boys walk by a newspaper stand. The front page of the paper features a picture of Spain's leader. The boys stop and raise their right arms in salute to the photograph.

¡Franco! El Caudillo de España.

Daniel snaps a picture.

The words and Franco's photo, in various configurations, appear everywhere. On the country's coins, postage stamps, trolley cars, and street signs. Daniel looks at the newspaper photograph. General Franco is short with a bland face and retreating hairline. His tiny mustache is perhaps his only distinguishable feature. Small in stature, his grip over the country looms tall, absolute.

"Dan's six foot one now," bragged his father recently. "Isn't that right, big man?"

Wrong. Height doesn't make a man big or powerful. He and his father look through different lenses.

As he exits Retiro Park, noise erupts like a clowder of screaming cats. Motor scooters blister down the scalding pavement, darting between wheezing buses and honking cars. A little girl in a ruffled dress sits on the handlebars of a motorcycle as her wild driver whips through traffic.

Daniel pauses on the sidewalk. Madrid roars with an exotic energy of deep colors. Cars and shoes are black, blending with street tapestries of charcoal, Goya brown, and dark currant. The churning scenes are accented by swirling exhaust and snaps of Spanish. His mother, born in Spain, is adamant he speak the language of her country. For the first five years of his life she spoke to him only in Spanish. Although the language is familiar, all else in Madrid is foreign.

On the corner near the entrance to the park, tired donkeys pull lumbering carts. Vendors hawk souvenirs. A pencil of a man stands behind an assortment of Spanish folding fans. He holds several at once, flicking them open to flutter like painted butterflies. The vendor motions to the badge hanging from Daniel's camera strap, asking if he's a journalist.

"¿Periodista? ¿Americano?"

Daniel nods at the half-truth and continues walking. The camera was a high school graduation present from his mother. The badge is from a local paper back home in Dallas.

"I want to be a photojournalist," he announced recently at the dinner table.

"Trust me, you'll grow out of it," said

his father.

He won't. Photographs are spontaneous and exciting, something that he creates, not inherits. They're a story of his own making, instead of an ancestral narrative steeped in oil fortune. He thinks of the typewritten letter at home in his desk drawer.

```
Dear Mr. Matheson,
Congratulations, you have
been selected as one of five
finalists for the 1957 Mag-
num Photography Prize.
```

His portfolio is due in September.

His father doesn't understand. Daniel won't tire of photography, but he is tired of frugal listeners who are generous with opinion. And the opinions are many:

He should pursue football instead of boxing.
Photography's a waste of time.
The family oil business will be his happily ever after.

Those who think they know him best

don't really know him at all.

Girls were no different. "Daniel Matheson. My, my, where have *you* been hiding?" joked the pretty debutantes crowding the jukebox at Nelson's.

He hadn't been hiding. He'd always been there but the girls had never noticed — until he returned as a senior, four inches taller and several yards stronger. His phone started ringing. They loved his truck, his photos, and hearing him speak Spanish with the waiters at El Fenix. Suddenly, he was "interesting." And suddenly, he was foolish enough to believe them.

After three months of dating Laura Beth, "interesting" no longer interested her.

"What about penny loafers instead of boots?" she suggested. "Let's take your father's Cadillac instead of your truck." And, "Oh, him? He's just a good friend of the family."

His school buddies at St. Mark's laughed. "What did you expect? She rides dressage. You ride rodeo. Everyone knows she's fickle. She's not worth the whiskey." Thankfully, it was his Spanish heritage

33

that ended the relationship with Laura Beth. He was "too ethnic." *Gracias, Madre.*

Daniel passes a café. The dry, windy air infuses with oil, garlic, and paprika. Heaps of prawns, eel, fried peppers, and spiced sausages fill the large glass window. He snaps a picture. The warm wind funnels through his hair. Madrid is as hot as Dallas. He turns a corner onto a narrow, cobbled street and tucks into a doorway. Daniel looks at his watch and then to the position of the sun. His parents are waiting at the hotel for lunch. His father will be annoyed with him. Again.

Approaching heels echo in the distance. Daniel raises the lens to his eye.

A nun.

Her steps are quick. Purposeful. She carries a small bundle wrapped in cloth. She looks constantly over her shoulder, as if she's being followed. Daniel remains in the doorway, unnoticed, waiting for the perfect shot. A breath of wind swirls the nun's black robes. She reaches down with a hand to tame them. As she does, the breeze lifts the cloth, revealing the contents of her bundle.

A baby's face, gray like smoke, stares at Daniel.

His breath hitches as he presses the shutter.

The child is dead.

The nun's eyes, wide with panic, snap to his lens.

Hammering the shutter produces nothing but an empty clicking. He's out of film.

His hand dives into his pocket for a new roll. He loads as fast as he can, but it's no use. When he looks up the nun has disappeared, replaced by two men in capes and wing-shaped hats. They're carrying rifles.

The Guardia Civil. The military force that serves Franco.

Daniel's favorite poet, Federico García Lorca, described them: *Who could see you and not remember you? Patent-leather men with patent-leather souls.*

"Steer clear of them," warned his father.

But their sinister appearance, like human crows, curls a beckoning finger toward Daniel's lens. He slides farther into the doorway to conceal himself. It's not illegal to photograph the Guardia Civil, is it?

Just one picture. For the contest.

Daniel presses the shutter. Did he get it?

A flap of wings. A silent bomb explodes.

The men are instantly upon him, slamming him against the door, yanking the badge hanging from his camera strap.

"¿Americano?"

"Sí, señor. Americano," replies Daniel, fighting the urge to shove them away. He tries to remain polite. *"Yo hablo español."*

The guard sneers. *"¿Y qué?* Because you speak Spanish you think you have the right to photograph whatever you please? Hand over the film. Now!"

Daniel fumbles nervously to open the back of his camera and remove the roll. Are they going to arrest him?

The guard rips the film from his hand. "Your badge is worth nothing here. Where are you staying?" he demands.

"The Castellana Hilton."

Wait.

No.

As soon as the words leave his mouth, Daniel wants to grab them, take them back, and hide them.

But it's too late.

. . . The system was very rigid. It was Franco's Spain. You did not want to fall under the hands of the Guardia Civil or the police. The jails were pretty bad and people were getting thrown in there all the time.

— ALEXANDER F. WATSON, U.S. consular officer, Madrid (1964–1966)

Oral History Interview Excerpt, September 1996
Foreign Affairs Oral History Collection
Association for Diplomatic Studies and Training
Arlington, VA www.adst.org

4

Puri holds a baby on her lap. She ties strings on the booties that match the pale rose of the child's cheek. This tiny girl loves sounds, so Puri makes popping noises with her mouth. The infant giggles and smiles in delight, alive with joy and wonder.

A brass medallion hangs from the child's neck by a white string. Puri turns the pendant over and runs her thumb across the engraving.

20 116.

20 116 is unaware she's an orphan. She doesn't realize she's been brought to the Inclusa, the orphanage in Madrid. She has no idea she is held by Purificación Torres Pérez, or that Puri wears a black apron bearing the red arrows of the Falange, the Spanish fascist movement.

"Your duty, your mission as a woman is to serve," lectured her school instructors. Puri is grateful to serve through working with children.

"We're going for photos. It will be fun," coos Puri to the infant.

20 116 is dressed in beautiful clothes that don't belong to her. Puri will take her to the small white room on the third floor. A man with a boxy black camera will come and hover in front of the orphan, capturing her portrait. Puri will soothe her after the spark of scary flashbulbs. She will make the popping noises.

20 116 will be returned to her ruffled bassinet in the nursery. The pretty clothes will be returned to the dark closet of Sister Hortensia.

One outfit for girls. One outfit for boys.

Sister Hortensia oversees each infant with sincere and devoted affection. Photos of the child will be shared with loving couples in Spain. Puri smooths the baby's downy wisps of hair, thankful there are so many families willing to adopt unfortunate children.

A large framed portrait of Franco hangs

at the front of the room.

"Our defender, *El Caudillo,* he is watching," Puri whispers to the baby. "He is taking care of us." She lifts the infant's tiny right arm in salute toward the picture. She bounces her in rhythm and sings the anthemic melody:

"He's Franco, Franco, Franco. Our guide and captain."

A nun from a local hospital sweeps frantically into the room, summoning Sister Hortensia. There are nods. Whispers.

"In the street. Yes, just now. And the Guardia Civil . . ."

Puri strains to hear.

20 116 begins to whimper. Puri makes the popping sound.

The two nuns look to Puri.

Puri turns her back.

5

Ana checks the register in her apron pocket for her assigned guest.

Daniel Matheson.

She knocks lightly on the door. No reply.

Using her passkey, she lets herself into the room.

Warmth. Quiet. The air-cooling is turned off and the door to the balcony stands open. The sheer pearl drape rises and falls on the hot breeze.

Most tourists want air-cooled rooms along with their ice. But this guest is different. This visitor welcomes the hot, dry breath of Madrid into the large suite. His clothes are not yet tucked into the drawers or closet. They spill from open suitcases on the floor amidst other litter of arrival. Stacks of newspapers and magazines sit atop the coffee table. A magazine title, *LIFE,* calls out to Ana. Resting next to the newspapers is a yellow box labeled GE PHOTO FLASHBULBS.

Hotel guests bring an array of expensive belongings. A man from Illinois works for a company called Zenith. He has "transistor" radios in a rainbow of colors, small enough to fit in your pocket. A musician down the hall has a portable record player housed in a suitcase. How do they earn the money to buy such things? The petit lobster appetizer on the hotel menu costs more than most Spaniards earn in months.

"They often leave food untouched, just sitting on the tray," she tells her brother, Rafael.

"Sure, it's not expensive for them," he explains. "American men have something called 'minimum wage' for working. One U.S. dollar per hour. And that's their lowest wage. Can you imagine?" Rafa leans in toward Ana. "Those rich Americanos are happy, not hungry. Put some lobster in your pocket for me," he says with a conspiring nod.

Ana laughs at her brother's teasing.

Their older sister, Julia, does not laugh. Julia worries. When not holding her baby, her hands hold each other, wringing twists of concern.

"We have five mouths at the table now. No one can lose their job," says Julia.

Ana loves her job, along with the English classes and the relaxed American atmosphere it provides. She could not bear to lose the position. But Rafa is right. Most guests at the hotel have never known hunger — not hunger for food, nor hunger for life.

Her family has known both.

An open magazine sits quietly on a chair. A photo of an American family stares at Ana. She gently sets down the towels and bends to pick up the magazine.

American girls wear cuffed socks with black-and-white shoes. They stare at pictures of singers who perform something called rock-and-roll music — music considered indecent in Spain. What would happen if Spanish girls wore pants on the street? Would they be apprehended? Would an unmarried woman in Spain ever be allowed a passport?

Ana dreams of travel, of one day leaving Spain. What lies outside the country's borders is untouchable for families like hers. For decades, Francisco Franco has believed that outside influence will corrupt Spain's purity and identity. The train tracks in Spain are purposely wider than the rest of Europe's to prevent unwanted entries and exits.

"Spain needs money and foreign investment, that's why Franco allowed the American hotel," claims Rafa. "*Ay,* a castle in Spain for Americanos," he laughs.

It's true. After years of isolation, select industries have been invited from America — tourism, motion pictures, and oil. Americans stay at the Castellana Hilton. But the Hilton has more than just hotel rooms. It has a business office. Ana's English is strong. Once she's worked at the hotel for two years she may apply for a position in a different department. The secretarial team from the business office travels with executives throughout Spain. They leave Madrid.

A key clatters in the lock. A tall young man with dark hair enters the room. They both jump, startled. The magazine flutters to the floor.

"Welcome back, *señor.*" Ana greets the guest as instructed.

The young man stands, holding a camera. He stares at her, then looks nervously about the room. His clothes are different from those Ana sees in magazines. Most Americans are polished and tidy. This boy is handsome but rugged. His hair has a mind of its own.

His low voice breaks the silence. *"Lo siento. No era mi intención asustarte."*

"You didn't scare me," smiles Ana.

"Oh, you speak English," he says quietly.

"And you speak Spanish very well, *señor,* but not Spanish from Spain. Perhaps you speak Spanish" — she pauses — "from Mexico?"

The side of his mouth lifts, almost reaching a smile. "Texas. Must be my accent. But my mother is from Spain." He points to the door. "My parents are in the suite down the hall." He attempts to smooth his tousled hair and that's when Ana notices. His sleeve is torn.

He sets down the camera and moves to retrieve the magazine. Ana reaches it first. She feels his eyes upon her as she swaps the magazine for the towels.

"Ah, yes. Your parents are the Mathesons of Dallas. You arrived yesterday. Welcome to the Castellana Hilton, *señor.* I hope you are enjoying your stay?"

"Yes, ma'am." He nods.

Unlike "sugar" or "doll," Ana has been told, "ma'am" is a term of respect, not endearment. She looks at the young man. At most, she is two years older.

"My parents," he says quietly. "Have they stopped by my room?"

"No, *señor.*"

His shoulders retreat with relief.

A knock sounds at the door. His blue eyes flash wide and a finger flies to his lips, requesting silence. Ana stands facing him, clutching the towels.

The knocking continues, followed by a woman's voice behind the door.

"Daniel, are you back?"

He looks to Ana and shakes his head quickly. His lips form the word *no,* followed by a sheepish grin.

Ana stifles a laugh, trying to contain her wide smile. She hates the spot of gold that tops her lower side tooth.

"Maybe he left the radio on and that's what you heard," says a man's voice.

Radio? Daniel mouths the word.

Ana points nearby. He leans across her and snaps it on low. He smells . . . nice.

After a few moments, Daniel cocks his ear toward the door. "I think they're gone," he whispers. He exhales deeply, as if trying to calm himself. "Sorry about that. I'm trying to avoid my parents."

"Yes, I can see that," she says with a laugh. She turns and takes the towels to the bathroom.

The telephone rings.

"Aw geez, now they're calling from their room," says Daniel.

She wants so desperately to be conversational, to discover why he's avoiding his parents, but heeds her sister's warning. "Is there anything you need, *señor?* If not, I'll be going," says Ana.

"No. Thanks a lot for your help." He

pauses, looking at her. "Say, your English is better than my Spanish. Are you from Madrid?"

Ana looks him straight in the eye. She smiles and lies.

"*Sí, señor,* from Madrid."

When I first went there, to Spain in '55, you had the feeling of depression when you got into Spain, repression. It was true. Everybody was careful what they said, what they did, how they disported themselves.

— WILLIAM W. LEHFELDT, U.S. vice consul, Bilbao (1955–1957)

Oral History Interview Excerpt, April 1994
Foreign Affairs Oral History Collection
Association for Diplomatic Studies and Training
Arlington, VA www.adst.org

6

" '*Rebellious, bohemian, vulgar.* These are the words used to describe Miguelín, the new bullfighter.' "

Rafael looks up from the newspaper. His friend Fuga sits on a crate in the cemetery shed and nods, urging Rafa to continue.

" 'Following his presentation at Las Ventas in Madrid,' " reads Rafa, " 'this *torero* assures audiences that he is one to watch.' "

Fuga points to the image of a matador in the newspaper.

"*Sí,* that's him, Miguelín," says Rafa. "Shall I show you how to write his name? I've told you, if you're going to be a famous bullfighter, you have to learn your letters."

The offer is ignored. Fuga teeters back

on the arthritic box, stabbing the dirt with a shovel. His mane of black hair, wild and unkempt, cannot conceal his feral eyes. Those who pass him look twice. They not only see him, they feel him. He is a gathering storm.

Fuga's gaze ticktocks between Rafa and a miniature plywood casket, the size of a large shoebox, that sits near his feet.

"*Ay,* another baby?" says Rafa.

Fuga says nothing, just stares at the little coffin.

Some friendships are born of commonality. Others of proximity. And some friendships, often the unlikely ones, are born of survival. Rafa and his friend are comrades of hardship. They refuse to speak of the boys' home in Barcelona. It was not a "home." It was a hellhole, a slaughterhouse of souls. The "brothers" and "matrons" who ran the institution took pleasure in the humiliation of children. The mere memory is poison.

The torments, like mental cockroaches, still crawl through Rafa's mind: holding a coin against the wall with his nose; kneeling on chickpeas; being held down and burned with cigarettes. He remembers pure fear causing him to wet the bed, then the brothers tying the soiled sheet around his neck, insisting he wear his cowardice like a cape for all to see. He remembers losing weight, losing his hair, losing his courage.

"¡Basta!"

Stop. The word reaches him before his friend's punch. The sting of pain is the customary antidote, a promise fulfilled when memory grabs hold. The memories are poison. Don't take the poison.

"Gracias."

Fuga nods, his fierce eyes softening beneath the wilderness of his hair. His hand suddenly extends from his pocket, offering a small mandarin to Rafa.

Rafa craves the citrus of the orange, but it's too generous. He can't take his friend's only meal. He shakes his head.

Fuga shrugs. *"Entonces,* ask her?"

"Her" means Julia, his older sister. The favor is one only she can fulfill.

"Sí, I'll ask her." Rafa tears the newspaper into a stack of neat squares. "Ana says they don't use newspaper in the American hotel. She says the guests are

provided rolls of soft white tissue in the toilets. When you become famous, *amigo,* you're going to buy us all white tissue for the outhouse."

Fuga stares at the baby's casket. "No," he hisses. "When I become famous, I'll unmask the evil homes and rescue the children." He stabs the shovel into the dirt. "Tell me the words from your book again."

He is referring to a thin volume that Rafa cherishes. It's a favorite book of his father's, containing the philosophy of Seneca.

"Gold is tried by fire and brave men by adversity," says Rafa.

"Sí," whispers Fuga. "I will emerge from this fire and when I do" — his head snaps to Rafa, wild eyes ablaze — "I'll burn them all down."

7

Daniel reluctantly takes a chair in his parents' suite. How could he be so stupid? Why didn't he tell the guards he was staying at the Ritz? They could have followed him there and no one would have known. The guards must have better things to do than chaperone a kid with a camera. It's not a big deal.

But if it's not a big deal, why is he still sweating? The images flash constantly through his mind.

The gray baby. The nun's face snapping toward the lens. Her look of shock as she scurried away. The sudden appearance of the guards.

Daniel stares at the camera in his lap. Thankfully, they didn't notice the roll in his pocket. Will the image of the infant appear on film as it remains fixed in his mind?

Bringing the camera to his eye, he frames his broad-shouldered father against the small hotel desk. His dad looks up and shakes his head. The disappointment presses Daniel's well-worn guilt button. Why can't he find passion in oil drilling like his father? It would be so much easier.

His mother evaluates her dresses and clears the annoyance from her throat.

"It was an accident, Martin. Daniel didn't know."

"I'm getting tired of these 'accidents,' María. Two days before our trip he got into a fight at the movie theater."

"I didn't pick a fight, Dad. I was defending a friend," says Daniel. He *was* defending a friend — while enjoying the opportunity to slug a longtime neighborhood bully.

"You're mighty lucky the Dallas police let you off with a warning. You're eighteen. You can be tried as an adult. And this?" His father opens his arms in query. "We've been in Madrid barely twenty-four hours, and the lobby manager tells me you were escorted back by the Guardia Civil?"

"I wish the valets wouldn't have seen," says his mother.

"I wish you hadn't bought him that camera," snaps his father.

"I wish you'd stop arguing," says Daniel.

"We're not arguing." His mother sighs and turns to Daniel. "Your father and I, we have weeks of engagements and trips, *cariño.* I thought it would be exciting for you to explore on your own. But maybe it's not safe. I no longer have family in Spain if something happens while we're away. And now you're so far from Laura Beth."

He still hasn't told his parents about the breakup. They'll ask all sorts of questions. Daniel examines his camera, dodging the topic of Laura Beth and wishing he had photographed the pretty girl in his hotel room. "I'm sorry. It was a dumb mistake. I'm completely fine on my own. Really."

He gives his mom an apologetic shrug.

Recently, his mother's tone has developed a tired edge. She's the one who begged to return to Spain, but since arriving, she seems nervous. Daniel recognizes his mother's reaction — it's her fear of not fitting in.

María Alonso Moya Matheson was born in the Galicia region of Spain but raised as a Spanish American in Texas. In public, his mother is the wife of an oil magnate and appears completely American. She baked fund-raiser cakes for the Eisenhower campaign. She supports the Hockaday School and the Junior League, and is accepted by the socialites of Preston Hollow and Dallas at large. At home, his mom speaks to him only in Spanish. He is *cariño,* darling, or *tesoro,* treasure. Many of their servants have Spanish heritage. His mother makes certain that Spanish food and customs are fixtures in his life.

"It's difficult navigating two cultures," she once told him. "I feel like a bookmark wedged between chapters. I live in America, but I am not born of it. I'm Spanish."

His mom is thrilled that oil business

has brought them to Spain. She wants to expose them to the country her late parents so adored. Pure Spain. Noble Spain. This is her plan.

His father snaps open his briefcase.

"I'm not here to bail you out of trouble, Dan. This isn't a vacation for me. Franco will only grant drilling rights to a few American companies. I'll tour the sites and close a deal before summer's end. *That's* the plan," says his father. "Do you understand?"

"Yes, sir," replies Daniel.

Daniel is freshly graduated from St. Mark's School of Texas. In the fall he'll enter Texas A&M University and following graduation he'll join the family oil operation — his college tuition is contingent upon it.

Daniel's thoughts return to the image of the dead baby; the photograph could anchor his portfolio submission. The cash award from the Magnum prize could easily pay for a year of journalism school instead of Texas A&M.

"We're invited to a dinner reception at the Van Dorns'," says his father. "They have a son your age and he's back from boarding school in Switzerland."

"The Van Dorns. Diplomats from Oyster Bay, the Long Island set," says his mother. "Several of these prestigious families have posts in the U.S. Embassy. Daniel, *mi amor,* please wear slacks and a tie. I wish you wouldn't wear those denims all the time. You look like a ranch hand." She grimaces. "Is your sleeve torn?"

Daniel quickly examines his shirt. "Oh, must have caught it on something."

The guards took his film *and* tore his sleeve? If that's how they treat tourists, how do they treat locals? He heads toward the door.

His mother gently takes his arm. "I saw they have postcards in the lobby. Make sure to mail a card to Laura Beth each day. Her family will expect that."

He exits the room with his camera, unwilling to cause a scene.

No need to worry his mother with the truth about Laura Beth.

8

Puerta del Sol. The heartbeat of Madrid.

Evening gathers tourists and locals who linger near the fountains and stairs to the Metro. The words GONZÁLEZ BYASS glow green from the TÍO PEPE sign atop a building, throwing an eerie radiance into the paling sky.

Ana walks down the narrow cobblestone street. The swallowed note is gone, but a taste remains.

I know what you've done.

She looks over her shoulder before slipping through the unmarked door. At the bottom of the darkened stairway, a soft light pulses beneath the entry. She pauses to listen, then pushes through the door.

A rainbow of color bursts with greeting. Glistening bolts of silk and satin climb from the floor to the ceiling. Shimmering fabrics in sea blue, deep amethyst, and gleaming gold cascade across worn countertops. Sketches and patterns are pinned across the walls. Three women sit at tables while two others work heavy material through machines.

Ana bends to retrieve a small pearl from the floor. In this snug space, ceremony is created. The beautiful fabrics and jewels are not for party dresses or wedding gowns. They are created and used for one person only.

El torero. The matador.

Traje de luces. Suit of lights. Named because the gemstones and beads sewn onto the fabric reflect and sparkle as if operated by a hidden switch. One suit is composed of countless pieces, taking months to construct, each detail completed by a different person. One woman specializes in pants, another in capes, and yet others in complicated threadwork. Her sister's specialty — beading and gemstones.

Like her brother, Rafa, Ana's cousin Puri loves the bullfighters. But Ana loves the bulls. She detests bullfights. Divided family loyalties are common, yet unspoken.

The workshop, generally full of chatter, is now devoid of voices. This means that Luis, the master tailor and owner of the shop, fits a matador in the next room.

Ana's sister, Julia, sits on a wooden chair in the corner. A lamp rings a halo of quiet light into her lap. She pushes a needle through the rigid seven-layer fabric, sewing one of hundreds of sapphire gemstones onto a cropped jacket.

Julia's fingers are silent narrators, embroidered with scars. Ana pulls an empty chair to her sister's side. She retrieves a small pair of pliers from a nearby table and sets a hand on her shoulder.

"Finish with these," whispers Ana. "Your hands, they'll bleed soon."

Julia nods gratefully, accepting the pliers to grip the needle.

Ana motions with her head toward the fitting room. Which bullfighter stands behind the door?

"Ordóñez," Julia whispers.

Ana looks to her sister. Julia's face, thirsty of color, needs rest and sun. Julia has a new baby girl, just four months old. The baby is not yet strong. Neither is Julia. She clings desperately to the child, and together they cry through the nights.

Fascist doctrine states that a woman's ultimate destiny is marriage, motherhood, and domesticity. For poor families, like theirs, hunger turns a blind eye to mandates. Many women from impoverished families take positions of manual labor.

But Julia is special. Her talent as a seamstress affords her the opportunity to work in a shop. Luis needs Julia's skills to please his matadors. Julia needs the wages to feed her family and pay their debts.

"We must pool our earnings," reminds Julia's husband, Antonio. "All wages and coins shall be deposited into this old cigar box."

To move from impoverished Vallecas to a small flat in Lavapiés — this is the plan. Julia rations and counts everything, pinching every last *peseta.* For now, four adults and a newborn baby share a dark, single room. But they are together. Which is what their mother wanted.

Ana has no memory of the war, but she remembers the tears of separation after her parents disappeared. She remembers crying desperately the day she left Zaragoza to be raised by her aunt and uncle in Madrid. Though her aunt and uncle have a daughter of their own, her cousin Puri is different. Obedient. Puri is free of heartache and shame. Free of secrets. Ana envies her.

"How was your palace today?" Julia asks.

Lies and threats. But don't worry, I swallowed them.

"The same. Ice and more ice," says Ana with a laugh. She tries to redirect the conversation. "I'll be on the seventh floor for the summer. I'm assigned to a very wealthy family, staying through August. They have a son about my age."

Julia nods.

"He's from Texas," says Ana. "He has American magazines."

Julia's expression shifts from fatigue to fear. "That hotel is not real life, Ana. Not for people like us."

"Julia, it seems unbelievable to us, but for them it's real life!" says Ana. "American women drive their own cars and fly around the world on airplanes. It's not considered sinful. They don't need *permiso marital.* They can seek employment, open a bank account, and travel without their husband's permission."

Julia glances over her shoulder before whispering, "Ana, please stop picking through trash in the hotel rooms. Stop reading those books and magazines! You know very well that the content is banned in Spain. This is not America."

Julia is right. In Spain, women must adhere to strict subordinate roles in the domestic arts. Ana remembers the teachings of the *Sección Femenina:* "Do not pretend to be equal to men." They also teach that purity is absolute. Women's bathing suits must reach the knees. If a girl is discovered in a movie theater with a boy but no chaperone, her family is sent a yellow card of prostitution.

Julia's brow buckles as she reaches for Ana's hand. Even her whisper is unsteady. "The world at the hotel is a fairy tale. I'm sorry, Ana, but that is not our world. Please remember that. Be careful who you speak to."

"It's my job to be conversational," says Ana.

"And that's fine, as long as it's a one-way conversation. You may ask questions but try not to answer any."

That might work. Guests enjoy talking about themselves. As long as she reveals little about her own life, there's no need for concern. Her stomach turns, digesting the note.

"Ana, is something wrong?" asks Julia.

"No." She smiles. "Nothing at all."

The life of every woman, despite what she may pretend, is nothing but a continuous desire to find somebody to whom she can succumb.

— SEMANARIO DE LA SECCIÓN FEMENINA, 1944

Throughout her life, a woman's mission is to serve others. When God made the first man, he thought: It is not good for man to be alone. And he made the woman, to help him and keep him company, and to be used as a mother. God's first idea was "man." He thought about the woman later, as a necessary complement, that is, as something useful.

— FORMACIÓN POLÍTICO SOCIAL (textbook), 1962

9

Daniel stands in the elegant parlor of the Madrid villa. Tall glass doors ornamented with flowering wrought iron stand open to the terrace and gardens below. The hands on the marbled clock approach nine. Dinner has yet to be served. Daniel looks through the viewfinder of his camera. His eyes scan the intricate inlay of the wood floor, the nineteenth-century furniture, and the exquisite handwoven carpets. His lens lands on Nicholas Van Dorn, the diplomat's son who greeted them upon arrival.

Through the crosshairs of the viewfinder, Daniel sees his parents were right; they're close in age. Nick Van Dorn has a suntan, slick blond hair, and quick brown eyes. He wears a blazer, pressed slacks, and expensive new loafers. His socks have the diamond pattern his mother loves. She says they're "argyle." His dad calls them "sissy socks." The viewfinder stops on Nick's hand holding a glass. Scabbed knuckles. A brawl? Interesting. The grated knuckles seem to contradict the rest of his appearance. Daniel snaps a picture.

"My friend hates being a diplomat's kid. I enjoy it. I get bored being in one place too long." Nick's gaze lands on the lens. "Hey, Dan, I'll show you a good spot for photos."

Nicholas leads Daniel away from the guests onto the tiled back terrace of his parents' villa. He gestures to Daniel's camera and then to the landscape. Illuminated fan palms cast fingered shadows that creep toward a glistening fountain. But manicured trees don't interest Daniel. People do. They are living, breathing landscapes. When captured at the right moment, truth reveals itself to the camera.

"Your father works for the embassy?"

Nick nods. "He's the U.S. public affairs officer. Madrid's a good post. There's a lot to do here. Great nightlife and wine is cheaper than water." Nick sips from his glass.

A servant with white gloves is suddenly at hand, passing a tray of olives cured in garlic. He disappears in the manner he appeared. Silently.

"And outside Madrid?" Daniel asks.

"Still pretty impoverished. That's why so many have poured into the city. It was brutal after the civil war. But things are looking up now. Spain allowed the Americans to build military bases here. But you probably know that. Your mom's Spanish, yeah?"

"Born here, but she's spent her life in the States."

Their conversation is interrupted by the appearance of Nick's father. White linen summer suit, pale blue tie, clean shave. He looks as if he's stepped out of a men's clothing catalog. "And you must be Daniel Matheson," he says, releasing a rehearsed smile full of warmth. Balancing a cigarette and cocktail in one hand, he extends the other for a handshake. "Shep Van Dorn. Welcome to Madrid."

"Thank you, sir."

Shep inhales deeply on his cigarette, looking at Daniel. Daniel notes the subtle appraisal, the perfect smile, the glow of a politician.

"That's a serious camera you have there, Dan. Is that the new Nikon? You must take some interesting shots. Your father tells me you've already had a run-in with the authorities."

As public affairs officer, Shephard Van Dorn works with the press. He is familiar with every camera, every news cycle, every reporter. He speaks the language Daniel is so desperate to learn. Why did his father have to say anything?

"I had a badge on my camera from our local paper. It caught the guards' eye," says Daniel, withholding the detail of surrendering his film. "The camera was my graduation present. I'm hoping to capture some good images in Madrid over the summer."

Van Dorn nods slowly, swirling the liquid in his glass. "There are a lot of stories here. Important ones. Just keep in mind that the geography itself holds a story. The differences between a Catalonian, a madrileño, and someone from

Basque Country are more pronounced than the difference between a New Yorker and a Texan. Be sensitive to that."

"I will, sir."

Van Dorn steps to the door, calling out to a man in the parlor. The guest sits alone, smoking, while wreaths of sweat bleed through the armpits of his dress shirt. His dark hair, frosty at the temples, is parted on the side and tamed with Brylcreem. From the shoulders up, the gentleman is "photo ready." But the middle of the man seems to have collapsed like a gusty exhale. His dress shirt flaps, untucked over his bulbous waistline. His slacks are wrinkled, as if they live in a ball, not on a hanger. Daniel sees two different portraits.

"Stahl, come join us," says Nick's father. The man picks up his drink and steps out to the terrace.

Mr. Van Dorn puts his hand on Daniel's shoulder. "Ben, this is Martin's son, Daniel Matheson. I've just learned that he's an aspiring newsman, in search of a story."

"Photojournalist," corrects Daniel.

"Ah, photojournalist, my apologies.

This is Benjamin Stahl. Ben's in the Madrid Bureau of the *New York Herald Tribune.*"

"Nice to meet you, sir," says Daniel.

"And, Ben, of course you know my son, Nick."

Ben adjusts his tie, bull's-eyed with a cigarette burn. "Oh yeah, Nick and I are pals," he says, grinning. Ben Stahl speaks as if he's chewing his words. He turns to Daniel. "I appreciate the civility, kid. I probably do look like an old bastard, but you don't have to call me 'sir.' I know 'sir' is mandatory in states like Texas, but you can save the tuxedo language for your oil parties."

Ben doesn't appear old to Daniel. Certainly less polished than Shep Van Dorn, Ben looks offbeat, like a stout philosophy professor who sleeps in his clothes.

"So, the spiffy son of an oil baron with an expensive camera and dreams of a Pulitzer, no doubt. Why should I care?" says Ben.

Nick laughs.

Silence hangs until Daniel accepts the

challenge. "The rich kid with expensive toys. Yeah, I've heard that. Actually, I hate tuxedos and fancy parties. I'm a finalist for the Magnum prize."

"Whoa, Dallas has a side of pride," says Nick. "I like this guy."

Ben Stahl whistles through his teeth. "Finalist for the Magnum at your age? That must have been some entry."

Daniel smiles, grateful.

"Well, I'll leave you newsmen to it," says Shep. "Ben, do his father and me a favor. Teach him about the press game in Spain so he doesn't get tossed in jail. And, Daniel, while you're here in Madrid, teach my son some of your Texas manners." He laughs and looks at Nick. " 'Yes, sir. No, ma'am.' Maybe going to Dallas would do you some good."

Nick's eyes narrow. "Dallas? What, Switzerland isn't far enough for you, Shep?"

Van Dorn ignores the pinch and enters the villa.

Nick paces the terrace.

Ben leans on the corner railing, framed by shadows of three towering palm trees.

"He's your father, Nicky. Let it go," says Ben.

Nick's fingers slowly tighten around the glass. "Let it go. Just let it go, Nick. I'm so tired of hearing that." He drains his glass and hurls it off the terrace. Daniel stares, listening for a crash that never comes.

Ben laughs and points to Daniel. "And there's the title for your next photo-essay.

"The silent scream in Spain."

The [military] base agreement had been negotiated in 1952 and I was helping implement it. Spain's objectives, unexpressed so far as I know, included some assistance from the U.S. in its political rehabilitation. Spain was run by Franco and was a bit of a pariah state. The U.S. in partial exchange for the base rights was willing, in effect, to help burnish Franco's image. This was a tough sell, because many in the U.S. simply were so anti-Franco that they blocked any opening to Spain.

— WILLIAM K. HITCHCOCK, special assistant to U.S. Ambassador, Madrid (1956–1960)

Oral History Interview Excerpt, July 1998
Foreign Affairs Oral History Collection
Association for Diplomatic Studies and Training
Arlington, VA www.adst.org

10

The baby finally sleeps. Puri watches her breathe, her tiny fingers pinching the thin blanket. Just a few months old, 20 116 is smaller than most. Puri has a special affection for the infant. Her disposition is always calm and sweet. 20 116 is *sin datos* — she has no data. Upon arrival at the orphanage, no information was included. After baptism at the Inclusa, she is now María, as are many of the baby girls with no data. But Puri has her own secret name for her. She calls this special girl Clover. She will be one of the lucky ones.

Arrivals to the orphanage take several forms. There are children, like Clover, who have no information. There are children who do have information, notes pinned to a blanket:

He has been baptized Manuel.
   Please hold her. She likes to be held.
      Baby will not eat. Cries constantly.
         God forgive me.

In addition to the children with and without data, there are new mothers at the Inclusa. The orphanage provides shelter for destitute mothers and their newborns. The women serve as wet nurses for the other infants.

Sister Hortensia says a priest from San Sebastián is coming for Clover. He will deliver her to adoptive parents. She will live along the glistening shores of the bay under the beautiful new statue of Jesus looking down from Mount Urgull. A lucky girl indeed.

Puri walks through the rows of ruffled bassinets. Dozens of babies, all under a year old. This is her favorite part of the job. *Auxilio Social,* Spain's social aid program, provides humanitarian relief — giving special attention to widows, orphans, and the poor. It is the duty of every good Spaniard to help those in need.

Puri longs to be a good Spaniard, to

support the noble country *El Caudillo* fought so hard to build. Her work at the Inclusa will prepare her for her ultimate destiny of motherhood. She loves the babies and they return her love. The doctors at the Inclusa advise that infants without physical bond or affection seem to progress more slowly. Puri's job is to interact with the babies. To rescue innocent children and give them a future — yes, she will be a good Spaniard.

Beyond the window, the sky darkens. Puri has stayed too long with the babies today. She hangs her pinafore apron on the hook and makes her way to the receiving office to collect her purse.

Puri's eyes land on the square opening in the wall near the door.

The box, it's called *el torno.*

Outside, on the busy street, is a private, walled entry to the Inclusa so visitors may access the *torno* without being seen. The door to the square hatch in the wall is opened and the infant placed on a large plate wheel. When the wheel is turned, the child spins from the outside wall to the inside of the receiving office. When the door to the *torno* closes, the child becomes an orphan.

This is the standard process Puri is familiar with, unless a nun or doctor brings an infant in through the back door. Like Clover.

Puri once asked about the backdoor arrivals, but was reprimanded. "Being nosy is a sin. Don't ask so many questions." She wasn't being nosy, just curious. There's a difference. But her mother also says curiosity is a sin.

Puri exits the building. She still has plenty of time. The *portales,* the large cast-iron gates of the apartment buildings, aren't locked in Madrid until ten thirty. After ten thirty, you must give three quick claps of the hands, calling into the darkness for *el sereno,* the night watchman.

Puri has never called for *el sereno.* She is never out late. She stays in, reading about her bullfighters in the newspaper clippings.

"*¡Espere!*" A woman on the sidewalk rushes to Puri. "Please, please tell me." She clutches Puri's sleeve.

"*Señora,* what is the matter?"

"My baby," the woman whispers. "They sent my baby for baptism. That was two days ago. I'm still waiting. Have you seen him?"

The woman's grip tightens on Puri's arm. Puri tries to pull away.

"Where is my baby? Is he inside?" pleads the woman.

"Of course not," replies Puri. "This is an orphanage."

Sister Hortensia appears in the front window.

"Come, why don't you speak to Sister," suggests Puri.

The woman quickly recoils and flees down the dark sidewalk.

Poor thing, thinks Puri. She's gone mad.

11

The table stretches the length of the entire dining room. As each course passes, the volume level grows. Twenty faces, illuminated by candles, shift and sway as they talk, creating patterns of light on the plaster ceiling. Summer homes, college alma maters, and who knows whom — each guest chatting, loading their side of the scale.

Ben Stahl, seated next to Daniel, sips his scotch and watches the guests intently. He leans in, his cigarette dangerously close to Daniel's sleeve.

"All right, newsboy. Give me one word. What do you see here?"

Daniel hesitates, pulling at the noose of his tie.

"Quick, what do you see?"

"Competition," says Daniel.

"Exactly!" Ben waves in agreement and, in the process, flings ash onto his plate. "A long, dark hallway of fragile egos. Come on, another word."

Daniel scans the guests. "Wealth?"

"Yeah, wealth, but that's not exactly on the nose. For accurate reporting you have to find the perfect word. The perfect word captures every subtlety. The perfect word shows true comprehension."

Ben's hand punches syllables when he says "perfect word," launching ash confetti to the tablecloth. Daniel stares at the glowing embers as they burn through the expensive fabric. He desperately wants to capture it on film.

"Are you listening, Matheson?"

"Yes, sorry. The perfect word."

"Correct. The word here isn't 'wealth,' Matheson. The word is 'fortune.' Think on that as you're taking pictures in Spain." Ben pushes his chair back. "I need to find a litter box."

Ben is right. The perfect word is like the perfect camera angle; it expresses the true nature of the situation. Change the camera position slightly and the picture tells tales. Daniel thinks of the photo he took of the nun and the baby. Maybe he should mention it to Ben.

Across the table, Daniel's mother is seated next to Mrs. Van Dorn. Their faces are animated, but they speak in whispers. His mother suddenly looks into her lap. She inhales deeply.

Daniel recognizes his mother's wearied look, her bookmark between chapters. She's trying to hide it from Nick's mom. He turns to Nick and searches for conversation.

"Do you have any siblings?"

"A sister. She's in New York. My mom leaves tomorrow to visit her."

"And your school in Switzerland. What's that like?"

"Le Rosey? It's better than a tired boarding school in the States. We spend weekends traveling. Lots to take pictures of. Plenty of visits to Madame Claude off the Champs, you know?"

"No, who's that?"

Nick laughs. "Do you have a girl back in Dallas?"

"I did," he says, eyeing his mother to

make certain she can't hear them. "It ended just before graduation."

"Well, that's lucky. Now you're single in Madrid for the summer. Tell your dad you need to rent a car from the hotel. My family's car is a diplomatic vehicle, so we can't use that. But with our own car and your connections," a sly grin spreads across Nick's face, "we'll have a big time."

"My connections?"

"Of course. It's all about connections, cowboy. Your father's an oil tycoon, negotiating drilling in Spain. Who do you think is authorizing that deal?"

Daniel nods just slightly.

"That's right. Franco. Sounds like your father's an influential fat cat. My dad said the embassy is processing your family's paperwork for the orphanage deal."

Daniel looks at Nick.

"Wait, you knew, right?" says Nick.

Daniel nods slowly. "Yeah. Of course."

12

Midday noise floats up from the street and through the balcony door of Daniel's room. Bands of sunshine wash over the chair where he sits with a book.

Orphanage.

"You're the only child, Dan. The family business needs you," his uncle had told him. But if their only child has no interest in the family business, they wouldn't adopt another, would they? Daniel laughs. No, that's ridiculous. Nick misunderstood. How would he know anything, anyway? But it pecks at him. It's an oil deal, not an orphanage deal. Isn't it?

A light tapping sounds at the entry to his suite. Daniel leaves his chair and pulls open the door. It's the girl from the housekeeping staff who was in his room yesterday.

"Buenos días, señor." She smiles sweetly. "Your mother has sent for you."

The blink of gold on her tooth matches the buttons on her sleeves. She is energetic yet graceful, with spirals of pretty, dark hair. He tucks the book under his arm and follows her down the hall.

"What's your name?" he asks.

"Ana," she says, glancing over her shoulder.

Her eyes are pretty too. He thinks of his camera.

"Something good?" Ana points to the book.

Daniel holds it up and nods. *Robert Capa. Slightly Out of Focus.*

Daniel's mother sits at the desk, compiling a list on a hotel notepad. "Your father's meeting has been changed, *cariño.* We're leaving tonight for Valencia. Would you rather stay here?" Without pausing for an answer, she points to a blouse on the bed and addresses Ana.

"A button fell off. Is there a chance you could mend it?"

"Of course, *Señora* Matheson." Ana

moves to inspect the blouse.

"Remind me of your name, dear?"

"It's Ana," says Daniel.

"I'm expecting a telegram. Can you see that I'm contacted as soon as it arrives, Ana?"

"Of course, *señora.*"

"Also, I'd like to take a gift to our dinner hosts in Valencia. Is there something lovely I could bring?"

Ana hesitates, thinking. "Perhaps candies from La Violeta? They are quite adored."

"Could I trouble you to pick up two boxes?"

"Mom, I'm sure she's very busy," says Daniel.

"You don't mind, do you, dear?" Mrs. Matheson scans her list.

"Not at all," says Ana. "I am assigned to help your family."

"Wonderful, because my son is looking for a camera shop."

Daniel gives Ana an apologetic smile. At home in Dallas, his mother's interaction with their household staff is more relaxed. The people on their estate aren't employees, they're family. In Texas, his mother is often described as "elegant Spanish." But here in Spain, her demeanor suddenly feels brash next to Ana's gentle sincerity.

As if sensing his unease, Ana quickly offers reassurance. "I often handle errands for guests. I know the owner of the camera shop. I'd be happy to take you, *señor.*"

Mrs. Matheson gives a syrupy sigh and turns in her chair. *"Señor.* Is my sweet little boy already a *señor?"*

Daniel rolls his eyes.

"Oh, forgive me, dear. Of course you're no longer a boy. You and Laura Beth are off to college in the fall."

No, we're not. We broke up. Should he just say it and get it over with? His mom's reaction can't be worse than the guilt he's starting to feel by keeping it a secret.

"*Perdón,* but we should hurry, *Señor* Matheson. Shops will close soon for lunch," says Ana.

"Sure, just let me grab my bag," says Daniel. He's in a hurry too. The sooner his pictures are developed, the sooner he'll see if he has a contest entry, a worthwhile story of his own, and — most important — a potential exit from oil.

13

Ana and Daniel stand in silence, waiting for the elevator to arrive at the seventh floor. Just as he thinks of something to say, the doors open.

"Buenos días, señor," greets the elevator operator. He waves a white glove to welcome them into the small compartment. His forest-green uniform features the gold Castellana Hilton crest between two rows of shiny brass buttons.

The elevator descends, stopping at the fifth floor. A corpulent, gray-haired gentleman with wire-rimmed glasses enters.

"¡Buenos días, Señor Lobo!" exclaims Ana. She quickly makes way for the guest, stepping back so far that she's brushing against Daniel. In the mirrored walls of the elevator, Daniel sees multiple angles of Ana. He lifts his camera and

takes a picture.

"Now, that will be a lovely photo, indeed," says the man, giving Daniel a wink. The doors open and the lobby staff erupts in greeting when the bespectacled guest emerges from the elevator.

"Who is that?" whispers Daniel.

"*Señor* Paco Lobo," replies Ana. "The hotel's most cherished guest. He's been here three years. *Señor* Lobo supports two orphan girls and recently adopted an entire village."

"He adopted a village?" asks Daniel.

"Yes, he adopted the people of Navalperal de Tormes, in the Gredos mountains. He's very generous and supports them financially."

Of course. That's what his parents are doing with the orphanage that Nick mentioned. They support all sorts of charities.

Daniel watches the beloved guest make his way through the lobby. Why would the man live in a hotel rather than a home or an apartment?

Ana signals to a young bellboy, dressed in a uniform similar to the elevator operator's. A round green hat, like a small drum, sits askew on the left side of his head.

The small boy sprints across the lobby to her side.

"*Hola,* Ana."

"*Hola,* Carlitos. *Señora* Matheson on the seventh floor is expecting an important telegram. When it arrives, deliver it to her directly."

The boy nods enthusiastically and turns to Daniel. *"¡Hola, señor!"* He points to the image on Daniel's belt buckle and bursts with excitement. "Tex-has!" He raises his fingers like guns. "Pow! Pow!"

"Yes, Texas," says Daniel, laughing. "How old are you, Carlitos?"

"Twelve." He beams, standing at attention. "Bellboys in Spain, we are called *botones* — buttons. Most guests, they call me Buttons, *señor.*"

"All right, then. May I take your picture, Buttons?" The boy obliges, striking a well-practiced pose.

"Carlitos, please tell the front desk that I am on task for the Matheson family," instructs Ana. Carlitos nods and marches away.

"He is a sweet boy, and very eager," says Ana.

A female employee appears, carrying a bucket of ice. Her lips are a shock of red against her pale skin and dark hair. Seeing Ana and Daniel, she raises her eyebrows and changes course toward them.

"*Hola,* Lorenza," says Ana. "Lorenza, this is *Señor* Matheson. His family is visiting from Texas."

Lorenza nods slowly, staring at Daniel. Her eyes travel south, taking in his jeans and cowboy boots. Her brows flash with interest. *"Bienvenido a Madrid, caballero."* She grins and saunters away.

Lorenza's self-confident swing reminds him of Laura Beth. Not worth the whiskey.

Summer heat swells and clings as they exit the building. Bellmen direct taxis collecting and delivering guests. Porters bustle, balancing stacks of colorful boxes and shiny bags from specialty shops in Madrid. Daniel scans quickly for the guards. They are nowhere in sight.

"Have you worked at the hotel long?" he asks.

"For nearly a year," Ana says.

"And before?"

"I worked for a family."

"Oh yeah? Which do you prefer?" asks Daniel.

"Actually, I'd prefer to hear about your camera. It looks very special." Ana smiles.

Daniel follows Ana through the crowded sidewalks lined with acacia trees, sharing details of his camera. He stops to photograph an old brick archway.

"That is the entrance to the Sorolla Museum, *señor.* You must visit. It's wonderful."

They approach a café adorned with brightly painted tiles. A sunburned tourist sits alone at a sidewalk table. He dozes, clutching a glass containing a final sip of wine. As he surrenders to sleep, the glass and remaining liquid tip dangerously close to his pants.

Daniel pauses.

Ana grins and nods quickly. *"Sí, sí."*

Just as Daniel snaps the picture, the

man opens his eyes, catching them in the act. They hurry away, laughing.

"Think he was drunk or just sleepy?" smiles Daniel.

"Both!" laughs Ana. "But which was the better photo? The sleeping tourist or our faces when he opened his eyes?"

"Great question! Wish we could see the two together. It's so easy to miss the good shots." Daniel's smile retreats as they pass two men in gray uniforms on the corner. They're holding billy clubs and sour expressions.

"There are also some shots to avoid, *señor,*" says Ana, her voice dropping in volume. "The police corps in the gray uniforms — *los grises* — and of course the Guardia Civil."

"Right. *Gracias.*" He nods. "Are there many Guardia Civil?"

Ana pauses, thinking. "Perhaps forty thousand?"

There's a clutch to his throat. "Forty thousand?"

"Yes, but you probably won't see them. They mainly patrol outside the city centers."

But he has seen them, *in* the city center. Why were they following the nun with the baby? Somehow, losing his film to them makes him want the picture even more.

Horns hoot and engine radiators bubble through the hot, congested streets.

"How did you discover photography?" asks Ana.

"My art teacher, Mr. Douglas. He convinced me to join the school paper."

Their conversation continues, alternating naturally between English and Spanish as they walk. Ana listens carefully, the first in a while to show interest in his photography.

"Sorry. I'm rambling about camera stuff," he says.

"You're not rambling. I asked, *señor.*"

Leading him down the wide cement stairs to the Metro, Ana explains how to purchase a ticket and which transit line they will take to cross the city. Although the glances aren't overt, Daniel feels the eyes of the locals. He also feels the eyes of Ana. Is it the jeans, the large belt buckle, or the boots that draw attention?

The Metro is a thrumming underground tube of white tile. Suspended lights illuminate colorful advertisements painted on the arched walls. The platform is clogged with passengers, but orderly. With such well-ordered society, are so many police and guards on the street really necessary?

"That's our train. Quick, let's catch this one before it departs." Ana pulls Daniel by the sleeve into a throng of people boarding a car. The door closes, sandwiching the passengers together.

Ana grasps the metal handrail overhead. The air inside the car is heavy with heat. As the car jerks forward, Daniel feels a trickle of sweat make its way from his hairline down to his ear. They stand so close a sheet of paper would barely slide between them.

"Is it too hot for you, *señor*?" whispers Ana.

He feels a wisp of her breath on his neck. He tries to wipe his brow. "No. It's pretty hot in Texas too."

"Do you have a Metro in Dallas?"

He shakes his head. "We have bus service."

Daniel thinks of his journalism project. Last year, the Dallas Transit Company announced its buses would be desegregated and the WHITE and COLORED signs would be removed. But they weren't. Daniel documented the delay, taking photos and reporting each week to the national headquarters of the Associated Press. He received an A on his project, but his efforts displeased many.

"You have subways in New York City, though," says Ana, interrupting his thoughts.

The train suddenly sways, jostling the passengers and pressing Ana against him. The feel of her so close, he nearly forgets to reply. "Yes . . . subways in New York."

"Grand Central is a big station."

"Oh, you've been to New York City?" asks Daniel.

Ana looks up, her nose nearly touching his chin. She shakes her head. "No, I've never been to New York. I've never left Spain, *señor.*" She pauses, then looks away quickly.

The sudden change in her expression,

he can't place it.

Is it sadness — or is it fear?

14

"*Ay,* Julia. It's just for a few hours."

"Rafa, I told you, no!" Julia shakes her head at her brother. Why is he so impossible?

"Just ask Luis. He'll understand. A *torero* can't go into the ring without a suit of lights."

"*Torero?*" Julia looks to the corner where a savage young man in rags is fast asleep across two broken chairs. He is barefoot, his face and arms covered with grime. Loud snores reverberate from his unhinged mouth.

"That miserable orphan is not a bullfighter. He's a gravedigger."

"Well, for now we're gravediggers. And for now I work at the slaughterhouse. But believe me, that man is a matador, Julia. He was the bravest of all at the boys' home. Do you know what they called him in Barcelona? They called him *Fuga.* 'Escape.' Each time he ran, the directors would drag him back and punish him. But he would escape again. He helped me find courage. He's the reason I made it out and found my way back. He protected me. If I'd been alone in those fields, I'd never have survived."

"Stop being dramatic," says Julia, wringing a wet diaper over a wooden pail.

"It's not dramatic. It's true." Rafa's voice drops in volume. "We were all so hungry, but Fuga vomited his food in resistance. He would rather starve than be fed by the hand that beat him. All the boys, we idolized him. We chanted his name under our breath, encouraging him. His fearlessness kept our spirits alive. And then one day I found myself locked in detention with him. I will never forget his first words to me. He looked across that dirt hole, and do you know what he said?" Rafa pauses. "*Voy a ser torero.* 'I'm going to be a bullfighter.' He has been fighting his whole life. He is not infected like so many. He doesn't carry the disease of fear."

"It's easy to be fearless when you have nothing to lose," says Julia.

Rafa throws his hands in the air. "He has everything to lose. He has been given an opportunity. That is so rare. Do you know what he's been fighting with? He has no red cape. He uses a blanket that he soaked with rusty bricks, and even so, I have seen him bewitch fifteen-hundred-pound bulls in a willow field. And now, after much pleading, Father Fernández has sent me to a man with connections. He is giving Fuga a chance."

Julia pauses. "If he wins, will there be money?" She thinks of her handwritten ledger and the sum needed to move the family.

"He may get a handful of grapes."

"A handful of grapes?"

"But, Julia, he will earn honor and the chance to fight again. This is a beginning. He must look like a *torero,* not a peasant. To rent a suit of lights would cost over five hundred *pesetas.* Every day you are surrounded by dozens of suits in the shop. Please, just ask Luis. Let us borrow an old suit. Just for a few hours."

"Where is this bullfight?"

"Near Talavera de la Reina."

"Rafa, that's over a hundred kilometers from Madrid. How will you get there?"

"I'm not worried about that. We'll walk from Vallecas if we have to."

And he will. Julia knows that. Although energetic and sunny in public, Rafa is brooding. He is the bull. He watches, quietly gathers pieces, and puts things together. But many pieces are still missing. The Crows carry pieces of her brother in their pocket. And he is desperate to win them back.

"I'll think about it," she says. "But if I speak to Luis, you have to do something for me."

"Anything."

"You have to speak to Ana."

"*Ay,* there's nothing to say to Ana. She's the smartest of us all."

"Rafa, she'll listen to you. That hotel is an American business. Male and female employees work together without chaperones. She's constantly looking at American magazines. She's a gorgeous young woman surrounded by a fairy tale. That makes her vulnerable again."

"What happened last year was not her fault," says Rafa.

He's right, but could they have protected her somehow?

"Trouble follows our sister wherever she goes," says Julia. "She's been so quiet lately. I'm worried she's hiding something."

Ripples of snoring cut through their conversation. The baby begins to cry. Julia turns away from her brother before he can state the obvious.

Of course Ana's hiding something. This is Franco's Spain. They're all hiding something.

15

Ana points to a tiny, elegant shop. LA VIOLETA. Curved windows set in polished oak arch from the sides of a tall glass door. Tucked within clouds of purple tissue behind the display glass are bonbons, boiled sweets, and jellied candies. A little girl in faded clothes stands outside, admiring the candy. Daniel snaps a picture behind her.

"You must come in," says Ana. "It's something very special."

Inside, the miniature shop smells of sugar. The shelves are lined with glass jars of purple sweets. Ana points to a crystal bowl on the counter with lavender-petal candies.

"Try one," she insists, popping one into her own mouth. She then selects two small boxes. She asks the clerk to wrap them and put them on the hotel account.

Daniel takes one of the small violet candies. "It looks like a purple clover." After a moment he grimaces.

"What do you think?" she asks.

"My mom will love it," he replies.

"But you don't."

He shakes his head. "It's like eating a flower."

Ana smiles as the portrait materializes. Daniel's jeans and boots, everything about him, clashes with the lavender interior of the shop. "May I take a picture, *señor*?"

"Sure. It'd be fun to have another pair of eyes." Daniel gives her the camera along with instructions, while the girl outside watches from behind the glass.

Ana looks through the viewfinder. "Okay, say, 'Texas boys like violet candy.'"

"Wait, what?" Daniel laughs.

And at that moment, when his smile is wide and eyes uncomfortably shy, Ana snaps the picture. "We have to hurry. Miguel will be closing the camera shop soon," she says, moving toward the door.

But Daniel is at the register, buying a candied chestnut wrapped in gold foil. "We'll give it to the little girl outside," he says, motioning to the window. "Do you think she'll like it?"

Ana nods slowly.

Of course she'll like it. Any girl would like it.

The camera shop is the size of a long closet. Room for one and cramped with two; a wooden counter divides the small space. Between rows of shelves that hold film and accessories hangs a black curtain. The acrid and wet metallic scent of photo-developing fluid exhales from the back of the shop.

"That smell, I love it," says Daniel.

"Ana!"

Miguel emerges from behind the curtain wearing a timeworn Panama hat. His darkroom hours give him a youthful complexion for a man in his late fifties, but his hair and eyebrows have tones of a black-and-white photo.

He greets Ana with a broad smile. "I

was just about to close."

"I'm sorry, Miguel. I have a guest from the hotel. He speaks Spanish, so we won't be long."

Miguel gives a wave of his hand, indicating that he doesn't mind. His eyes shift to Daniel's camera. "*¡Caray!* That's a serious camera for a young man. Do you know how to use it?"

"You'll have to be the judge, sir." Daniel removes a roll of film from his bag and winds a second from the camera.

"I've only seen a couple of these new Nikons. Both with American journalists. They told me they paid over three hundred U.S. dollars for that camera. I hope it's worth it."

The familiar pang of sadness thuds within Ana's heart. Three hundred American dollars? That's eighteen thousand *pesetas.* Eighteen thousand *pesetas* is more than the average Spaniard earns in five years. The cost of Daniel's camera could move her entire family of five from their leaky hut in Vallecas to a decent apartment in Lavapiés, closer to the city center. The cost of the camera could eliminate the debts and threats that strangle her life. She thinks of the note she swallowed in the hotel basement. A shiver trills up her spine.

"Yeah, it's probably too nice for me," says Daniel. "It was a gift for my graduation. But really, my old camera was swell." He removes a portfolio from his bag. "I took these with my old camera."

Miguel slowly turns the pages of the album. *"¡Ave María Purísima!"* He points to a picture.

"Sí," says Daniel. "There was a tornado in Dallas last April. It obliterated sixteen miles and hundreds of homes."

Ana stares at the massive, twisting tornado. It's positively demonic, unholy. And he was in front of it. "Weren't you terrified?" she breathes.

"I didn't have time to think about it. I really wanted the shot," says Daniel.

Miguel continues to page through. He stops on a photo of dozens of men in cowboy hats. They stand in the dark, one light overhead, hands raised in the air. Fatigue and sunburn line their weathered faces.

Ana peers at the photograph. "Who are they?"

"Braceros," says Daniel, "manual laborers from Mexico working in Texas. At the end of the day they're inspected and searched, to make sure they haven't stolen anything."

Miguel pauses, absorbing the image in front of him. *"Qué duro,"* he says quietly. Daniel nods in agreement. Rough.

"This is Texas?" asks Ana.

"Not all of it. Just part of it." Daniel flips the portfolio forward several pages. "This is also Texas."

Ana stares at the black-and-white photos. A parched landscape dotted with oil rigs, bathed in a sunset of fire. The photo is so evocative she can imagine the colors. He turns the page. A lavish garden party. Carpets of thick grass surround a swimming pool that sparkles like a suit of lights. Groups of glamorous people cocktail and make merry against the backdrop of a massive estate.

Miguel points to a young woman lying by the pool in a bikini. "She would be reprimanded in Spain."

"My mother claims some should be reprimanded for wearing them in America," says Daniel, laughing.

Ana eyes the picture. The woman looks beautiful, relaxed. There is nothing offensive about a bikini, but of course she could never say that aloud.

Miguel picks up the rolls of film that Daniel has set on the counter. "What's your name, Americano?"

"Daniel Matheson."

Miguel reaches over the counter to shake hands. "I'm Miguel Mendoza. You have a clear eye, Daniel. You see many angles."

"*Gracias, señor.* I had a great teacher at school. Those photos were part of a contest I entered. So maybe it's not fair. I'm showing my best work."

"Who knows," says Miguel, holding up the two rolls of film. "Maybe this is your best work. They'll be ready in a day or two."

Their words are muffled noise to Ana. She stares at the photo of the Texas garden party, absorbing every detail. Tables of endless food. Cardigan sweaters, strings of pearls, the nice teeth, glowing faces, the vibrancy of freedom. Young girls and boys stand around a phonograph, holding record albums. Women are smoking. Dozens of carefree people — happy instead of lonely — oblivious to the camera. And then she sees it. In the corner of the frame, a beautiful girl with beckoning eyes stares straight into the lens. She looks like a movie star. She's blowing a kiss to the photographer.

"I should return to the hotel," says Ana. "I have to mend your mother's blouse."

"Sure," says Daniel, sliding the portfolio into his bag. They bid goodbye to Miguel.

Ana rushes through the street, back to the Metro station. Daniel jogs to catch up. "Sorry about that," he says. "I'm taking too much of your time. I'm sure you have a lot of work to do."

Ana shakes her head. "My work is helping your family, *señor.* The hotel has assigned me to you. And besides, I really like your pictures." Ana's steps slow. She turns on the sidewalk, looking up at Daniel. "May I ask you a favor, *señor?*" She pauses, gathering strength. "The picture you took this morning in the elevator. Please don't give my picture to anyone."

His eyes are upon her as the hot breeze lifts her thick hair. "No, I would never share your photo without your permission. I'll give it to you."

Ana exhales relief. They resume their steps toward the Metro. After several yards, Daniel volleys back. "Ana, can I ask *you* a favor?"

"Of course, *señor.* What is it?"

"Don't call me *'señor.'* Call me Daniel."

She pauses, waiting on the reluctant words as they rise to the surface. "I'm sorry, that's impossible, *señor.*"

Ana looks away, confident that concealing her face will conceal her truths.

16

Puri sits on the grass, wearing her black pinafore apron embroidered with a cluster of arrows. A little girl points. "Look, the arrows on your apron match the arrows on the building."

"Very good!" Puri looks up to the familiar emblem etched into the exterior of the Inclusa.

The Inclusa spans three large stone buildings, positioned in a U-shape, with a plaza garden in the middle. Puri likes to mentally remove the exterior walls and imagine the Inclusa like a dollhouse. The lower floors house dining areas, administration offices, a medical wing, and learning rooms. The upper floors are divided into sections with the capacity to house five hundred children and a hundred mothers.

Puri looks to the basement windows at ground level. In the farthest corner of the basement is a private file library. The file room is locked, accessible only to the nuns and doctors. She can't help but wonder — why is it always locked?

"¡Toro!" yells a boy, racing by Puri.

Most children delight in being out-doors, anxious to run and jump. On sunny days, Puri and the mothers bring the children outside in shifts. The doc-tors advise that without adequate sun exposure the orphans may develop rick-ets, skeletal deformities that cause bones to soften and bow. Fortunately, medical care is rigorous at the Inclusa. But Puri hears some physicians lament that mor-tality rates of newborns in Spain are particularly high. Cases of polio increase each year.

"Other countries have a new vaccine for polio. Why aren't we using it in Spain?" asked one of the young mothers.

"Maybe other countries need a vaccine. They don't have the faith to pray it away," replied Sister Hortensia. "The Holy Spirit will see to polio."

Will it?

Puri wonders. She wonders so many things but is reprimanded for her questions.

When the radio broadcasts announce, "Spain is the chosen country of God," does that mean that God has abandoned other countries? And if foreigners are indecent, why is Spain catering to them as tourists?

"Why must you question everything?" scolds her mother. "Have you no faith?"

She most certainly has faith, but she also has questions. Can't she have both? Puri turns to watch a group of six-year-olds sitting under the silvery leaves of an olive tree. She worries about the older children. Newborn babies are the most desirable for adoption. It is more difficult to find homes for the older orphans. If the child's parents or grandparents were known to be Spanish Republicans, those who opposed Franco during the war, then the child must be rehabilitated and reeducated as a rational human being. Puri heard one couple tell Sister Hortensia that they didn't want a child who had been "circling the drain." They said they wanted an infant — "a bright, fresh canvas."

It made no sense to Puri. Shouldn't the most vulnerable children be rescued first? When she asked her mother, even she agreed.

Puri knows all of the six-year-olds by name. Soon they will be gone. If a child reaches seven and is not adopted, they are taken out of the Inclusa and sent to separate boarding schools for boys and girls. The orphan girls receive more assistance. Puri hears that at the age of fourteen, a matchmaking process secures husbands for the girls.

"Isn't fourteen young?" she once asked.

"Enough questions. One is never too young to honor their country," replied Sister Hortensia.

Thankfully, the children ask as many questions as she does.

"Are the arrows on the building a scar? I have a scar," says a boy, pointing to his arm.

"No, *chico,* that's an etching on the building. Your scar is special. It's warrior skin, very strong," Puri assures the boy, rubbing his thin arm and wishing she could remove all of their scars.

To Puri, the children's beauty certainly eclipses her own. Her frame is so much wider than her mother's. Her brown hair is not shiny like other girls', not nearly as pretty as her cousin Ana's. It seems unfair that Ana and Julia received all of the family beauty. But she would not trade places with either of them. Their parents were Spanish Republicans. In school, Puri learned that Spanish Republicans killed many priests during the war. How could someone kill a priest or a nun?

Sister Hortensia appears in the garden. She walks slowly around the edge of the grass, hands hidden beneath her thick white robes. Only her face is exposed, framed by the starched coif of her habit. Are nuns also susceptible to rickets?

Sister Hortensia is squat, with a strong jaw softened by gentle eyes. Sister devotes her entire existence to the protection and care of the orphans. She is firm with the children, yet kind. Some young mothers at the Inclusa whisper about Sister Hortensia. They prefer Sister Pilar, a woman of their own age, with a loving laugh and patient heart.

Although Puri respects Sister Hortensia, a tiny part of her fears her. If what the young mothers whisper is true, Sister Hortensia has tremendous power. And now, out of the corner of her eye, Puri watches the wooden rosary swing from Sister's robes as she moves closer. A small boy tugs at Puri's hand, pulling her attention to the children. A little girl tries to braid her hair. A third child climbs onto Puri's back.

"Good afternoon, Sister," greets Puri. Sister Hortensia nods and then stops, staring at her. Puri feels the nerves beneath her skin begin to tiptoe. She glances down at her apron. It's smeared with diaper cream and talcum from the nursery. Cleanliness is a sign of spiritual purity. "I'm sorry, Sister."

Sister gives a forgiving nod, turning her gaze to the row of olive trees. She speaks without looking at Puri. "I saw you from the window yesterday. A woman approached you on the street. What did she say?"

Puri is eager to share the odd experience. Perhaps Sister will have answers.

"She was confused. She was told that her baby had been taken for baptism. The child was never returned to her. She asked if he was here."

"And what did you tell her?"

"Well, I explained that he could not be here, that this is an orphanage. And then she scurried away. I think the poor woman was suffering emotional distress."

"Indeed," agrees Sister Hortensia. "Pray for her," she says, and walks away.

Puri nods. She wants to ask if emotional distress can be prayed away like polio, but tucks the thought aside. She asks too many questions.

17

"Welcome back, *señor!*"

Carlitos greets Ana and Daniel at the entrance of the hotel. "No telegram yet," he announces.

"*Gracias,* Carlitos," says Ana.

The round upper lobby of the hotel brims with people, all chattering in English. Daniel sees his mother, as well as Shep Van Dorn and Ben Stahl, the reporter.

"It's the monthly luncheon for the American Club of Madrid," whispers Ana.

A voice appears from behind. "And what are you two doing?"

The voice belongs to Nick Van Dorn. He stares intently at Ana. "Hello, Ana," he says, and then nods to Daniel.

Daniel nods in reply, noting Nick's unbroken gaze toward Ana.

"Buenas tardes," says Ana quietly. After an elastic pause, she adds, "I was on errands for the Mathesons. I'm sorry, but I'm in a rush. I have a task to finish for *Señora* Matheson."

"Thanks again for your help," says Daniel.

"My pleasure, *señor.*" She turns and darts through the crowd.

"How do you know her?" asks Daniel.

"Just a friend," replies Nick. "Come on, have lunch with us."

Daniel eyes the men in suits and ties. "I'd better change first."

"Nah, then you'll be boring like the rest of us. Let the girls think you're the Marlboro Man."

Daniel follows Nick to the circular upper lobby, where beverages are being served. Waiters balancing silver trays of sangria thread through dozens of well-heeled guests. Nick helps himself to a drink.

"Most of these people are families of

American diplomats or officers from the U.S. air bases," explains Nick. "The hotel is constantly hosting functions for them."

Daniel spies Paco Lobo, the hotel's resident guest, petting the bilingual parrot that serves as the lobby mascot. He's about to reach for his camera when he hears the laugh.

It belongs to his mother. It's not her real laugh, it's the one she uses when she's nervous. Turning toward the counterfeit sound, Daniel sees Shep Van Dorn regaling his mother with a story.

Nick lets out a breath of disgust upon seeing his father. "Where's your dad?" he asks.

Daniel shrugs. "Probably working. He's always working." And somehow always working against me, thinks Daniel. He'd love to tell his father about Miguel and the camera shop but knows he'd dismiss it as a waste of time.

He follows Nick through the crowd toward Ben.

"Do you know who Ben's talking to?" asks Nick. Daniel shakes his head.

"That's Max Factor Jr., the Hollywood

cosmetics mogul. He and his wife are staying at the hotel. Franco allows some of the Hollywood studios to shoot movies here." Nick approaches, close enough to listen but not interrupt.

"When I saw the black winged hats and long coats, I assumed it was a costume and they were filming," says Factor with a laugh. "I was going to mention our new product line."

"Trust me," says Ben, "the Guardia Civil are not actors. Where did you see them?"

Daniel takes a step closer. His stomach drops a step back.

"Around the corner an hour ago, speaking to a hotel employee. Thankfully, the little bellboy stopped me before I pitched Hi-Fi to them. It's a new foundation that's lighter than our Pan-Cake makeup used for Technicolor. Don't imagine you'd be interested in covering the new Hi-Fi line for the *Tribune,* would you, Ben?"

Ben's hair is immaculate but his dress shirt is missing a button and shows freckles of a prior meal. His generous stomach makes his tie appear short.

"Sorry, Max, I focus more on world news," says Ben.

Max sees the drift of Ben's gaze and turns to Daniel.

"Well, howdy there, partner. Are you straight off a movie set?" asks Factor.

"No, sir, just inappropriately dressed for the function," says Daniel.

"Nonsense. Nothing wrong with being comfortable, young man."

But he isn't comfortable. Despite Mr. Factor's compliment, he knows his mother will be annoyed that he's under-dressed.

"Let's get this kid into a Hollywood picture," says Factor.

"Dan's a photographer, not an actor," says Ben.

"Really? Sure seems like he belongs on the other side of the lens."

Daniel fights the impulse to roll his eyes. Why does everyone need to catego-rize him, and incorrectly? Laura Beth had a particular talent for that.

"Excuse me, I'm going to head up to my room," he says. Inappropriate dress aside, mention of the Guardia Civil nearby makes him uneasy.

"Dan, wait a minute." Ben Stahl follows him. "I'm not going to the luncheon either. We can have lunch in the hotel coffee shop. It's the only place in Madrid to get a burger and a milkshake."

Daniel hesitates, sizing up Ben's invitation. Is this generosity or just another one of his father's chess moves? He decides to find out. "Sure, a burger sounds good."

18

Ana sews the button onto *Señora* Matheson's silk blouse. The white label on the neckline declares it's from Neiman-Marcus. An assigned guest once told Lorenza all about Neiman-Marcus. The lavish store, established in Dallas, sells luxury items to oil-rich Texans. Ever since Franco granted drilling rights in Spain, the hotel has been flooded with Texans. Oil fortune brings talk of debutante balls, fancy summer camps, silver dollars, and something called pimento-cheese sandwiches.

The image of Daniel with the candied chestnut floats back to Ana. The little girl, bouncing on her toes, stared at the treat like it was a diamond. Diamonds are also something common on Texans. Is Daniel a common Texan? He's certainly different from other guests at the hotel. He looked at her when she spoke. He opened the door for her. He carried the bag from La Violeta as if it were his job, not hers. As nice as Nick is, he's never done that. She thinks of Daniel's photos and his worn jeans. He's unusual. Was it rude that instead of answering his questions, she posed her own?

Carefully folding the blouse, Ana places it next to the suitcase packed for Valencia. She positions the two boxes of candy from La Violeta on the desk. She stares at the wrapping, recalling the enchanting atmosphere of the shop. How lucky the recipient in Valencia will be.

Valencia. City by the sea, birthplace of her favorite painter, Sorolla. Hotel guests speak of Valencia's tranquil beauty, fragrant orange trees, and rolling blue waters. What does a large body of water sound and smell like? Ana wonders. Landlocked, fenced by circumstance, she has never seen the sea. She sees Spain only through images on postcards that guests collect in their rooms. If she transfers to the hotel business office, perhaps one day she too will walk along the beach in Valencia. Ana will need letters of recommendation for her application. If she does a good job, perhaps Daniel's family might consider it? A letter from an influential American family could expedite consideration.

Ana straightens the room, thinking of oranges, thinking of Valencia. On the chest of drawers she sees a bright turquoise package.

NEW!

Out of color TV research — a great make-up discovery:

Max Factor **Hi-Fi** Fluid Makeup

Lorenza has whispered that Max Factor and his wife are guests at the hotel. Ana can't wait to share her findings of the new cosmetics.

She moves to empty the trash. The small bin contains only one item: a squat, green glass bottle. Ana inspects it and immediately wishes she hadn't. She doesn't need Texas secrets. She has enough of her own.

Madrid today has got more Texans than Spaniards. The barroom in the Castellana Hilton sounds like roundup time in the Panhandle.

So far in Spain no Texan has leaped into the Plaza de Toros and attempted to show the Spaniards how a real man can bulldog a beef. I have seen no horses ridden into lobbies lately. My friends, riches are weakening the strain that made you exceptional. Constant association with Yankee businessmen is turning you sissy. I blame it on the ladies, largely. They are trying to live up to Neiman-Marcus and are forcing their will on husbands who used to wear spurs to the square dance. The girls say: "Now, you behave!" And the old boys are behaving.

— ROBERT C. RUARK

from "World Travel Is Turning Texans into Real Sissies"
Abilene Reporter-News, *Abilene, Texas,*
July 30, 1954

19

Ben chooses a booth in the small alcove restaurant.

"Quieter here," he says. "No one talking about makeup." He yanks at the knot in his tie, loosening it, and lights a cigarette.

"This hotel is deceptively huge," says Daniel. "It doesn't seem that large from the outside, but once you step inside, it's massive."

"Deceptive. Good word," says Ben. A waiter appears and discreetly slides an ashtray under Ben's hand, forecasting the gray snowfall from his cigarette. "I've gotten lost in here and I've never even made it to the labyrinth beneath. The location is strategic, you know."

"What do you mean?"

Ben sighs. "Come on. An American

hotel in a country ruled by a fascist dictator? It's no coincidence that the U.S. Embassy is practically across the street. There are several levels belowground in this place. Ask the pretty girl that you came in with." He grins.

"She's assigned to help my family. It was just a visit to the camera shop."

"Which one?"

"Miguel Mendoza's."

"Miguel," nods Ben. "Great guy. Great little darkroom as well. I'd invite you to use the bureau's darkroom — ours is light-tight — but then you'd have to deal with the censors."

"Miguel seems nice. I'm happy to give him the business. He's developing a couple rolls for me and also looked at my portfolio."

"All right, my turn. Hand it over."

Daniel quickly retrieves the album from his bag and slides it across the table. It's a great opportunity. The man in front of him reports for one of the largest newspapers in the world.

Nothing about Ben Stahl is fast. It takes him forever to order from the menu, even though he knows what he wants. It takes him even longer to look through the portfolio. He turns the pages slowly, analyzing each image as if it were a coded message.

Daniel shifts. It's uncomfortable watching his work reviewed. Ben knows it. He gets to the end of the album, studies the final photograph, and closes the portfolio. Ben takes a long, silent drag on his cigarette. He looks up at Daniel.

"You're a fraud, cowboy."

"Excuse me?"

"Your father told me that you're going into the oil business. But the truth, it's here. You have as much interest in oil as I do in Hi-Fi makeup."

"I don't want to be an oilman."

"So why'd you tell your father that you do?"

"I didn't. He knows I love photography. I want to be a photojournalist, but my dad doesn't support it. He'll only pay for college if I study engineering at Texas A&M."

"A&M? No, you should go to J-School."

Daniel looks at Ben, grateful. "I want to go to journalism school. I've been accepted at Missouri but my dad won't pay tuition for J-School." He pauses. "Speaking of payment, is my dad paying you to keep an eye on me?"

"Your dad? No." Ben looks at him. "But Shep and the embassy might slide me a few favors if you keep to a darkroom instead of a jail."

Daniel nods. Of course. His father has an arrangement with Mr. Van Dorn and the embassy. A quiet safety net in the event of trouble. But there is no trouble. Is there? Ana said the crow-like guards don't patrol the city center. But . . . Max Factor says he saw them today?

"Listen, forget about your dad's motives," says Ben. "People discouraged me from journalism too. But clearly, you've caught the bug. The stuff in this portfolio is as serious as my blood pressure." Ben wipes sweat from his hammy brow. The speed of his lecture accelerates.

"Sincerity. It's important. If you take photos with this type of sincerity you may as well be holding a gun. There's a meaningful story here in Spain, a human story. But it's virtually impossible to tell and even harder for an outsider to understand. You need to be smart about it. This is a dictatorship. Franco's regime censors everything. Freedom of the press doesn't exist here. And you better believe the censors read everything I write before I send it to New York. I'm too visible. But you . . . You!" Ben slams his hand on the table. A waiter comes running.

"We're fine. Sorry, Pepe," he tells the waiter.

He leans in to whisper. "But *you.* You can capture a real story here — a photo essay to show a different side of Spain than the one on the postcards. All the foreign correspondents are chasing the same threads — that Hitler survived and Franco smuggled him to South America; that Texaco secretly fueled Franco during the Spanish Civil War."

Daniel's eyes expand. "Are those things true?"

"Who cares if they're true. That's the wild boar everyone's hunting so one day they'll run it down. But they're missing something. What about the people of Spain? What is life like under a dictatorship? What's it like for young people when textbooks are government sponsored? What are their hopes and dreams when there are no free elections and only one religion?"

The waiter delivers their hamburgers and milkshakes. Ben gestures to the plate with his cigarette. "Everyone seems to understand what 1950s Middle America is like. They say it's hamburgers and milkshakes, right? For years I've been trying to explain to the world what it's like for the average person in Spain."

Daniel looks at Ben, not certain he understands. Is he baiting him or trying to inspire him? "But life seems fine here. My mom's Spanish and she claims Franco's sympathetic. Nick says things are better now."

"Franco's an architect," whispers Ben. "Maybe things are better than when the war ended, but wages here — they're still lower than what they were in 1936. But that's not the point." Ben drills his finger on the cover of Daniel's portfolio. "You're a photographer, a storyteller. In a dozen pictures, you showed me ten layers of Texas. Choose an angle and show me ten layers of Madrid."

Daniel stares at Ben, trying to interpret his comments. "And you'll print my pictures in the *Herald Tribune?*"

"Hell no. I can't do that. I'm the visiting correspondent here. I have to play by the rules. I'm knuckled by the censors. Why do you think it's been so hard to tell this country's story?" He pauses, looking over his shoulder. "But meaningful photos, human beings enduring hardship, that'll get the attention of the Magnum judges. That'll win you the cash prize and get you to J-School. And who knows, when you get back to Dallas you might happen to stumble upon a contact for *LIFE* magazine. Madrid through the eyes of a young American — pretty interesting stuff, don't you think?"

LIFE.

Daniel sits, frozen, not willing to believe what Ben is suggesting. A potential photo essay in *LIFE* magazine? Robert Capa, Eugene Smith, Gerda Taro — all of his heroes shot in Spain. *LIFE* printed their photos. The image of the nun with the baby returns to Daniel. Why is he hesitant to tell Ben about it?

Ben takes a wide bite of the hamburger. He removes a package of Bisma-Rex antacids from his pocket and sets it on the table. His voice returns to a whisper.

"Focus your lens on the Spanish people," Ben lifts his cigarette and points it at Daniel, "but don't be stupid. There is a dark side here. Sure, they're selling sunshine and castanets to the tourists. But that's not all Franco's selling. One wrong move and the police will be on you. You'll be dead in a dirt pit."

The major thrust, I think, of the Political Section was to give to Washington an idea of how the ordinary Spaniards were living under the regime, how they felt toward it, and what the regime's relationships with the European countries were. Obviously, Spain's relations with us at that time were somewhat controversial since there were many people in this country, particularly in the Congress, who felt strongly unfavorable to the Franco regime.

— STUART W. ROCKWELL, U.S. political section chief, Madrid (1952–1955)

Oral History Interview Excerpt, October 1988
Foreign Affairs Oral History Collection
Association for Diplomatic Studies and Training
Arlington, VA www.adst.org

One of the amusing things to me was that there was a ministry called The Ministry of Information and Tourism headed by an old line Falangist who I am sure hadn't had a new idea in a long while. On the one hand he was the chief censor, that's what information meant. Information did not mean giving out information, it meant control of information.

— FRANK ORAM, U.S. public affairs officer, USIS, Madrid (1959–1962)

Oral History Interview Excerpt, April 1989
Foreign Affairs Oral History Collection
Association for Diplomatic Studies and Training
Arlington, VA www.adst.org

20

Julia carries a package wrapped in stiff brown paper. Before she arrives at the open door, she hears the baby begin to cry. "*Mamá* is coming, Lali."

Her husband, Antonio, carries the infant back and forth across the earthen floor. The slight drag of his left foot is a teenage souvenir, courtesy of the Guardia Civil. At fourteen, Antonio and his friends thought they were mature. They shared cigarettes, analyzing Spain's political straitjacket, and whether Franco was using memories of the war to control the population. Their secret conversation resulted in brutal beatings that cost one boy an eye, another his teeth, and Antonio his gait.

Julia closes the door. A tin kerosene lamp dangles from a wire stapled to the sagging ceiling. Absent the daylight from the door, the only remaining light in the room comes from the primitive lamp and a small broken window.

"Why are you home so early?" asks Antonio, concern striping his face. "And why are you closing the door? It's too hot."

Julia kisses her husband and the baby. She sets the papered bundle on a chair and reaches into a crate for a piece of folded fabric. With a flick of her wrists the fabric billows and settles over the scarred wooden table. "Luis sent us out of the shop. An American actress wanted to discuss a custom cape. She requested privacy."

Antonio releases a sigh of relief. "Let me guess. Ava Gardner." He shakes his head. "Poor Luis. A request from one of her bullfighter boyfriends, no doubt."

Julia moves the fat bundle to the table. "*Sí,* but this is why I closed the door."

She pulls the twine and the corners of the starched paper flower open like an envelope magically unfolding itself. Even in the dim space, the stack of garments shimmers and glows like electric starlight.

148

"*¡Maravilloso!*" breathes Antonio. "It's beautiful."

Julia nods, picking up the *chaquetilla,* the matador's ornate, cropped jacket. "No sleep tonight. I must finish the beading that lines the edges. Ordóñez comes for it tomorrow."

Antonio points to a stack of turquoise fabric still in the paper. "And that?"

Julia smiles. "For Rafa's *torero.* "

"No! Luis let the wild orphan borrow a suit of lights?"

"Not exactly. Last year, Rafa buried Luis's brother at the cemetery. Luis says this favor is for Rafa, not the *torero.* It's quite big. I'll need to alter it to fit."

"In the spare time that you don't have. You are a wonderful big sister."

Julia folds the paper back over the blue suit to conceal it. She reaches for the baby.

"She's better today," says Antonio, placing Lali in her arms. "Getting stronger. Her voice is louder."

"I thought so this morning, but then wondered if I was imagining it." Julia cradles the infant and sits on a chair for feeding. Lali squeals and bats her tiny fists.

"And you, *mi amor?*" asks Antonio.

Julia nods. "I'm getting stronger too."

She wishes he could believe her. Julia knows his arms ache with sadness. She wonders if Antonio feels her pain through their embrace as she feels his, as she feels Lali's. The baby's cries are haunting, heavy with separation.

Antonio pours water from a bucket into a clay mug and brings it to his wife. He then pours a mug for himself.

Julia looks around the small room and sighs. Strands of hair, wet with sweat, cling to her face. "I tell myself this is temporary. But we work ourselves day and night, and nothing changes. No wonder Ana and Rafa dream as they do. No wonder Rafa idolizes his fellow grave-digger. Rafa says they call him *Fuga.* Escape." Julia looks down at her daughter. "Of course they want to escape. I often wonder what Mother and Father would tell us to do."

"They would tell us to stay together,

that here in Vallecas we are with our people."

"But they were teachers, Antonio. *Mamá* would hate Rafa working two jobs and digging graves. He should have gone to university."

"*Sí,* and my father was a bookseller, murdered in his very own shop. He would hate me being a trash collector," says Antonio. "He would also hate knowing that his children inherited the pain and punishment of a war. But the tourism coming to Spain, it's helping the economy. Exposure to foreigners helps too. It makes the people here realize that the restrictions in Spain — it doesn't have to be like this."

"But what if that realization is dangerous? Look at Ana."

"Sometimes the truth is dangerous, Julia. But we should search for it nonetheless." Antonio sighs. "We'll keep our heads down, save for a bit longer." He points to Lali, now fast asleep in her mother's arms. "And count our little blessings."

A group of loud male voices approaches from outside. The door opens a crack and

Rafa's voice booms in.

"Antonio! I'm going to the fountain to wash. Then I'll take Lali."

Antonio dresses for work and the family shift change. The family works quietly, but in concert. Ana stays at the hotel two nights per week while Rafa helps with Lali. Prior to Lali's birth, their hardship and debt were manageable. Julia remembers the sober face of the doctor she saw during her single pregnancy visit.

"Your difficulties exceed your good intentions. How will you manage all of this?" he had asked them, shaking his head.

"As we always have," responded Antonio. "Together."

But with time, their debts increase. Families must pay rent on a burial grave. Although the location of their father's body is unknown, they are responsible for the rent on their mother's costly plot. If they can no longer afford the rent, *Mamá*'s remains will be hacked up and tossed in a common pit. Julia cannot bear the thought. After their mother's torture in prison, knowing she rests quietly in her own private space is of deep comfort.

Rafa returns, shirtless and wet from the waist up, water dripping from his dark curls. Antonio hands him the family's sole towel as he departs for work.

Upon seeing his sister, Rafa freezes. "*Ay*, Julia, why are you home? Is something wrong with Lali?"

"Nothing's wrong. Luis closed the shop early for a meeting. I'll finish the jacket for Ordóñez here tonight."

"Ordóñez?" Rafa's eyes light up and he moves toward his sister.

"Stop! You must dry off completely. I don't want you dripping anywhere near this jacket."

Rafa uses the small, threadbare towel and furiously rubs at his hair and skin. His eyes are glued to the sparkling fabric in his sister's lap.

"Look at that! *¡Sensacional!* There must be a thousand jewels on that coat. That fabric is so strong, like a shield. How many needles did you break?"

"Too many," says Julia, looking at her ravaged hands. When needles break, the pieces lodge in her fingers.

"And the pants are in the package?"

asks Rafa, pointing to the paper bundle.

Julia shakes her head. "Something else." She motions for Rafa to open the package.

He peels back the paper and lifts the turquoise jacket. He looks to his sister.

"From Luis. For your *torero.*"

Rafa's bright smile turns to shock. He carefully lays the old suit on the table, ever so gently, as if it were made of glass. He stands, staring in disbelief.

"Julia," he whispers. "*Gracias,* Julia."

Rafa slowly brings a hand to his face. He begins to cry.

21

Daniel wakes to the bleat of a car horn. The clock says 1:00 a.m. His body has still not adjusted to the time change in Spain. The open balcony door welcomes the cooler night air into the hot room. He steps out onto the terrace and looks down at the bustling patio. In Preston Hollow, the entire neighborhood is dark by 10:00 p.m. Here in Madrid, the city's alive at 1:00 a.m. as if it were barely dinnertime.

He wonders if his parents have arrived in Valencia.

"We'll only be a few days, *cariño.* You can reach us at the Hotel Alhambra," said his mother, kissing him goodbye.

"I arranged the car rental you asked for," said his father gruffly.

Daniel's stomach complains, reminding

him that he missed dinner. He pulls on his jeans and boots. He'll make his way downstairs and find something to eat.

The hotel lobby buzzes with music and guests.

"Still quite a party here," he says to the lobby clerk.

"*Sí, señor.* The quiet time is early morning. The city comes alive at night."

Near the elevators, a narrow opening in the sidewall catches Daniel's eye. He peers down and sees a stairway. Perhaps it leads to one of the restaurants?

Ben's words return to him. *I've gotten lost in here and I've never even made it to the labyrinth beneath. . . . There are several levels belowground in this place.*

Labyrinth. The description is too intriguing. Daniel heads down the stairs.

He arrives at the first basement and, sensing a lack of activity, continues down farther. The second basement is darker. The air thicker. Unlike the sparkling upper floors of the hotel, this lower level is not glamorous. Stretches of weathered gray stone line the walls and floors. Gaslight flickers in the primitive fixtures, not yet converted to electricity. It's more interesting than the fancy lobby. He contemplates turning back for his camera.

After passing several stockrooms, a uniform supply closet, and a large laundry facility, he arrives at a classroom. Rows of chairs face a long chalkboard. A world map, wrinkled with age, is taped to the wall. As he continues down the stone corridor, he passes a bathroom and janitorial facilities.

At the corridor's end, a light glows behind a square of glass set within a door. Daniel walks toward it and peeks inside. Staff members, clearly off duty, smoke and play cards at a table. In the far corner, a girl sits alone. Her wet, dark curls hang down over her face. She is reading a magazine. The square of glass in the door is a perfect frame. Why didn't he bring his camera? The girl loops her hair behind her ear and that's when he realizes. The girl is Ana.

"*¿Qué hay, amigo?*" A pair of hands grabs Daniel.

22

Daniel stumbles through the swinging door into the room.

"Two more for the card game."

Ana jumps from her chair. "*Señor* Matheson." She looks from Daniel to the men playing cards. "This gentleman is a hotel guest."

The men drop their cards and stand at attention.

"My apologies, *señor,*" pleads the man who drove him into the room. His eyes, taking in Daniel's clothes, expand with fear. "We have hundreds of employees at the hotel. The corridor is very dark. I assumed you were staff, longing to join the game, but too shy to ask. I did not mean any offense."

"None taken," says Daniel.

Everyone stands in awkward silence.

Ana looks to the clock on the wall and then to Daniel. "Can we help you with something, *señor*?"

Daniel shifts his feet, searching for an answer. "Sorry, I think I'm lost."

The men's shoulders, up near their ears, slowly retreat. They look to Ana.

"*Sí,* I'll take him back." She instructs Daniel to follow her into the hallway. "Wait here a moment."

Ana disappears behind a door. When she reappears, her wet hair is pinned back and she is wearing a green apron with the hotel's golden *C* crest.

"I'm sorry. I'm putting you back to work. Did you just return from a swim?"

Ana looks at him and laughs, the small gold of her tooth visible. "A swim? Of course not. You are so funny."

"I am?"

Still smiling, Ana lowers her voice. "Employees are not allowed in the hotel pool, *Señor* Matheson. Those facilities are reserved for guests."

"Oh, I thought . . . then why is your hair wet?"

Ana swallows hard. She looks to him and changes the subject. "You arrived very recently. You're not quite adjusted to the time difference. Why don't I take you back up to the lobby?"

Ana leads Daniel through the double basements. It's an underground village with countless hallways and alcoves, like Ben described. The late-night pace of the downstairs world is a production all its own. They pass two bustling kitchens, a dedicated pastry workshop, and an entire room housing an enormous machine that makes ice.

Daniel eyes the food in the kitchens.

"Are you hungry, *señor*? Shall we send dinner up to your suite?" asks Ana.

"I can eat here." He shrugs.

"I'm sorry, guests may not eat in the kitchen. They'll bring a proper meal service to your room. It's no trouble."

Daniel hesitates. "Are you hungry?" he asks.

Ana's eyes widen. She takes a small step back.

"Oh, I don't mean to put you in an awkward position," says Daniel quickly.

"It's just, my parents are gone. I don't know anyone here yet."

Ana nods slowly. She speaks to the kitchen staff and upon receiving permission, begins to fill a plate. "Follow me," she says, carrying a loaded tray. She directs him into the empty staff cafeteria and chooses a small table near the door.

"Maybe we can sit over there?" He points to a larger table in the corner. "Quieter."

Ana looks to the secluded corner, hesitating. "Well . . . I guess that's okay. I am assigned to your family."

Daniel stares at the tray Ana has prepared. Galician bread rubbed with garlic and topped with grated tomatoes and olive oil. Iberian ham and fire-roasted piquillo peppers.

He grins. "How did you know?"

"Your mother is Spanish. Traditional favorites. What are some traditional favorites in Dallas?"

"Chicken-fried steak, barbecue, pecan pie." Daniel looks at her. "Why are you smiling?"

"Your Texas accent is really heavy when

you say, 'chicken-fried steak.' "

"Is it?" says Daniel. "What does it sound like?"

Ana's attempt at a Texas accent results in a fit of laughter between them.

"If that's what I sound like, no wonder people are looking at me," laughs Daniel. "That's terrible!"

While Daniel eats, Ana's questions drive the conversation. "And why photography?"

"I'm not great with words, but I discovered I can say a lot with a photo," shrugs Daniel. "Each roll is an adventure, waiting for the images to be developed. My mom supports it but my dad doesn't."

"No?"

"Nah, he wants me in oil. He needs to steer everything. When I was fifteen, I was too small to play American football. Dad feared I wouldn't be able to hold my own so he enrolled me in boxing — anything to get me away from cameras and art. I was good at sparring and loved the technique behind it. But now that I'm a lot taller he's suddenly decided he doesn't want me boxing either. He says

162

it's not a good college sport."

"Which college will you attend?" asks Ana.

"Well, I'm supposed to go to Texas A&M, but just between you and me, I've been accepted to journalism school," says Daniel. "I'm competing in a photo contest, and if I win, the prize money would fund the journalism program. But my parents aren't exactly in the know about that yet."

Ana nods.

"Now that you know my secrets," says Daniel, grinning, "it's only fair that you tell me one of your own."

Ana lowers her voice and gives a quick glance over her shoulder. "My secret," she whispers, pausing to pull out the suspense, "is that I'm very good at keeping secrets." She laughs and leans back in her chair. Daniel throws a piece of bread at her.

Keeping secrets. He's noticed. When he asks Ana questions, she quickly diverts. Their discussion sways like a dance. He steps forward with a question. She pivots back, holds for a moment, then moves in closer with a question of her own. Despite her caution, Ana has enthusiasm that's natural, a shine underneath.

She leans in, changing topics. "Tell me, why do Americans love ice?"

Daniel leans in, challenging her earnestness. "Tell me, why do you ask such difficult questions?"

"Stop," laughs Ana. "I'm being serious, *señor.*"

He shrugs. "I guess ice is just one of those things you get used to."

Ana nods. "I imagine there are many lovely things to get used to in Texas."

Daniel rocks back on the chair, looking at her expression of solemn curiosity. He wishes he could photograph it.

Ana opens her mouth to ask something else but changes her mind.

"What?" Daniel grins.

"I love reading American magazines and newspapers. It helps my English. I recently read something in a magazine. What does this mean?" Ana's brow creases as she recites. " 'Rustproof aluminum shelving . . . controlled butter-ready.' " She lets out a tiny exhale when she reaches the end.

"Those sound like features of an American refrigerator," laughs Daniel. Ana smiles and laughs too. He looks at her. They're close in age. She's easy to talk to, but she's holding back. He thinks of Ben's comments. *What about the people of Spain? What is life like under a dictatorship?*

"Ana, do you always work so late?" he asks.

"No. I stay overnight two days per week. Sometimes I babysit for the guests who —" She stops speaking and quickly begins to clear the dishes. "Let's get you back upstairs."

Daniel looks toward the door. Why did she halt the conversation?

They head up the staircase side by side. Daniel tries to catch her eye, but Ana stares straight ahead. "I feel like I've told you a lot about Texas. I'd like to know more about Spain," he says.

"I'm not really the person to ask. The concierge can be of great help, though," says Ana.

They arrive at the lobby and Daniel is certain — Ana is exactly the person to ask. She's full of questions. Is it curiosity or is she gathering information? Regardless, he feels more comfortable with Ana in one day than he did after months of dating Laura Beth. There's something inside Ana that's natural and fun, but she's roping it in. Is she following hotel rules, or someone else's? Or maybe she's following the master in Spain that Ben spoke of.

Fear.

23

There's so much Ana wants to say. So much she wants to ask. Is she being rude? He's a hotel guest. Should she apologize for not answering his questions? She thinks of the swallowed note, of Julia's warnings, and decides to say nothing. She must remain silent.

Silence is so tiring.

"Now that you've found your way out of the basement" — she points down the hallway — "perhaps you'd like to visit the Rendezvous Room, *Señor* Matheson? It's the hotel's nightclub. It's open until four a.m."

"I'm not really interested in a nightclub."

"Are you sure?" Ana smiles. "Nick is probably there."

"Don't you mean *Señor Van Dorn?*"

jokes Daniel.

Color drains from Ana's face. She stares at her feet. "Yes, of course. *Señor* Van Dorn. My apologies."

"Ana, I'm joking. You call Nick by his first name. I want you to call me by mine."

She stares at his boots, unable to meet his eyes.

"Ana, I wasn't reprimanding you. You know that, right? I was only kidding." He reaches out and touches her arm.

A desk clerk approaches. "A telegram has arrived for *Señora* Matheson."

They both reach for it.

"Your mother asked me to deliver it to her room," explains Ana, pulling the telegram in her direction.

"I have a key. I'll put it in their room," says Daniel, tugging it back toward him.

Ana's breath quickens. "But your mother, she was very insistent. She might call from Valencia for the message."

"Don't worry. I'll give it to her."

Ana struggles to find words. "It felt like it might be important."

"Then you can definitely trust me with it." Daniel pulls the folded paper into his possession. "Thanks for everything, Ana. And please know, I was only joking."

Ana nods slowly, watching Daniel make his way across the lobby with the telegram. He reaches the elevator and gives a wave. The fleeting sensation of fun from the basement disappears. The gold elevator doors close, leaving Ana with her one and only companion.

Loneliness.

24

They're looking at 20 116, Puri's favorite, the girl she calls Clover. Sister Hortensia grimaces. She stands next to Clover's bassinet, arguing with a doctor. Across the room, Puri changes a baby's diaper and strains to hear the conversation.

"It's been nearly a month. I deserve an explanation," says Sister Hortensia.

The infant wiggles under Puri's grasp. She returns her attention to the little boy. He's a diaper fighter. His short legs are rolls of pink fat. He's jousting with them and enjoying every minute of it. It makes Puri laugh.

"Purificación!"

Puri stiffens at the sound of her name. She quickly pins the diaper and lifts the baby from the changing table. Worn from combat, he rests his tiny head on Puri's shoulder.

She smiles and turns to Sister Hortensia. "He's tired himself out."

"Put the child down and come at once."

Puri doesn't want to put the child down. She wants him to rest upon her shoulder, to feel comfort, safety, and love after the diaper fight. She fears if she puts him down he might develop the trauma of loneliness the doctors describe. But she does as Sister Hortensia instructs. Her first duty is to follow orders.

Puri leans over Clover's bassinet. The girl immediately responds to her, eyes wide and mouth curving into a smile.

"See, that's lovely," notes Sister Hortensia.

"She's beautiful. Well, they're all beautiful," says Puri quickly. They're not supposed to have favorites. The doctor nods and exits.

"Apparently not beautiful enough. The priest in San Sebastián informs me that there has been a change," says Sister Hortensia.

"Oh no," says Puri. "They're not going

to adopt her?"

Puri attempts to conceal her distress. Clover is a special girl who must have a special life. To live amidst the velvet-green mountains of San Sebastián, looking out upon the churning cobalt sea, this is the plan.

And then Puri remembers.

She recalls the article and her parents' hushed conversation in the kitchen. The floppy Basque beret versus the jaunty military beret. The reported sign, illegally posted on a wall in San Sebastián, that says, PLEASE REMEMBER, THIS IS NOT SPAIN.

The Basque people are an indigenous population with their own language and heritage. *El Caudillo* wants to unite everyone as Spaniards so the Basque language has been banned and some of their schools have been turned into jails.

Is this the reason Clover is no longer going to San Sebastián? Confused while eavesdropping and even more confused now, Puri wonders. Why is it all so complicated?

"Purificación!" scolds Sister Hortensia.

"Stop daydreaming. We'll need different photos. Have them focus on facial portraits this time." She points to Clover, swaddled in a pink blanket. "See, like that she's perfect."

Sister Hortensia sighs and exits the room.

What does she mean, *like that*? Puri wonders.

25

Ringing.

It comes in intervals. It begins, stops, then begins again. Daniel's eyes flutter. His body feels nailed to the bed, his limbs too heavy to lift. Just as his eyelids close, the shrill sound resumes. Drunken with sleep, he stumbles from the bed to the sitting room of the suite. Daylight peeks through the heavy drapes covering the sheers. He locates the phone and lifts the receiver.

"Daniel? Is that you, *cariño*?" His mother's voice peals as shrill as the ringing.

"Yes, ma'am."

"I've been calling and calling."

"I've been sleeping."

"It's already midday," she announces.

"You must still be on Texas time."

"Or maybe I'm more Spanish than we realized."

"I called the front desk. They said that my telegram arrived."

"I have it. I'll go get it."

"No, no," says his mother. "It's business, well, of the womanly sort. I know how you hate that kind of thing."

She laughs. The fake laugh. The nervous laugh.

"You don't need to open it, dear. There's a cable office downstairs in the hotel. Take it there and have them forward it to me at the Hotel Alhambra in Valencia."

Daniel yawns, looking back toward the bed. Fatigue pulls harder than curiosity.

"Did you hear me, Daniel? You don't need to open it. I'll be here waiting."

"Yes, ma'am. I'll send it. Goodbye." He stares at the bed. It beckons. Her voice is still chirping through the handset as he hangs up the phone.

More ringing.

Daniel looks from the pillow to the clock. He's been asleep for two more hours. Anticipating his mother's reprimand, he doesn't answer the phone. Instead, he heads for the shower but stops midway. He sees the telegram on the table and recalls the urgency in his mother's voice, along with Ana's desire to deliver it.

It felt like it might be important, said Ana.

You don't need to open it, his mother insisted.

Daniel retrieves his camera. He snaps a picture of the telegram on the side table, the stormed bed looming in the background. He sets down his camera and picks up the telegram.

And then he opens it.

26

Miedo. Fear.

It lingers in the blood. Of that, Rafa is sure.

He arrives at *el matadero,* the cavernous slaughterhouse, and changes into his issued work clothes: white pants; white shirt; white apron; and wooden clogs. The same clothes are worn for the entire workweek. On the sixth day, employees bring their uniform, stiff and rank with decay, home to wash.

Each Sunday, Rafa rises with the sun. He carries the galvanized tub to the well. Using castile soap and lemons, he scrubs at the scents and smears of blood, feces, and innards living in the clothes. He watches the remnants of death seep from the fabric into the water. When he is finished, the tub is a bath of muddy chestnut, the clothes closer to their original selves, and the apron a pale shade of dead blood that smells like citrus.

Fuga says there is good death and bad death. Fear brings bad death, it leaches into the organs and skin. Butchers claim it affects the product. Good death, peaceful or unaware, quickly separates the Holy Ghost from the suitcase of skin holding the bones.

The cemetery is full of bones. At first Rafa was afraid of them. Most are sealed in coffins, but there are mass pits with the poor and the older pits with the Protestants. The cemetery and slaughterhouse require Rafa to face his fear of death. That's why he endures them. "You see, by facing fear, I am cleansing myself, straining my past of the horror that infects me," he tells Fuga.

Each day, Rafa chooses a brave and happy smile. He faces fear and wins. The temporary victory is silent, but sings through his soul.

"Rafael!" his supervisor calls out to him. "Are you still trying to get to Talavera de la Reina for the bullfight?"

"*Sí.* The Sunday after next."

"We have an offal transport to a cosmetics factory the day before. They might be able to drop you on the way."

Rafa runs to his supervisor. "Is it confirmed?"

"Not yet, but if things fall into place you will arrive in Talavera de la Reina on Saturday night. Would you have a place to stay?"

"We'll sleep outside."

"Your *torero* will be okay with that?" asks the supervisor.

"You don't know Fuga," smiles Rafa. "But you will. *Por favor,* without transportation we'll have to walk or hitchhike. We don't have money for a bus."

"What sort of promotion are you doing for this bullfight?"

"Word of mouth. Tell everyone you know that on Sunday next the people of Talavera de la Reina will witness history. They will see a star rise." Rafa hears a rising swell of chants in his head. He must get to the cemetery and tell Fuga of the transport.

"But what's his name? You can't call a

torero Fuga."

Rafa pauses to think. His name? For years he's answered only to "Fuga."

His supervisor shakes his head. "If you want word to spread, start with his name. I'll know something about the transport in a couple days. Now get to the floor."

Rafa ties his apron and heads to work. An offal transport to a cosmetics factory. That means they'll be sitting in the bed of a truck with heaps of animal brains, skin, hair, bones, hooves and whatever else is used to make cosmetics. Bad death, but better than walking.

His boss is right. Promotion for the bullfight is essential. Why didn't he think of that? Word must spread about Fuga, the dark storm. He struggles, reaching into his memory for his friend's birth name. The name does not return to him.

But the voices of the past do.

Do others in Spain have ghosts in the attic of their mind? Do they try to face them as he does? The door to the attic creaks constantly, beckoning Rafa with a long, crooked finger back to his childhood. Back to the war. On the dark attic stairs he passes buildings exploding with bombs, a man with a crater for a nose, bellies swollen with hunger, and the "brothers" from the boys' home, rubbing their fat palms together.

Come closer, Rafa.

They're not real, he tells himself. You can beat them. At the top of the stairs is a whispering graveyard, full of unquiet bones and unmarked graves. His heart hammers. His body vibrates with sweat. None of this is real. It's not real.

Come closer, Rafa. We have something to show you. Closer.

The crooked finger points to a small, wiggly mass on the ground. Sprouting from his father's brains . . . is the flag of the Falange.

Boo.

I had a conversation with Ambassador Griffis before he left here and informed him that Franco's attitude in these matters is exceedingly obnoxious to me. There was a time, and I think it still exists, when Protestants couldn't have public funerals. They are forced to be buried at night and are allowed no markers for their graves. They are buried in plowed fields like potter's fields. I think in these modern times when we are doing everything we possibly can for religious freedom that it is a very bad example to be set before the world.

— HARRY S. TRUMAN, 33rd president of the United States

August 2, 1951, Memorandum from President Harry S. Truman to Secretary of State Dean Acheson
Acheson Papers — Secretary of State File Truman Library Archives

27

Daniel walks back to the lobby, his mind tangled in the telegram he forwarded to his mother. The words in the message belong to their priest in Dallas. Father Brodd has been part of the family for decades.

WESTERN UNION TELEGRAM

— VIA CABLE

SENDER: CATHOLIC DIOCESE OF DALLAS MRS. MARIA MATHESON, CASTELLANA HILTON MADRID WILL FORWARD DOCUMENTATION RE-QUESTED. WITH RECENT MISFOR-TUNE URGE REFLECTION AND PRAYER.

IN DOMINO, FR BRODD

"Recent misfortune"? Has something

happened with his father's business? What sort of documentation would his mother need from the Catholic Church?

He wishes he'd never opened it. If his father's business is struggling, there may be more pressure to join the company.

"*Hola,* Texano!"

Carlitos, the bellboy, sprints to Daniel's side. He plants his right foot and stands at attention. "I have a message for you! *Señor* Mendoza called. Your photographs are ready."

Daniel perks up. "That's great. Thanks, Buttons." He fishes in his pocket and tips the boy before heading upstairs.

In his short absence, the suite has been cleaned. The flowing drapes are corded back. The twisted sheets are now taut; the bed dressed and respectable. On the bench at the foot of the bed sits his belt, carefully coiled around the large buckle. He lifts the belt and something flutters beneath. It's a newspaper clipping.

Madrid today has more Texans than Spaniards. The barroom at the Castellana Hilton sounds like roundup time in the Panhandle.

A notation added in the margin says, *And some boys from Dallas are "getting lost" in the basement.*

He laughs, looking at the feminine handwriting. Ana's pretty *and* clever. It's his turn to reply. He grabs a magazine from the table and begins to search.

The elevator doors open to the lobby. The seemingly ever-present Paco Lobo, the man who adopted a village, stands in the corner, chatting with staff. Upon seeing Daniel, he waves.

Carlitos appears and points to the envelope in Daniel's hand. "Shall I mail your letter for you, *señor*?"

"You can deliver it for me. What is Ana's last name?"

"Ana here at the hotel? She is Ana Torres Moreno."

Daniel retrieves a pen from his camera bag. He adds Ana's last name to the envelope adorned with the hotel crest.

"How long have you been speaking English?" asks Daniel, as he hands the letter to Carlitos.

"Over a year." He waves Daniel forward

186

with a conspiratorial grin. "There's a classroom in the basement of the hotel. *Señor* Hilton is very good to his employees."

Daniel nods, furthering the covert conversation. "I saw the classroom. I was down there last night. You must also study courtesy. Everyone here is so polite. They insist on calling me *señor.*"

"But of course! We must refer to everyone in that manner."

Everyone. So apparently to Ana, Nick is not "everyone"?

"Say, Buttons, if you can deliver this letter privately, I'll give you a good tip when I return."

Carlitos clutches Daniel's sleeve and pulls him close. "Of course, *señor.* Privacy is one of the first words we learned in the classroom. After all, a hotel is a house of secrets."

Daniel hates secrets, but his are quickly multiplying. The photo of the nun with the baby, the breakup with Laura Beth, his plan for J-School, and now, the opened telegram.

He takes a breath, acknowledging the reality:

A secret never stays secret for long.

28

Carlitos makes his way into the basements in search of Ana. His cheery whistle dances off the walls as he winds through the underground maze. She is nowhere to be found. He heads to the staff break room. Lorenza stands in the doorway, smoking a cigarette. Women in Spain don't smoke, especially not in public. It's considered vulgar and indelicate. But while working at the hotel, some employees exploit American customs. Lorenza seems to exploit all of them.

"Have you seen Ana?" he asks.

Lorenza exhales a scarf of smoke, leaving a lipstick print the color of murder on the cigarette. "*Sí,* she was requested upstairs in the *Placita.* Why?"

"No reason. If you see her, tell her I'm

looking for her."

Lorenza snaps the envelope from his hand. "Who's it from?"

"*Ay,* Lorenza, give it back."

She lifts the envelope to the light, trying to peer into it. "Don't worry, *pequeñín,* I'll give it to her."

"No, the guest asked me to deliver it myself."

Lorenza pulls the envelope to her chest and lowers her voice. "It's from a guest? Which one? Is it Max Factor?"

The boy's face wrinkles with concern, as if he's committed a grave error. "It's private, Lorenza. If you interfere I might not get a tip." He clasps his hands together in a begging plead.

"Fine, *chico.* I'm just trying to help Ana. We don't want her to get into trouble again."

The boy's eyes widen. "Ana was in trouble?"

Lorenza pulls another drag on her cigarette. "*Uy,* you didn't hear that from me. But let's just say that Ana's sweet smile might not be so sweet after all."

"*Ay,* stop." Carlitos grabs the envelope and leaves Lorenza to her cigarette.

He takes the service elevator up two levels to the shopping *Placita.* The *Placita* is a large cobblestone rotunda, surrounded by a circle of expensive stores. Originally a palace courtyard, the shopping area now features a men's hat shop, a hair salon, a Spanish specialty store, and the couture boutique of renowned designer Pedro Rodríguez.

That's where he finds Ana.

Carlitos peers through the storefront window and sees a slender woman wearing a long pink gown, covered with crystal flowers. Ana assists the tailor with a fitting. Carlitos stands by the door, unwilling to step into the underworld of sequins and silk. The fabric finery isn't the only reason he is bashful. In most department stores in Spain, clothing is displayed on flat silhouettes. The mannequins in the hotel shop have a human female form, with curves and bumps. Some of the curvy mannequins wear revealing dresses.

"I have a delivery," he calls out, looking away.

Much to his despair, the tailor waves him into the shop.

Ana kneels on the floor near the hem of the dress, taking instruction from the tailor.

"What do you have?" asks the tailor. His speech is garbled through fitting pins held in his mouth.

"A letter."

He extends a hand to Carlitos.

"No, *señor,* not for you. For Ana."

Ana's head snaps to the boy. "For me?"

"It will have to wait. We're nearly done," says the tailor. "Isn't she gorgeous?"

Carlitos gives a thick swallow. "Nearly done? But half of the dress is still missing, *señor,*" he whispers.

"It's not missing. It's a plunging back."

Carlitos pretends to understand. "Oh. Where is she plunging?"

"No, *chico,* it means the back is open," says Ana. "The dress is for the fashion gala at the American embassy."

"*Ay,* the dress is for Americans. That's good, we must keep Spanish girls like you out of trouble," says Carlitos, doing his very best to sound mature.

"Ana, in trouble?" The tailor laughs. "Ana's too nice to cause trouble."

29

Trouble? Has someone seen the notes? Ana spies the envelope clutched tightly in the boy's damp hand. The gold emblem. Her heart drops.

An official hotel envelope.

How could this happen? She swallowed the note days ago. She told no one, not even Rafa. She snatches the envelope from Carlitos and stuffs it in her apron pocket.

"*Bueno,* you may carefully remove the dress," the tailor tells the woman, unzipping the side.

Ana follows the model to the fitting room and helps her remove the gown.

"*¡Ay!* You're poking me with the pins. What's wrong with you?" snaps the woman.

"*Perdón.* I'm sorry, *señorita.*"

"You should be sorry," huffs the model. "I can't have scratches on my skin wearing a dress like this." She hands the garment to Ana and orders her out of the fitting room.

Ana looks at the beautiful pink gown, a gown she could never afford, a gown too revealing for Spain. The letter from the hotel peeks out of her apron pocket and her sister's nervous warning floats back to her. She cannot lose this job. They have five mouths to feed.

Ana heads to the back of the shop, and after laying the dress on the tailor's table, she slips behind a rack of jeweled dresses. She stares at her name on the envelope.

The handwriting is artistic, unique. Fingers trembling, she opens the flap, frightened to look inside. She removes the paper. It's not a termination letter. It's an advertisement.

Ana recognizes it immediately. It's from *LIFE* magazine, an issue she peeked at in Daniel's room.

The illustration features a handsome family around a table in an American kitchen. Everything sparkles, especially their smiles. But the ad is annotated. A large arrow points to an appliance. Above it is written, REFRIGERATOR — ELECTRICALLY WARMED THERMOSTAT, CONTROLLED BUTTER-READY. Thought bubbles are drawn over the family members' heads, exclaiming:

"Ana! We like ice!"

"Have any more ice?"

"Hooray for ice!"

And over the man's head is written, "Ana, I have an idea!"

Relief floods through her. It's a joke. From Daniel. She smiles and begins to laugh. A mirror on the wall hands back her reflection and the laughter knots into a catch of breath. The jeweled gowns shimmer next to her dark hair and olive skin. Expensive fabric has never touched Ana's body, has never draped across her shoulders. She suddenly thinks not of herself but of someone else.

There are photographs. Her mother in gowns and beautiful jewelry. Attending elegant events. Dancing alongside those who will later order her arrest and imprisonment.

How different things could be. Why

didn't her family flee to Mexico or France like some of the others? She doesn't speak of it, but on occasion tourists do.

"The little general is doing a fine job here," they say. "Spain's economy is picking up. See, things aren't so bad here after all."

It takes all the force within her to remain silent, to resist the reminder that they weren't in Spain after the war. They haven't seen hope eaten by hunger and dignity destroyed. And now, in describing Madrid, the new guidebook says: *Everyone who isn't a maid has one.*

Yes, Ana is a maid. Temporarily. Soon she'll move to the business office. But for now that's a secret dream. She once made the mistake of sharing a dream. How many notes will she have to swallow because of it?

Ana's gaze returns to the mirror.

What possessed her to leave Daniel that magazine clipping? He's a hotel guest. Yes, she's assigned to his family but initiating private jokes with an American boy who lives the life of a prince? Foolish. But he's so kind and they communicate so easily. It was just a bit of fun. She's supposed to be conversational, isn't she? It was rude to ignore his questions in the cafeteria. His family won't give her a recommendation if she's rude.

No. Why is she trying to rationalize? Because he's handsome? She's kidding herself.

Even in a country where both God and peasant are called *señor,* the line between "have" and "have not" is deeply carved. A singular truth shines revealing light.

Her sister is right.

The life and liberties Ana sees at the hotel do not belong to her. The war's outcome will forever dictate her future. But . . . it's just a bit of harmless fun.

She folds the envelope from Daniel and puts it back in her apron pocket.

No one needs to know.

30

The three-hour *siesta* is ending. Shutters part or rattle up, revealing storefronts awakening for business. Daniel makes his way to the camera shop. He looks for photo opportunities along the way, distractions from his mother's telegram.

Madrid is a city of hardened soil. Amidst the heat and dryness, spots of color draw his lens. Hues emerge from the palette of children. Girls skip rope down the street in beautiful dresses. Boys bounce brightly colored balls.

"Children — they're treasured in Madrid," Ben told him during their lunch. "Contraception is illegal. Franco's family policy laws reward parents with the most kids. Six to ten children is not uncommon. Big family photos."

Daniel's family photo is small. When

he was little, he asked constantly for siblings. One night his father sat on his bed and gently explained that asking for siblings made his mom very sad. "Let's not talk about that, okay, partner? We don't want to make Mom sad."

But many years later, his mother still seems sad. Perhaps that's why they're supporting an orphanage now.

There are colors of beauty in Madrid, but also colors of hardship. Ghosts of war walk the streets in Spain. Daniel passes blind lottery vendors, citizens missing limbs, young people using canes. Should he look directly at them and acknowledge their sacrifice or look away and honor their dignity? Are veterans treated differently in Spain than they are in the States? When Daniel was five, he told his parents he wanted to join the soldiers and fight in Germany. They bought him a toy helmet and plastic grenades. His father, however, did not fight in the war and seemed relieved to have flat feet.

The wooden door to Miguel's small shop stands open, but unattended.

"Hola," calls Daniel, as he sets his camera on the counter.

He turns to the framed photos on the wall. One catches his eye immediately, pulling him closer. Young children sit on a sidewalk, playing a game. Behind them is a ruin of a building with ammunition holes the size of grapefruits. The door of the building is caved in. Stone shrapnel covers the area where the children play. The photo is signed in black ink.

Robert Capa.

"Do you know his work?" Miguel asks, entering from the street.

"*Sí,* very well," says Daniel. "How did you get a signed photo?"

"I developed it." Miguel smiles, and his eyebrows, a winged mix of black and gray, rise as if they could take flight.

"You met him?"

"Many times. Some rolls with personal photos — he didn't want them developed by the newspapers or magazines. We speak of film; let me get yours." Miguel disappears behind the curtain.

Capa fascinates Daniel. Robert Capa was born Endré Friedmann, a Hungarian Jew, who fled to Paris. While exiled in Paris, Endré and his girlfriend created the identity of "Robert Capa." They sold their photos to news agencies under the guise of an American photographer.

"Did you know him as Endré Friedmann or Robert Capa?" Daniel asks.

Miguel's voice calls from behind the curtain. "Ah, you know the story. To me he was always Capa. His ruse was eventually discovered and abandoned, but the name 'Robert Capa' endured."

Daniel considers the concept of alternate identity. What name would he choose?

"Do you know what his motto was?" calls Miguel from the back.

"*Sí.* 'If your pictures aren't good enough, you're not close enough,'" says Daniel.

He returns his gaze to the photos on the wall. Capa's photos make Daniel feel as if he's inside them. But how close is too close? Three years ago, Capa died stepping on a land mine in Indochina.

Miguel returns with an envelope. "Photographs are personal. Perhaps you'd like to see them privately."

"Not at all," replies Daniel. "I'm a

finalist in a photography contest in the States. I'd welcome your help." He opens the paper sleeve and begins removing the photos. He doesn't look at them. Instead, he quickly lays them on the counter, like he's dealing from a deck of cards. Once all of the photos are displayed, Daniel steps back to evaluate. He immediately realizes: One photograph is missing.

The photo of the nun and the baby. It's not among the pictures. He swears he pressed the shutter. The photograph should be there. He sees Miguel eyeing him from behind the counter.

Daniel quickly selects one picture and sets it off to the side, facedown. He chooses two more and moves them to a different position. He then creates two groups, arranged in lines. Miguel watches Daniel with fascination, as he assembles a narrative with the pictures.

"¿Qué piensas?" Daniel asks Miguel for his thoughts.

Miguel studies the squares like a chessboard. He opens his hands, asking for Daniel's permission.

"Por favor." Daniel nods.

Miguel moves the photo of the hungry

girl outside the candy shop next to a shot of the Van Dorns' lush dinner table.

"*Sí,*" agrees Daniel. "That's good."

Some lines create a narrative with pictures from the same setting. Others build a story by the positioning of opposites.

Daniel and Miguel stand in silent evaluation, arms crossed, brows creased. Daniel suddenly jumps to the counter. He pulls the photos of children and creates a new line. The poor girl at the candy store window, Carlitos posing proudly in the hotel lobby, and the small son of an American diplomat in a miniature suit and tie.

"*Sí,*" applauds Miguel. "The next generation. The future." Miguel then takes the photo of the American child and positions it between the two Spanish children.

"That's it," says Daniel. "America within Spain."

They both smile, satisfied with the story threads they've created.

Miguel steps back from the counter. "*Muy bonito.* Is this how you always do it?"

"It's not how I do it; it's how I see it," explains Daniel. "A single photo has to be powerful to tell a story on its own, like Capa's. I haven't mastered that yet. For now, I create stories by positioning things side by side. But —" Daniel reaches into the envelope for the negatives. "One photograph seems to be missing."

"*¿Ah, sí?*"

Miguel remains silent while Daniel inspects his negatives. It's there. The image is there. Why didn't Miguel develop it?

Before Daniel can ask, Miguel points to the single photo that sits alone outside the groupings. He turns it over. It's the photo of Ana, her bright smile reflecting amidst the multiple mirrors in the elevator.

"And this one? Where does she fit in?"

Daniel looks at the picture. It's perfect. Natural and fun, like their conversation in the basement. "I guess that one's a story all her own." He begins to gather the photos.

Miguel bellows a hearty laugh, loud

enough to float outside and bounce among the balls on the street. "That's what Rafael would say."

Daniel slides the photos back into the paper sleeve. "Rafael's her boyfriend?"

Miguel watches Daniel avoid his eyes, yet wait for a reply.

"No, Texano," he says quietly. "Rafa is her older brother." And after a pause, "She has an older sister too."

Daniel nods without raising his glance. He reaches for his wallet to pay. "*Gracias*, Miguel. But . . . I think you missed one frame on the strip."

Miguel takes the money from Daniel and drums his tobacco-stained fingers on the counter. He disappears behind the curtain. When he reappears, he's holding a photo. "*Ay*, I thought perhaps this one was a mistake." He sets it on the counter.

The swirling robes of the nun. The empty stare of the dead child. The image is there, just as Daniel remembers it. It's haunting, unsettling. There's a story, but what is it? He should have paid more attention to his surroundings, to the buildings on the street.

Miguel clears his throat. "You're very talented. But remember, Spain is not your country. Be careful, *amigo.*"

The Guardia Civil delivered a similar message. Daniel knows the words of caution are meant to dissuade him. They should.

But they don't.

Mr. Capa, specialist in the shot-and-shell school of photography, was the kind of close-up lens artist who made veteran combat troops blink in uneasy disbelief. . . . He jumped with paratroopers into Germany; he landed on the Normandy beachhead on D-Day; he was one of the advance arrivals on Anzio. And he shrugged away the risks with the remark that "for a war correspondent to miss an invasion is like refusing a date with Lana Turner after completing a five-year stretch at Sing Sing."

"Cameraman Capa Killed in Vietnam: Photographer for LIFE *Dies in Explosion of a Land Mine — At Front Only Few Days*"
The New York Times, *May 26, 1954*

31

Ana stands on the sidewalk near the hotel, laughing at her inquisitive cousin.

"*Ay,* don't laugh," says Puri. "Julia must know Ordóñez. She makes suits for all of the famous matadors. Has she met him? Just tell me."

Ordóñez. To her cousin, he is Spanish perfection. Bullfighter, husband, father.

"Julia doesn't speak of the customers. You know that," smiles Ana. Puri is remarkably naïve. *La Sección Femenina,* the women's section of the fascist movement, is succeeding with her cousin. Women should aspire to the ultimate cultural archetype — the Virgin Mary.

For some girls, nature dissolves doctrine once they're noticed by boys. Ana wonders when Puri's innocent world might become more complicated. Daniel's photograph of the Texas party and the sultry girl blowing a kiss to his camera returns to Ana. Is that his girlfriend?

"Is it true that Rafa's friend will fight near Talavera de la Reina?"

Ana wipes a meandering hair from her cousin's eyes and takes her hand. "Puri, in the few minutes we have, let's speak of something other than bullfights. How are Aunt and Uncle?"

"They're fine," she says with a sigh. "Mother would like to see Julia and Lali. It's been a month."

Ana nods. Puri's mother is her aunt Teresa, her mother's younger sister. Aunt Teresa took care of Ana while her mother was in prison. She longs for details of her mother's final days, but her aunt still refuses to provide any. Is it too painful or too dangerous? Ana avoids the alternative: It is too shameful.

"*¡Dios Mío!* Ana, look. The tall one. Is he a famous actor?"

Ana raises her eyes to the street. It's not an actor. It's Daniel. He sees her and waves. She waves back.

"He's a hotel guest," whispers Ana.

"*Ay, mi madre,* you know him?" Puri quickly smooths her hair and skirt.

"Howdy. Taking a break?" asks Daniel.

Ana nods. "This is my cousin, Purificación. We're visiting for a few minutes. She doesn't speak English."

Daniel introduces himself to Puri in Spanish.

Puri's eyes expand. "Where are you from?" she asks.

"Texas. But my mother is from Spain. Galicia."

"*El Caudillo* is from Galicia," says Puri with a bob of approval.

"Oh, really?" says Daniel.

Puri nods, appraising him. "How old are you?"

Ana shoots an apologetic look, but Daniel smiles. "Nineteen soon."

"Nineteen," nods Puri. "In Texas, are you Catholic?" she asks.

"Puri!" gasps Ana.

"I've heard that some Americans aren't Catholic."

"Many Americans aren't Catholic," says Daniel.

"Why?" asks Puri.

"Because some are Protestant, some are Jewish. There are quite a few religions in America."

Puri's brow knits in confusion.

"I'm sorry, *señor,*" says Ana, trying to reroute the conversation in English. "She hasn't met many Americans. She's just curious. She doesn't mean any offense."

"I'm not offended. My mom is Catholic. My dad had to convert to marry her. Kind of an ordeal in Texas."

Puri frowns at their English, excluded from the conversation.

Daniel looks at Ana. "Say, I just picked up my photographs from Miguel."

"Are you pleased?"

"I think so. I'd like your opinion. But I better be careful." Daniel lowers his voice. "Did you hear? Boys from Dallas are getting lost in the basement."

Ana raises her eyes to his. "Yes, I heard. Probably hunting for ice."

She glances casually to the street, trying to conceal the blush deepening down the length of her neck. She hopes he does not see it.

He does. His grin says so.

Ana notes Puri trying to decode their exchange, trying to rejoin the conversation. Puri's eyes land on Daniel's boots. They're the color of toffee, have a squared toe, and are well past the effort of a shine. "Do you ride a horse in Texas?" she asks.

"I do. We've got a bay quarter named Tony."

"You have a horse named Tony?" Puri bursts into a nervous fit of giggles.

Daniel looks to Ana. "I guess that's funny? Well, I'm going to head up to my room." He gives a wave to the girls and departs down the sidewalk.

Puri grabs Ana's arm. "I just met an American," she whispers.

"Yes, you did."

"Nice to meet you, Daniel!" Puri calls after him.

"Nice to meet you too, Puri." He points to Ana and switches to English. "She called me Daniel. Sounds pretty good, don't you think?" He smiles and shrugs his shoulders.

"What did he say?" asks Puri.

"He said goodbye," says Ana quietly, watching the retreating figure of Daniel Matheson cast a tall shadow on the sidewalk.

32

Puri stares at her cousin. Ana is lying. Again.

The American boy said more than goodbye. Does Ana speak with many boys at the hotel? Is she properly chaperoned in their rooms when she cleans? Ana's cheeks are flushed. The look in her eyes, is that what Puri has been warned about?

Puri thinks of all that Ana might see at the Hilton. Are some of the guests Protestants and Jews, like Daniel mentioned? Sister Hortensia says Americans are known to be indecent and libertine. Puri thinks of it with equal parts pity and fascination. What, exactly, defines indecency? Was it indecent of her to call out to Daniel on the street?

Her parents whisper about Ana. They

say it is not her fault. They say Ana is a beautiful girl, punished by her father's blood.

Spanish Republican blood. The "Reds" tried to pull Spain away from virtue. But what does that really mean? wonders Puri. And why won't anyone answer her questions?

"Thanks for coming to visit me," says Ana sweetly.

Puri wraps her arms around her cousin. Poor Ana. But perhaps all is not lost. Perhaps Puri can help Ana like she helps the orphans at the Inclusa.

Perhaps she can save her.

The sensual woman has sunken eyes, flushed cheeks, transparent ears, pointed chin, dry mouth, sweaty hands, broken waist, insecure step and a sad overall being. . . . Only her damaged imagination remains active with the representation of lascivious images which fill it completely. The sensual woman should not expect serious work, serious respect, clean feelings or welcoming tenderness.

— FATHER GARCÍA FIGAR
Medina, *magazine of the* Sección Femenina, *August 12, 1945*

33

Rafa finds Fuga in the cemetery work shed. On most nights, when Fuga's not roaming the pastures or visiting Rafa, this is where he sleeps. In the corner of the corrugated metal hut between stacks of shovels sits a lantern and a pallet of straw. Apart from his tattered clothing, Fuga has only two possessions that Rafa knows of — a magazine clipping of a Miura bull and a small gold pendant with a serene, hand-painted likeness of Blessed Mother Mary.

The energy in the shed has a brewing, cyclonic feel. *"¿Qué pasa?"* asks Rafa.

Fuga paces the small space, nostrils flared, fingers splaying and clenching. Anger courses through his body with such force that the vibration is visible.

"Cálmate. Tell me what's wrong."

Fuga slowly raises his hand and points.

A miniature plywood coffin sits in the dirt. It's for an infant.

"*Ay,* it's very sad," agrees Rafa. "Poor *niño.*" Rafa understands his friend's frustration. Whether sick, disabled, or orphaned, vulnerable children trigger deep feelings of injustice within Fuga. He wants to protect them. "No one protected us. No one," he often says.

"I'll help you bury it. It will be quick with two of us." Rafa takes a step toward the coffin, but Fuga moves to block him. He looks down at Rafa and shakes his head.

"*¿Por qué?*" asks Rafa.

Rage explodes from Fuga. He kicks the baby coffin with all of the force inside him. It rockets across the shed, smashing into the wall.

"STOP!" screams Rafa. "What are you doing?"

Fuga resumes pacing.

"*¡Ay, no! ¡Ay, no!*" gasps Rafa. He runs to the wall and begins searching among the broken pieces for the corpse. He picks up a scrap of dirty muslin and looks frantically around. He finally stops, his breathing labored and panicked. "Fuga, where is the child?"

Fuga shakes his head.

"Where is the baby? What did you do with the baby?"

"No baby," hisses Fuga.

Rafa's heart beats wildly. He takes a deep breath, trying to keep the voices behind the barrier. It's not working. The memories are crawling over the fence.

"The box is empty! There is no baby!" Fuga begins to push and punch him, screaming, "Do you understand? There is no baby!"

Rafa takes his friend by the shoulders. "*Tranquilo, amigo.* I don't understand. They asked you to bury an empty coffin?"

Fuga nods. He walks to his bed of straw and kicks it, creating a swirl of dust.

"Who brought it to you?"

Fuga stares at the wall of the shed. "Clinic. Many coffins they bring are too light."

"The maternity clinic is asking you to

bury empty coffins? I don't understand. Why?"

Fuga whirls to face him. "Because the babies aren't dead."

34

"Delivery for room 760."

760. Daniel's room.

"Gracias," says Ana. The hospitality manager drops a box into her basket.

Once in the elevator, Ana steals a glance at the small box. It's a roll of tape. Grateful for the opportunity to see Daniel, she plans her apology for Puri's questions.

He opens the door on her first knock.

"Hola, señor. Hospitality asked me to deliver this." Ana extends the small box.

"Thanks." Daniel props the door open with his boot. "Come in for a moment?"

Ana stands, frozen in the hallway. "Does your room need servicing, *señor?"*

"Servicing? No, I'd like to show you my photos."

"Perhaps your drapes need adjusting?"

"No, they're fine."

Ana remains outside the door, smiling, until Daniel realizes. She isn't allowed into his room without a service request.

"Oh, can you help me open the door to the balcony?"

"Certainly, *señor.*" Ana shifts the basket from her hip and enters. The suite, already warm, will be sweltering within minutes. She slides the glass door open anyway.

On the floor near the wall is a mosaic of pictures. Daniel waves her over.

"I put them together with Miguel," he explains. "Each grouping should tell a story. They'll be easier to see once I tape them to the wall."

Ana nods, staring at the photos. They do tell a story. In fact, they tell many stories.

"Do you like them?" he asks, wiping a bead of sweat from his forehead.

"*Sí.* Very much, *señor.* Especially the photos of the children."

Ana mentions the children, but she is

staring at the photos of the Van Dorns' dinner party. She gazes at the long, elegant table, the sparkling crystal goblets, the tangles of fresh grapes roped between sterling candelabras. He's captured it all.

The air in the room is suddenly thick, creeping and pressing in around Ana. She removes a small accordioned fan from her apron pocket. "Is it too hot with the door open, *señor*? Shall I turn the air-cooling on?" she asks, fluttering air toward her face.

"No, I'm fine." Daniel tugs at the center seam of his western shirt. The pearl snaps create a soft pop as he pulls them apart. "So, you got my note."

"Yes, more ice." Ana gives a weak laugh, willing herself not to look at him.

Daniel's gaze is upon her. She can feel it, serious, as if he were trying to capture the moment on film.

"In the note I mentioned an idea," he says.

"Yes. This is a very good idea," says Ana. "I like the way the photos are organized."

"Oh." Daniel pauses and runs a hand through his sweaty hair. His voice drops in volume. His eyes fasten to hers. "Actually, that's not the idea I was referring to."

Alarm bells crash in Ana's head, while a mixture of hope and fear beats through her chest. Daniel steps in close. His plaid shirt hangs open, revealing a damp white T-shirt beneath.

"I was thinking, well, I guess I was hoping . . . ," he says quietly.

Ana stares at the photos instead of Daniel. She knows she should step away, but her feet have grown roots through the floor. She should not allow him so close. She should not inhale the smell of his expensive aftershave. But the roots are growing, snaking all the way down to the dark, stone basements.

"I was hoping you might work on a project with me," says Daniel.

"A project?" Her voice is a whisper. Her fan bats like a butterfly.

"I'd like to create a story about life in Spain, but through the eyes of people our age."

A story. About Spain. The roots snap. Ana's heart freefalls into her stomach. Disappointment and relief flood through her in equal parts. "Why?" she asks, tucking the fan and her hope back into the apron.

"To illustrate differences and similarities between us, between the U.S. and Spain."

Ana steps away from Daniel.

What similarities could he possibly see between them? Daniel can travel anywhere in the world. He is heir to an oil dynasty, lives a life of privilege, and enjoys every freedom imaginable. He can vote in an election, pray to any God of his choosing, and speak his personal feelings aloud in public.

"We could remain anonymous," says Daniel quickly. "Like Robert Capa and Gerda Taro. You could be Jane Doe."

"Jane Doe?"

"*Sí, Jane Doe* means 'an anonymous woman.' As Jane, you could provide a lens into Spain that I can't access on my own. We could work together. You're a good subject and a good photographer.

227

Look." Daniel points to two photos on the desk. One is the photo of Ana in the elevator. He hands it to her.

She grimaces. "Is my mouth really that big?" She despises the gold tooth on the bottom side of her mouth. She puts the photo back on the desk.

"It's not a big mouth. It's called a bright smile. You don't want the picture?"

She shakes her head. Next to her picture is the photo she took of Daniel in the candy shop. The left side of his mouth lifts in a grin, on the brink of laughter. He looks into the camera with eyes so honest, yet so evidently out of place amidst the pretty sweets. The photo she took *is* good. It's beautiful. But it has nothing to do with her photography.

His project — if Daniel made a formal request to her manager — could they work together on it?

Her sister's warnings whisper loudly.

Ana lifts the basket and makes her way toward the door. "I'm very sorry, *señor,* but I don't think I can help you with your project. The hotel keeps me so busy."

Daniel stands, hands in the back pockets of his jeans. He nods in understanding.

As Ana passes the coffee table, she stops. The image in the Hilton hotel magazine sends a wave of chills across her neck.

The massive granite cross.

It's perched on a hilltop northwest of Madrid within jagged fangs of stone. It towers one hundred fifty meters high and can be seen from over thirty kilometers away.

El Valle de los Caídos. The Valley of the Fallen.

The magazine text barks and beckons:

Nearly twenty years in the making, the Valley of the Fallen approaches completion. Visitors will soon experience this beautiful place of rest and meditation in memory of all those who fell in the glorious crusade.

The reeds of the basket crack beneath her grip. She points to the magazine. "Do you know what this is?"

"Yes, the site where tourists will learn

229

about the Spanish Civil War."

"Is that what you think?" gasps Ana.

"Is that wrong?" he asks. "I was thinking of visiting to take photos. See, this is why I need your help. I don't understand, but Jane Doe can explain it to me."

Ana stares at him, a lump rising in her throat. So, this is how the world sees Spain? Do they think the Valley of the Fallen is a place to buy souvenirs? It's being built by Republican prisoners.

Ana returns to the photos on the floor, to one that instantly caught her eye. She picks up the photo of the nun and the baby and tosses it on the coffee table. "Sometimes there is no explanation, *señor*. Good evening."

Ana exits the room, fighting for breath. She turns the corner in the hallway, slumps down the wall, and wills herself not to cry.

There is a thriving temporary village at the Valley of the Fallen which houses two thousand workers and their families. . . . A marvelous combination of grandeur, magnificence, and simplicity. We strongly recommend a visit.

Castellana Magazine, *Hilton Hotels, July 1957*

35

They walk in darkness. Madrid's night sky stretches deep and wide. Their footfalls issue soft calls on the dry sand of the dirt road. Rafa tries to make conversation, but Fuga marches ahead in a trance. He utters only one word: *mentirosos.*

Liars.

That afternoon they had exhumed the corpse of a four-year-old boy for lack of payment. The family, too poor to pay rent on the cemetery plot, stood crying as the child's remains were churned and reburied in a common trench. The grandmother wailed curses.

"Please, *señora,*" explained Rafa. "It is not our fault, only our job. If we do not work, we do not eat."

"May you choke on the bread you earn

from this," spat the bereaved woman.

"Fuga, she wasn't blaming or cursing us," says Rafa. "She was grieving for the child." Rafa knows that Fuga not only grieves for the boy, he sees himself in every poor child, in each pit heaped with bones. With each trench of the shovel, he is burying himself.

"Mentirosos," hisses Fuga.

"Think of your own words to me," says Rafa. "You say we mustn't allow ourselves to be poisoned by circumstance. Your plan is honorable."

Fuga nods and spits on the side of the road.

Rafa thinks of his friend's pledge. Fuga says he will fight for the child — the innocent, the unwanted, the lost children of Spain. He will use money earned from bullfighting to pay rent for the cemetery plots of children. He will save destitute boys from the evil "homes." This is his plan.

Fuga stops and motions for silence. Was it a voice or a bird? They run to a nearby row of cypress trees. Lying on their stomachs, they listen.

Rafa hears only Fuga. Nostrils flared for fight, Fuga is aflame with determination. The mantra of bullfighting is "To become a bullfighter, you must first become a bull." Fuga has long been a bull. He has courage and strength to battle any man or beast and remarkable finesse while doing it, but sometimes Rafa worries his friend lacks the inherent grace required of a *torero.*

The pasture of Don José Isasa Cuadros is not far. Rafa hopes it's an owl Fuga heard. He hopes at this late hour the Crows are asleep on their barrack cots. So despised are the Crows that they do not serve in the region where they live. The risk to their families is too great.

"Perhaps we train another night," whispers Rafa.

Fuga says nothing. After several breaths, he stands and resumes walking. Rafa follows his friend toward the pasture, the moon's glimmer their sole guide.

Most matadors are gentlemen, classically trained *toreros.* Joselito, Belmonte, and Spain's beloved Manolete — Rafa reveres them all. When Manolete died, a piece of Spain died with him. He was gored through the thigh, and the teams of special surgeons couldn't save him. He and Fuga have no special surgeons. There is no one supporting them.

They trudge on, into the closing dark. Rafa issues the reminder.

"The world we seek entrance to, it is a world of men with fat cigars, expensive automobiles, and relationships over many generations. You know that. But it is also a world where courage and skill transcend ancestry, Fuga. If a matador is truly talented, the blood running through his veins is not judged. It is protected."

Fuga nods.

To practice with bulls in a breeder's pasture is highly illegal. If caught, punishment will be immediate — and final. Rafa will go to confession before Mass on Sunday. He will again ask their priest in Vallecas for forgiveness and courage. Rafa pledges that once he earns money as part of Fuga's *cuadrilla,* his entourage, he will secretly compensate the breeders for tainting their bulls. This is his own plan.

They arrive at the pasture. The rumbling exhales and stomps of the bulls pass loudly on the still night air. Fuga unrolls his rusty blanket. He looks to Rafa and nods.

"In the name of the Father, and of the Son, and of the Holy Ghost, amen," recites Rafa. He makes the sign of the cross.

They crawl through the fence.

36

A six-year-old boy sees Puri and gestures frantically.

"What is it, *chico?*"

He lifts his small right hand, pinched tightly into a fist. He waves Puri to the corner and opens his fingers.

In the center of the boy's palm sits a tooth. Puri claps in delight.

"Wonderful! Let me see," she says.

The boy smiles proudly, revealing a large gap in the front of his mouth.

"You know what this means, don't you?" asks Puri.

The boy nods.

"Sí," says Puri. "Tonight you will put the tooth under your pillow. Ratoncito Pérez, the mouse that lives in a box of cookies, will visit while you sleep. He will

take the tooth and leave a surprise for you."

Puri wraps the child in a hug as he bounces with delight. The older children at the Inclusa have less chance of being adopted, so Puri dotes on them whenever possible. She loves playing Ratoncito Pérez.

A nun whisks by Puri. "Don't dawdle. Diapers need changing, babies need bathing and feeding."

Puri makes her way to the nursery, anxious to share the news of the tooth with Sister Hortensia.

Sister Hortensia stands at Clover's bassinet, engaged in conversation with a pregnant woman and her husband. Puri enters unnoticed. She tends the babies nearby and eavesdrops in the process.

"My wife is tired of wearing a pillow around her stomach. We're not sure this feels right," whispers the man.

Puri is desperate to look at the woman, but knows better.

"This child could be the answer," replies Sister Hortensia. "She's still very small."

"She's small, but too large to be a newborn, especially if we're claiming a premature birth. For the large sum we're paying, we want a newborn."

"And you shall have one," whispers Sister Hortensia. "I only present this as an option because your wife feels uncomfortable with the current situation. Let's discuss this in my office."

Puri counts their retreating footsteps on the tile floor. She turns to look. It is not the first time this has happened. Sister Hortensia tells her that some couples feel ashamed they cannot conceive. She says societal pressures are such that on occasion, a woman prefers to fake a pregnancy rather than admit adoption. When that happens they must protect the woman's secret at all costs. It is a sin to reveal someone else's secret.

Puri thinks of Ana's family. As children of Republicans they must carry many secrets. How, then, did Ana manage to get a job at the big American hotel?

Clover cries and Puri moves to inspect her diaper. She is relieved the couple did not choose Clover. The man was dough-faced and grim. She did not like the way he mentioned the large sum of money, nor how that prompted Sister Hortensia to ensure his satisfaction. Clover must have a handsome and kind family. She wishes that one of the brave matadors would adopt the child. A notable Spanish family adopting an orphan would be incredibly touching.

The thought triggers last night's dream. Puri reaches into her memory, trying to retrieve the quickly fading narrative. A tall matador walks toward her, handsome and graceful. He wears a suit of lights in royal sapphire, covered with glimmering gold accents. She looks up at him and smiles. He smiles back. And that's when Puri realizes. The matador in the dream is not Ordóñez. It's Daniel, the Texas cowboy she met on the street.

37

Why does the Valley of the Fallen upset Ana?

Daniel stares at the photos, now taped to the wall of his hotel suite. He shouldn't have asked her to work on the project. It made her uncomfortable. But when they're speaking and she's smiling, he forgets that she's a hotel employee.

He turns to his father, seated on the small sofa. "How was Valencia?" he asks.

"Wonderful city. Beautiful sea. I would've stayed an extra day, but your mother wanted to return for the fashion show at the embassy. Speaking of, you should get dressed. Suit and tie tonight."

Daniel nods.

Martin Matheson rises from the chair. He stands, looking at his son's photos affixed to the wall. Please. Just one compliment, thinks Daniel.

Instead, his father starts to laugh. He points to the photo of Nick Van Dorn's scabbed knuckles. "Pretty undiplomatic for a diplomat's son. That kid's a handful, huh?"

Daniel shrugs.

His father clears his throat. "What do you make of Ben, the newspaper man?" asks his dad.

"I like him. Seems like a smart guy. Intense about his job."

"Most journalists are. They want their story and will do anything to get it. It's a vicious business. Remember that." His father makes his way to the door.

The word *business* reminds him of the telegram. "Say, Dad. There's something I want to discuss."

His father stops. "I know."

"You do?"

He nods, face full of apology. "Dan, I'm sorry."

His father's sincerity smooths his annoyance.

"I was waiting for you to tell me," says

his father. "I understand hiding it from your mother. She loves Laura Beth. She'll be so hurt."

Laura Beth? His dad thinks he wants to talk about Laura Beth?

"Dad —"

"I know all about it. Someone told your uncle. Laura Beth, she's just confused. Graduation was overwhelming. You two make a fine couple and she's from an excellent family. Don't fret, I'm certain — quite certain — she'll change her mind."

A fine couple? They had nothing in common. They only dated a few months, during which she also kissed other guys. Does he know that Laura Beth felt his mom was "too ethnic" and therefore their families weren't a suitable match?

"It's okay, Dad, there were problems."

"Every relationship has problems. Speaking of . . ." His father pauses, as if carefully gathering words. "Daniel, your mother and I have had a bit of a tough time lately. Give her a little extra room if you can. It's important to her that you're happy here in Madrid."

The request takes Daniel by surprise. A tough time? What does that mean? His mind returns to the telegram. He wants to ask questions but something about his father's expression tells him not to. His dad's tone, it's kinder than usual, intentionally easing up on him.

"Okay," says Daniel.

"Thanks, partner. We'll leave for the embassy in fifteen minutes." He exits the room.

Daniel stares at the door. His father can be headstrong and, sure, their father-son dynamic has been tense for the past few years. But things have never been strained between his parents.

What did he mean by a tough time?

38

The American embassy is built of blocky white sandstone. Its posture conveys a mix of durability and refinement. A large red, white, and blue flag, along with its forty-eight stars, salutes above the entry.

"Welcome to the embassy, Daniel. So glad you could join us."

Nick's father, Shep Van Dorn, greets them in a formal receiving line at the entrance. Van Dorn shakes his hand and looks to Daniel's mother.

"Good evening, María. My, you look gorgeous. Are you sure you're not in the fashion show tonight?"

Ever polished and professional, Shephard Van Dorn is cut from different fabric than his son. Nick stands amidst a group of pretty young women in the corner, and when he sees Daniel, he whistles loudly. The girls laugh at his inappropriate gesture. Nick's father does not.

"Well, how about that," laughs Nick. "Cowboy traded his boots for a suit. Lookin' good, Dan." Nick's enthusiasm, fueled by wine, entertains the group through introductions.

"I've arranged to bend the rules. They're going to play some Elvis in the hotel club tonight. You should join us," says Nick.

Like bikinis, Elvis and his gyrating hips are considered indecent in Spain.

Daniel nods absently and looks around the room. He longs for his camera to capture the tight feel of the event. Although it's a diplomatic affair with attendees from many different countries, the atmosphere feels distinctly American to Daniel, as if he could be at an event in Dallas.

The young women, wearing crisp taffeta dresses and white gloves, are debutante daughters of American diplomats, moguls, and military officers. They attend colleges like Wellesley and Bryn Mawr. Their dresses are different colors, but Daniel fears their destinies are probably similar. They will make advantageous marriages and be listed within the coveted Social Register in their city of residence. But is that what they really want?

Daniel looks at his mother. He's grateful that she's different, that she maintains Spanish customs at home, even though he knows it makes things difficult for her among the Dallas society crowd.

"Your mother, is she descendant from nobility in Spain?" the society writer from the *Dallas Morning News* asked during his job at the paper.

Attachment to a sovereign title significantly boosts your intrigue in society circles. Some Dallas residents hire genealogists hoping to unearth a long-dead baron in the family who might grant them admission to the right club.

Women in Dallas follow society news like a trader follows stocks. Laura Beth spoke ad nauseam of the forthcoming debutante ball for Henry Ford's granddaughter. Daniel knows his association with Laura Beth's family brought a sense of society connection to his mother. It brought him a sense of fatigue, as does the embassy fashion event.

He spots Ben Stahl at the edge of the room, deep in conversation with Paco Lobo. Just as Daniel starts toward them, he's ushered into the main hall.

Waiting in the large salon are over a hundred chairs, neatly ordered in rows. Daniel seats his mother and takes the aisle chair next to his parents. A host introduces the event and the fashion designers. The lights dim.

"Isn't this wonderful?" says his mother.

Daniel nods, but disagrees. It must be incredibly hard to be a diplomat. He would be terrible navigating endless formal events and discussions. As women sashay down the aisle in a myriad of dresses, his mind wanders to the pictures taped to the wall in his hotel suite.

The audience releases an audible gasp.

"Stunning," whispers his mother.

Daniel returns his focus to the front of the room. A young model in a shimmering pink gown has taken center stage. She turns slowly, showcasing the narrow dress, and this time Daniel pulls a breath.

The posterior of the dress is missing, revealing the woman's entire back and waist. The fabric clings to the sides of her slender torso and dips suggestively, meeting in a shallow V just above the sacrum of her lowest vertebrae. Her olive skin is flawless and glistens under the lights. Daniel's eyes are fastened to her back. He's desperate to photograph the subtle curve and gentle hollow. She rotates and his eyes travel across her small waist, up to her neck. She glows, as if lit from within. Her black hair is swept away from her face, with a few spiraling pieces left to frame her high cheeks, dark eyes, and full mouth.

She walks down the center aisle.

She turns every head.

She is undeniably beautiful.

And then he realizes.

She is Ana.

39

Daniel leaves his seat before the lights return. The models thread through a door at the front of the room, and he trails their exit. Others have beaten him there. Shep Van Dorn, the U.S. public affairs officer, corrals the media for photos. A designer poses with the women in front of an official photographer.

"Wish you had your camera?" asks Nick, stepping in beside him.

You have no idea, thinks Daniel.

"You know they won't kiss you," says Nick.

"What?"

"Here in Spain, the girls won't kiss you. Proper Spanish girls kiss only on the cheek until they're married. All dates are chaperoned. They grow up slow here," explains Nick. "My mom thinks it's great. Seems strange to me. But don't worry. There are plenty of eager American girls here to choose from." Nick drains the glass of sherry, noting Daniel's gaze. "Do you recognize her?" he asks.

Daniel nods.

"Apparently the model was sick. The dress fit Ana, so they had her wear it. C'mon, let's get ourselves in a picture." Nick strolls confidently toward Ana.

"Hey, pretty girl. Well done," says Nick, giving a well-oiled smile to the camera. The photographer snaps a photo of the three of them.

"Gracias," says Ana. She gives Daniel a polite smile. *"Buenas noches, señor."*

"*Hola,* Ana. You look lovely."

"It was all last minute. The dress, the makeup — I was very nervous."

"You didn't look nervous," says Daniel.

"Really?" asks Ana. Her smile widens.

"Really, you looked very comfortable," agrees Nick.

Shep Van Dorn steers a gaggle of people toward them. "And this showstopper, she's just a maid at the Hilton, can you

251

believe that?" says Nick's father.

Just a maid. Ana's smile retreats.

"What we can believe, Shep, is that sometimes you're an ass," says Nick.

The silence is instant, uncomfortable.

Shep Van Dorn gives an exaggerated laugh. "Don't mind my son. I think Nicky's sweet on her. But, holy smokes, how could we blame him?" The adults laugh.

Nick glares at his father and shakes his head. He storms off.

"Want some fresh air?" asks Daniel.

"Please," says Ana quickly. Daniel leads her through a tall glass door into a quiet inner courtyard.

Ana looks at the darkened sky. "I've found the answer," she says quietly.

"What's that?"

"Why Americans love ice. Here in Spain, we drink wine. But Americans have fancy cocktails that require ice. Gin and tonic, scotch and soda —"

"Ana."

She turns to him.

"I'm sorry I asked you to work on the

photography project. I could tell you were upset. I've felt awful about it since yesterday."

"Don't feel badly, *señor.* Your photographs are beautiful. It's just difficult because —"

"There he is." Shep Van Dorn leads Daniel's parents into the courtyard.

"We're heading back to the hotel, Dan," says his father. "We have to be up early."

"*Querida,* you are simply stunning," breathes Daniel's mother, rushing to Ana's side. "I'm María Matheson."

Daniel looks from Ana to his mother. "Mom, it's Ana."

"So nice to meet you, Ana," effuses his mother, clearly unaware that Ana is the employee assigned to her at the hotel. "I see you've met my son."

Daniel and Ana exchange looks.

"Nice to meet you, *señor,*" says Ana to Daniel. He smiles, stifling a laugh.

"And what a shame you don't have your camera," says his mother. "I'd love a photo of this gown."

Mr. Matheson touches his wife's elbow,

eager to depart.

"You were just lovely this evening. So pleased to make your acquaintance, Ana," says Daniel's mother. She gives an approving nod before exiting.

How embarrassing. He can only imagine how Ana feels. "I'm sorry about that."

"Don't worry, *señor.* I'm not in uniform . . . I don't look like myself."

"You look exactly like yourself. I'm the one who looks different," says Daniel, loosening his tie.

She scans his expensive suit. "I think I prefer the jeans."

"Good. Me too. Do you need an escort home?"

Ana looks at Daniel. She opens her mouth to speak but stops.

"Such a gentleman." Mr. Van Dorn slaps Daniel on the back. "Kind of you to offer, Dan, but we've arranged for the embassy car to take all the girls home."

Ana stands, motionless. Daniel tries to decipher her odd expression, her eyes.

"So, see you tomorrow?" he asks, hoping she'll say yes.

She takes a single, deep breath. The way Ana looks at him, it makes him want to reach for her. She turns and hurries away.

Daniel watches her retreat, stares at her beautiful back, and curses himself. He knows he's just made a mistake but he's not sure what it is.

40

Ana sees the note, but pretends she doesn't. The white corner peeks out of her purse pocket, a small arrow purposefully left to call her attention. She tries to determine when it was placed. Was the note already in her purse when she left the hotel?

Her hand runs a path over the green skirt of her hotel uniform. The uniform is the nicest piece of clothing she owns. But suddenly the fabric feels coarse and stiff, so different from the silky dress. The model was sick. The boutique was desperate. They begged Ana's manager for permission.

It was a fluke. Nothing more. Like Mr. Van Dorn said, she is just a maid. She pulls a faded handkerchief from her pocket and wipes her mouth, careful to remove all traces of the expensive lipstick.

But despite her sister's warnings, Ana does not regret the evening. She wore a beautiful dress, a dress she could never own. She spoke to a handsome boy alone in a courtyard and was respected by his mother. For a few hours, she felt beautiful. And for that brief moment, beautiful felt possible.

The pavement ends and the car continues onto the dirt road.

"Pull over, please," says Ana.

"Are you sure?" asks the driver. "It's dark. It's no trouble to drive you in."

"*Gracias,* but I'd like some air. I'd prefer to walk the rest of the way," says Ana.

The driver pulls over and Ana exits the vehicle.

A shiny diplomatic car would draw too much attention in Vallecas. Small children would chase it, men would become suspicious, and the women — Ana thinks specifically of the women — the women would run to Julia with questions and opinions.

She wishes she could tell Julia about

her evening. Needlework is Julia's passion. She's spent years studying the designs and patterns of Spanish designers like Pedro Rodríguez and Cristóbal Balenciaga. Ana would love nothing more than to give her sister every detail of the beautiful gown. But it's not possible. The event was at the American embassy. Julia will worry.

The black sedan pulls away. Ana walks alone down the dirt road, and when the sound of the engine has entirely left her ears, she grabs the note from her purse.

This will be the end of you.

Ana rips the note to shreds, scattering pieces as she walks. She blinks back the oncoming tears and looks over her shoulder, making certain no one is there. Making certain no one sees the trail of threat crumbs, leading straight to her door.

41

Two thirty in the morning.

Daniel sits at a table in the corner with his camera, observing the crowd. The hotel nightclub pulses with music, conversation, and cigarette smoke. Dead bottles of champagne, with their foil collars wrinkled and torn, laze in sterling coolers. Ben Stahl is tomato-faced with perspiration. He shambles around the dance floor, flaming cigarette in one hand, scotch in the other. His rhythmic moves are disjointed from the music, as if he hears a different song entirely. Ben's having a grand time, seemingly unaware that he's dancing by himself. Daniel snaps a picture.

Nick drops into the chair next to him.

"Don't want to dance, Danny boy?"

"I'm having a fine time with the camera. Lots of great shots here."

"In Texas do you have formal dance classes like we do in New York?"

"Two full years," nods Daniel.

"Do you dance those crazy Texas dances?"

"Best kind. If I have to dance, I'm most comfortable dancing in boots."

Nick takes a swig from his glass. "So, what happened with your gal in Dallas? Was it serious?"

"She was very serious . . . about trying to change me."

"Ouch. Good riddance." Nick laughs.

"Doesn't matter. There were other problems." Daniel seizes the opportunity. "And what about you? Your dad said you're sweet on Ana. Are you guys an item?"

"Nah. I don't like to be tied down. Diplomats move around every couple years. Why get attached when I'll just have to leave? Besides, she's not exactly an accepted girl on the Social Register."

"So you and Ana never dated?"

Nick sets down his glass. "Why are you

so curious about Ana?"

"No reason. She's assigned to help my family here at the hotel. She seems interesting."

Nick stares into his emptied glass. A smile suddenly curls at the corners of his mouth. "She is interesting. Actually, Ana lives in a very unique part of Madrid. It's a great place to take pictures. You should stop by her house."

"Really? Wouldn't that be an imposition?"

"Nah, she'd love it. She can't really socialize at work. There's always someone looking over her shoulder, you know?"

Daniel thinks back to his exchange with Ana. Maybe Nick is right. She said the hotel keeps her busy. She can't enter his room without an assigned task.

"Do you have a pen?" asks Nick. "I'll give you directions."

Nick scratches information on a cocktail napkin and tosses the pen on the table. "I'm thirsty. You thirsty?"

Daniel looks at the cocktail napkin. "Nah, I think I'll turn in soon."

Nick nods and disappears into the

crowd. Daniel spends another fifteen minutes snapping photos and declining invitations to dance. He's making his way to the door when Ben grabs him.

"Dan, hurry. It's Nick." Ben pulls Daniel through a back door into an alley behind the hotel. Nick writhes on the cobbled ground while two men hover above kicking and punching.

"Hey!" yells Ben, approaching. "Knock it off."

"Not your business, *culón.* Go back inside."

The assailant, charged with adrenaline, shoves Ben while the other continues to punch Nick. His fist makes an awful cracking noise across Nick's jaw.

"Oh Christ," says Ben, stumbling, "they're gonna kill the kid. I said, knock it off!"

Nick has clearly surrendered, overpowered by the two men. Daniel hands Ben his camera. "Come on. That's enough," he says, advancing between them. He pulls the man off Nick. As soon as he does, they both turn their attention to Daniel.

"Look, I have no problem with you," says Daniel. "You should leave."

One man nods to the other. *"Nenaza."*

The word creates a strange pulse at the base of Daniel's throat. He doesn't want trouble with his father. He doesn't want trouble with the guards. But, no, he's no sissy. Daniel's feet move into stance.

The men lunge toward him, fists swinging. His coach's voice is in his ear.

Hands up. Elbows low. Move your head.

Left-hand jab to the face, right-hand punch to the body. *Dodge. Breathe out when you punch.* They're brawlers, not boxers.

Broken nose. First man down. *Keep your feet moving. Always look at your target. Pivot. Stay alert but stay calm.*

Throw the hard punch when you're sure you can land it.

He lands it.

Ben grumbles from the back seat of the taxi. "Jiminy Christmas, Nicky. What did you get yourself into this time? What a pounding. And the night was just getting started. It's barely three a.m." Ben lights a cigarette. "Hey, Dan. Dan! You okay up there?"

Daniel turns around from the front seat. His face is streaked with sweat. "I'm fine, but will they call the police?"

"Don't worry, the hotel knows to call Shep with Americans, not the police," says Ben.

"Really, they can't call the police," stresses Daniel.

"You got a rap sheet, cowboy? Relax, they won't call the cops," says Ben.

Nick groans. He's slumped next to Ben in a heap of bloody towels. His face is battered and swelling. Daniel raises his camera and looks through the viewfinder.

Ben nods. "It's a good shot. He won't mind. Not after what you did, Matheson."

Daniel snaps a picture as they speed to the hospital.

42

Ana turns and looks over her shoulder. Her wavy, dark curls swing gently, taking flight. The crystal flowers on her pink gown create shards of colored light, as if glowing through a prism. They glisten upon her bare back. Daniel snaps a picture.

"Dan. Wake up, fella."

Daniel opens his eyes. Shep Van Dorn stands in front of him. Crisp blue suit, red tie, shoes with high shine. Daniel rubs his eyes.

"Where's Ben?"

"He left. You were sound asleep," says Shep.

"Is Nick okay?"

"He'll recover." Shep sits down. "Dan, I can't tell you how much we appreciate what you did. The doctors said one more blow and the damage could have been permanent or fatal. Ben said you fought hard to defend Nick."

"Why did they go after him?"

Shep lowers his voice. "Nick's had a rough couple of years. It's difficult being a diplomat's kid, hard to make true friends when you're moving so often. But sometimes Nick's his own worst enemy. He recently fell into some gambling debt. Of course I never imagined it would come to this and that you'd be dragged into it."

Van Dorn takes a measured breath. "Your father's going to have my hide when he hears of this. He was adamant about keeping you out of trouble. I owe you one, Dan. If there's ever anything I can do for you, please don't hesitate to ask. I mean that."

"No one's going to call the authorities, are they?" asks Daniel.

Shep shakes his head. "As public affairs officer, I manage American affairs privately — if you know what I mean. Franco's men are trained to shoot, no questions asked."

Daniel takes a breath. No questions asked. It feels like the mantra for Spain.

Before leaving the hospital, Daniel stops to look in on Nick. His face — the color and shape of a deformed plum — is monstrous with swelling.

"*Hola,* prizefighter," says Nick. "They'll discharge me by tonight, in time for us to go back to the club. Think my face will be ready by then?" He laughs and then winces in pain. "Did my old man find you?"

"Yeah. We spoke."

"He's worried that your dad will be angry."

"My father knows I fight. I've done some boxing in Texas."

"Really?" Nick shakes his head. "You're a riddle, Matheson. I owe you one."

Why do both Nick and his father speak so freely of "owing"? Daniel wonders. "You don't owe me anything. Get some rest."

"Take a picture. I know you want to. I'll hang it in my dorm room."

Daniel looks through the viewfinder of

his camera. Lying in the hospital bed is a young man with every opportunity. Despite being a slick diplomat, Shep seems reasonable and would probably pay for J-School or any school Nick wanted. Father-son dynamics. A complex portrait, indeed.

Daniel snaps a picture.

43

"*¡Buenos días, señor!*" Carlitos meets Daniel at the entrance to the hotel, bouncing with enthusiasm.

"*Hola,* Buttons."

"May I see?"

"See what?"

Carlitos points to Daniel's hands. "Texhas! Pow! Pow!"

Daniel slides his hand into his pocket. "How do you know about that?"

"Everyone knows, *señor.*"

"Who's everyone?"

"The hotel staff at the nightclub saw. The two bad men who hurt *Señor* Van Dorn tried to hurt you too. They say you punched them both, while the newspaperman was smoking. Did they have big knives?" asks Carlitos, pointing to the blood on Daniel's dress shirt.

Daniel walks into the hotel. Carlitos trails close behind, peppering him with questions. If Carlitos knows, has the news already reached his parents? He dreads his father's reaction. He'll tell him the truth. But what is the truth? That it felt good to fight?

The morning quiet of the lobby falls even more still as Daniel walks across the chessboard-marble floors. Employees cease talking and silently watch him make his way to the elevator. A young porter points and whispers.

The elevator climbs to the seventh floor. The attendant does not make eye contact. Instead, he clings to the wall, keeping distance from Daniel. In the mirrors of the elevator, Daniel sees his reflection. His left hand is caked with freshly clotted scabs. His dress shirt is torn and bloodied. He's missing his tie.

Daniel holds his camera to the side and snaps a self-portrait in the mirror.

Hoping to avoid his parents, he quickly walks past their suite and quietly enters his own. A note has been slipped under the door.

AT MEETINGS. HEARD ABOUT YOUR NIGHT. LET'S KEEP IT BETWEEN US. YOUR MOTHER IS RESTING. WE LEAVE FOR TOLEDO THIS AFTERNOON IF YOU'D LIKE TO COME ALONG.

— DAD

Let's keep it between us. No reprimand? No anger?

The suite has been cleaned. Has Ana been there? A large silver tray sits upon the table in the center of the room. Fresh juice, coffee, a large plate of *churros* with a cup of chocolate, and a small bucket of ice. Daniel puts several ice cubes in the cloth napkin and presses them against his torn fist. He leans back in the chair, exhausted. He is about to close his eyes, but then he sees it. A newspaper, strategically folded and propped next to the coffeepot, displays a photograph.

He's in it.

44

There is a category of unspeakable things, a dark drawer where inexpressible truths live in exile. Julia knows them well.

Don't speak. Don't tell.

Estamos más guapas con la boca cerrada. We are prettier with our mouths shut. That's what her aunt Teresa says.

Julia sits in the corner of the shop, repairing a pair of trousers for a matador. The ornate embroidery that scrolls down the outside of the leg is expertly designed and measured to flatter the matador's frame. Julia tugs at her thread, pulling it taut.

When life is hectic, Julia is able to keep thoughts and questions tucked in the back of the drawer. Today, during a rare quiet of early morning, her thoughts turn gently inward as she works. Each stitch a meditation.

What is the cost of silence? If she remains quiet about her suspicions, is she granting acceptance of what is happening? If she imposes silence upon Ana and Rafa, what is that telling them? That she is ashamed of their parents? Their parents did nothing wrong. They were academics, hardworking, sophisticated people. Their father wanted to create a school outside of the Catholic Church. That is all.

Her mind reaches deeper into the drawer. That is not all.

After the Francoists killed her father, Julia's mother joined the resistance. Despite the pleas of friends and family, her mother secretly sewed Republican flags for nearly a year. When Franco's troops arrested her, no one came to her aid. Neighbors hid behind their curtains, full of fear and panic. Those who shared her convictions did nothing to protect her. The price was too high.

They shaved her head in prison. They branded her bare flesh with the yoke-and-arrow symbol of the Falange. They force-fed her castor oil so she would soil herself. They paraded her mother through the streets, human dignity excreting down her legs for all to see. Their mother, a teacher, became a human billboard:

This is what happens when you become a *Rojilla,* a little Red.

There is so much heartache, so much pain. Tired of being fearful, tired of being hungry — most days Julia is too tired to fight. But keeping the drawer of secrets tightly locked doesn't mean she condones the dictator or the Falange. It means she wants to protect all that remains. So she repeats Aunt Teresa's mantra: *Estamos más guapas con la boca cerrada.* We are prettier with our mouths shut. Life is prettier with its mouth shut.

Her siblings feel otherwise. Full of energy, they long for truth and justice. It is difficult for the younger generation. Rafa believes he can liberate himself through the conquering of fear. He will assist the gravedigger matador. The bullring will become his theater of courage. Ana believes she can author her own destiny and eventually leave Spain. But her sister's dreams are too large. Too dangerous. Ana thinks Julia does not see her pain. She does. Last night Ana cried herself to sleep after returning from her day at the hotel. Her sister's tears, the audible famine of isolation, it made her cry as well.

"Julia."

The drawer of thoughts closes. Her boss, Luis, stands at the front of the workshop. "May I speak with you?"

Julia follows Luis through the workshop to his small office. He closes the door and motions for her to sit.

"I want you to see this, before someone else does." He hands Julia a newspaper and points to a photo.

The caption reads:

America's Distinguished Sons — Nicholas Van Dorn, son of embassy diplomat, and Daniel Matheson, son of Texas oil baron, attend the fashion gala at the U.S. Embassy. The model wears a gown from the Pedro Rodríguez boutique at the Castellana Hilton.

Julia stares at the photo. Some people appear awkward in glamorous clothing.

Ana is not one of them. She wears the expensive dress more naturally than her threadbare clothes or hotel uniform.

Julia looks at the tall, dark-haired Texan. Ana mentioned that she is assigned to his family for the summer. She did not mention his looks. Handsome. His suit is expensive, privately cut, and expertly tailored to his strong frame. His tie is imported from Italy; Julia can tell by the size of the knot.

The photo speaks a private language. Ana leans toward the Texan. The Texan leans toward Ana.

"I saw the photo and nearly fell off my chair. At first glance I swore it was your mother. She looks so much like her," says Luis.

Julia smiles softly. "She looks exactly like her. She's beautiful."

"And that one. He's the one you told me about?" asks Luis.

Julia sighs and points to Nick Van Dorn. "Yes, he's the one."

45

"I have an important meeting. I am not to be disturbed. Do you understand, Purificación?"

"Yes, Sister," says Puri. "But . . . did the boy find my surprise from Ratoncito Pérez?"

"Indeed. He was overjoyed." Sister Hortensia removes a small envelope from her desk drawer and hands it to Puri. "I'm going to trust you with something important. While I am in my meeting, take the tooth downstairs and put it in the boy's file. The file number is on the envelope. Are you responsible enough to handle this?"

"Yes, Sister." Puri slips the small envelope with the tooth into the pocket of her apron.

"Good." Sister removes a large ring of

keys from her rope belt and extends a key to Puri. "You will give the keys to Sister Pilar when you are finished."

Puri swells with pride. She has won Sister's trust. As long as Puri can remember, her parents have been overprotective, not allowing or trusting her to explore on her own.

The locked file room, located underground, is generally off-limits to anyone but the doctors, nuns, and priests. The dark basement is much cooler than the upper floors. The heavy keys echo in the windowless space as Puri unlocks the door. Her hand feels along the rough stone wall for a light switch. She pushes the button and a dim, caged light glows from above. Puri decides it's best to do her work in private. She shuts the door.

Rows of wooden filing cabinets create aisles in the room. Puri walks down the lines of cabinets, looking for the range of numbers that will house the envelope in her hand. She finds the drawer and pulls it open. The files are neatly arranged in numeric order.

"There you are," says Puri, retrieving a file. She puts the envelope with the tooth in the file. She pauses, curious. What sort of information is kept in the files? She begins to leaf through. The file contains the child's arrival form, annual medical summaries, classroom reports, and various other notations and correspondence. A postmarked envelope addressed to Sister Hortensia is included in the file. Should she? Puri peeks inside.

Thank you for your letter, Sister. I am happy to hear that José is a good little boy and that you feel he is gifted and smart. Unfortunately, we cannot accept him back at home. We have seven other children and no means to care for them. José will be better off with an adoptive family. Since he is smart, he will be able to make his own way in life.

Puri's heart sinks. How could parents not want their son back? How can a six-year-old make his own way in life? Adopting couples and families want newborns, perfect infants they can raise as their own. Chances are very slim that a family will adopt the sweet boy. This means that José may never feel truly wanted or loved. She returns the file to the cabinet and closes the drawer. Puri is grateful for the information. She will dote on little José. It is her duty to serve the children.

Heartsick, Puri suddenly thinks of Clover. She makes her way down the cabinets and looks for 20 116. She finds files for 20 115 and 20 117. The file for 20 116 is missing. Perhaps Sister Hortensia has the file in her office because she is so actively looking for a good home for Clover?

Near the door, Puri spies a table with several files. Maybe Clover's is among them. She opens an unmarked file and sees columns with the assigned numbers that correspond to each orphan. In a row to the right of each number is a list labeled ADOPTION FEES.

They can't be correct.

Puri looks at the numbers more closely. The figures are astronomically high.

She scrolls the list to find 20 116. She runs her finger across the line and lands on Clover's adoption fee. There has to be a mistake.

200,000 *pesetas.*

46

Rafa steps into the dark confessional box. He kneels and awaits the priest. Bound by the sacramental seal of confession, Rafa knows the Vallecas priest will not divulge his sins. The words spoken in confession are guarded by complete confidentiality.

The small square window slides open and through the latticed screen, Rafa sees the silhouette of Father Fernández. He greets the priest with the sign of the cross.

"Hail Mary the Purest."

"Conceived without sin," replies the priest.

"It has been seven days since my last confession." Rafa takes a breath. "*Padre,* I have trespassed upon another's property."

"And where were these sins committed?"

"In the pasture of Don José Isasa Cuadros, *Padre.*"

The priest remains silent.

"Oh, and I fibbed again to my sisters. They still don't know about my girlfriend."

Rafa clears his throat. "For these and all my sins, I ask pardon of God, penance, and absolution of you, *Padre,*" he recites.

Rafa hears the priest breathing behind the screen. He issues the penance.

Rafa begins. "I am deeply sorry for all of my sins and for offending Thee, my God, who art deserving of all my love. I detest my sins and will make efforts to do better."

"May God bless you," replies the priest.

Rafa exits the confessional. He feels lighter, grateful to be absolved of sin.

Rafa loves confession.

47

Julia kneels in the confessional.

"Hail Mary the Purest."

"Conceived without sin," says the priest.

"It has been two weeks since my last confession. *Padre,* I am withholding truth from those I love in an effort to protect them."

"And these truths you are withholding, do they relate to your own actions?"

"No, *Padre.* They relate to actions during the war . . . and current actions by those of authority in our beloved country of Spain. I have told no one what I suspect. The risk is too great. As a result I am forced to be dishonest with my siblings in order to protect them. But each lie leads to another lie. The pressure is mounting and soon it may all explode."

"You are not alone, my child."

"But, *Padre,*" says Julia. "The children of Republicans — we've been alone for years, frightened and hiding, punished for something we had no role in."

"But you are not alone in your hardship. You are safe in the arms of Vallecas."

Fear is Julia's constant companion. But with Father Fernández, she feels peace and freedom to unburden all that troubles her. Since it is presumed difficult, some clergy avoid Vallecas. But so moved by the desperation and needs of the people, Father Fernández wrote to the bishop. He asked to delay his next assignment in order to stay with the flock in Vallecas.

The priest issues Julia's penance of three Hail Marys.

She is grateful for Father Fernández.

Julia is grateful for confession.

48

Ana steps into the confessional.

"Hail Mary the Purest."

"Conceived without sin," replies Father Fernández.

Ana pauses. Could she ever be truthful about her sins? She imagines the confession:

Bless me, *Padre,* for I am full of rage. I am seen by many but understood by few. My heart, so capable of love, is instead lined with hatred for our country's leader. I detest that the coins I earn bear his image and the phrase "Caudillo by the grace of God." I detest that my future is determined by the past. I detest that I am made to feel unworthy and unable to pursue my heart's desires. I dream constantly of leaving Spain, of being wanted, yet the hands that have reached for me have never loved me. My sole intimacy is with silence and the taste of tears. Where, dear *Padre,* is the Grace of God for the children of war, the children judged so unfairly? Am I allowed to ask that?

The priest clears his throat. "Shall you make a good confession today?"

His voice revives Ana from her daydream.

"*Sí, Padre.* I told two lies, gossiped once, and engaged in flirtatious behavior with an American boy."

Ana is too frightened to confess her true feelings to anyone but herself.

Ana fears confession.

49

Puri parts the heavy drapes and enters the confessional of the Madrid church. She kneels and her pulse begins to tick. If faith is so easy, why is confession so difficult? She clears her throat.

"Hail Mary the Purest."

"Conceived without sin," responds the priest.

"It has been one month since my last confession."

At the priest's invitation she reluctantly begins.

"I judge the behavior of others. I am resentful of parents who forsake their children. It angers me when people are ungrateful for all that our great country offers them." Puri prattles on until the priest interrupts her.

"You speak easily of the sins of others.

And what of your own sins?"

Puri stares into her lap. She cannot bear to look at the shadow of the priest before her. She has tried so hard. Puri knows it is her sacred duty to defend purity. Those before her have confronted it successfully. Saint Francis of Assisi rolled in the snow, Saint Benedict threw himself into a thornbush, and Saint Bernard plunged into an icy pond. Why, oh why, thinks Puri, is it all so hard?

"I've had . . . impure thoughts," she whispers to the priest.

Puri loves being a good Spaniard. Puri loves the Catholic Church.

Puri hates confession.

50

Staying at the hotel, instead of traveling to Toledo with his parents, is conditional upon his mother's one requirement: Daniel must attend Mass on Sunday.

The concierge provides a list of three churches. Daniel selects the one closest to the hotel. He arrives before Mass in order to give confession.

"Bless me, Father, for I have sinned. It has been two months since my last confession. I accuse myself of the following sins: I entered an argument that was not my own and caused bodily harm to two men while defending another. I opened a telegram with private information, I harbored anger toward my father, and" — he lowers his voice — "there's a girl I can't stop thinking about."

"It is not for you to fight the battles of

others," says the priest. Following penance, the priest imparts absolution. "Through the ministry of the Church, may God give you pardon and peace. I absolve you of your sins, in the name of the Father, and of the Son, and of the Holy Ghost."

"Amen," says Daniel.

Daniel appreciates confession but feels most content when sharing truths with someone he feels close to.

As he parts the drapes and exits the wooden booth, Daniel has a strong feeling that what he's about to do could send him back to the church.

Daniel may need confession.

Despite his success, Hernando remembers growing up in hunger-stricken post-war Spain as if it were yesterday. He lived in a tin-roofed shack in Vallecas, a working-class quarter of Madrid. "We were always hungry," he says. "I had to rummage for food in the rubbish dump like the other children. I ate banana skins and cheese crusts from the bins outside the houses of the rich." To feed his five children, his father hunted rabbits at the gates of Franco's El Pardo palace; had he been caught he would have been beaten by the Guardia Civil.

— ALFONSO DANIELS

"Property in Spain: Castles in the Sand,"
The Telegraph, *February 19, 2009*

51

"*Ay, no, señor,* that area is not for tourists," cautions the concierge with a wagging finger. "Do not go there. Instead, enjoy this Sunday weather and go to Retiro Park or the Prado Museum."

The words of the hotel concierge are lost on Daniel. He looks at the directions from Nick and studies the route on the map. It's not far. Perhaps twenty minutes.

"*¡Ahí no!* Do not go there. It's not for you, *señor.*"

Daniel thinks of Ana. The way she looked at him in the embassy courtyard. He slings his bag over a shoulder and retrieves the keys to the rental car from his pocket. "I'll be fine. This isn't a tourist outing. I'm visiting someone."

The black Buick is unnoticeable in the

city center, but as Daniel reaches the outskirts of Madrid, the sedan becomes a boat in the desert. Luxury hotels and shops disappear. Manicured landscaping and paved lanes give way to dirt roads, scrubby bushes, and the occasional scoliotic tree. The roads wind through ashen landscape, dusty and bleached by the sun. There are no knife grinders or lottery vendors on the street, just tired men with frowning shoulders and sagging donkeys pulling wagons of terra-cotta pots.

Daniel approaches two Guardia Civil on horseback with rifles. Despite the heat, they wear black patent-leather hats and long capes. Their trancelike faces are instantly menacing. He grips the steering wheel as a distinct feeling emerges. He is venturing out of bounds. It's a sensation that's uncomfortable, foreboding. The nerves at the base of his neck ignite, sending caution signals to his mind.

Patent-leather men with patent-leather souls.

One wrong move and they'll be on you. You'll be dead in a dirt pit.

No. They've forgotten all about him by

now. But he will find a way to photograph them for the contest. He drives past the Crows, tense, grateful that the car has air-cooling that allows him to keep the windows rolled up.

A few miles later and certain he must be lost, Daniel stops the car on a dusty road to consult his directions. He is well outside of Madrid amidst a large slum of squalid shacks. He checks the address that Nick gave him against the map.

Vallecas.

This can't be it. Would Nick purposely send him to the wrong location?

Daniel glances repeatedly at the notes. The paper in his hand vibrates as a small patting swells to a pounding and hordes of children run toward the vehicle. In an instant, the car is surrounded, faces pressing against the glass, distorted, like reflections in a ghoulish fun house. The children shriek and wave, playful and exuberant. He waves back. Their faces are clean, but their clothes are faded and patched. Daniel looks out the windshield and sees a group of men walking toward the car. One carries a club. The sea of children parts for the men as they survey the Buick and walk to the driver's side.

Daniel takes a deep breath. He rolls down the window.

"*¿Qué haces aquí?*" demands the largest of the group.

"I'm visiting a friend," replies Daniel in Spanish.

"Trust me, you have no friends here. Leave," says the man.

"I'm looking for Ana Torres Moreno. Does she live around here?"

The man pauses. "If you're her friend, you would know where she lives."

One man pulls another aside for an exchange of words and nods.

"Leave your car and come with us. We'll take you to Ana and see if she knows you."

Caution speaks, needling across the back of his neck.

He exits the car. The rabble of children, tempered by the man with the club, stand back with wide eyes. They whisper and point at Daniel's large belt buckle, jeans, and boots.

"Americano?" gasps a small boy.

"*Sí.* Americano," says Daniel. "Texas."

The children give a collective *"Ooh."*

Daniel locks the car and follows the men. He considers the possibility that he has completely lost his mind. What is he doing here and why isn't he turning around?

Thoughts of Ana lasso and pull. He slips his camera bag over his head to hang across his body, leaving his scabbed fists free. He may need them.

The men, positioned on both sides of Daniel, begin their march. The three locals are all less than six feet tall, but he's outnumbered. The procession of fledglings and whispers trails down the street laden with pits and holes. Daniel imagines the scene from overhead. He imagines the photo.

The pale dirt road is lined with small *chabolas,* crumbling barrio shacks, connected by crisscrossed clotheslines. Daylight shines through the threadbare clothes pinned to the lines. They look more like gauze than garments. Elderly residents with thick brows and faces engraved by hardship rest on chairs outside the doors. They watch as a savage-eyed cat scratches wildly at nothing in the hardened soil. A woman appears and dumps a bucket in a trench on the side of the road, sending streams of reeking sewage rolling down a well-worn canal. A naked infant sits in the dirt near the sewage trench, joyfully playing with a stick.

Snatches of flamenco guitar float over the crumbling roofs, interrupted by the irate screams of a woman. At the end of the dirt lane is a fountain, surrounded by people with buckets, jars, and galvanized tubs. A tiny girl with a raven plait down her back and holes in her shoes skips up to Daniel and takes his hand. After a few steps she stops, yanks off her shoe, and dumps out rocks.

The men continue on, finally halting at a squat cement shack. Its sole window is broken. The roof is in such collapsing decay it is nothing but a strainer for rain. The splintered door stands open, askew in a tired frame that has long given up. One of the men grabs Daniel and pushes him into the doorway.

He squints into the small space. A dull

light gives the appearance of a conjurer's cave. Bundles of dried herbs and aromatic roots hang suspended from a beam across the ceiling. A scowling young man with dark skin and blue-black hair stands shirtless, wearing the turquoise trousers of a matador. A woman, on her knees upon the dirt floor, works on the pants. Two men sit at a small table. The address is correct. He's sure of it. Because barefoot in the corner is Ana. Daniel's stomach seizes.

She is holding a baby.

She looks to him. The mixture of shock and shame on her face is evident.

They all turn and stare at him, standing in the crooked doorway, stealing their small bit of rationed light.

A small boy tucks in beside Daniel.

"Americano!" he announces.

Daniel knows he has made a terrible mistake. He wants to leave. To run.

But it's too late.

52

The man with the club shoves Daniel aside and addresses Ana for validation. "Is it true? You know him?"

Ana nods silently.

Arguing briefly ensues, but a smiling young man with curly hair gives a broad wave. "*Bienvenido,* Americano! What is your name?"

Daniel takes a breath, trying to swallow enough regret in order to speak. "Daniel Matheson. I'm sorry. I don't mean to intrude. I'm spending the day taking photographs and Nick assured me it was okay to stop by."

"Nick?" says Ana from the corner.

"Photographs?" The young man beams. "Well, you are lucky, Americano. I'm Rafael and standing in front of you is the next great matador! We call him Fuga but soon he'll have a new name."

The shirtless Spaniard with hostile hair stares at Daniel, taking in his height and clothes. His black eyes drill holes, issuing an unspoken warning.

"I can see this is an imposition. I'll leave. I'm parked just down the street," says Daniel.

Rafa jumps from his chair. "You have a car?" He runs to Daniel's side. "No need to leave so quickly. It's not an imposition. You speak very good Spanish. Come, sit down." Rafa steers him deeper into the shack.

Daniel stares at Ana and the baby. "I brought you a few things. I'll leave them."

From his bag, Daniel retrieves a bottle of wine, two packages of American cigarettes, and a small bundle of white paper tied with string.

Everyone stands in stunned silence until Rafa and Fuga lunge at the table. Rafa tears open the cigarettes and Fuga rips at the white bundle. Yelling and fighting continue until Ana speaks up.

"Stop!"

"Well, if the package is open it can't be

sold," says Rafa.

"Sold?" says Daniel. "No, these are gifts. The dried meat is from Texas. It's called beef jerky."

"I love beef jerky!" bellows Rafa.

"You don't even know what it is," says Ana.

"It's food, so I love it." Rafa shrugs.

Ana emerges from the dark corner, her voice soft amidst the chaos. "It's very kind of you, *señor.*"

Her faded dress hangs like a thin scarf on her petite frame. Despite the change in wardrobe and location, she is entirely the same girl from the hotel and the fashion show.

"*Señor* Matheson, this is my sister, Julia, and this is her daughter, Lali." Ana hands the baby to Julia.

Daniel nods slowly. The baby is her sister's.

The family resemblance between Julia and Ana is evident. The worry and responsibility Julia carries is also evident, appearing through deep lines on her forehead and around her mouth. Daniel notices Julia's grated hands. They are hands of hard work, similar to those he's photographed in the Texas oil fields.

Ana continues the introductions. "This is Julia's husband, Antonio. And this is my impolite brother, Rafael, and his friend."

"Fuga's going to be famous. You should photograph him. We need pictures for promotion," says Rafa.

Fuga says nothing.

"*Lo siento,* we weren't prepared for guests," says Julia flatly.

"No, soy yo el que lo lamenta," says Daniel, apologizing. "I'll be going. Nice to meet you all." He reaches into his bag and takes out two small lavender boxes. "They're from the shop you took me to," he tells Ana. "You liked those clover candies so I brought some for you and your sister." He sets the ribboned boxes on the table.

The quiet weight of awkwardness suddenly materializes, elbowing and crowding its way in. The silence is thunderous. Rafa digs at the dirt floor with the toe of his shoe. Fuga remains frozen, hands

302

balled into fists by his side.

Ana stares at the beautiful boxes from La Violeta. She looks to Daniel. Her eyes fill with grateful, unspoken sadness. Her expression produces a heavy pressing upon his chest. Daniel knows she won't accept them. He turns to leave before she can object.

"Rafael," says Julia. "Take *Señor* Matheson to his car. Make sure it's parked in a safe place. Take the buckets to the fountain for water. When you return, we'll all have a glass of *Señor* Matheson's wine together," says Julia.

Rafa runs to grab the buckets. "Hurry, Americano, before she changes her mind." He rustles Daniel toward the door. "And you will take the photographs?" asks Rafa.

"If that's what your friend would like."

Fuga remains silent.

"Of course he'd like that. Julia, don't let anyone eat that beef jerky without me."

Rafa leads Daniel out of the shack.

53

Rafael is a burst of energy. He talks nonstop of his matador friend.

When he pauses for breath, Daniel breaks in. "How long have you lived here?"

"In Vallecas? *Ay,* several years. It's a special place, especially here in El Pozo del Tío Raimundo." He swats a fly from his curly hair. "Where in America are you from?"

"Dallas, north Texas."

The men who'd approached Daniel's car stand at the nearby corner.

"They don't like outsiders," whispers Rafa. "But really, we're all outsiders. Here in Vallecas we are from many provinces of Spain — Andalucía, Extremadura — but Vallecas is a family of its own. We have to share with our family."

Rafa sets down the buckets and removes the package of American cigarettes from his pocket. He gives one cigarette to each man on the corner before heading to Daniel's car.

"You must be brave," says Rafa. "One Texano against three Vallecanos."

"Bravery and stupidity are sometimes interchangeable."

Rafa lights up. "Yes! But fear brings dimension to our lives. Without fear we will never meet courage."

Daniel thinks on Rafa's words, on the dimension he sees before him in Vallecas. Beneath his exuberant exterior, Ana's brother radiates sincerity and heart. "Rafa, would it be okay if I take some pictures?"

"Sure, why not." Rafa stops walking. "*¡Madre mía!* Is that your car?" Rafa sprints to the vehicle. "Texano, take a picture of me with the car!" Rafa abandons the buckets and leans against the car with a casual air. "Wait! I have to be holding the keys."

Daniel tosses Rafa the keys and photographs him with the car. His smile is bright, like Ana's, and contains two gold teeth.

"I'll give the photo to my girlfriend," says Rafa. His smile suddenly disappears. "*Ay,* don't mention my girlfriend to my sisters," says Rafa. "Julia doesn't want us to socialize outside of Vallecas. Besides, if I'm part of Fuga's *cuadrilla,* I won't have time for girls. And what about you?" Rafa grins. "Do you have a girlfriend?"

Daniel shakes his head.

Daniel and Rafa move the car to a nearby cemetery, where Rafa assures him it won't be disturbed. They carry the buckets to the fountain for water, and Daniel takes photographs along the way. Amidst the poverty, there is beauty and camaraderie in Vallecas. People in the street stand tall, unapologetic. They wave Daniel forward with his camera.

The line at the fountain snakes down the road.

"It's Sunday, the day we wash clothes and bathe," explains Rafa.

Children crowd around Daniel, slipping their tiny hands into his pockets fishing for coins. When they reach the fountain, Rafa pumps the long arm, sending water sloshing into a wooden pail held by a shrunken white-haired woman.

"Should we carry the bucket for her?" asks Daniel.

"She won't let you. Besides, that woman is stronger than both of us combined," says Rafa with a laugh. They fill their buckets and make their way back to the shack.

"Have you heard of Agustín García Malla?" asks Rafa. Daniel shakes his head.

"Malla was a bullfighter from Vallecas. In his very first fight, the bull tore his mouth apart. But he was very brave and continued to fight. He lacked the elegance of some matadors but he was long on courage. In the end, Malla was gored through the heart during a fight in France. You see, Texano, there are many here in Vallecas with rips and tears like Malla. When I need advice or time to think, I go to Malla's grave. Sometimes I find answers there."

Daniel thinks on Rafa's comments. He feels guilty. He doesn't have to visit a grave for answers. When he has questions, he goes to his parents or teachers. When he is thirsty, he goes straight to his faucet. "And your parents?" he asks.

Rafa looks to him, grief rising quickly to his face. He shakes his head. "War is a thief, isn't it?" He coughs to clear the emotion from his throat. "And now," says Rafa, kicking a stone in the road, "we work day and night to pay for our mother in the grave, even though we can never have her back. Life is a strange story." Rafa's head and shoulders twitch, as if he were trying to clear pesky flies of memory from his mind.

Daniel has never known theft as Rafa does. He has never sipped from a bucket or bathed in one. He was unprepared for Vallecas. Presumptuous. What an idiot. Did he assume that everyone in Spain lived in apartments or villas? Why didn't Nick say anything?

He must tread carefully. There's a thin line between helpful and humiliating. He does not want to humiliate them.

As Miguel warned him, Spain is not his country.

54

Ana's niece sleeps in a wooden crate instead of a cradle.

"Would you take a photo of Lali, *señor*? I know that film and developing are very expensive, but my family would cherish a photograph of her," says Ana.

Daniel quickly obliges and takes a portrait of the sleeping child.

Four peeling chairs and two wooden crates are placed on the dirt floor around the table. Everyone takes a seat and Antonio pours wine into chipped glasses and dented enamel mugs. Fuga, still wearing the trousers from the suit of lights, does not sit. He stands behind Rafa.

"Again, my apologies for interrupting," says Daniel. "In Texas, we sometimes visit friends on Sunday."

Ana nods. Her loose curls are now pinned back and her face freshly scrubbed. Daniel sits across the table from her, making it impossible to avoid each other's eyes.

"This wine . . . I've never tasted anything so delicious." Rafa sighs.

"It is lovely, thank you, *señor,*" says Ana. She recognizes the wine. She's seen it in the *Placita* shop of the hotel. The bottle costs more than she earns in two months. She can't help but think of the money she could have earned from selling it. It must be painful for her sister to drink. Each delicious sip is a step backward from their new apartment.

Julia insists Ana sell all gifts from hotel guests. She eyes the two lavender boxes of candy on the table, desperate to keep them. She reaches across, pulls the ribbon on one and opens it. Julia kicks her under the table. Ana pretends to misunderstand and holds the open box to her sister. Reluctant to offend, Julia takes one of the violet clovers from the box. Perhaps she can retie the bow and still sell it as new.

"In Spain, we generally meet in cafés,

not in the home," says Antonio.

Julia smiles, softening the reprimand. "How is it that you speak Spanish so well?"

"My mother was born in Spain, *señora.* She's from Galicia," replies Daniel.

The table falls quiet.

Fuga leans over to Rafa. He whispers something and points.

"My friend has a question," says Rafa. "He's heard that in Texas you don't fight the bulls, you ride them. Is that true?" Fuga pokes his shoulder. "Oh, and he wants to know what happened to your hands."

"Yes, bull riding is popular in Texas." Daniel avoids Fuga's menacing stare and the question about his hands. "When is your friend's bullfight?"

"A week from today. Near Talavera de la Reina."

Daniel seizes the opportunity to expedite his exit. "That's soon. We better take the photos now, in time for developing."

"Yes! Good point," agrees Rafa. "Julia, we need the rest of the suit for the photos."

Julia and Fuga are both apprehensive, but Rafa rushes around the small space, gathering pieces of clothing. Ana instructs her brother's friend to sit. She removes a comb from her pocket and tames his wildly snarled hair. Daniel snaps a picture as Ana dips a soft cloth in the bucket of water and gently cleans the matador's face.

"The light will be better for the portrait outside. I'm going to find a spot," he says.

Antonio intercepts Daniel in the doorway.

"Mucho gusto," nods Daniel.

"Nice to meet you too." Antonio lowers his voice. "For interesting photos, you should explore the city center. Take your camera to the Inclusa or the hospitals in Madrid. People love photos of children but can't afford them."

It's an odd suggestion. Why would a hospital or orphanage allow him to take photos? Is Antonio being sincere or is it a veiled dig about his expensive camera and being so out of place in Vallecas? The word *Inclusa,* it sounds familiar. Daniel thanks Antonio and steps outside the shack.

A woman standing nearby eyes him as he walks down the dirt road, her stare thick with suspicion.

"Don't you hurt our Ana," hisses the woman.

Daniel looks over his shoulder. Is she addressing him? The woman nods and viciously points a finger.

He reaches for a reply, not sure what to say.

"No, *señora,* I would never hurt Ana."

55

Rafa bursts from the shack and runs to Daniel. "Texano, it is decided. You must come to the bullfight next Sunday!"

"I'm not sure your friend would like that," says Daniel. "He hasn't been too friendly."

"*Ay,* that's just his way. Like many, the war has stolen his trust. His pain makes him not so friendly, but a very brave bullfighter. Please come with us. It will be a great adventure for your photography."

Daniel considers the idea, photos for his contest submission.

"Also, I must be honest with you," says Rafa. "We need transport to Talavera de la Reina. My boss at the slaughterhouse said we could ride in a truck with dead animal parts, but that is not confirmed.

If we could ride in your nice big car, we could make a grand entrance."

Ana emerges from the shack with Fuga. His face is clean. His hair, the color of black crude oil, is parted on the side and slicked expertly back from his strong, architectural face. The turquoise suit of lights throws sparkles with each small movement. The man who looked like a murderer now looks like a matador. Julia leans against the doorframe, a small smile upon her face. Rafa cannot contain his excitement.

"*Ay,* look at the maestro! Quick, let's take the photos before the children come running. Ana says film is expensive, but could you take two pictures?"

Daniel positions Fuga in the center of the long dirt road. The late afternoon sun throws golden light onto the young man's face. Rafa is right. Fuga looks handsome and regal in the suit of lights. But he eyes Daniel with such contempt it won't make for a good portrait. So Daniel instructs Fuga to look toward Ana, who stands nearby. Fuga's expression eases and Daniel snaps the photos in profile.

"Please, Texano, say you'll drive us in

your car."

"Rafa, stop," says Ana. "Perhaps *Señor* Matheson has plans next Sunday."

"I don't," says Daniel. "I can take you if you'd like."

"*¿Sí? ¡Gracias!*" Rafa showers Daniel with gratitude and discusses details. He then follows Fuga, who has stomped back into the shack. Daniel says goodbye to Julia and Antonio.

"Ana, will you be going next Sunday?" asks Daniel.

"No, *señor.* I know it must sound strange, but I don't care for bullfights." She sighs and looks off in the distance. The sun transforms her faded dress and kindles highlights in her hair. Daniel snaps a picture.

"Okay, Robert Capa, let's walk you back to your car," says Ana.

They walk without speaking. Daniel smiles. He feels so comfortable with Ana, there's no need to fill the space with conversation. But when the car is in sight, she asks the inescapable question. "*Señor,* why did you come here today?"

Daniel lets out a breath. "I'm so sorry.

Nick told me he thought it was a good idea."

Ana nods stiffly and continues walking. "I'm grateful to you," she says, arriving at the vehicle.

"It was nothing, just some small gifts. I know you like the purple candy."

"I do," says Ana, looking up at Daniel. She reaches out and touches his scabbed fist. "But I'm grateful to you for saving Nick."

"Oh." Daniel takes a moment to swallow. He's not sure what to make of the gesture. Ana's touching him, but she's speaking of Nick. He looks at her fingers resting upon his hand. "I didn't save him."

"That's not what I heard," says Ana.

"It wasn't a fair fight."

"Life isn't a fair fight."

They stand by the car in silence. Echoes of gypsy guitar rhythms climb in the distance. Her sudden expression of quiet sadness — it's the same look he saw at the embassy, the look that pulled and spoke without speaking.

"Ana, is there some way I can help?"

She gives a soft laugh. "No, *señor*. Everything is fine here. But perhaps now you understand that I wasn't swimming that evening at the hotel. I am allowed to bathe there twice per week." She looks up at Daniel, full of both sincerity and humiliation. "Do you see? I am so fortunate to work at the Castellana Hilton. I could never jeopardize my job to help you with your project" — she pauses and her voice drops to a whisper — "even though I desperately want to."

Her hand slides from his. She turns and departs down the dirt path toward the shack.

Daniel stands, watching Ana. As the distance between them grows, his thoughts call silently after her.

Ana, if you desperately want to, then please don't walk away.

56

Fortune.

Born into, unearned. The mute accomplice of fate that determines futures and carves lines to divide. It's the word Ben mentioned the very first night, the word that Daniel thinks on during his drive back to Madrid.

Upon his return to the hotel, the lobby feels opulent to Daniel. Too opulent. It's the way he feels when he returns from the oil fields to their estate in Preston Hollow.

Ben Stahl gives a beckoning wave from the upper lobby. He's sitting with Paco Lobo.

"Have you two met? Dan, this is Fred Wolf, but everyone calls him Paco Lobo."

The portly, bald gentleman wears wire-rimmed spectacles and nurses a fat cigar as if it were his last meal. He's the man that Ana says has adopted a village. Is his village similar to Vallecas?

"I've seen you, but we haven't been introduced. Nice to meet you, sir."

"Nice to meet you, Daniel. Are you enjoying your stay in Madrid? That is, when Ben isn't dragging you into brawls."

"I dragged him outside, but the brawling was all his," laughs Ben. "Your paws doing okay, Dan?"

"They're fine."

Paco Lobo stands. "Well, I'm off. Ben, give some thought to our discussion. This one might be easier than you think. We just need the right team."

Paco Lobo departs and Ben's posture eases. He sits back in his chair and reaches into his blazer for cigarettes. The package is empty. He crumples it and tosses it into the ashtray. He runs a nervous hand over the back of his neck and looks across the room. He motions to Lorenza, who is circulating the lobby, selling cigars and cigarettes.

"So, what did you do today?" asks Ben.

"I went to church, gave a good Catholic confession, and then went to Vallecas."

Lorenza arrives at their chairs. Ben selects a package of cigarettes. "Vallecas, what the hell were you doing out there?" Ben puts a wrinkled bill on Lorenza's tray. "Thanks, doll face, keep the change."

"*Gracias, señor,*" says Lorenza. Instead of leaving, she hovers nearby.

Ben leans in to Daniel. "I think she likes me."

"I think she's eavesdropping," whispers Daniel.

"Could be." Ben waits for Lorenza and her red lipstick to saunter off. Once she's out of earshot, his words come freely. "Don't tangle with her. She gets away with a lot but there's a reason. Word from the bird is that her dad's a Guardia Civil."

"He is?" Daniel looks off toward Lorenza.

"Keep that between us. Hotel management knows but the employees don't. Like I said, steer clear of those fire engine lips. You don't know who she's flapping them to."

"Don't worry, she's not my type."

"So, what pulled you out to Vallecas?" Ben repeats.

Daniel hesitates, wondering whether he should tell Ben. After all, Ben's the one who told him to peel back the layers of Madrid. "Nick gave me directions to Ana's, the girl here at the hotel. He assured me it was fine to visit."

"You went to her house? Oh, Dan, people don't do that here. This isn't Texas."

"So I've learned. But it worked out okay in the end. I think I got some great shots for the contest."

Ben's head lifts from the cloud of cigarette smoke. "Really? I'd like to see those. I might be able to use them. Boy, you're my kind of guy, Matheson. Most photographers would beg Max Factor to get them onto a movie set. But you head out to Vallecas." Ben points his cigarette at Daniel. "Intrepid. That's the perfect word for you. I like it."

"Thanks. It definitely showed me a face of Spain that I haven't seen here in

Madrid. I'll take the film to Miguel tomorrow. Say, Ben . . . what do you know about Valley of the Fallen?"

"The Valley? The paper sent me out there, but I haven't reported on it yet. Don't think I will."

"Why not? It's a symbol of reconciliation, right?"

Ben laughs hard and loud, which leads to a fit of coughing. "Reconciliation? Where'd you hear that, Matheson?"

"I didn't. I was just wondering. The hotel magazine makes it sound like it's a tribute, but it seems to upset some people."

"Sure it does." Ben lowers his voice. "It's being built by Republican prisoners. Forced labor. Some have died building the Valley. And now there's talk of exhuming mass graves all over Spain and bringing the remains to the Valley. When it's done, the forest floor could hold over forty thousand exhumed bodies. Imagine that walk in the park." Ben shakes off a shiver.

"Bodies from both sides of the war?" asks Daniel.

Ben looks at Daniel carefully. "Yes, bodies from both sides of the war. But since the war ended, there's only been one side, Matheson. You were in Vallecas today. You saw. There are so many villages like that throughout Spain." Ben lowers his voice. "For years Spain was collapsing, people were starving, and Franco, he was spending money on this monument?" Ben shakes his head and takes a deep drag on his cigarette. He speaks as he exhales. "After World War II, even Germany, our archenemy, was a recipient under the Marshall Plan, but Spain?" Ben forms a "zero" with his hand. "Spain was the only major Western European nation excluded from the economic recovery plan. What do you think that says?"

"I'm not sure what it says," replies Daniel. "That's why I'm asking questions."

"It says the topic of Spain is very controversial. Look, you study Hitler and Mussolini in school, but you don't study Franco," whispers Ben. "Because he's still alive. The history hasn't written itself yet, Matheson. But you're capturing it as we speak with your photos. Exciting stuff."

Ben's mention of his photos makes Daniel uncomfortable. And something else makes him uncomfortable — the fact that Franco and his men personally invited his father to Spain to discuss a collaborative project. Why is his family doing business with a dictator?

"You're asking good questions, Dan. I hope your photos are as interesting."

Daniel nods absently, his mind cluttered with confusion. Despite his better judgment, he decides to ask one last question.

"Say, Ben, do you think Nick likes Ana?"

Ben exhales a sleeve of smoke and chases it with the last of his scotch. "Likes her? Oh no, cowboy, he loves her."

While the Americans have been using their time establishing shopping centers and supermarkets, the Spanish people have been working to build a monument and tomb. It now rivals the greatest works of the Pharaohs.

This monument, known as the Valley of the Fallen, has been opened to tourists for two years. The Spaniards put sixteen years of hard work into its construction and they expect it to become one of the world's prime tourist sights.

This tomb, conceived by General Franco, is estimated to have cost six million dollars. It is located in Cuelgamuros, 30 miles from Madrid. It is longer than St. Peter's Cathedral, which is the largest church in the world. It has often been claimed that the gigantic monument will be Franco's tomb, but no one is yet certain of this. Some twelve tons of bones of soldiers killed during the Spanish Civil War will be buried behind the Chapels. The Valley is dominated by a great cross, higher than the Eiffel Tower, which can sometimes be seen in Madrid. The Valley of the Fallen is just another of the examples showing the magnificent abilities of the Spanish people.

"Spaniards Complete Gigantic Monument"
The Rosebud News, *Rosebud, Texas,*
May 6, 1960

57

Ana looks at the box of violet clovers from Daniel. She has no choice. She must sell it and give the money to Julia for their debts. After much morning pleading, Julia allowed her to keep the other box.

A waiter at the hotel eagerly buys the discounted candy for his wife's birthday. Ana pinches a few *pesetas* from the sale and requests permission to make a phone call. When she hears Nick's voice, she contemplates hanging up.

"Ana, I know it's you. You always hesitate, as if you might change your mind. Don't worry, no one's here," says Nick.

"How are you feeling?" asks Ana.

"I look worse than I feel."

Ana stares at the telephone. "Nick . . . why did you do it?"

There's silence on the line. "Did he actually show up in Vallecas?" asks Nick.

"You knew he would. You told him to. He even brought gifts. Rafa adores him and talked him into driving them to a bullfight on Sunday."

"Ana, I'm so sorry," replies Nick. "I was lit. You have every right to be mad. We were sitting at the table and Dan was asking about you, and suddenly I thought, Wait, why not? Ana deserves some fun for a change. I pegged Dan for a coddled rich kid, but he's not. He'll speak his mind and, man, he'll take on a fight. I think he's a really good guy."

"He *is* a good guy, Nick. So just leave him alone. Please don't create problems."

"Ana, I don't create problems. I try to solve problems. You know that."

She does know that, but it doesn't matter. She quickly hangs up the phone.

58

"*¡Buenos días, señor!*" calls Carlitos. He sprints to the front door to meet Daniel. "A telegram has arrived this morning for *Señora* Matheson. Does she want it delivered to her room or shall I give it to you?"

Daniel sees the telegram and tries to resist. He can't. "Thanks, Carlitos. I'll give it to her." He puts it in his back pocket and exits the hotel.

"Texano!" says Miguel. "I didn't expect to see you so soon."

"Me neither. But I have some photos that need rush processing. They're for Ana's brother." Daniel sets two rolls of film on the counter.

"Photos for Rafa?"

"Yes, his friend is an aspiring matador."

"Aren't they all," laughs Miguel.

"Well, this one has an amateur fight on Sunday. So when I was in Vallecas, Rafa asked me to take some photos."

Miguel looks intently at Daniel. "When you were there, did you see it?" He points to the Robert Capa photo of the children in front of the bombed building. "That photo you admire. Capa took that in Vallecas."

"Really?"

Miguel nods. "There are many unique frames in Vallecas." He looks at the film on the counter. "I generally let the prints dry for several hours. If you want to come back before I close, they might be ready."

"That's fine. I'm heading to take photos of the Inclusa."

"What sort of photos could you take at the Inclusa?"

Daniel shrugs. "Ana's brother-in-law, Antonio, said I might find it interesting."

"¿*Por qué?*" presses Miguel. "I think you misunderstood."

"Something about people not being able to afford photos. I guess I'll find out."

Daniel heads to O'Donnell Street. The Inclusa, a large buttercream-colored building, spans an entire block. Flanking both sides of the arched sandstone entry is an inset figure of an infant with empty eyes, arms outstretched, and palms open. Although large and imposing, the building is otherwise unremarkable. Why would Antonio send him here? There is nothing to photograph. Perhaps, as Miguel suggested, it was a mistake?

He walks down the side street of the Inclusa. A chorus of young voices jingles in the distance. As he reaches the edge of the building, he sees dozens of children at play in a large garden. Young women wearing white dresses and black pinafore aprons supervise the children. The children are clean and tidy, their hair neatly combed or tied in ribbons. They are jubilant and appear healthy, a much brighter scene than orphanages in America. Maybe that's why Antonio sent him? Could this be the orphanage his parents are donating money to?

Daniel snaps a picture.

A billow of black and white appears in the distance within his viewfinder. A nun.

He turns and quickly walks away before anyone spots him. Was that the sister he saw with the dead child? He looks at the surrounding buildings. They are medical facilities. Clinics. Hospitals. Was the nun with the baby walking to a clinic or to the Inclusa? Were the Guardia Civil escorting her?

As he turns back onto O'Donnell Street, Daniel sees a small boy, standing near the entrance of the Inclusa. His shoulders quiver and his face is streaked with tears.

"*¿Estás bien, chico?*" asks Daniel.

The little boy shakes his head. His trembling lips, holding tight to his sorrow, open and release a deep sob.

Daniel kneels quickly to the boy on the sidewalk. "Hey, there. *¿Qué pasa?*"

The boy clutches a wrinkled note in his shaking hand. He extends it to Daniel and through a rush of tears issues the heartbreaking pronouncement:

"My *mamá* doesn't love me anymore."

59

Puri rushes through the aisle of file cabinets, hoping to find more information. She must hurry. If she doesn't join the other aides outside, someone may notice she's missing.

The questions remain fixed in her mind, but she's limited in whom she can ask. If the Inclusa wants to find homes for the children, why are the adoption fees so high? What are the huge sums of money used for? Were the dough-faced man and his wife with the pillow willing to pay two hundred thousand *pesetas* for a child?

Perhaps she could ask the priest these questions. But the priest may reprimand her again for speaking of others instead of herself. Or maybe she can ask the doctor who brings newborns through the back door of the Inclusa? She cannot ask Sister Hortensia. If she does, Sister will know that she looked at a file without permission. But Puri's concern for the children surpasses any guilt about snooping. If her access to the file room continues, perhaps she can reference files from some of the recently adopted children.

Puri knows she can't ask her mother. She will scold her curiosity. She will say what she always says:

Estamos más guapas con la boca cerrada. We are prettier with our mouths shut.

She opens the last cabinet on the end. The folders are labeled GENERAL CORRESPONDENCE. Near the back of the drawer are multiple files marked RESOLVED. Puri pulls a file.

She flips through memos and arrives at a handwritten letter addressed to a doctor.

Dear Dr. López,

I send another letter, not to disturb you, kind Sir, but simply to appease my conscience. My wife said the child she gave birth to was bald and had a red birthmark on his arm. The deceased infant shown to us was larger than our son, had a bit of dark hair, and did not have the marking on his arm. You and Sister Hortensia advised that grief over our child's death was clouding our recollection. But is it possible that perhaps there was some mistake? Perhaps it was the child of another couple that died? Of course we infer no accusation of you or your clinic, simply an honest error. We anxiously await your reply and hope you will help us pursue the matter in more detail.

Puri looks at the next letter.

Dear Sister Hortensia,

In contemplating our finances, we've found that 300,000 pesetas to adopt a newborn is simply not within our means. You had suggested payments of 30,000 pesetas over ten years but that is also beyond our reach. Unfortunately, we will not be able to pursue adoption of a newborn. With gratitude for your understanding. ¡Viva España!

Three hundred thousand *pesetas*? Puri looks at the letter. It's dated several months prior. The next letter is unsigned and contains only a few handwritten sentences.

You stole our child.

God forgive me if I am wrong. If I am right, there is no forgiveness for you.

Puri looks at the first sentence.

You stole our child.

What does that mean? Who stole their child?

Puri thinks back to the woman who stopped her on the sidewalk. She said her child had been taken for baptism but was never returned. Her tone was insistent, desperate, but also full of fear.

A noise sounds in the hallway. She must return to the garden. Puri rolls the remaining letters from the correspondence file and puts them down her blouse, where they are secured by her undergarments and hidden by the apron.

Heart pounding, she dashes up the

stairs. As she passes the receiving office, she hears a male voice.

"I found him crying on the sidewalk. He was holding this note."

"Thank you for bringing him inside."

Puri stops in the doorway. A boy with tearstained cheeks and holes in his pants is perched upon a chair. A young man crouches in front of him. He rises to leave and she gasps.

"Daniel?" exclaims Puri.

The young man looks at her, confused. Sister Hortensia shares his expression.

Puri brings a hand to her chest. "It's me, Puri. Ana's cousin."

But the words are hardly audible. When Puri's hand touches her chest, a crunching of paper sounds from beneath her apron.

60

"He seems nice enough," says Antonio. "Maybe a bit naïve."

"Of course he's naïve. Arriving in Vallecas uninvited? He's from a rich American family. He knows nothing of Spain." Julia lifts Lali from her crate for feeding.

"That's not true, his mother was born here. He speaks Spanish well," says Antonio. "And he seems generous. It's kind of him to take the boys to the bullfight."

"I'm not worried about the boys. I'm worried about Ana. Did you see the way he looked at her?"

"Most everyone looks at Ana like that. You should be more concerned about the way Ana looked at him."

Antonio is right. Julia noticed the way Ana downplayed her excitement while scrubbing her face and pinning her hair. She also noted the silent rhythm between her sister and the Texan. She wishes she could encourage and support Ana instead of blocking her at every pass.

"*Ay,* even if he is nice, he's a hotel guest. She mustn't jeopardize her job," she tells Antonio.

The infant wiggles in Julia's arms. She looks at her daughter. She's still so small. Another woman in Vallecas has a two-month-old child who's already larger than four-month-old Lali.

"*Mi amor,* we'll be short again this month," says Antonio. "Is there any way Luis could give you an advance?"

Julia releases a deep sigh. "I can't ask Luis again. Take the candy from La Violeta to work. See if you can sell the box somewhere along the way."

"Didn't you tell Ana that we would keep one box?"

She did. Ana promised to sell one box at the hotel but begged Julia to keep the other.

Julia recalls the way Ana hugged the ribboned box to her chest, pleading, "Just this once, Julia. *Por favor.* For me."

She hates disappointing her sister, but hates poverty more. Why did she open the wine? It would have brought a dear sum. They've been saving money to move and every *peseta* counts. By Julia's calculations, in two months they will be close to having the money.

"*Mi amor,* tell me the truth. Is it the candies you want to get rid of — or the Texano?" asks Antonio.

He means to tease, but fatigue has stolen her humor. "We don't have the luxury of candies, Antonio. Please, sell it. We need the money." Julia recalls the conversation.

The war is over. We must accept our fate and make sacrifices. Pursue peace and stability above all, Julia. Leave truth for some distant day in the future, her mother had said.

How distant is that day? It's been nearly twenty years since the war ended and truth still clings to the shadows. But Julia reassures herself that even if withholding the truth is painful, it is the right thing to do. It keeps the peace. It is what her mother wanted.

342

61

Daniel takes the Metro to Puerta del Sol, reflecting upon what transpired. The nun in the office, who introduced herself as Sister Hortensia, was older than the nun he photographed with the baby. Ana's cousin seemed happy to see him, but suddenly began to cough and quickly excused herself to the garden.

"How do you know our Purificación?" asked Sister Hortensia suspiciously.

When Daniel explained that his family was staying at the Castellana Hilton where Puri's cousin worked, the nun suddenly became inquisitive.

Thinking about the episode gives Daniel an uncomfortable feeling, similar to the feeling in confession. As he exits the Metro, he sees police in gray uniforms surround a young man. No one dares to look. Pedestrians pass quickly with their heads down. He does the same. He walks briskly and turns down Calle Echegaray.

Rather than return to the hotel, he decides to wait until his photos are developed. A faded green sign pulls Daniel in off the street. Men in flat caps stand at a bar under a fly-specked light bulb, while the barkeep marks their tab in chalk on the wooden counter. The chemistry in the room changes the moment he walks in. Clearly, tourists are not frequent visitors.

Rows of dust-smeared bottles line the shelves behind the bar, but the drink selection is small. *Jerez* and tap water only. Daniel orders a Manzanilla, his mother's favorite. It is the only drink he recognizes and he remembers it smells good.

He selects a table in the back and sets his bag behind a chair. A gruff man delivers a complimentary plate of crisp green olives and sausage marbled with ivory-colored fat.

Daniel reaches in his back pocket for the telegram that Carlitos delivered at the hotel.

He places the folded envelope on the table in front of him. It's addressed not only to his mother but to his father as well. He turns it over. Half of the envelope flap is not sealed. He eats an olive and tries to distract himself. It's none of his business. Opening someone else's mail is illegal. He'll have to go to confession again. But maybe it will provide answers.

The temptation is too great. Daniel slides his finger under the flap. He gently loosens the remaining adhesive and removes the telegram. The Western Union form is the color of onions. The cabled message is printed on thin white tape affixed to the form.

```
WESTERN UNION TELEGRAM
                    — VIA CABLE

    SENDER: BUD MATHESON —
           DALLAS, TX

MR. AND MRS. MARTIN MATHESON
— CASTELLANA HILTON, MADRID
PRIEST SHARED NEWS. HAVE YOU
TOLD DANIEL? WORRIED WILL BE
```

HARD ON HIM. WILL PREPARE THE
HOME STAFF FOR CHANGE.

Daniel stares at the message from his uncle. His father's brother is a pragmatic man, who rarely expresses emotion or concern. His worry ignites fear in Daniel, bringing back the questions — the edge in his mother's voice, her emphatic desire to come to Spain, his father's mention of a "tough time." Has he gotten it all wrong?

Could his parents be separating?

62

Daniel makes his way back to Miguel's shop. His feet move but feel detached from his body. He spent hours staring at the telegram and the plate of olives. With no one to talk to, he came up with theories of his own.

His parents' strange behavior suddenly makes sense. The fight with the two men in the alley had no consequence with either of them. They were too concerned with their own problems to reprimand him. Shortly before their trip to Madrid, he heard his parents arguing in their bedroom. His mother was crying. Why didn't he pay attention? His mother's gift of the camera and her support of his photography frustrate his father. Did that cause their "tough time" and is he to blame?

He thinks of all that could change. Will his mother move back to Spain? Is that why his father mentioned the importance of his happiness in Madrid? The timing with his recent graduation can't be co-incidental. Have they been waiting until he leaves for college to separate? Will he be forced to choose who he spends time with?

Daniel knows of only one divorced family in Dallas. Considered pariahs, they were removed from the Social Register. Divorce is not an option for Catholic couples. Instead, his parents will remain married but live apart. Several couples in Dallas reside in different residences. The husband lives in the summer home and the wife lives in the Preston Hollow estate. They are seen together at social events and remain on the Register. On the outside, all remains intact. But everyone knows the truth: Behind closed doors, life lies in pieces. And that's how his head feels.

"Texano!" Miguel bellows as Daniel enters the shop. "I think you will be very pleased. Your photographs are *excelentes!*"

The compliment should fill him with joy, but barely registers. "That's great. And thanks again for developing them so quickly." Daniel retrieves his wallet. "How much do I owe you, Miguel?"

"You don't want to see them?"

"Not right now," says Daniel.

Miguel eyes him with concern as he accepts payment. *"¿Estás bien, amigo?"*

"Ay, I've got a lot on my mind."

"Ya lo veo. I see that. Well, when you are feeling better, please return. I would like to discuss these photos with you."

"Sure, I'd like that too." Daniel takes the large envelope and exits the shop.

The hotel is alive with music and guests. Hundreds of young men in stark white uniforms fill the lobby. Daniel doesn't want the distraction of a party. He longs for privacy. Quiet.

Ben Stahl speaks to an older man in uniform and takes notes on a small pad. Lorenza and Ana orbit the group, selling cigars and cigarettes. Ana sees Daniel on his way to the elevator and makes her way to him.

"*Buenas noches, señor.*"

"*Hola,* Ana. Looks like a big party."

"The U.S. Air Force cadets are visiting Madrid during their summer tour. The embassy is holding a reception here," she says.

"Well, I'll leave you to it."

Ana's brow creases. "*Señor* Matheson, are you okay?"

Daniel looks at her. Ana's concern is so genuine. He wants to tell her everything. Instead he gives a weak smile. "I'm fine. I think I'll have an early dinner in my room tonight."

Her voice quiets. "Of course, *señor.* I'll have the room-service operator call up right away."

"Thanks, Ana. I appreciate it." He makes his way to the elevator, holding the envelope of photos.

"Seventh floor, *por favor.*"

The elevator climbs. Daniel's heart sinks.

63

The room-service trolley sits in his room, the silver dome unmoved from the entrée plate. A soft knock sounds at the door. Daniel opens it and finds Ana in the hallway.

"Forgive me for disturbing you, *señor.* I will soon leave for the night. I wanted to inquire if you'd like turndown service?"

"Oh, thanks. That's fine." Daniel steps aside and allows Ana to enter. He slumps back in the chair as she flutters around the room.

She lifts the silver dome from the dinner plate. "You haven't eaten. Did the meal not please you? We can request something different."

"I'm not hungry."

Ana walks over and sits down next to Daniel.

"Forgive me for intruding, *señor,* but you are clearly not yourself."

Daniel looks at Ana. She leans toward him, concerned and eager to help. Her brown curls lie in perfect waves across her shoulders. Her eyes search for answers.

"Ana, if I tell you something, will you promise not to tell anyone?"

"Señor," says Ana, smiling wide, "be assured that I am someone who can keep a secret."

Daniel nods. He points to the telegram on the coffee table. "Read it."

Ana lifts the paper and scans the message. "I don't understand."

"This is the second telegram. I know I shouldn't read them. I guess it serves me right, swiping their secret."

Ana pauses, examining Daniel. "And what, exactly, do you think their secret is?"

"I think they may be separating."

Ana pulls back in bewilderment. "No,

señor. They're not."

"I wish that were true."

"*Señor,* I —" Ana pauses, as if choosing her words carefully. "*Señor,* the housekeeping staff is witness to much at the hotel. I can assure you that your parents are not separating."

"Do you know something?"

Ana closes her eyes and releases a frustrated exhale. "Hotel privacy forbids me from saying more." She leans forward and puts her hand on Daniel's. "*Señor,* your parents are not separating. I am so certain of it, let's make a wager. If I am wrong, I will help you with your project."

"You'll be Jane Doe?"

"No, I will not," says Ana. "I'll be Tom Collins."

"Who's Tom Collins?"

"Tom Collins is a drink on the lobby bar menu. It's a drink with lots of ice." She smiles sweetly.

Daniel laughs.

"But we needn't speak of your project because I will win our bet," says Ana.

Daniel stares at Ana's delicate hand on

353

his. She's touching him, just as she did near the car in Vallecas. He slowly rotates his palm. Their fingers graze and gently thread together. A rush of heat flows down to his hand.

Ana's eyes flutter and close. "I . . . are those your photos from Vallecas?" She rises and their joined hands surrender. She walks to the display of photographs on the desk.

Ana stands, silent, with her back to Daniel. He runs his nervous palms down the thighs of his jeans.

"Miguel developed them today."

One image has been enlarged. It's the portrait of Fuga and it's stunning.

"¡Dios Mío!" exclaims Ana. "Look at Fuga. He looks like a real *torero*! Rafa will be thrilled."

Daniel approaches behind her. "I'm glad you like it. Take it to Rafa. I know he needs the photograph to promote the fight." Daniel puts the photo in the envelope.

"He will be so pleased, *señor. Gracias.* You have been very kind to my family." She looks up at him. "I should be going.

Just call room service if you need more ice." She gives a flustered laugh and makes her way to the door.

He doesn't want her to leave. "I saw your cousin today."

Ana stops. "You saw Puri? Where?"

"At the Inclusa. Antonio suggested I go there to take pictures."

Ana's face clouds with concern. "The Inclusa?" Her mental processing is visible. "I'm sorry. I must go. I can't miss my transport back to Vallecas. Perhaps I'll see you tomorrow. I know your parents return from Toledo in the morning."

Daniel nods. "Thank you for talking with me, Ana. I hope you're right."

"My pleasure, *señor.*" She steps outside into the hallway, then pops her head back around the door with a big smile. "I know I am right."

64

Rafa waits until lunchtime. His announcement will have more impact if all are gathered together. He peeks at the photograph in the envelope, trying not to soil it with fingerprints.

Fuga stands in profile. His figure is in sharp focus but the long road behind him is soft, creating the imagery of a path to destiny. The elegance of the suit is contrasted by the power of his strong jaw and vaulted cheekbones. The photo captures the power, the internal freight train that is Fuga.

The Americano is not only a nice guy, he's a good photographer.

Rafa passes the bloody aprons hanging from their hooks. He walks to his coworkers, seated at the lunch table. Their sleeves and shoes are smeared with death.

Rafa shakes the voices from his head, focusing.

"*Caballeros,* you have heard of my *amigo* who will fight this Sunday near Talavera de la Reina."

"You mean your *amigo* whose bowels will be punched open by a mangy bull calf?" The men at the table laugh and one interjects with a tale. "I once knew an amateur *maletilla.* His intestines were gored out. He was so desperate to fight he had a friend stuff his guts back in his belly and sew him up with twine. The hurried stitches were too loose. A piece of his intestine was hanging out."

The table issues collective groans and nods.

"*Sí, sí,*" says Rafa. "We have all heard tales of young men pursuing this dream — seeking victory on a Sunday after-noon. For four hundred years, this dream has led Spain's sons to the grave, has it not?"

The men all nod in agreement.

"We know that it is spectacle and tradi-tion that drives men with money to the ticket window, but it is often hunger and desperation that drives a *torero* onto the sand."

The men issue supportive chants of *sí, sí.*

"These amateur village *capeas,* we know they are the only way to be seen by benefactors and ranchers. They are often the only way for an amateur to meet a bull. The road to Las Ventas arena in Madrid is long, *amigos.* But for one aspiring *torero* who seeks a benefactor and entrance into the world of the *corrida,* it begins this Sunday. Support this young bullfighter at his first *capea.* Support him in hopes that he may soon come to *el matadero* and train here alongside the other aspiring *toreros.* When he does, we shall claim him as our own."

Rafa receives a round of applause.

"Does he have a name yet?" asks the supervisor.

"He does." Rafa steps forward. *"Caballeros,* you will remember this day, the day you first saw his face. I present to you . . . *El Huérfano!"*

He removes the photograph from the envelope and proudly displays it to the table. The group of men erupts in loud cheers and applause. Rafa beams with pride.

"El Huérfano. 'The Orphan'?" mutters his supervisor.

"*Sí,* he chose the name himself," whispers Rafa. "During one of his stays in jail a nice cellmate referred to him as El Huérfano."

The men begin to chatter.

"Have you ever seen a *maletilla* with such a photograph?"

"Or with such a suit of lights for a village *capea?*"

Rafa's supervisor pats him on the back. "*Bien hecho.* Great job. But, Rafa, are you sure you want to be part of this man's *cuadrilla?* You are a natural promoter."

"*Gracias,* but this has always been our plan. When we were younger, he helped me. Now I will help him."

Rafa will wear only a modest black suit of lights. He will always walk behind Fuga, not next to him. No one will ever ask for Rafa's autograph, nor will he be allowed to eat at the same table as his matador. But he will stand on the sand. He will protect his friend.

He will face fear. And he will win.

65

"He's fine."

Sister Hortensia assures Puri that the newly arrived orphan enjoyed a comfortable first night and that the other young boys have welcomed him warmly.

"I wish there was something we could do for the older children," says Puri.

"Whatever do you mean?" demands Sister Hortensia. "We are housing them, feeding them, bathing them, clothing them, and seeing to their education. Most are children of degenerates! But here, they feel a sense of community and will grow into very fine adults."

"Yes, most are very happy. But they have no parents."

Sister exhales her annoyance. "It is better to have no parents than the wrong parents."

Puri thinks on Sister's statement. She had a hard time sleeping, thinking of the crying boy, abandoned on the sidewalk. Many families have eight or ten children but no way to support them. She thinks of José, the little boy who lost his tooth, and the letter from Sister Hortensia to his family, explaining how gifted and smart he is. But they did not want him back. They are the wrong parents. José is fortunate to live at the Inclusa. He will grow into a fine man. Puri thinks of little Clover, her favorite. What if no one wants her?

Puri knows she is lucky to be an only child and receive her parents' full attention, but one child does not satisfy the Francoist mandates for large families. She once tried to discuss it with her mother. When Puri commented that being an only child like herself was a rarity in Spain, her mother became deeply offended and stomped off to her room.

Sister Hortensia's mouth softens. "You care very deeply for the children, Purificación. The doctors and I see that. We are grateful for your tender heart. It is a virtue. Like you, we want each child to have the best chance to succeed in life."

Puri nods emphatically. "Yes, Sister. That's it. I just want these children to have an opportunity." Puri thinks of the letters she smuggled out in her uniform. Two were from Spanish Republican families, desperate to locate a child they suspected had been taken from them at birth.

"Of course," says Sister Hortensia, nodding. "And that's exactly what we want too. The opportunity for a fine life, a devout life, a life rehabilitated and liberated from sins of the past. I'm very pleased with your dedication. We have plans for you, Purificación."

Plans for her? Pride swells within Puri's chest.

"For now, take this folder downstairs and file it accordingly." She hands Puri a file and also a small slip of paper with two numbers. "Locate the files listed on the paper and bring them to my office."

Elated for the opportunity to return to the file room, Puri rushes to the basement.

She retrieves the papers from beneath

her apron, the papers she smuggled out the day prior, and returns them to their files. Thankfully, her fit of fake coughing diverted notice of their crunching sound. She looks at the folder Sister Hortensia asked her to file.

Questions. Why does she cling so tightly to questions? Why can't she open her fist and let them fly away? Together with doctors, bishops, and priests, Sister Hortensia devotes her entire existence to the orphans. It is disrespectful to question their authority.

Yet something nags at her. Hesitation. Doubt. She is ashamed by it, yet compelled to probe further. Puri returns to the RESOLVED files and continues to read through the letters. There are hundreds of them, dating back nearly twenty years.

Most of the correspondence is polite and cautious. But why is the file marked RESOLVED when they are not resolved at all?

A woman gave birth to a healthy baby but was later told that the child was choked by the umbilical cord and died. Could there have been a mistake?

A doctor told a couple they were having twins but upon delivery the nuns claimed there was only one baby. Could there have been a mistake?

Many letters are from families asking where their deceased infants are buried. The letters reference the "generous insistence of the clinic to handle burial of the deceased child" but the parents would now like to visit the grave.

Puri moves quickly. The two files Sister has requested are for recently adopted newborns *sin datos.* As she scans each file she sees that the infants did not enter via the *torno,* the box in the wall. One came directly from the hospital and the other came from a medical clinic nearby. One of the infants was sent to a requesting priest in Bilbao. The file on the other child is more cryptic.

Puri retrieves the unmarked file from the desk to cross-reference the adoption fees for each child. As she does, she notices that Clover's listing has been amended.

200,000 *pesetas* is crossed out. It now says 150,000 *pesetas,* pending.

66

"Welcome back, *Señora* Matheson. I hope you enjoyed Toledo," greets Ana at the entry to the suite.

"We did, thank you. It was lovely and very warm. My father used to say, 'When God made the sun, he hung it over Toledo.' "

"Yes, I've heard that too," says Ana. "You telephoned that you'd like assistance unpacking your bag?"

"Please. My husband's as well. We've just returned and Martin is still downstairs." She steps aside to allow Ana into the room.

As she points out the luggage to be unpacked, Mrs. Matheson notices the telegram, placed squarely on the desk. Her voice falls tense. "Oh, when did this arrive?"

"I am not certain, *señora,* I did not deliver it."

Daniel's mother opens the telegram and quickly scans its contents. She turns her back to Ana. She stands motionless for several minutes.

Ana thinks of Daniel and how upset he was about the telegram. She recalls the touch of their fingers as his hand turned to grasp hers. What if she hadn't let go? When he confided in her she wanted to do the same. She wanted to explain things, the threatening notes, to tell him everything.

Ana moves *Señora* Matheson's expensive shoes to the suite's closet. The jeweled satin pumps are marked PERUGIA in gold scroll along the instep. Her black hat has a label that reads SCHIAPARELLI. Ana turns from the closet and María Matheson stands, hands nervously clasped as if she's on the brink of tears.

"*Señora* Matheson?"

It takes a moment for her to begin. "Ana, I owe you an apology. I didn't recognize you at the fashion show. Martin, my husband, advised me of my error after we left. It must have been horribly uncomfortable with me showering praise and introductions when in fact we had already met and interacted on several occasions."

Ana does not want an apology. She does not want the lump swelling in her throat.

Daniel's mother continues. "It's bothered me for days." She extends a hand and steadies herself on a chair. "Ana, I've been consumed with personal difficulties of late, and my preoccupation has obviously left me insensitive to others. I'm so sorry. My dear, please believe me when I tell you that you are beautiful, no matter what you are wearing."

Ana's eyes expand with shock and tears. *"Gracias, señora,"* she whispers.

They stand, absorbing the exchange. Daniel's mother reaches for the desk and seats herself in the chair.

"Oh my," says Daniel's mother. "Look at us, both emotional. We can't have that."

"No, *señora.*"

"Well, then." She takes a deep breath. "Let's move on. My husband and I would like to take our son somewhere special for dinner tonight. What do you know of Lhardy?"

Lhardy.

Señora Matheson has mentioned the one restaurant that Ana is desperate to visit.

"Lhardy is magical. It's been open for over a hundred years. They say that Queen Isabel II used to steal away from the palace just to eat at Lhardy. Of course, I've only been on errands to the foyer for a cup of broth or a croquette, but the doorman and staff are always lovely. At Lhardy, everything is refinement, *Señora* Matheson. Waiters stand behind screens, so not to interrupt the guests but to watch and tend to their every need."

Ana realizes she is blathering. "Of course, you must consult the concierge for his opinion as well," she says.

"I see no need. Not after that glowing recommendation. Please ask the concierge to make a reservation for nine p.m."

"Yes, *señora.*"

Lhardy.

Tonight Daniel and his parents will dine at Lhardy. Tonight they will taste the delicious *cocido a la madrileña* under flickering gaslight and sip a full-bodied *Rioja*.

Ana swallows hard. Tonight Daniel may learn the truth.

67

"*¿Estás ahí,* Miguel?" calls Daniel into the empty shop.

Miguel emerges from behind the curtain. "*Hola,* Texano. Feeling better?"

"*Sí, gracias.* I'm sorry I left so quickly yesterday. You said you wanted to discuss my photos?"

Daniel removes the stack of pictures from his bag and lays them on the counter in pre-organized configurations.

"I'd like to discuss your photographs, but also how you captured these images."

Daniel shifts his feet. "Oh, the photos from Vallecas?"

"*Sí.* I recognize Ana and her family. They invited you?"

"No. That was an error on my part. Someone gave me the address and suggested I visit. I didn't know it was inappropriate," Daniel says. "I do now."

"And how did you earn these people's trust to allow you to photograph them?"

"We talked as I walked through the village. They seemed happy to have their pictures taken. That's one of the reasons I came back so soon. I'd like to have reprints made so I can give each person their photo this weekend."

"That's very generous of you," says Miguel, as Daniel hands him the negatives.

"Thank you for making the enlargement of Rafa's friend. I gave it to Ana."

"I couldn't resist. The image called for it. Who is he? In your photo he looks like a true matador."

"He's a friend of Rafa's, someone he trains with."

Miguel's large brows descend over his eyes. "Trains? Trains where? They're not entering breeders' pastures, are they?"

"I don't know."

Miguel looks at Daniel's photos, spread out before him. "It's a hard life there. I'm sure you saw. There's no running water, no facilities, only fountains. There is beauty in Vallecas, but you have to have the eyes to see it. Your photos, they show a strong human spirit. I hope the judges of your contest will recognize that."

Daniel looks at the photographs. They're portraits of everyday life. People in lines at the fountain, a woman weaving a basket in the doorway while a cat prowls a hole in the roof. The raven-haired girl examining a cut on her knee. Ana washing Fuga's face. Her baby niece asleep in a wooden crate.

"What are your intentions with these photos, *amigo*?" asks Miguel.

"My intentions?"

"*Sí*. You are assembling a story. Are these really for the contest you mentioned or for something else?"

"They're for the contest," says Daniel.

Miguel nods. "Just remember that images without explanation are easily misinterpreted."

"Like the nun with the baby?"

Miguel puts up his hands and steps back from the counter. "*Ay,* I know nothing of that."

Can that be true? Miguel lived through the war. He's developed thousands of photos. He understands that the images that speak the loudest are often the most curious, controversial, or dangerous.

"Miguel, I really want a photo of the Guardia Civil for my contest submission. They're so menacing, like human crows, pecking at the population. The right image could make a real statement about authority and power in Spain."

"It could also land you in jail. Don't even try."

"I did try, but was apprehended."

Miguel's face loses color. His voice is a whisper. "You were apprehended? Trust me, you don't need that photo. *Por favor.* Forget about it."

"Forget about it? Is that what Capa would have done?" asks Daniel.

"We don't know. Remember, Texano, Capa's dead."

68

The moment Daniel is seated with his parents at Lhardy, a waiter appears and ceremoniously lights the ivory taper candles on the table. His mother loves extended meals. Three to four hours is not uncommon and that's a long time to be in a suit. Daniel appreciates fine food, but prefers Texas backyard suppers where he can relax in the grass and wait for the stars to reveal themselves.

Thick red curtains drape the windows in the mahogany-paneled dining salon, while gaslight dips and quivers in lamps suspended from the walls. His mother orders a glass of sparkling cava; his father, vermouth from the Lhardy tap.

"Daniel," says his mother. "You don't have to keep your hands under the table. I know everything. The Van Dorns sent a beautiful Spanish fan as a gift of gratitude."

The Van Dorns sent a *thank-you* gift for a fight? Is that a common occurrence in their family? Daniel slowly lifts his hands from beneath the tablecloth. The small remaining scab is now a deep black.

His mother releases a gentle smile. "Really, *cariño,* a mother always knows."

But knows about what, Daniel wonders. Does she know her telegrams have been opened? Does she know about Laura Beth?

"I received a few cables from the office," says his dad. As his father recounts the updates from his colleagues in Dallas, Daniel considers what his friends at home might be doing. The guys are probably seeing a picture show at the Majestic. The girls are probably at Titches Tea Room.

Although he thinks about it, Daniel doesn't miss it. His genetic connection to Spain feels deeply inscribed. He loves the narrow, cobbled side streets of Madrid, the plate-glass windows with piles of pink shrimp, dried tuna, and advertisements for squid cooked in their own ink.

He loves that the walls of every café on the Calle de Victoria are pasted with faded posters of bullfights and portraits of matadors. He appreciates the convenience of the Metro and that so much of life in Spain is lived outside, instead of inside. He enjoys his photography mentor, Miguel, the monologues from Ben, and most of all, his exchanges with Ana. In Madrid, Daniel finally feels adult, free to pursue what inspires him, and able to navigate the world on his own.

His mother reaches across the table, interrupting his thoughts. She takes his hand. "I've begged your father not to tell you, but perhaps you've figured it out. I've been sick, *tesoro*."

69

Daniel stares out the window of the taxi. It's well after midnight. Lights and life sparkle in Madrid. He'd prefer to walk on his own, but fears it will offend his parents.

Sick.

His parents are not separating. His mother had what she calls an "incident." They assure him all will be well. In time. After the "incident" she was sick and there may still be a "procedure." But she is recovering and wanted to visit Spain. She has no remaining relatives in the country, but it is her country. She gathers strength and grounding here. It will aid her healing.

She shared the cryptic news in a restaurant. This is her way. It would be unacceptable to become emotional in public.

So the details were conveyed over cava and vermouth at a candlelit table, where they could be explained flatly, without tears. The plan seemed to work until he began to ask questions.

"Mom, I had no idea you were sick. What's wrong?"

His mother is silent. After a moment, she looks to his dad.

"There was a baby," whispers his father.

A baby. Was. Past tense.

"Your mother had wanted another child so badly. We tried through the years but then gave up. A few months ago your mother became pregnant. We were both shocked and elated but said nothing. It seemed too good to be true and we wanted to consult the doctors before sharing the news."

His mother takes a breath, her lips quivering. "And it *was* too good to be true. I lost the child."

His father reaches across the table and gently takes his mother's hand.

Daniel looks at his parents' clasped fingers. He fumbles for words. "Mom, I'm so sorry."

His mother quickly moves her hand to his shoulder. "No, no. I'm okay, *tesoro*. Really. I'm suffering most from the injustice of it all. It seems incredibly unfair that such a blessing and dream were given and then lost. My spirits were terribly low and so your father has brought us along to Spain. It's already done a world of good."

"Why didn't you tell me?"

"I was devastated, emotionally and physically. The last thing I wanted was to worry you or for anyone back home to know. I made your father swear the doctors to secrecy. I've confided only in the priest and your uncle."

"Mom, you can't keep all of this bottled up."

"I will not plague our family with indecency or gossip."

"A miscarriage is not indecent."

"*Shh.* People talk, Daniel. You must know I hear the whispers and jokes. That we're a 'mixed marriage,' that your father married a Spanish dancer. You don't understand, dear."

He does. He hears the jabs too. Oil

money is new money. His family is nou-veau riche. Laura Beth's family claimed they weren't a good fit because his mother was "too ethnic." Considering the news, he's relieved he didn't tell her about the breakup.

"Mom, forget about other people. Your health is what's important, right?"

The tension at the table is palpable. His mother sits wholly erect, as if a yardstick had been placed down the back of her dress. She holds the stem of her glass delicately, with her thumb and two fore-fingers. Her large diamond rings reflect and sparkle amidst the bubbles through the glass.

The stiffness, it's the American part of his mother and it pains him.

"Excuse me." She smiles and departs for the restroom.

Daniel fiddles with the fork on the table. His father releases a deep sigh.

"What did the doctors say?" asks Daniel.

"An issue with the uterus. They may eventually have to remove it. It'll all be fine, partner."

"Really?"

"Yes, really."

The nervous edge in his mother's voice, the crying behind closed doors, his parents supporting an orphanage, the pieces complete the picture. He and his father sit, silent, until Daniel speaks.

"Now I understand — the orphanage deal," he says. "Nick mentioned it."

"That kid's a loose cannon. No wonder he's getting beat up. Nothing's been decided. I need to close this drilling deal first." He flags a waiter for another vermouth.

His mother returns to the table full of smiles. "I just love this restaurant, don't you? It's a shame you didn't bring your camera. We could have taken a family picture. You look so handsome in a suit."

Her enthusiasm is genuine. But he knows his mother. She uses happiness as a shield. She's trying to protect him or prepare him. Maybe both.

Daniel unlocks the door to his suite. On the coffee table is a plate with round chocolates bearing the gold crest of the

Castellana Hilton. Neighboring the plate are several notes and messages. The first is a folded piece of paper. He hopes it's from Ana.

¡Amigo! My sister is bringing you this note. Thank you for the photograph. It's fabulosa! Everyone is impressed by it. Fuga is now El Huérfano, isn't it great? Please don't forget us on Sunday. We will be waiting for you and your big car. See you soon, Texano!

— Rafa

The next notes are message slips from the hotel operator.

8:25 p.m. From Benjamin Stahl
Call me at the Bureau. An opportunity.

8:30 p.m. From Nicholas Van Dorn
Meet us at Taberna de Antonio Sánchez.

9:45 p.m. From Nicholas Van Dorn
Eating at Botín. Join us.

11:10 p.m. From Nicholas Van Dorn
Heading for Pasapoga club on Gran Vía.

11:15 p.m. From Tom Collins
Sleep well.

Tom Collins. He smiles. The message was an hour ago. Is Ana home in Vallecas now? Or is this one of the days she stays overnight at the hotel? He thinks about stealing down to the basement to check.

At the very bottom of the stack is a Western Union telegram. The envelope is sealed and addressed to Daniel. Is it from his uncle? He tears it open.

```
WESTERN UNION TELEGRAM
  — VIA NIGHT LETTER CABLE

SENDER: LAURA BETH JOYCE —
DALLAS, TX MR. DANIEL MATHE-
SON, CASTELLANA HILTON, MADRID
CAN WE TALK? I'M SORRY. I WANT
TO COME TO MADRID.
```

70

Daniel calls to have the breakfast dishes picked up, hoping to see Ana. Just as he hangs up the phone, there's a knock at the door.

Ben Stahl leans on the doorframe, tie wrestled loose. Pieces of his normally slick hair stand in exclamation points. His flapping shirttail is stained with red wine. "I called you." Ben's voice sounds like he's gargled with gasoline.

"I got back after midnight. I figured it was too late," says Daniel.

"Late? You're joking, right? I haven't been to sleep yet. But the word *late*, let's think about that word. It's such an important one, isn't it? Late — often paired with regret or disappointment." Ben's lungs chime in, hacking up a nightclub of cigarette smoke.

"How did you know what suite I was in?" asks Daniel.

"I've got connections to get me where I need to be. Listen, I need a photographer on Monday. My guy has to be in Barcelona. Are you available?"

Daniel's heart hops. He tries to act casual. "Sure. What's the assignment?"

"You'll be perfect for this. But I don't have a budget so there's no pay."

"That's fine," says Daniel. As the words leave his mouth, he knows he responded too quickly.

Ben nods. "That's fine because you're stinkin' rich or that's fine because you understand the value of an opportunity?"

Daniel accepts the challenge. "First, *I'm* not rich. If I were, I'd be on my way to J-School. Second, if you need a free shoot it sounds like you're the one who grasps opportunity value."

Ben laughs. "There he is, swingin' those punches. Hey, can I use your john?"

Without waiting for an answer, Ben pushes past Daniel into the room. He sees the wall of photos and stops.

"Actually, I'm not ready to share those

yet," says Daniel.

"You're not ready? Looks like you've got your own exhibition here." Ben scans the photos. He moves in, pushing his face close to the pictures. "Holy hell, Matheson."

A knock echoes at the door. Daniel opens it and finds not Ana, but Lorenza, lips candied like an apple, hip swung to one side.

"*Buenos días, señor.*"

Unlike Ana, Lorenza enters without invitation. Her eyes are instantly glued to the photo wall. Ben's eyes are instantly glued to Lorenza.

"Hi there, sweet cheeks."

Lorenza gives Ben a wave and turns to Daniel. "Do you like flamenco, *señor?* You should photograph some flamenco dancers." Lorenza stares at him. Her beckoning gaze reminds him of Laura Beth and how her every expression looks staged, like she's posing for a camera.

"Flamenco, sure. Say, Lorenza, could you have Ana bring up some towels?" asks Daniel.

Lorenza makes a clucking with her

tongue. *"Ay,* no. Ana is very busy, *señor."* Lorenza slaps the back of the chair with a cloth, as if she's dusting it, sauntering closer to the photos.

"Ay, look at the matador. Oh and Ana, washing his face. *Qué bonito.* Oh, look at the *pequeñines!* Sweet little ones. How did you get such photos?"

"It's what we do. We're journalists," says Ben. "Excuse me. Gotta drain the radiator." Ben closes the bathroom door.

Daniel is equally honored and unnerved that Ben is referring to them together as journalists. He's also unnerved that so many people are in his room.

"If Ana is too busy, shall I call the manager to make the request?" he asks Lorenza.

Lorenza stiffens. "No. I'll get her now. Towels, you said?" She scurries toward the door.

"And the breakfast dishes?" says Daniel.

"Señor, you must call room service for the dishes."

"I did. I thought they sent you. Isn't

that why you're here?"

The door clicks shut.

Ben emerges from the bathroom, returns to the photos, and lights a cigarette.

"Really, Matheson. I'm impressed. The Magnum judges will be too. These are better than anything in your portfolio. I might even be able to use some."

Daniel accepts the compliment.

"Has anyone seen these?"

"Just my dad," replies Daniel. "And Miguel, who developed them." He doesn't mention that Ana has also seen them. All of them.

"Keep your negatives in a safe place," says Ben. "Meet me in the lobby of the hotel Monday at nine a.m. I've gotta get some shut-eye." He gives a wave and exits.

Daniel still has no idea what the assignment is.

71

Lorenza dashes into the supply room. "Ana, where have you been? *Señor* Matheson has requested towels. I told him you were very busy this morning. He became impatient and said he's going to complain to the manager."

"What? Why?"

"Because you weren't doing your job. *Ay,* why is he so serious all the time? Max Factor is much nicer. He gave me the prettiest bottle of perfume. It's a cat with a feather boa and — Ana, are you listening? What's wrong with you?"

"Nothing," says Ana, grabbing two towels from the shelf.

"*Bueno.* I thought maybe you were sick." Lorenza edges closer with a curling grin. "Lovesick."

Ana ignores the remark and rushes by

Lorenza to the elevator. When she arrives at Daniel's suite, a room-service attendant is removing the breakfast dishes.

"*Señor,* whatever is the matter? Lorenza said you are calling the manager?"

"No. I didn't mean to scare you. Lorenza said you weren't available. I didn't believe her. I don't even know why she was here. I wanted to share the news." Daniel leans against the chair. "I was hoping you'd lose the bet and we'd be working on the project together, but you were right. My parents aren't separating." He smiles.

"See! I told you, *señor.* Your parents are very affectionate with each other. They have no troubles together."

Daniel says nothing about his mother's condition. Have they told him the truth? Ana knows that Daniel thinks in frames. Has he considered the portraits she's seen when servicing his parents' room? Medicine bottles in the trash. Doctor's orders next to the bed.

She stares at the wall. "You have so many beautiful photos."

"Thanks. I have the images, but what I

don't have is context." He points to the photo his father mentioned, the one of Nick's grated knuckles. "My dad's caption was 'Pretty undiplomatic for a diplomat's son.' "

"No. That's incorrect." Ana looks at the photo. Her voice is steady and lyrical. "Fighting phantoms. There are some problems that even money can't solve."

Daniel nods. "Wow, Tom Collins is good at this." He points to the photo of her niece, Lali, asleep in a box meant for oranges.

Ana looks at the photo for a long time before she begins.

"No money, no cradle. Earnings pay rent on their mother's grave." Ana's voice catches as she continues. "If payment is not made, her body will be dug up and thrown in a common trench."

"No. Would they really do that?"

She nods, her eyes filling with sadness.

"Ana, I'm so sorry." He steps closer. "I had no idea."

"How could you know?" she whispers. "It's impossible for outsiders to understand. There is a tension that exists between history and memory, *señor.* Some of us are desperate to preserve and remember, while others are desperate to forget. We all have our reasons. Does your mother ever speak of that?"

Daniel shakes his head. "No, she doesn't."

Ana takes a breath and points to a picture of his parents on the wall. "Your turn."

Daniel looks at the photo. "The caption is . . ."

When he finally speaks, his deep voice has thinned. "They say everything will be fine. But what if it's not?"

The vulnerable tone in his voice. Her hand reaches, gently touching his back. He turns to her. When Ana realizes what she's doing, she draws quickly away. "I must return to work." She manages a small smile. "Just call if you need more towels, *señor.*"

Daniel follows her to the door. "Ana, are you sure you can't come to the bullfight on Sunday?"

"*Sí.* That is my brother's passion. But it's very nice of you to take them. It's just a *capea*. The animals won't be harmed, but the amateurs might be. Make sure you bring towels for your car."

"For what?"

Ana looks at him with surprise. "For the blood," she replies.

72

Puri sits at the front desk of the clinic, nervously rolling her apron between her fingers. It is her new assignment, the plan of Sister Hortensia. One day per week, she will work at the maternity clinic down the street from the Inclusa.

"Special cases are handled here," explains Sister. "Difficult and high-risk pregnancies are brought from the hospital for direct attention. You must be sensitive to the fact that women at the clinic have been informed of a possible complication. They are often fearful, which is understandable. Labor and childbirth can be a lengthy process, so the doctor may ask you to sit with the women to calm their nerves. During labor they are administered an anesthetic. You may also have to sit with them after the birth until they are fully awake."

Puri's nerves roil, releasing a chilled sweat on her palms. The tour of the clinic was too brief. The doctor heaped so much information upon her. How is she to remember it all?

There are already two women in labor in the clinic. One is a young, unwed mother. When Puri sat with her, she expected the girl to wail with remorse for her carnal sins. Instead, she told Puri she was an actress and was anxious to take her child to Barcelona.

"I'll pray for you," Puri assures her.

But Puri doesn't pray for her. She sits and wonders whether the woman really is condemned. The girl is excited both to be a mother and to pursue her interests in Barcelona. Does she not remember the teachings about motherhood and her duty to Spain?

Puri looks at her notes. She is expected to ferry supplies if needed. Water, towels, basins.

Basins. Where did the doctor say the metal basins were?

Puri walks quietly down the gray tile

floor of the hallway. The clinic feels cold and sterile, not homey like the Inclusa. The Inclusa smells of baby powder, soap, and bleached diapers. The clinic smells . . . what exactly is the smell? Puri locates the room with the towels and laundry. Farther down the hall is a room that looks familiar, similar to the bottling room at the Inclusa. Is this where the doctor said the basins are stored? Puri enters.

Perhaps the basins are in the metal cabinet. She pulls the handle on the silver door. A rush of cold air flows out, causing her to blink. Her knees lock. Her hand flies to her mouth, muffling a scream.

The refrigerated cabinet does not hold a basin.

It holds a dead baby.

73

Rafa waits at the end of the road. He shields his eyes from the sun, watching for the shiny black car. Ana assures him the Texano will come, that he won't forget. He paces the road, hoping she's right. Without a ride, he and Fuga will miss the *capea* entirely. The truck with the dead animal parts left yesterday.

Rafa gave confession this morning and professed regret for a mixture of trespassing and fibs. Following the issuance of penance, the priest leaned forward toward the latticed screen.

"Today is your *capea*."

"*Sí, Padre.*"

"At the back of the sanctuary, I have left three votive candles. Take them with you. Help your matador follow the proper ritual."

"Sí, Padre. Gracias, Padre."

Fuga has been absent for two days, but it does not worry Rafa. He knows that his friend was in the cemetery, practicing with the cape, becoming El Huérfano. Early this morning Fuga walked silently into Vallecas, just as Rafa knew he would.

Most matadors begin training very young. Will they ask how old he is? Fuga doesn't know. When they lived in the boys' home and Rafa had asked his age, Fuga just shrugged.

"Well, when's your birthday?" Rafa inquired.

"What's a birthday?" asked Fuga.

Following their escape, they traveled the roads, begging. Outside of Barcelona they came upon a small town where an old Catalonian woman shared kindness and food. That night they lay on their bellies in the dirt, peeking through a crack in the stone wall. The villagers were assembled in a dark building to watch a flickering film. The hero of the movie was Currito de la Cruz, "Curro," an orphan from the slums of Sevilla who becomes a bullfighter. They couldn't hear the sound, but they didn't need to. The visuals told the story. That night Fuga did not sleep. He lay on the grass next to Rafa, staring at the darkened sky.

"Is it really possible for us, *amigo?*" Rafa had asked.

Fuga nodded. It was.

That night, Rafa pledged support and protection to his friend. They shook hands.

Now there is pulling, a twisting in Rafa's stomach that for once has nothing to do with hunger. Life has never offered him triumph. Despite his hopes and dreams, he cannot shake the shadow of guilt that has followed him since the death of his father. He had sat in the bushes, frozen with fright. He did nothing to help his *papá.*

Although Rafa is determined to face fear, a quiet part of him worries that he may be luckless. What then? If they actually take part in the *capea* today, the participation alone will be the most fortune he has ever known. As he considers the potential for victory this afternoon, an overwhelming sense of joy emerges. The voices in his head, the questions — they are his own. They are not voices from the shadows, creeping forth to taunt him.

A black bull suddenly appears in the distance.

It's the Texano's Buick.

74

"Hola," says Daniel. "Ready to go?" Rafa slaps him into a huge hug.

Daniel is not alone. Asleep in the front seat is Nick Van Dorn.

"He wanted to come. I hope that's okay?" whispers Daniel.

Rafa stares at Nick. He finally shrugs. "Sure, your car."

"Is your girlfriend coming?" asks Daniel.

Rafa throws a quick glance over his shoulder. *"Shh.* No. Just us. I'll get Fuga." Rafa turns and makes his way toward the encampment of crumbling shacks. Daniel follows.

Only Fuga, Julia, and the baby are present in the shack.

"Buenos días, señora," Daniel greets Ju-

lia. "I brought you a couple of pictures." He hands Julia the photo he took of Lali and also the picture of Julia fitting Fuga's suit of lights.

"Gracias, señor. I will cherish these. I saw the photo you took of our matador. It's *fabulosa."* Julia shoots Fuga a prompting look. Fuga shrugs.

"I have photos for some of the people in Vallecas," says Daniel.

"¡Qué fantástico! You can share them upon our triumphant return!" says Rafa.

Julia hands Rafa the bundle of clothes. She whispers to both young men and gives them each a kiss. She then lifts the stiff cape from the table, prepared to follow them.

"No, you needn't come," says Rafa quickly, blocking her from the doorway.

"Lali is sleeping. She'll be fine. I just want to see you off."

Rafa whispers to Julia. Her face shrinks with alarm. "Nick? What is he doing here?"

Daniel tries to conceal his frustration. Why didn't he trust his instincts and just say no to Nick?

"I'm sorry. I didn't realize there was a problem. He wanted to come along," says Daniel.

Julia gives a tired wave of her hand. "Just go. Go!"

The three men trudge from the shack.

"It's a long story," says Rafa. "And not mine to tell."

They take a few steps and are bombarded by teams of shrieking children, grabbing at the bundled suit of lights.

"*¡Basta!*" yells Rafa. "Enough. But if the afternoon goes well, we will all celebrate," he assures them.

Daniel opens the trunk of the car so Rafa can put in the clothing. Seeing crates of food, the children squeal with delight. *Tortilla de patata,* oranges, and Manchego cheese.

"I thought we might get hungry," says Daniel.

Rafa slams the trunk. "No food. Not until after. He's on a restricted diet."

A boy tugs at Daniel's sleeve. "The *torero* must have an empty belly. That way it's easier for the doctor to sew him back together if the bull tears holes in him." The little boy smiles and nods, proud of his macabre knowledge.

"It's true," says Rafa. "But there will be no specialized surgeon today. No doctors or chaplains standing by."

Daniel gets in the car. He is grateful he took Ana's advice and brought towels.

The children surround Fuga's side of the car, waving and pushing their faces against the glass. They wish him well, bubbling with joy and excitement. The faintest hint of a smile emerges on Fuga's lips. He takes his finger and touches the window, replying to the girl with the raven braid, who is kissing the glass. Daniel grabs his camera from the floorboard and takes a picture.

Daniel spent the night reading a book he bought on the history of bullfighting. In ancient times, bulls were revered as mythological gods. Those who stood before the bulls and presented their life for sacrifice were considered high priests. Symbolically, in facing a bull, some believe a matador achieves closeness with God and unifies himself with death.

Daniel looks in the rearview mirror. Fu-

ga's eyes are closed, a quiet smile cross-
ing his face. He is composed. Ready.

The Buick pulls slowly out onto the
road.

75

Ana makes her way down the corridor of the seventh floor.

Do guests realize that personal details reveal themselves in a hotel room? Lorenza shared her daily brief earlier in the basement:

The man in 615 eats in bed (crumbs in the sheets), has high blood pressure (medicine in the bathroom), and plays Casanova (leaves his wedding ring in the room while out for the evening).

The woman in 248 secretly likes gin (bottles under the bed), sleeps with her makeup on (evidenced by her pillow), and has a penchant for mystery (books with "Murder" in the title by someone named Agatha Christie).

Ana unlocks the door to 760.

Daniel's suite is not neat, but also not

messy. Coins, expensive cuff links, and a fountain pen sit exposed on the bureau. He is trusting. She looks to the undressed bed. The hotel coverlet lies bunched at the foot of the mattress. He sleeps with only a sheet, his head on the left pillow. Most American guests have pajama sets or nightclothes. He doesn't. She blushes. On the nightstand sits his Capa book. Daniel reads before going to sleep.

Ana opens the narrow closet and runs her hand across his clothes. His jeans are not from Neiman-Marcus. They have a leather patch on the back pocket that says Blue Bell Wrangler. She tries to adjust the jumbled hangers but they put up a fight. As she removes the hanging clothes, she discovers the cause. Stacked from top to bottom in the back of the closet are the countless towels Daniel has requested — requested so she would come to his room.

She smiles and removes them so he'll ask for more.

His toiletries in the bathroom are housed in an expensive leather travel kit. A single bottle, his shaving tonic, sits on the bathroom counter. Ana brings the glass bottle, marked *Old Spice Holiday Edition,* to her nose. It's the scent she smelled the very first day in his room, the scent she smelled on the Metro, and the scent she smelled in the courtyard at the embassy. It's masculine and steady, like Daniel. It smells of leathery cloves and herbal woods, with hints of sweet tobacco. Ana removes a thin handkerchief from her apron and dots a tiny pop of the aftershave on it.

Holding the fabric to her nose, she walks into the living area of the suite. She's happy that Daniel is with Rafa and hopes she'll get to see him when they return to Vallecas. If only Julia could understand. Daniel is different. He's kindhearted, genuine, and honest. He didn't have to share his fears about his parents but he did. Each time they're together, Ana cares less about the recommendation letter and more about Daniel. Thoughts of Julia's disapproval bring the threatening notes to Ana's mind. She whisks the thought away.

A lone chair is placed in front of the wall containing Daniel's photographs. Ana sits in it. The images are evocative, full of story and truth. The captions come to her immediately. She walks to the desk to retrieve a piece of hotel stationery. And that's when she sees it.

Sitting in the trash is a Western Union telegram. It's addressed to Daniel from someone named Laura Beth.

It's torn apart.

76

While the others prepare, Daniel and Nick stand at the back of the car, eating lunch from the trunk.

"Ben has a photo assignment for me tomorrow," says Daniel.

"That's swell. What is it?"

"He wouldn't tell me. But I trust him. Ben's on the up and up."

"Yeah, he's definitely not on the up and down, if you know what I mean. Poor guy won't admit it, but he's been desperate to find a girlfriend in Spain. He hangs on at the clubs even after I've left. So that tells you something."

"He works hard. He probably needs to unwind," says Daniel.

Nick removes a flask from his shirt pocket and takes a swig.

"Rafa seemed surprised to see you," says Daniel.

"Yeah, it's been a while."

He turns to face Nick. "So, let's hear it. Why'd you send me out to their house last weekend? Kind of a wise-guy move, if you ask me."

Nick laughs. "Sorry if I embarrassed you."

"Not me. It was embarrassing for Ana."

"Nah, she loved it."

Daniel shifts his feet. "She loved it or you loved it, Nick?"

Nick raises his hands in nervous surrender. "Honest. I could tell you were interested, but she can't socialize at the hotel. Did it all turn out okay?"

Daniel nods. "Listen, if you have eyes on Ana, be a man. Tell me to step aside."

Nick speaks slowly and directly. "We're just friends. I've told you that, Matheson."

"So you won't mind if I spend time with her?"

"No. But remember, this isn't the States. You can't just drive up in your nice car, sweet-talk the parents, and take a girl out. All dates have to be chaperoned. Families are involved, the whole thing."

Daniel thinks of his parents. "Ana's family, what's the story there?"

"Her parents were part of the intellectual crowd who opposed Franco. They both wound up dead, and the kids are terrified they'll eventually be punished as well. Let's face it, Franco wasn't exactly forgiving after the war. Ana's older sister had to carry the load. And Rafa." Nick whistles and shakes his head. "He had it the worst. He was sent to some reformatory joint up near Barcelona. He and his crazy matador friend were there together. From what I gather, they were tortured. And I'm not talking beat up in an alley by some debt-collecting thugs. I mean really tortured. The two of them escaped somehow and nearly died in the process. We're a couple of pansies next to those two."

Daniel thinks on Nick's words. Rafa was tortured? He exudes such warmth, enthusiasm, and determination. He doesn't have an ounce of bitterness.

Nick lights a cigarette. "Listen, Ana is beautiful. But if you've got some rich boy fantasy of a girl from the other side of the tracks, step back. You and I both know our parents want us with debutantes from families on the Social Register. But if you're looking to have a real conversation and you're willing to take it slow, Ana's a girl that you'll never forget — if you can get around her sister and brother-in-law."

Daniel nods. "The brother-in-law, Antonio, already sent me on a fool's errand. Probably hoped I'd get lost and never return."

"Oh yeah?" Nick laughs.

"Yeah. He sent me to some huge old orphanage. He said I might find a story there to photograph."

Nick's eyebrows lift. "Even if you did, you wouldn't be able to prove it."

"Prove what?" Daniel asks.

Nick exhales a mouthful of smoke. "That some of the babies they're selling aren't orphans."

We also had the Basque-Spanish orphans program. We sent a couple of orphans to the United States, alleged orphans. They were no orphans, no question about that. It wasn't that they didn't have family to take care of them. That was an interesting time.

— WILLIAM W. LEHFELDT, U.S. vice consul, Bilbao (1955–1957)

Oral History Interview Excerpt, April 1994
Foreign Affairs Oral History Collection
Association for Diplomatic Studies and Training
Arlington, VA www.adst.org

77

Puri cannot eat. She cannot sleep. Why is a dead baby in the freezer at the clinic instead of the morgue? She sits on her bed, knees to her chin, arms spiraled around her legs. There are explanations:

The corpse is being used for medical study.

The infant recently died. Burial is forthcoming.

She is mistaken about what she saw.

Could she be mistaken?

The doctor found Puri in the bathroom, a pale heap near the toilet.

"Bad eel. It will pass," she assured him.

But the nausea hasn't passed and neither have the questions. Instead, the words from the filed letters scroll through her brain.

My wife is certain there must be a mistake. She said the child she gave birth to was completely bald and had a red birthmark on his arm. The deceased infant shown to us was larger than our son, had a bit of hair, and did not have the marking on his arm.

And the letter that still haunts Puri:

You stole our child.

The question clings. Whom does the child in the freezer belong to?

For the first time, Puri eagerly seeks confession.

"Hail Mary the Purest."

"Conceived without sin," replies the priest.

"I am deeply troubled, *Padre,* by a question that plagues me. I ask for your wisdom and guidance to soothe my heart. In our beloved country of Spain, is it better for a child to have no parents than the wrong parents?"

"Are you with child?" asks the priest.

"No, *Padre!*" gasps Puri. "I ask only because I am committed to the preservation of our noble country."

"We owe it to our children and our future to protect Catholic values and morals."

"So that means," leads Puri, "it is better to be raised by the right parents, even if they are not the birth parents?"

The priest gives a tired exhale. "You seem to have answered your own question."

No, I haven't, thinks Puri.

But I will.

78

The miniature, portable ring has been
set up at the edge of the village. The *maletilla* amateurs stand in a stone shed.
Rafa kneels on the earthen floor, secur-
ing the bottom of Fuga's trousers. There
will be no picadors or *banderilleros* today.
Only half a dozen young men who have
come to brave the bulls and prove themselves to anyone who may care to notice.
Only one other participant wears a suit
of lights. He is a boy of sixteen or seventeen with a husky frame. He dons an ill-
fitting amber suit. But Rafa sees that the
cloth is cursed. There's a faint smear of
blood across the thigh. The other boys
throw worried glances at Fuga. His suit
of lights, age, and demeanor raise expec-
tation.

Although the suit is old, Julia has

altered it so perfectly that it appears to be expressly for the *torero* wearing it. Fuga's frame is tall and hungry. He is cut from the same strong wood of the olive tree he has slept beneath for so many years. The strength of his form is lean legs. His extended gait lends drama to his every step. His long arms, ungainly for a common man, are an asset for a *torero.* The *muleta* cape handles more easily and melodically with elongated arms.

Rafa looks at the beautiful silver embroidery that climbs and vines the outside of the trousers. He gives thanks for Julia and for her boss, Luis. No other tailor creates suits as special as his.

"Comb your hair," instructs Rafa. "Do it the way Ana did for the photo."

Fuga spits thick saliva on the small comb and rakes it through his hair.

Uncertain what to do, the cluster of other boys press and lunge into leg stretches because they have seen photographs of famous matadors doing the same.

Rafa removes the priest's votive candles from his pocket. He positions them upon a shelf in the shed and strikes a match to light them. He pulls out a small faded portrait of the Virgin, salvaged from an outdated pocket calendar, and carefully sets it behind the glow of the candles. Another boy contributes a broken mirror and balances it on the shelf.

Reflected in the quivering candlelight is a motley assembly of young men before a makeshift altar. If they succeed today, they may pick up a *peseta* or a handful of grapes. If they do not succeed, they will be laughed at and dismissed. If they are gored, Rafa hopes someone will be generous enough to squirt alcohol in the wound.

Rafa says his prayers and allows the others to do the same. Each young man leaves the shed until only Fuga is left.

"I'll give you a moment of privacy," he tells his friend.

They exchange a formal handshake. Rafa issues a message of luck.

"*Suerte,* Huérfano."

79

Fuga stares into the cracked mirror.

He is not frightened.

He is not frightened of the bulls. He is not frightened of the breeders. He is not frightened of the Crows. He is not frightened of poverty or hardship.

He is not frightened of Franco.

Fuga's death came as a child, at the hands of a monster in the boys' home.

He stares at his reflection and begins the internal conversation.

It is impossible to kill a man who is already dead. The mirror is broken, but the reflection is intact. Resurrection is possible, Huérfano. You fight for the forgotten, the abused, the hungry, and the unwanted. You fight for your one and only friend, just as he fights for you.

He takes the wrinkled card of the Virgin and kisses it.

Without hesitation, he walks out of the shed.

80

Rafa stands with Daniel and Nick amidst a small crowd at the edge of the ring. They watch as the ragged troop of young men emerges from the shed. The burly boy in the amber suit yanks constantly at the waistband of his trousers.

"Oh, boy," says Nick. "This could be unpleasant."

"Ana says the animals won't be harmed," says Daniel.

"*Sí*. This is just a *capea,* a caping," replies Rafa. "As you can see, the audience is less than a hundred people. If we were at Las Ventas in Madrid, there'd be twenty-five thousand people in the arena and it would be very different."

Daniel stands with his lens on the shed, waiting for Fuga. Rafa nervously assures the men that there is one remaining matador.

"Wait, El Huérfano is coming."

"Maybe Huérfano has chickened out," says a man. But there is no time to laugh. At that moment Fuga emerges from the shed in the turquoise suit of lights, silver embroidery shimmering beneath the afternoon sun.

Women nearby chatter. Men issue commentary and judgment.

"Nice suit."

"*Ay*, he's too old."

"Why such a suit? It's just a *capea*."

"I think I've seen him somewhere."

Fuga walks to the ring, radiating reverence and strength. He is not arrogant, but calmly disconnected from all that titters around him. Rafa recognizes the spell. It is the same trance he has seen in the dark willow fields, when the world seems to fall away and a solitary light shines only on Fuga and the bull.

The group of animals is less ragged than the *toreros* but still disappointing. Rafa was relieved when he saw them, but he knows Fuga will be disappointed. Fuga has faced full-grown bulls in the fields. He hopes Fuga does not complain when he sees the collection of scrawny, dull-coated bulls, young bull calves, and a restless Corriente cow with massive horns.

The first young man enters the ring, holding a newspaper as a cape.

"Ten *pesetas.* He'll last less than two minutes," Nick wagers with a nearby attendee.

The young bull calf is released into the ring. It runs around and the boy dodges it, flapping the newspaper. The energy is frantic. The calf chases the boy in circles. Nick wins the bet. The next *torero* is the same. The third ends up running from the ring amidst a serenade of boos. The husky boy in the floppy suit of lights marches into the ring. He is arrogant and demands to face the irritable cow with the big horns.

The cow enters the ring and simply stands there. The *torero* moves closer to the animal but it does not respond. The boy begins jeering and taunting the animal, flapping the cape, looking for a reaction. Without warning, the cow charges at the boy. He tries to spin away but the animal's horns catch on his loose jacket.

"*¡AY!*" The boy is lifted from the ground and yells in a panic.

Rafa jumps into the ring. He has pulled Fuga from clips in the fields. Rafa and another man dislodge the boy from the cow and escort him from the ring. The boy wails as blood spills through the sleeve of his suit. The cow's horn has punctured his shoulder.

The cow is angry, snorting, and rearing.

Fuga jumps into the ring. The crowd pulls a collective breath.

The animal is not calm.

But Fuga is.

With slow and graceful steps, El Huérfano emerges. His gaze is strong and steady, showing reverence to the animal, acknowledging the exchange about to begin. He allows adequate distance and gives the cape a subtle twirl. The cow charges. At the last possible second, Fuga snaps the cape high and away, allowing the cow's horns to pass so close to his torso that Nick gasps. Subsequent passes are completed with similar strength and grace, eliciting an *"Olé"* from a few men.

The cow becomes tired. Fuga comes alive.

The cow is exchanged for a young bull. Fuga exhibits similar resolve. He performs a set of *tandas,* a series of passes, displaying his skill and form. His respect for the bull is evident. He continues the passes with the young bull until the animal achieves *sentido,* the knowledge that Fuga is his challenger, not the cape. Each pass then becomes more dangerous. The animal suddenly charges straight for Fuga. He drops to his knees in front of the bull. Left hand on his hip, he guides the young bull with the cape extended in his right hand. The crowd issues *"Olés"* and applause. The breeder corrals the bull from the fight.

Fuga crosses the ring toward Rafa.

"No, walk the ring!" Rafa whispers. Fuga's face is blank. But Rafa recognizes the stare. It's presence.

Fuga has a keen readiness but no fear. What he has experienced in life is far worse than anything that could transpire at a *capea*. In the streets he is ignored and denied. He is labeled a wild orphan, a mad gravedigger. Fuga reveals himself to the animal only. In life, he falls to his knees for the animal only.

At Rafa's insistence, Fuga walks the small ring, collecting *pesetas*, grapes, and most of all, respect. He says nothing, interacts with no one, just turns and walks to the stone shed.

Rafa runs to Daniel. "Did you get photos?"

"I did. Wow, your friend is very talented."

"*Sí*, he is very brave." Rafa lowers his voice. "This was nothing. An angry cow and a young calf. Wait until you see El Huérfano with a real bull."

A man in a wide felt hat approaches Rafa.

"How old is your friend?" he asks.

"We don't know. He's an orphan."

"So, that's part of your pitch, huh? He's faced bulls before, that's obvious."

"Well, *señor,* we have an old wheelbarrow. We tied a set of horns to it. I run it around so Huérfano can train."

The man looks at Rafa, clearly skeptical.

"That is why we are here, *señor*. We were lucky to find these Americanos to pick us up and drive us here. With the recommendation and backing of a fine man such as yourself, Huérfano can begin to train properly as a *novillero*. I work part-time at the slaughterhouse, but a *torero* must have a sponsor to train there."

"So, you're telling me that this — Huérfano — has never faced a bull." The man chews on his cigar, staring at Rafa.

Rafa skirts the question. "He has yet to face his destiny, *señor.*"

"And what about that suit? Did he steal it?"

"No, *señor*. My dear sister works for the best tailor in all of Madrid. The suit must be returned tomorrow."

The man extends a business card to Rafa. "Don't return the suit just yet."

Rafa breaks out in a grin.

Daniel snaps a picture.

81

Daniel turns the Buick onto the dusty path. The youngsters spot the car and stampede toward it. Rafa hangs out the window, waving wildly as the children explode into cheers, jumping up and down. Elderly residents awaken in their chairs. Neighbors emerge from their shacks. The community pours into the road to watch the big black car glide toward Rafa's house.

Antonio stands in the doorway, holding Lali. Julia and Ana appear just as the car pulls to a stop. Rafa jumps out, stands in the center of the street, and hoists the business card above his head.

"*¡Novillero!*" he yells.

The crowd gives a huge cheer.

Ana looks to Daniel, her mouth open in surprise. Daniel nods.

"*¡Toro! ¡Toro! ¡Toro!*" scream the children.

Rafa walks to the rear door of the Buick. "Vallecanos, congratulate our friend, El Huérfano!" Rafa opens the door and Fuga steps out amidst the chaos.

Still dressed in the suit of lights, Fuga looks princely, strong. He ignores the adults but acknowledges the children, giving them his grapes. He then walks straight to the door of the shack, carefully cradling a handful of coins.

Fuga bends to one knee and bows his head. He raises his hands and offers his winnings.

To Ana.

82

The worthy opponent is someone you respect, someone who has similar goals, and someone you must overcome. Daniel looks at Fuga.

He is a worthy opponent — and he has caught him completely off guard. As he snaps the picture, it all rolls back at him.

Fuga's glares. Instant. The moment he entered the shack Daniel felt Fuga's eyes upon him, saw his hands ball into fists. While taking his photo, Fuga's menacing stare softened only when he glanced — toward Ana. At the time, Daniel thought nothing of it. Was his lens biased? Did he dismiss Fuga because he was a gravedigger? The most dangerous adversary is the one you underestimate.

The crowd disperses. Fuga enters the shack with Rafa and the family.

Nick whistles and scratches the side of his head. "Well, there's a humdinger. I never saw that one coming."

"We should leave," says Daniel.

"Nah, there's generally a dance on Sunday night. We should stick around."

How does Nick know there's a dance on Sundays?

Ana emerges from the shack and approaches the car.

"Ana, I'm trying to convince Dan to stay. There's a dance tonight, isn't there?" says Nick.

"Yes. Do stay, *señor*. Rafa will want you here to celebrate. He's so excited."

"Looks like El Huérfano is the one who's excited." Nick laughs. He gets down on one knee and holds his flask up to Ana.

"Stop it, Nick! I was just as surprised as you were." Ana looks nervously to the door. "Stand up. It would be very hurtful if he saw you teasing like that."

Nick gets up. "So, you and the matador aren't courting?"

"Of course not. He's barely spoken to

me." Ana steps closer, hands on her hips. "Even if we were, you have no right to my personal life. You might be surprised to learn, Nick, that I've moved on from the Van Dorns." Ana walks back toward her house.

"Yeah? Don't need my help anymore?" he calls after her. "Got yourself a beau? Who is it?"

Ana stops at the door and whirls to face Nick. "Yes, I do. His name is Tom Collins." She gives a sweet shrug and walks through the door.

Nick scratches his head, confused. "Well, that's a sorry break, Dan. Sounds like you'll have to get in line behind this Tom character and then you'll have to fight our pal Fuga."

Daniel smiles. Nick's wrong. Tom Collins just passed him a private message.

He's definitely staying for the dance.

83

Puri stands on a chair in her mother's closet, reaching for the box she knows is there. She has snooped before, but at the time, the box didn't interest her. Jewelry and lipstick were more interesting than files and correspondence about the war. But now more than ever, all things locked and hidden pull Puri. Tonight her parents are with friends for dinner. There's plenty of time.

She pulls the metal box from the far corner of the shelf and sits down in the closet.

Although the photos are faded, Puri recognizes her aunt. Ana looks much like her. Two sisters — her mother and Ana's mother — stand together, arms linked, smiles wide. The smile on her mother's face is spontaneous and carefree. Puri doesn't recognize the easy expression. It's foreign and makes her feel uncomfortable, as if her mother used to be a different person. A thick square of folded paper sits in the box. It's stained and without envelope. Puri unfolds the paper.

Dearest Sister,

Forgive my hurried hand. Each time I write, it is with the knowing that the end draws closer. The guards remind me daily that the best cure for my suffering is death.

Yet I cling to life. It is my final resistance.

But if you receive this letter, Teresa, I am gone.

Although you are far away in Madrid, you must hide your grief. Hide it well or you will be marked a sympathizer. You will not be alone in your silence. Our country has entered a period of memory hibernation and I fear this "winter" could be long.

You once asked if new schools were worth dying for. I told you they were. I still believe that. Our husbands stood on opposite sides during the war, each defending their convictions. I hold no grudge. But I never fathomed that brutality could exist to this extent. The war is over but the torture continues. A hunting permit is required to kill a rabbit, yet each day I see women tortured and killed at whim. Today, the young daughter of a journalist was dealt such bestial blows she died choking on her own blood.

In many ways, it is the children of our country who will pay for this war — my own included — and for that, I cannot forgive myself. Teresa, there are so many children who are desperate and orphaned. I have seen them tear newborns from a mother's arms just prior to execution. I know you have long tried for a child of your own, but if you could find it in your heart, dear sister, please give shelter to any that you can. Build a family from the broken pieces.

I've begged Julia to stay away but she has found ways to communicate. She will get this letter to you. What indescribable sorrow it causes me, knowing that my elder daughter will sacrifice her childhood to take care of the family. Julia will contact you when appropriate. She understands the necessity of silence.

Take comfort that this silence is not yours alone, Teresa. In the fields, across the mountains, under the streets, and beneath the trees lie thousands of souls, condemned to silence. But one day, far into the future when the pain is less sharp, the voices of the dead will find harmony with the living. They will make a melody. Listen for the music, Teresa. I sing for you, for my children, and for the better day I know will come. Until then, I send you all my love, sister, and my eternal gratitude for helping my children.

Yours, Belén

Puri stares at the faded, handwritten letter. The sorrowful note provides no real answers, but raises an additional question.

I know you have long tried for a child of your own, but if you could find it in your heart, dear sister, please give shelter to any that you can. Build a family from the broken pieces.

Was Aunt Belén telling her mother to adopt a child?

Puri swallows. Broken pieces. Is she one of them? No. It can't be true.

Or could it?

84

A schoolhouse on weekdays, the dilapidated building now serves as a sweltering dance hall. There are no crystal chandeliers, no champagne fountains, no circulating hors d'oeuvres, and everyone is having a grand time.

Antonio looks through the lens of Daniel's camera.

"*Sí,* like that. Turn it slowly to focus," instructs Daniel. He looks around the room to see what Antonio might see. Fuga stands in the corner in what appears to be an angry exchange with Lorenza. Does Lorenza live in Vallecas?

"I won't take a picture. I know that film is expensive," says Antonio.

"That's okay. Take pictures if you'd like. Do you see Julia?" Daniel points. Antonio finds his wife in the crowd of dancers and snaps a photo.

"Have you taken a lot of pictures in Madrid?" asks Antonio. He hands the camera back to Daniel.

"I have." Daniel fiddles with the camera, his foot tapping to the music. "I went out to the Inclusa like you suggested." Mention of the Inclusa triggers Nick's comment about babies not being orphans. Could that be true? Does Antonio know something?

The lines on Antonio's forehead lift in surprise. "The Inclusa, was it interesting?"

"A boy came crying on the sidewalk. He had a note from his mother, sending him to the orphanage. I felt badly for him. He was only five."

Antonio nods attentively. "Did you take any photos inside?"

"No, it didn't really feel appropriate."

"They might be pleased for you to take photos. You can show America how wonderful Spanish social programs are. You should ask."

Daniel is only half listening. His eyes are on Ana. She's dancing with Nick, whose steps are clumsy. Spaniards hold their drink. If Nick weren't holding on to Ana, he'd probably be stumbling.

Antonio follows his gaze. "Texanos don't dance?"

"We do." Daniel hands his camera to Antonio and walks out onto the dance floor. He taps Nick on the shoulder to cut in.

"Time for the switch, cowboy?" Nick's voice brims with false enthusiasm. He steps aside and makes a grand gesture of departure to Ana.

"Think you can stand a Texas two-step?" asks Daniel.

"If you show me, I'll try to follow."

"Do we need a chaperone?"

Ana laughs, her smile glowing. "We have a hundred chaperones here, *señor.*"

Daniel slides his right arm under Ana's left, placing his hand on her shoulder blade. He takes her hand. She looks to the floor, following his steps. *Quick, quick, slow, slow. Quick, quick, slow, slow.*

Daniel slides in to her ear. "Look at me, not your feet. It works best if you feel it, not think it."

She looks up at Daniel. Eyes clasped, he guides her and they fall in step.

"I think I've got it." She smiles.

"Yeah? You got it?"

She nods.

His arm is suddenly over her head, spinning her away, then pulling her back in. Each time he pulls her back, it's tighter, her smile wider. When their bodies finally meet, he holds her close, moving her into the steps.

Girls in Texas wear fabric chaperones — stiff dresses and petticoats that rustle and crunch with each movement. Ana's dress is handkerchief light and sways silently as she moves. Daniel turns Ana away from him, sliding his hand across her waist. When he twirls her back in, her dance-thrown hair presses against the side of his face. She smells like lemons. Her dress is so thin it's like touching her skin. Can she feel his belt buckle through her dress? Ana's mouth is suddenly to his ear.

"*Ay,* I think we need a chaperone." There's a light pull at his earlobe.

Did she just kiss him?

Ana kissed him on the ear.

Did she?

The song ends and Daniel steps back quickly, putting respectable distance between them. He nods politely to Ana as he would a partner in a Texas dance hall. Her black hair, full and tousled from the turns, hangs in wild, loose spirals around her face. She looks at Daniel and throws her head back with laughter.

"What's so funny?" he asks.

Ana shakes her head. "You. Your expression."

Nick approaches, holding Daniel's camera retrieved from Antonio. "Didn't you say you had a photo shoot tomorrow?"

Daniel nods, staring at Ana.

"Well, it's late," says Nick. "We better get going."

"You're worried about staying out late, Nick? That's a first," says Ana.

Daniel runs a hand through his sweaty hair. "Actually, he's right. I told Ben that I'd shoot for him tomorrow morning."

He looks at Ana. "But maybe sleep is overrated."

Ana nods, grinning. "It is late. I'm sure turndown service was completed in your suite long ago. Perhaps I'll see you tomorrow at the hotel. *Buenas noches, señor.*" Ana turns and walks away.

"Let's get out of here," says Nick. "Looks like Fuga's planning his own 'turndown' service for you. Man, that guy is scary. Did you ever notice that he actually looks like a bull?"

Daniel hasn't noticed. Why did Ana laugh at him? He was trying to be polite and respectful. Did he come off as an amateur?

Nick falls asleep the moment the car leaves Vallecas. But Daniel is wide-awake. He drives through the dark Spanish night with all the windows rolled down. He feels her whisper upon his ear. The melody of Ana plays on in his head.

85

Julia watches her sister from across the room. Ana is flushed, aglow after her dance. The Texas boy is trouble. His jeans, his boots, his dancing. Trouble.

Antonio wraps a comforting arm around Julia. "*Ay,* don't worry so much. He'll go back to Texas soon. They're just having fun."

"Exactly. Remember the intensity of everything at that age? It results in bad decisions."

"It's fine. He's gone for the night. *Mi amor,* would a rich Texano really be such a bad decision?"

"Yes, Antonio. He's not serious about her. He's just another American who thinks he can take whatever he wants." Julia sighs with concern and looks to her husband. "He's going to break her heart," she whispers.

Antonio shakes his head. "You're wrong."

"I am?"

He nods. "She's going to break his."

86

Daniel pulls the Buick onto the apron of elegant pavers in front of the hotel. A man in a green-and-gold uniform sprints to the car.

"Welcome back, *señor.*"

Nick yawns, groggy. "You want to get something to eat?" he asks Daniel.

"No, I'm gonna head up."

Daniel briefly checks the lobby to see if his dad might be there. His father is not in the lobby, but Paco Lobo is, peering over a wrinkled map spread out in front of him. He waves Daniel over.

"Hello. I was just checking to see if my father was here."

"Your parents had drinks with Max Factor. They went up about an hour ago," says Paco, looking up at Daniel through his glasses. "Say, my eyes are so bad, I can't see the small print. On the coast, south of Valencia, can you find a city named Dénia?"

Daniel leans over the map. "Here." He points to a city in the Costa Blanca region. "Are you adopting another village?"

"No," Paco Lobo says with a laugh. "I have to visit for work."

"Oh, I thought philanthropy was your work."

He shakes his head and pushes the wire frames higher on his nose. He puts a finger to the map. "Yes, there it is. Thank you."

Daniel notices a small notepad near the map. "The names and words you've got there, they're German, aren't they?"

"My, your eyes *are* good." Paco Lobo quickly slides his notes beneath the map. "Daniel —" Paco speaks without looking at him. "During cocktails, I overheard your father tell Max Factor that you met the Guardia Civil. He sounded proud, said you held your own. I'm sure it was nothing, but Franco's police and guards"

— his eyes leave the map and lock to Daniel's — "they're thorough. Have a good night."

The statement is a dismissal. Is it also a warning? Daniel wonders as he heads for the elevator. His father and Max Factor — the makeup mogul. They couldn't be more different. The cocktail conversation must have been lacking if his father had to bring up the incident from the first day in Madrid. And proud? No. That's not a word he'd use about his son being reprimanded. Perhaps Paco Lobo is the one who had a few drinks.

Daniel enters his suite; it's quiet and comforting with just a glow of the desk lamp. A telephone message sits squarely within the lamplight.

11:45 p.m. From Benjamin Stahl
Lobby 9:00 a.m. Pros wear suit and tie.
100
ASA. Bring your passport.

100 ASA is for bright light. The shoot is probably outside. Why does he need his passport?

Daniel takes off his shirt and tosses it

over the back of a chair. Ana was right. Turndown service has been completed. Did she do it herself before leaving for the night? Daniel turns and finds the answer. Taped under each photo on the wall is a small strip of paper. A caption.

From Tom Collins.

He snaps on the lights.

The picture of Nick, face bludgeoned, slumped in the back of the taxi:

Sometimes, when there's nothing left to burn, we set ourselves on fire.

The happy girl from Vallecas with the raven braid and holes in her shoes:

She has a name for the tapeworm that lives inside of her. She calls him Chucho.

The hairy-chested tourist asleep at the sidewalk table:

The drink he spills costs more than many earn in a week. Who benefits most from tourist dollars in Spain?

Shep Van Dorn, entertaining guests at

the dinner party:

> Expensive clothes or cheap drapes of
> emotional poverty?

Rafa, smile beaming, standing by the Buick:

> The lashing scars on his back live like
> veins above the skin. But sometimes,
> a good smile can chase the memories
> away.

Each caption provides a new lens into the image, peeling back invisible layers to reveal a human story. He can't wait to discuss them with her. As he scans the wall, his eyes land on the picture that Ana took of him that day in the candy shop.

The caption is just two words, but says everything.

> Hola, Daniel.

87

Rafa removes his bloody apron for lunch. A fellow slaughterhouse worker passes behind him.

"Rafa. Supervisor wants to see you. By the way, I heard about yesterday. Sounds like your *torero* made an impression. *¡Felicidades!*" he says, patting Rafa on the back.

"*Gracias, amigo.*" Rafa smiles. His colleagues have been generous with words of encouragement and congratulations. His announcement and their enthusiasm have made for a very happy Monday. He heads to the office and knocks on the frame of the door.

"*Adelante.*" His supervisor waves him into the small, windowless room with brick walls. "A gentleman called this morning asking about you. Did you tell someone at the *capea* that you work here at *el matadero?*"

"Just the man in the big hat. The one who gave me his card."

His supervisor nods. "He asked me to confirm that you are employed here and then he asked a lot of questions about your *torero.*"

"Questions about El Huérfano? What kind of questions?"

"About his training, his background. Questions I couldn't answer. But I told him I do know you and that you're a good worker."

"Ay, ¡gracias!" says Rafa.

"He wants to see your friend fight again."

"When? We'll be ready!"

"Sunday. Just said he'll be in touch about a fight in Arganda del Rey. But if he's calling around the morning after the *capea,* seems like a good sign to me."

A tingling spreads across Rafa's back. It is a good sign. It's a great sign. He'll head straight to the cemetery after work to tell Fuga.

Last night Fuga was restless. He insisted they must return to the pastures to train. "No," said Rafa. "If the promoter is interested, he will help us find proper training."

"There are a million reasons this rich man could change his mind," argued Fuga. "But I'll prove it to him. I'm better than everyone else."

It's pointless to argue with Fuga. But maybe he doesn't know Fuga as well as he thinks? Fuga doesn't smile for many, only children and bulls. So why did he give his winnings and smile to Ana? Sure, he's asked about his sister before, but never in a way that implied he liked her. Aspiring bullfighters shouldn't have girlfriends anyway. As the saying goes, a married bullfighter is a finished bullfighter. Success requires complete focus. He explained that to his girlfriend yesterday when he broke up with her.

Rafa scratches his head, recalling her furious reaction. Her anger had surprised him. He didn't realize she cared so much. Women are so confusing. His sister Julia is the most confusing. Last night she huffed around, saying she'd rather Ana end up with an amateur bullfighter like Fuga than the rich Texano.

What did she mean? What could be so bad about the Texano?

88

Puri dries the dishes at the sink, devising a way to raise the topic with her mother.

"I think I'd prefer not to volunteer at the clinic," announces Puri. "The Inclusa is a much happier place."

"It's not your choice. Sister Hortensia has assigned you to the clinic because she believes you will contribute there. You will serve as instructed, dear."

"But it's all so distressing. Women can be so irrational."

Her mother turns from the table. "Excuse me?"

"Of course, not you, Mother. But the other day as I was leaving the Inclusa, a woman stopped me on the street. She was frantic. She said that her baby had been taken for baptism and was never returned to her. It was very strange, as if she thought someone was hiding her baby inside the Inclusa. She gripped my arm so hard it hurt."

"She took hold of you?"

"Yes. I saw Sister Hortensia in the window and suggested the woman speak to Sister."

"Did she?"

"No." Puri shrugs, trying her best to appear casual. "She ran away."

Her mother turns slowly back to the table. She speaks to Puri over her shoulder.

"Did Sister mention seeing the episode?"

"Yes, we discussed it. We agreed the woman was suffering some kind of mental collapse. Sister told me to pray for her."

"Yes, you should," replies her mother quietly. "There is so much misfortune in the world. We must help whenever we can, Puri."

"Of course. You and Father have set a wonderful example. You took care of Ana and now Julia appreciates all the things you send for Lali. It must be so difficult for Ana without parents. But Sister says that it's better to have no parents than the wrong parents. I think about that each day when I'm with the children at the Inclusa. I wonder, though: Once children are adopted by the right parents, should they ever know about their wrong parents?"

Puri steals a glance over her shoulder. Her mother sits, a block of erect silence, slowly stirring the spoon around and around in her coffee. And that's when Puri realizes.

Silence has a voice of its own.

89

Lens: clean.

Film: loaded.

Spare: three.

Flash: just in case.

Suit coat. Tie. Wallet. Passport. Notepad and pen.

A beat pulses through Daniel's mental checklist. He's excited, but calms himself with assurance. Ben would only trust him for a minor assignment. There's no pressure.

Carlitos greets him in the lobby. "You look very nice, *señor*! But, *ay*, where is the cowboy belt buckle?" The bellboy pistols his hands.

"Don't worry, it'll be back soon. Say, Buttons, can you send word to my parents that I'm with Ben Stahl and will return in a couple hours?"

"*Sí, señor.* I'll see that they get the message."

Ben leans against a marble pillar in the lobby. His clothes are fresh but Ben is not. He hasn't seen his bed.

"Are you okay?" asks Daniel. "You look rough."

"Fine. You're starting the day, I'm finishing it. Just waiting for a pack of due backs and then we can leave."

Lorenza approaches with the package of cigarettes.

Ben drops a large bill onto her tray. "Thanks, toots. Keep the change." He turns to Daniel. "So, you nervous?"

Daniel opens his mouth to speak but Ben interjects.

"Don't mess this up, Matheson. I'm taking a chance on you so you better be on the stick. You have your passport?"

"Yes, but why do I need —"

"You'll see soon enough. Here, take this." Ben hands Daniel an official press pass from the *Herald Tribune.* "This is worth more than gold here. But I'll need it back as soon as you take the picture. Can't have you running around Madrid with a *Trib* pass. You'll have to wind the roll and give me the film as well."

If Daniel wasn't nervous before, he is now. He follows Ben outside. Ben tips the doorman who is holding a pre-arranged taxi.

"So, sounds like Nick returned the favor in Vallecas, eh?" Ben rubs his index finger across his teeth, brushing them. "I saw him at the club last night. He said you guys were at a dance in Vallecas and some crazy bullfighter wanted to kill you."

Nick went to a club when they got back? He was practically passed out in the car.

"Nick was drunk," says Daniel.

Ben nods. "Okay, newsboy. Pop quiz to prepare. Who's the U.S. ambassador to Spain?"

"John Lodge."

"Correct. Decent fella. He cares. Who are some of Franco's guys?"

"Franco's guys? You mean the Guardia Civil?"

"No, some of his ministers. His minister of information, minister of transportation."

Daniel shrugs.

"Do you know anything about Franco?"

"Sure. He's been in power since 1939. Devout Catholic."

Ben rolls his eyes. "So? He also loves fishing and Fanta. Who cares?"

Daniel thinks back to Ana's captions and things he's overheard. He begins to recite: "He's building the Valley of the Fallen and it's going to cost millions of dollars. Under Franco, there is no longer freedom of religion. Protestant and Jewish religious services are not allowed outside the home. Nor are their weddings or funerals. It's a military dictatorship. People in Catalonia and Basque Country are not allowed to speak their native languages. The people are obedient because they're emotionally exhausted. There's a tension that exists between history and memory. Some people are desperate to remember but others are desperate to forget."

Ben nods. "Nice. Anything else?"

Daniel recalls Nick's offhand commentary and adds, "Franco aims for a 'Spain of Spaniards' only. Nick mentioned that some babies being adopted in Spain aren't really orphans."

"Whoa, whoa. Nicky told you that?"

Daniel nods. "He said that Franco feels that Republicanism is a heritable disease. So, to rout it out, kids must be raised by Francoists whenever possible."

Ben's face is obscured by a cloud of his own cigarette smoke. "Don't go repeating that on the street. It's an allegation, a piece of a much bigger story. Look, you didn't hear this from me and I don't know where Nick heard it. But yeah, there are whispers of babies disappearing. It began after the war. Children of Republicans were taken as punishment to the parents. But some claim it's still happening now, that parents are told their baby died when that's not really the case, that they're being given or sold to a family that's deemed more worthy."

"Are you going to break that story?"

"I'd love to break that story. But right now there is no story. The laws of the dictatorship state that the adoptive parents are the sole parents."

"What are the birth parents doing about it?"

"Their hands are tied. They can't challenge authority here. If a doctor or a priest tells you something, you accept it."

Daniel decides to tell Ben. "On my first day here I took a photo of a nun. She was carrying a dead baby."

"And?"

"The nun became upset when she saw me taking pictures."

"Well, it's pretty macabre to take pictures of a dead baby, Matheson. It's not the St. Paddy's Day parade. She was probably taking the kid to a morgue."

Daniel thinks on the incident. The nun's expression wasn't one of privacy; it was one of fear. Nick repeatedly says that many people in Spain live in fear.

"Say, Ben, if Franco is such a tyrant, why is America doing business with him?"

"Various reasons. But I look at it like this: We're a chisel. We're slowly tapping our way into the rock. If we get deep enough, maybe we'll crack it a bit."

Daniel thinks of the visual, taking a chisel to Franco. It doesn't work for him. From the photographs, Franco seems small and fleshy. It would be like chiseling rubber.

The taxi pulls to a stop.

"You ready, cowboy?

"Are we here?"

"We are. Welcome to El Pardo Palace. Get ready to photograph Franco. We're gonna win you that contest."

Some felt that the US Government should not be "cozying up" to this "fascist," as they saw it; that we should not have signed the 1952 Bases Agreement; that we should not be giving aid to Spain; and that, like the Europeans at the time, we should be virtually boycotting Spain economically and politically. (It has since been amply proven in my estimation how wrong this point of view was.)

Our policy at the time was to emphasize that the United States was cooperating with Spain and its government to benefit the people of Spain, as well as our own interests. Our public pronouncements would seldom, if ever, mention Franco himself as head of state or his single-party régime, but would always center on the Spanish people.

— J. EDGAR WILLIAMS, consular officer, U.S. Embassy in Madrid (1956–1958)

Excerpt from "Ambassador Lodge Corrects the Record"
American Diplomacy *(journal), February 1999*
The University of North Carolina at Chapel Hill

90

Daniel follows Ben to a security checkpoint where dozens of military officers stand guard. Their identification and press credentials are checked against a list. Before being allowed through the gate, their bags are thoroughly searched.

A wide cement drive flanked by sculpted gardens carves a straight path to an expansive, two-story blond palace. Dozens of balconied windows line the front of the façade. Small dormers peek out from the gray slate roof, which is capped with over twenty chimneys. Daniel stops to take a photo.

"It used to be a hunting lodge," says Ben. "Photo will be at the front entrance."

Shep Van Dorn stands amidst the grouped media. He sees them and approaches. "You brought the kid. Aw, you're such a softie, Stahl." Van Dorn reaches for a handshake. "Good to see you, Dan. If Ben uses your photo, make sure he doesn't run away without giving you photo credit. This is a real opportunity for someone your age."

Daniel lets the camera hang from his neck momentarily while he puts his hands in his pockets. They're clammy. He draws a breath. What would Capa do? He would try to get inside the photo. Get as close as possible. Daniel looks at the cluster of photographers and media. He notes the position of the sun. He wants to give Ben a good angle, something different from all the other photographers. But this is journalism, not an art project. Keep it simple. Make sure to get the shot. "Mr. Van Dorn, what's our working distance?"

"Maybe ten to fifteen feet. You'll only have time for a few frames before the general steps back inside."

Daniel looks at the entrance. The red-and-gold flag of Spain hangs over the arched front gate. If he positions himself slightly to the left, he may catch a wider angle of the flag with Franco underneath. But would a profile make a good press shot?

The fortuity is not lost on Daniel. Van Dorn is right. To photograph a country's leader in front of his palace is an incredible opportunity. He thinks of the photographs he's seen of Hitler, Mussolini, and Stalin. He will have a photo of a dictator in his portfolio, a leader whose crushing wake he has personally seen evidenced in and around Madrid.

But only if he gets the shot.

A clanging sounds behind the gates.

"Showtime," says Ben, exhaling a lungful of smoke.

Van Dorn trails the embassy photographer, giving back-seat instruction.

Three men step outside the entrance. Daniel's chest constricts. He looks quickly to Ben for explanation. "Stay focused!" snaps Ben.

Just over five feet, General Franco is the shortest, dressed not in military uniform, but in a drab brown suit. Ambassador Lodge wears a navy suit and a warm expression. Daniel counts his shots as he presses the shutter. He tries to concentrate, noting the remaining frames on the roll. Over six feet tall, the man standing on the other side of Franco towers over him. The short leader and tall man suddenly turn to face each other. They shake hands. A small breeze billows the bicolor Nationalist flag, exposing the crest in the center.

Daniel presses the shutter. He pulls a breath. He presses the shutter again.

Franco and the ambassador disappear back through the door.

Daniel looks at his camera. His shot will definitely be different from the other photographers' because the tall man shaking the general's hand —

It's his father.

"Surprise," says Ben. "This is a story in itself. A young photographer captures his father sealing a deal with Franco. Great, right? The photo credit will be Matheson and the name in the caption will be Matheson. Great for your contest entry *and* your family scrapbook." Ben reaches out and gives Daniel's shoulder a swat.

Shep Van Dorn approaches with Daniel's father in tow.

"Dan, I didn't expect to see you here," says his dad.

"It's all Stahl's doing," says Van Dorn.

Ben lights a chaser cigarette, clearly proud of himself. "Thought it would be a special father-son opportunity to capture the signed oil deal. Your kid's a serious talent, Martin." Ben turns to Daniel. "You did get the shot, didn't you?"

"I got several."

Ben flaps his hand, indicating he wants Daniel's camera. He hands it to Ben, expecting him to wind and remove the film.

"All right, gentlemen. Let's get Preston Hollow at El Pardo." Ben snaps a photo of Daniel and his father, with the palace behind.

"Father-and-son photo. Some journalist. You're more sentimental than a girl, Stahl," chides Van Dorn.

"And you're more bitter than a jilted lover, Shep," replies Ben with a stare. He winds and removes the film and hands the camera to Daniel. "Well, I suppose you and your pop may want to have a celebratory brunch or head back to the hotel. I myself am headed to sleep."

But Daniel isn't thinking about celebrating. He's unnerved. He knew they were in Madrid for an oil deal. He knew that Spain would be different from Texas. But he didn't anticipate feeling so conflicted. And right now, he can't shake the unsettling feeling of seeing his father smiling and clasping the hand of Francisco Franco.

91

Ana walks down the seventh-floor hallway, the steel passkeys hanging heavy in her apron pocket. What time did Daniel leave for the photo assignment? She lets herself into his room. Has he thought of the dance as she has? Julia's lecturing was nonstop.

"He's a rich boy from Texas and a guest at the hotel. *Ay,* what are you doing, Ana? It's some sort of fling for him. For you this could have terrible consequences. What about Fuga? He seems to have . . ." She searched for a word. "Potential."

"Fuga has more potential than Daniel?"

"I see. Now you're on a first-name basis with *Señor* Matheson?"

"Stop. I've never given Fuga a thought before today and you haven't either. He's a bullfighter, Julia. You believe there's a safer future with a bullfighter than with an American boy?"

"You're from the same culture. You share similar struggles. Common ground paves for smoother relationships. Antonio's parents suffered the same fate as ours. He understands me. Deeply."

Her sister means well, but her objections have grown tenfold overnight. Julia knows her well enough to see that she's feeling something. And she is. She loves spending time with Daniel. She feels safe with him.

Ana thinks on her sister's words. "It could have terrible consequences." She pulls the note from her pocket. It was in her apron when she arrived this morning. Just when she thought perhaps things were changing, threats fading, they return as if she's being watched from every corner.

You are a liar, little mouse. Do you know what happens to liars?

She's tried to forget the notes. She's ignored the notes. But today, she's angered by them.

Ana looks to the wall of photos. What did Daniel think of the captions from Tom Collins? Did he even notice them? Did he see her caption under his picture? As she nears the wall, she knows that he did see the message. The caption, *Hola, Daniel,* is gone. In its place is a new caption that now says, *Hola, Ana. Would you like to dance?*

She thinks of Daniel's question near the car in Vallecas, if there was a way to help.

Julia reminds her constantly of silence, but Daniel reminds her there are those who will listen. She wants to leave him a note, but what should it say? Ana's expected to cower and cave to demand, keep everything from everyone. What if instead of what's expected, she does the unexpected? A secret isn't a secret if you share it.

She's going to tell Daniel everything.

92

"Join us in the embassy car. We'll drop you at the hotel," says Mr. Van Dorn.

"That would be mighty kind of you," says Daniel's father.

Daniel had hoped to be alone with his father. His questions have been fast accumulating. But there is something Van Dorn can weigh in on.

"Mr. Van Dorn, may I ask a question?"

"You bet."

"What's America's position on the dictatorship?"

"Well, that's a big question," intercepts his father.

"But a fair one," says Van Dorn. "Daniel's probably seen enough of Madrid to observe a disparity. The administration feels that bringing American commerce to Spain will help the Spanish people in the long run, more than it will help the dictatorship."

"And the U.S. air bases here?"

"Strategic positioning. Keeping us all safe from the Soviets." Van Dorn winks.

The answers seem fair, even if well rehearsed. But of course they're well rehearsed. Journalists and photographers capture stories and, as public affairs officer, Van Dorn positions them in the best frame and most flattering light.

"Have you made any friends so far in Madrid?" asks Van Dorn.

"A few," says Daniel. The minute he responds, he regrets it.

"Really?" says his father. "Your mother will be pleased. Who are they?"

Daniel fiddles with his camera. "Well, Nick and Ben, of course. It was nice of him to bring me today. And Miguel at the camera shop. I'm learning a lot from him."

Van Dorn turns from the front seat. "And maybe a pretty maid at the hotel?" He gives another wink and laughs.

"Dan is a gentleman," says his father

flatly. His tone is curt. Implication hangs in the car. Is his father stating that Nick isn't a gentleman? Or is his father implying that his son wouldn't fall for a maid?

"Of course he's a gentleman," says Van Dorn. "A boxing photographer of a gentleman. He must take after his mother . . . or an uncle." Mr. Van Dorn extends the dig with a smile and offers a smoke to his father. "Cigar to celebrate your big deal?"

"Mighty kind, but no thank you, Shep."

Van Dorn turns back around and stares out the windshield.

What just happened? In a matter of seconds, his father and Mr. Van Dorn have faced off. The hum of tension in the car is louder than the traffic. Daniel lifts his camera to load a roll of film. Hanging from his camera strap is the press badge. Ben forgot to take it back. Daniel quickly stuffs it in his pocket.

93

"You opened a coffin?" whispers Antonio. He steals a glance at the orange crate where Lali sleeps. "Why didn't you mention this before?"

"Well, we didn't open it. It sort of . . . broke," says Rafa. "When Fuga saw it was empty, he exploded. He often says that the infant caskets feel too light, but I never paid much attention."

"Caskets? There have been others?"

"*Ay,* many infant coffins. They brought another one yesterday."

"Who brings them?"

"Fuga says the clinics. I'm generally at the slaughterhouse when they arrive."

Antonio limps across the dirt floor of the shack. Rafa's knee bobs as if powered by its own interior motor. Should he have told Antonio? He needs to keep Fuga focused. He thought perhaps Antonio would have suggestions.

"Fuga insists we must do something about the empty coffins. It's distracting him and that's dangerous. A distracted bullfighter ends up gored."

"What does he think is happening?" asks Antonio.

"The 'brothers' who ran the boys' home in Barcelona always told Fuga he was worthless, that if he was an infant they'd at least be able to sell him to Franco. He thinks babies born to Republican or poor families are being stolen, that the Church wants the children redeemed and raised by Francoists. *Ay*, I need him to forget about the cemetery and the coffins. We finally have a promoter interested."

Antonio shakes his head. "Fuga's not sidetracked. He's engaging more deeply. You speak often of Fuga's dedication to children. You say he goes hungry, he gives his own food away. This is what propels him. He's fighting not for himself, but for others."

Maybe Antonio is right. Could this be

Fuga's approach to fear? Fuga fears nothing for himself but wants to be the protector of others.

Antonio stops pacing. His expression softens, untangled by an idea. "The Texano and his camera. He's taking pictures back to America."

"So?"

"Images are powerful. They convey truth. Why do you think our media is censored? Ask the eager Texano to come and take photographs at the cemetery. He'll have record of what's happening. That may calm Fuga."

"*Ay,* no. Talk of the Texano does not calm Fuga. It angers him. If I bring the Texano to the cemetery, Fuga may want to fight him. It's all such a mess."

"But the way you describe Fuga, he doesn't look to fight. He looks to defend."

Rafa thinks on Antonio's words and Fuga's recent behavior. Immediately following the *capea,* Fuga gave his winnings to Ana. Initially, he thought that meant Fuga had feelings for Ana. But does it mean he thinks she needs protection — protection that money can provide? Rafa scratches the back of his neck. Does Fuga see something dangerous around his sister that he missed? Something about the Texano?

Antonio tucks in his shirt. "I have to leave for work," he says. "But, *por favor,* Rafa. Do not tell Julia about the empty coffins. Promise me."

"*Ay,* do you think I'm crazy? I would never tell Julia."

94

Bringing American commerce to Spain will help the Spanish people. That's what Van Dorn said.

Franco's an architect. There is a dark side here. That's what Ben said.

Which is true? And whose side is his father on? Daniel wonders as he and his dad arrive back at the hotel.

His mother waits in the lobby wearing a blend of haute couture and apprehension. Her face brightens when she sees her husband and son.

"I didn't expect to see you together," she says.

"Nor did I," says his father.

"Ben Stahl needed a photographer," explains Daniel.

"And he chose you? Daniel, how wonderful!" She means it. Despite his father's disinterest, his mother has always supported his photography. She then lowers her voice and his parents speak below their breath. "So, how did it go?"

"Swifter than I imagined. We signed."

"It's done?" his mother gasps. "How marvelous!"

"Yes. Installation dates for the equipment must be arranged, but at this point, that's just a technicality."

His parents are clearly thrilled. But . . . marvelous. Is it really? Daniel questions.

His father smiles at his mother. "You look lovely. Ready to go?"

Carlitos appears at their side. "*Hola, Señor* Matheson. I have some messages for you."

Daniel's father extends his hand.

"No, not for you, *señor,* for your son." Carlitos hands a few message slips to Daniel.

"My, my, you're popular," says his mother. "Who are they from?"

Daniel folds the messages and puts them in his pocket without looking at them.

"Aren't you going to read them?" presses his mother.

"*Ay,* he knows they're from the owner of the camera shop," says Carlitos. "*Señor* is consumed with photography. Pictures, pictures, and more pictures."

Daniel nods to the boy in silent gratitude. "Shall we have lunch?" he asks his parents.

"Oh, I'm sorry, *cariño.* Your father and I have an engagement. We'll be back soon." His mother gives his hand a squeeze. "I can't wait to see your photos from this morning."

His parents depart and Daniel tips Carlitos. "Thanks, Buttons."

"It's nothing, *señor,*" says Carlitos, his high voice full of humor. "Remember, here at the hotel we understand the importance of privacy."

Once in the elevator, Daniel pulls the message slips from his pocket.

9:45 a.m. From Tom Collins
Request meeting. Important.

A meeting with Tom Collins. Instant smile.

488

10:30 a.m. From Nicholas Van Dorn
Come over for my birthday lunch
around 2:00 p.m.

The corridor of the seventh floor is quiet. He removes the photo badge from his pocket and reattaches it to his camera strap. Hopefully he can take to the street and snap some photos before Ben wakes up. With an official badge, the guards — those Crows — won't be able to stop him. He lets himself into his room. It's warm and sunny. The balcony door is open just as he likes it.

His jeans and plaid shirt are waiting on the bench at the end of the bed, as if Ana knows the first thing he'll do is abandon the suit. He looks to the wall, wondering if she has seen his new caption. Is that why she wants to meet? Then he realizes.

His picture and caption are still on the wall, but several of the photos aren't.

They're gone.

95

Daniel rushes to the hotel lobby. Of course Ana took the pictures, but why? He spots Carlitos near the entrance of the hotel.

"Buttons, I need a favor. It's important."

"*Sí, señor.* Tell me."

"Find Ana and give her this message. Tell her, 'Room 760 needs towels.' "

"*Ay, señor,* but I see Lorenza just over there. She can get one for you now."

"No, tell Ana only. Just Ana."

Carlitos's small mouth puckers in an attempt to understand.

Daniel hands a one-dollar bill to Carlitos. The boy's eyes expand.

"*Sí,*" nods Daniel. "This is an important one, Buttons. Just tell Ana that I need towels."

Carlitos quickly crunches the bill in his palm, so it can't escape. "Room 760 needs towels. Tell Ana only." He takes off running, as if the building is on fire.

Daniel returns to his room. The phone rings. It's Nick.

"I'm having people over for lunch at the villa. Join us."

"Yeah, I got your message." Daniel hesitates. Everything with Nick feels like a trap.

"It's casual. No ties." He then adds, "And no parents. C'mon, it's my birthday!"

There's a knock at Daniel's door.

"Maybe I'll stop by." He hangs up and heads for the door.

Ana stands in the hallway, glowing and radiant. "I was told you needed towels, *señor?*"

"Sí."

She steps into the room and Daniel quickly closes the door.

"You received my message?" she asks.

"Yes, and I saw that the pictures are gone."

The smile slips from Ana's face. "What do you mean?"

"You took a few of the pictures."

"No, I didn't." She sets down the towels and runs to the wall. She lifts her hand, fingers scanning across the images. She turns to Daniel. "One photo of Rafa, one photo of Fuga, and . . . the nun with the baby."

"You didn't take them?"

"No." Ana's face blanches with concern. "I was here in your room until after ten. All of the photos and captions were still here." She goes to Daniel's jeans, folded on the bench. She reaches into the pocket and removes a note.

"Is that for me?"

She nods and takes a step back. Her fist closes tightly around the paper, her voice drops to a whisper. "*Señor,* this is very bad. Someone has been in your room. The captions that I — that Tom wrote. They were too honest."

"What do you mean?"

"I'm the only one assigned to your room unless you call downstairs. Did you request anything?"

"I wasn't here. I just got back."

Daniel runs to the closet. He grabs his cowboy boot and reaches inside. His hand reappears, holding the negatives. His shoulders exhale in relief.

"No one knows you wrote the captions, Ana. They'll think I wrote them."

"Who is 'they'?"

"Whoever's been in my room."

Tears pop and stream down Ana's face.

"No, hey, don't cry." He moves to Ana and reaches for her hand. "They're just photos. I have the negatives and I'll reprint them. Ben probably took them. He mentioned he could use them. Really. Please, don't cry."

"But this is dangerous."

"Dangerous? You mean it's dangerous for you to help me?"

"Yes . . . and no. It's not just the photos." She extends the crumpled note to Daniel.

Can I talk to you?

He reads the message; his eyes shift to

493

her. "Ana," he says quietly.

"Not here," she whispers, as if someone were listening. "I have a break at five. Meet me in the garden of the Sorolla Museum." Ana looks up at him. "I'll be on the bench near the secret fountain."

"The secret fountain?"

"*Sí,* look for the fountain of whispers."

She squeezes his hand and runs from the room.

96

Puri looks at the clock in Sister Hortensia's office. After lunch she is to report to the clinic. But first, she hopes to get to the file room.

Sister sifts through notes in front of her. "20 123, 20 121, and 20 116. Make sure they are all clean and fed before you go to the clinic."

20 116. Clover.

"What for, Sister?"

Sister Hortensia stares at her, stone-faced.

"I'm sorry. I meant, right away, Sister." Puri flees from the office.

Puri sees to Clover first. She recalls the note in the file. One hundred fifty thousand *pesetas.* Pending. "Maybe," she whispers to the baby, kissing her head.

She wants Clover to have the right parents, but are the right parents only paying parents?

The other two orphans are boys. Also *sin datos.* Neither came in from the *torno,* the box on the street.

Puri bathes the infants. She takes them to the mothers who live at the Inclusa and serve as wet nurses.

"Someone coming to see these three?" asks one of the mothers.

"I guess so," says Puri. She watches the young woman feed Clover.

"They'll take the boy I just fed," says the mother. "He's the youngest and cutest."

Puri exhales in defense. "He is not the cutest. She is. Maybe they'll want a girl."

"No. People prefer boys. Boys are easier to raise. They can work and help as they get older."

"Girls can be helpful too!"

"But they're not considered providers." She sighs. "If you love this one so much, why don't you take her?"

Puri stares at the young woman in

shock. "I'm a single girl," whispers Puri.

"So am I," says the young mother. "And I love my daughter just as much as any couple would."

How could the young mother who lives at the Inclusa compare herself to Puri? Should she be offended? Once Clover has finished feeding, Puri returns her to the nursery, wrapped in a fresh pink blanket.

"Ah, there she is." Sister Hortensia stands with an elegant couple near the ruffled bassinet of 20 123. "Purificación, bring the darling girl to us."

Sister's voice leaks exaggerated sweetness. The couple is well dressed and the father has a warm smile.

Puri looks down at Clover. "Look, we have visitors." She carries Clover across the room and makes popping noises with her mouth. By the time she reaches the couple, Clover's face is alive with joy.

"*¡Oh, qué chiquitita!*" exclaims the woman.

"Yes, she's still tiny," replies Sister Hortensia. Sister puts 20 123 back in his bassinet.

Without asking, Puri hands Clover to

the woman. She eagerly accepts the child.

"She's such a sweet girl with a very calm disposition," whispers Puri. "She loves to smile and giggle. Make this sound and you'll see her react."

The woman imitates Puri and Clover immediately responds. Her tiny hand appears from beneath the blanket. The man leans in and Clover grasps on to his finger.

"*¡Cúcú!*" says the husband.

"She loves peek-a-boo," says Puri.

The couple is clearly comfortable with an infant. Do they have children of their own? The pair not only looks lovingly at Clover, they look lovingly at each other. The woman wears the largest emerald ring Puri has ever seen. They are elegant, wealthy, kind, and in love. And they are Catholic. They wouldn't be here otherwise.

Puri sees Sister across the nursery, picking up 20 121, the other little boy. She feels time slipping.

Puri speaks quickly, almost blurting. "She is a sweet one. She's the sweetest one. She's engaged, alert, and so affectionate. She's the very best child here and I know all of them, I promise. You should choose her. Good day."

Puri bobs and turns from the couple. Sister Hortensia stands, holding the other baby boy, giving a questioning glare to Puri.

"Have a nice afternoon, Sister. I'm on my way to the clinic." Puri smiles, suddenly feeling like a very good Spaniard.

97

"Look who's here. *Hola,* cowboy!" says Nick, rising from the table. He greets Daniel in the entry to the breezy villa dining room.

"Happy birthday."

"Thanks. You remember these folks from the event at the embassy, don't you?" Daniel eyes the girls in dresses and the young men in ties. Once again, Nick has led him astray. "I thought you said it was casual," he whispers.

"It is! Look at me. I'm not wearing a tie. I can't help that they did." Nick walks to the table and makes an announcement. "My friend feels he's underdressed. Would you please assure him that his Dallas ranch wear is just fine?" Nick lifts a glass in a toast. "To comfort, Daniel Matheson."

A girl at the table perks up. "Your people are the Mathesons from Dallas?"

"My people? Uh, yes," he says.

The girl gives an immature squeal. "Then you must know my parents' dear friends? The Joyce family from Preston Hollow? They have a daughter our age, Laura Beth."

Society's noose casts long shadows. Half a world away and this girl knows his family and also Laura Beth's? His mother would be thrilled. Of course they know the Joyce family. Everyone does.

"I'm sorry," says the girl. "Did I say something to offend?"

"Not at all," recovers Daniel, realizing that his face gave him away. "Just looking for a place to put my camera."

"Unlike the rest of us loafers, my pal Dan's been on assignment this morning. He's an award-winning photographer and a finalist for a big photography prize."

Nick actually sounds proud. His mention of Daniel as a pal feels genuine.

"Holy cow, that's impressive," says one of the guys. "What did you photograph this morning?"

Five faces stare at him from the fancy lunch table, waiting for a response.

"I photographed Franco," says Daniel quietly.

The table erupts with impressed chatter.

"I see you've got the press badge to prove it," whispers Nick. "How'd you swing that? Shep says those are worth gold."

"I'll be returning it to Ben after I leave here," says Daniel.

"Sure you will." Nick nods with a grin.

Daniel moves to place his camera on a nearby table. Behind is a wall of shelves holding dozens of framed photos — Nick with his Le Rosey rowing team, Mr. and Mrs. Van Dorn with President Eisenhower, Mr. Van Dorn with Conrad Hilton. There are also several group photos and family photos. One image catches his eye. He moves closer. Standing in the back row of the group is Nick. Standing next to him is Ana.

Nick approaches from behind. "Evaluating the photo technique?"

"Nope. The people in the photo." Daniel points to Ana. He looks at Nick.

"I told you, we're friends. Nothing more," whispers Nick. "Come on. Let's eat."

But Daniel has lost his appetite.

98

Ana stands in the office of her supervisor. "This message just came through the hotel operator. It says it's urgent."

Urgent? Ana's mind pulls to Julia and Lali.

"If it truly is urgent, you may use the phone in my office. But do not make this a habit, Ana. The hotel cannot take calls for employees. Do you understand?"

"*Sí, señor.* Of course. *Gracias.*" She looks at the telephone message:

4:30 p.m. From Nicholas Van Dorn
Urgent. Please call.

As unpredictable as Nick can be, he's never claimed urgency. Ana looks at the clock. She has just ten minutes before meeting Daniel on her break.

"You may call while I'm gone." The supervisor exits the office.

A servant answers and Ana requests Nick. She twists the telephone cord, anxious.

"Hi." Nick's voice lacks the usual bravado.

"I got your message."

"Yeah, listen. Dan was here for lunch. He saw the photo of our family. The one with you in it. This is getting ridiculous."

"Why do you still have that photo?"

"I don't know. It was on the shelf. But look, he's asking questions. I watched you two last night at the dance. He likes you. He really likes you. Do you like him?"

Ana pauses, debating what she should share. "Nick, there's something I haven't told you. Please don't be mad."

"Oh, am I the last to know?"

"It's not about Daniel." Her voice lowers to a whisper. "I've been getting notes again."

There's no response.

"Nick, are you still there?"

Nick's voice is deep, measured. "Why didn't you tell me?"

"Well, I wasn't sure who was writing them," says Ana.

"You weren't sure? You mean you have multiple men threatening you?"

"No. I thought maybe he put someone up to it. Part of me wanted to just let it go."

Nick laughs in disgust. "Why do people say that, like it's so easy. 'Let it go, Nicky, just let it go.' I'm so tired of hearing that."

Ana hears Nick inhale, trying to contain his anger.

"Tell me, Ana. What do the notes say?"

She takes a breath. "He says I'm a liar, Nick. That he's figured it out and it will be the end of me. He must know about the bracelet. He's threatening consequences."

"Consequences. Yeah, there'll be consequences. I'll tell my mom. I'll tell the ambassador. I'll write to President Eisenhower and broadcast that my father, Shephard Van Dorn, the dashing foreign affairs officer, is a louse and a first-class creep."

"Nick, no. We agreed. And please, let's keep your mom out of this. You promised. But . . . I want to tell Daniel."

"You do?"

"At least part of it. The day I took Daniel to the camera shop he asked about my job before working at the Hilton. I told him I worked for a family in Madrid. But I didn't tell him it was your family."

"I didn't tell him either," says Nick. "I told him we were friends but didn't elaborate."

"Exactly, but it's not fair. I'm not delusional. I know that I'd never be able to have a boy like Daniel. Trust me, Julia reminds me every day. But I respect him and I want to be honest with him."

"Just say it. You're falling for him. I saw it from a million miles away, Ana. And he likes you too. Why do you think I sent him to Vallecas?"

Ana looks to the door, making certain she's alone. "He's a guest at the hotel, Nick. I can't lose my job. I'm trying to work my way up. You know that!" she whispers. "Your father claims I led him to believe we had an arrangement, but it's not true."

"Of course it's not true. This is his notch-in-the-belt game. He's such a child."

"He's not a child. He's a powerful man who could hurt my family. I love my job and we can't survive without the income. Please, we have to be careful."

"And what — hope Shep finds someone else to toy with?"

"I won't mention your father. I just want to tell Daniel that I used to work for your family. That you're like a brother to me and you saved me from bad circumstances and got me the job at the Hilton. That's all I'll tell him."

Ana hears a deep inhale and exhale through the receiver. "All right. Fine. But I kinda did like Matheson thinking that I was competition." Nick laughs.

"Well, now he'll know the truth. That you're a knight in shining armor."

"Yeah, right."

"Are you doing something special for your birthday?"

"Mom's in New York and Shep forgot.

Big surprise, right? I threw a celebratory lunch for myself."

Ana stares at the receiver of the phone. "Happy birthday, Nick. You're a true friend."

"I'm only trying to help. I know your family hates me."

"They don't hate you. They're frightened of what your father could do to us."

"They're not the only ones," says Nick.

99

Daniel steps through the brick-walled archway of the Sorolla Museum. The entry strikes him as an exit, a quiet pause from the bustling outside world. The artist's villa is margined by a courtyard garden that's expansive yet intimate. Daniel hesitates to take a photo, as if Sorolla himself puts a finger to his lips for breath and reflection.

He walks quietly around the courtyard. Birds twitter and chirp amidst the ferns and climbing twists of purple wisteria. Pathways of clay tile rowed by box hedges lead to trickling fountains, pergolas, and ponds with hand-painted ceramic tilings. The imagery on each tile tells a story. They could give texture to his photo essay. He takes a picture.

The fountain stands in front of a semicircular room of glass projecting out from the rest of the building. It depicts two figures in long robes. One leans toward the other, as if whispering secrets while the trickling water masks the sound.

A wooden bench, crisped from years of Spanish sun, is tucked into a nearby corner behind a thick banana palm. Hidden from view, Daniel can't see who is entering the courtyard. So instead of sitting, he stands beside the palm.

Why is Ana in the Van Dorns' family photos? Is it a game that Nick and Ana are playing with him? Whatever it is, he's fed up with it.

Ana appears in the courtyard and hurries toward the bench.

"*Hola, señor.* I only have a few minutes."

"*Hola.*" Daniel moves to sit next to her but she stops him.

"Would you mind standing to keep watch?" she whispers. "My hotel uniform is very recognizable."

Daniel gives a frustrated exhale.

She raises a hand to stop him. "Please, let me explain. The day I took you to the

511

camera shop, the first day we really spoke, I told you that I used to work for a family in Madrid. The family I worked for was the Van Dorns. They treated me very well, made me feel like I was truly part of their family. I have never dated Nick, nor am I attracted to him. He's like my brother."

Like a brother. Daniel attempts to conceal his happiness. "So why the secrecy? Why didn't either of you just tell me that?"

Ana's hands bunch, grasping the skirt of her uniform as if it's a railing and she's about to fall.

"Because something happened," says Ana. She looks up from her lap and squarely at Daniel, honesty tumbling forth.

"Someone accused me of something I didn't do. They threatened me. I had to make changes. Nick offered to help and promised to keep it a secret. He got me the job at the Hilton, where I can work my way up to a better position. I was grateful to you for defending Nick in the fight because he saved me. He gets himself in trouble, but he's not a bad person.

And you, you are a wonderful person. You're kind and fun and talented. You've been very respectful to me, *señor,* and you deserve the same."

Daniel looks at Ana, processing what's most important to him. She isn't dating Nick. She's in trouble. A charge flows to his fists. Who is threatening her?

"Is anyone nearby?" asks Ana.

Daniel peeks around the palms. He shakes his head.

"The dance last night . . ." Ana lowers her voice. "It was special, dancing with you. I just wanted to tell you, well, in case you were wondering."

He smiles. What he's wondering is when he can kiss her.

"But the missing photos — I'm frightened," says Ana. "Who was in your room and why did they take them?"

He's concerned too but doesn't want to worry her. "I don't know. I hope it was Ben. When someone steals a photo, there's a reason. That's good news for my contest entry but bad news for hotel security."

"It's bad news for me too. Those captions were personal." Ana stands to leave. "My break is nearly over. I must get back. I'm babysitting for the next few hours and staying at the hotel tonight."

"Ana, have dinner with me. We'll figure this out together."

"*Señor,* I cannot be seen dining with a hotel guest."

"You won't be seen. I'll order room service for us. Say you're visiting Puri and her family. I'll give some excuse to my parents."

Ana hesitates. "I don't think so. I mean, no, I can't."

"Please? How can I figure this out by myself?" He gives an imploring look.

"Oh, stop."

"Say yes. But only if you want to."

Ana shakes her head. She looks over her shoulder and then suddenly blurts, "Okay, maybe. Yes. I'd like that. I have to go. But promise me you'll go inside the museum. It's magical. Sorolla is my most favorite painter."

"Really? Why?"

Ana smiles widely. She is lighter, unburdened by sharing a truth with Daniel.

"When I look at Sorolla's pictures of the seaside, I feel the wind and the water. I can feel what it might be like — to be free."

100

Rafa hacks the shovel into a patch of dry earth, waiting for Fuga. Madrid's soil is untender, strong and enduring like many who walk upon it. He reviews his rehearsed points. If the Texano takes pictures of the empty coffins, the story will be captured. It will bring Fuga peace and he can focus on bullfighting. This is the plan. But now he must convince his friend.

Fuga appears in the distance, walking over a hill, shovels on each shoulder. The image is solitary, quiet, like Fuga. How can courage be so still, when fear is so powerful? For Rafa, fear wears many faces. It may arrive through a nerve, fluttering upon his eyelid like a moth to a light. Sometimes it's a hand that awakens him in the night, reaching through a seam of sleep to punch his tired mind. When he asks Fuga about his stillness, his friend shrugs and says, *"El momento."*

The moment.

To Fuga, the past no longer exists. The future is yet to exist. Fuga pledges loyalty to the "is," not the "if." When he meets a bull, he is fully present. Fuga is passionate but exists in the moment, gives himself to the moment. Rafa envies his friend's singular presence.

Rafa wipes the sweat from his brow and looks out amidst the graves. Families of Republicans are not able to publicly mourn those they have lost. Even if the location of his father's body was known, they could not visit the grave. Rafa is lucky to have a job as a gravedigger. He is able to whisper words to his mother each and every day. And sometimes, she whispers back.

Fuga arrives and gives a nod to Rafa.

"I have news. The promoter called. You will fight in Arganda del Rey on Sunday."

Fuga's habitually knitted brow rises. A small smile emerges on his cloudy face.

"Sí. Es fantástico," nods Rafa. "But we

have just a few days to prepare. You must listen to me, *amigo*. You must be focused."

"*¿Yo?*" Fuga points to his own chest, offended.

"*Sí, tú.* You can't lose your temper and break coffins. You'll end up in jail and then everything we have worked for is lost. When you become a famous matador, you will save many children and support the orphanages. But as you often say, the future is yet to exist. We exist right now. And right now you must work to become a famous matador."

Fuga chews on a piece of grass, gazing upon the cemetery, content within his silence.

Rafa begins his rehearsed speech. "Antonio had an idea. I think it's a good one. The Texano —"

Fuga turns to Rafa with a glare.

"*Tranquilo.* Listen. The Texano has a camera. He wants to be a photojournalist. If the Texano takes pictures of the empty coffins, he can take photos back to his big papers in America. The issue is no longer silent. Let him share these dangerous stories and the consequences.

You stick to the bulls."

Fuga pauses, digesting Rafa's words. He then jams his shovel into the dirt and begins to dig.

Dig. Throw. Dig. Throw.

Rafa's conscience calls out a warning. Dangerous stories. He didn't imply that the Texano would be in danger, did he? That's not what he meant. Should he have said important stories?

Fuga pauses, wiping sweat that weeps from his brow. "*Sí*. Bring the Texano," he mutters.

Rafa nods, noting the snap of intense determination within his friend.

Fuga returns to his shovel and digs with vigor.

The grave opens like a jaw.

101

Puri walks down the gray tile floors of the clinic. They look cold, like wet concrete.

The clinic serves only one woman today. She's been in labor since Puri arrived, moaning and asking for her husband.

"You must calm yourself, *señora,*" instructs the doctor. "Hysterics put undue stress on both mother and baby."

Puri thinks on the doctor's comment. The woman is in pain but she isn't hysterical. Perhaps it's less dignified to moan about, but giving birth must be extremely difficult. Puri once asked her mother if giving birth was painful. Her mother cringed and waved away the question as if it was not only painful, but too painful to discuss.

Puri takes her place at the front desk. She studies her own frayed cuticles, blocky black shoes, and saggy nylon stockings. Adoption would explain her lack of resemblance to her parents or Ana's family. Could she really be adopted? If so, did her mother wear a pillow like the woman who came to the Inclusa? Is that why she waved away the questions about childbirth?

After two hours, Puri hears the loud wail of a newborn. The cry is strong and fortified. Good lungs. Vitality. Puri wishes all the orphans at the Inclusa had the strength of this newborn. Especially Clover. Will the handsome couple decide to adopt her?

A man rushes through the door of the clinic. His face is flushed and glistens with sweat. "I came as soon as I was able. My wife is *Señora* Sánchez. How is she?"

Puri knows that only the doctor can provide information. During her training that rule was drilled repeatedly. She was quizzed on it.

"I'll let the doctor know you are here." Puri smiles, wishing she could share the happy news with the perspiring father.

She heads through the door and down the hall to the nurse's area. A nun, still wearing a birthing apron, holds the bundled newborn in a white swaddle. The doctor stands next to her.

"The father has just arrived," announces Puri.

"And what did you tell him?" asks the doctor.

"That I would inform you of his arrival."

"Very good," he nods. "Purificación, as I explained, the mothers are given a sedative during the birthing process. This helps them rest. Please sit with *Señora* Sánchez. You are to come to me if you note any changes in her color or breathing, or if she wakes up."

Puri enters the room quietly. The woman lies tucked in bed, a starched white sheet pulled up to her shoulders. She's very pretty. Her color is quite good and her breathing is steady and deep. She is fast asleep, probably dreaming of her new baby.

Puri sits in the chair next to the bed. Over an hour passes. The woman's eyelids begin to flutter.

"*El bebé.*"

"*Sí, señora,*" says Puri. "I'll get the doctor."

Puri rushes down the hallway to the doctor's office. She finds him sitting behind his desk, making notes in a file.

"The mother is awake, Doctor."

"*Gracias.* You may return to the front desk."

Puri makes her way to the front desk. The baby's father sits in the lobby, face cupped in his hands. His shoulders wrench up and down. He is crying.

"*Señor,* whatever is the matter?"

The man looks up at Puri, his face red and swollen with grief. "I don't know how I'm going to tell my wife."

"Tell her what?"

"That our baby . . ." He can barely speak. "That our baby has died."

Puri backs away from the man, as if the words he speaks are from the devil himself.

No, it is not possible.

She heard the healthy lungs for herself.

523

No.

She sat with the mother, whose cheeks blushed with fresh roses. Puri bangs through the door and spots the doctor in the hall.

"Doctor!"

The doctor puts a calm, pale finger to his thin lips, calling for silence.

"But . . . the baby's father," whispers Puri. "He thinks the child has died."

The doctor puts a hand on Puri's shoulder.

"I can see you are shaken. That is entirely understandable. If eel so easily disrupts your constitution, an incident of infant death will of course take its toll. Go home and rest, my dear."

Puri shakes her head slowly. Her feet are anchored to the floor.

The doctor's voice pulls taut. "You must steel yourself against these tragedies. Sadly, they're not uncommon," he says. "Many of these mothers, they don't take care of themselves during pregnancy. They don't eat properly. Some drink in excess. That weakens the fetus. But some are lucky. God will smile upon them and grant them another chance, another child. Perhaps they already have other children. But for now, the punishing consequences of their own neglectful behavior are difficult to accept."

Puri stares at the doctor.

He nods. "Yes. You must pray for this young mother. And speak of it to no one. If you are strong of faith, you will not even mention it to your parents. Remember, Purificación, it is a sin to reveal someone else's secret."

102

"*Lo siento,* Puri. Ana is working. She can't take a break right now," explains Carlitos on the sidewalk.

"But did you tell her that I was here?" asks Puri.

"*Sí.* I told her. Why don't you speak with her brother?"

Puri turns to see her cousin Rafa heading toward them on the sidewalk.

"Rafa!"

"*¡Hola,* Puri!" Rafa kisses his cousin on both cheeks. "*Hola,* Carlitos. I need to speak with Ana."

"*Ay,* she's busy, Rafa. I just told your cousin the same thing."

Rafa looks out at the street, as if the traffic sends him advice. "Well, actually, I hoped to get a message to her friend, the

Texano. I don't imagine he's around?"

Carlitos raises a finger. "*¡Sí!* He is having a milkshake in the restaurant. I will go get him." The small boy races off.

"How do you know the Texano?" asks Puri.

"Purificación, how do *you* know the Texano?" teases Rafa. "Have you been meeting with American boys?"

Anger rises. She has questions and is only looking for answers. "No! I am not doing anything wrong!"

"*Ay,* Puri. *¿Qué pasa?*" asks Rafa. "I was only teasing."

Puri sighs. "Nothing's wrong. I'm just tired."

"Still working at the Inclusa?" asks Rafa.

Puri nods.

"Still a steady flow of orphans?"

"Of course there are. There are always people who don't want their children."

"No," says Rafa. "People always want their children. But sometimes life commands other things."

Is Rafa talking about his own mother?

She thinks of the letter she saw in the file at the Inclusa. *José will be better off with an adoptive family.*

Rafa is wrong. Not everyone wants their children.

103

Daniel appears on the sidewalk, carrying his camera. He smiles while chatting with the bellboy, and Puri notices his white teeth against his deeply tanned skin. His plaid shirt hangs open, revealing a white T-shirt stirring atop his large belt buckle as he walks. Daniel lifts a hand in a wave. He is so handsome. Almost as handsome as Ordóñez, thinks Puri.

Almost.

"*Hola,* Rafa. *Hola,* Puri," smiles Daniel.

Rafa puts a hand on Daniel's shoulder. "Texano, I have an opportunity for you to take pictures."

"Oh yeah? Where's that?"

"At the graveyard."

"What's to see at the graveyard?" asks Daniel.

"Ghosts," whispers Carlitos.

Rafa hesitates. He looks at Puri and Carlitos before replying. "Well, you see . . . I thought it might be interesting. You could photograph me and El Huérfano." As if the ignition switch to his idea finally catches, Rafa speaks quickly. "To capture raw portraits of an aspiring matador working in a cemetery. Life before stardom in Spain. You would have pictures of Fuga digging graves contrasted by your pictures of him in his suit of lights. It would be a great story."

"Your matador is El Huérfano? The orphan?" asks Puri.

"*Sí.* Texano took great pictures of him," says Rafa.

Daniel nods. "That's a great idea, Rafa. I'd like that."

"Good. Come tonight."

"Tonight? Oh, I've made some plans for tonight. How about tomorrow? I'll need light for the pictures."

"Okay. I'll come to the hotel after my shift at the slaughterhouse. We can go together."

"Any chance I could photograph you

at the slaughterhouse?"

Rafa lights with joy. "*Sí,* come to *el matadero!* There is much to photograph there."

Puri listens to the two boys as they exchange details and location information. Rafa and his bullfighter work at the cemetery. Do they ever bury infants? Are dead children held in the freezer until they're sent for burial?

Puri thinks back to her orientation at the Inclusa. One of the doctors mentioned that infant mortality rates in Spain are high, too high, in his opinion. He seemed annoyed about it. Are the mothers truly that careless about their health? Would Rafa be able to tell her anything? No, she'd best not ask Rafa. Like her mother says, Rafa talks too much. He shares information with the charcoal delivery men in Vallecas and his friends at the slaughterhouse. Rafa thinks life is prettier with mouths open rather than shut.

"Give Aunt Teresa a kiss for me," says Rafa. He leaves.

"Give her one from me too," laughs Carlitos as he scurries back to the hotel.

"Are you here to see Ana?" asks Daniel.

Puri nods. A thought suddenly occurs to her. Could she ask Daniel? He doesn't know anyone at the Inclusa or the clinic. Could he give her advice?

"May I ask you a question? Do you . . . go to confession?" asks Puri cautiously.

The question takes Daniel by surprise. "Yeah, but not as often as I should."

"Me neither. I hate confession. They say I ask too many questions."

Daniel shrugs. "It's good to ask questions."

"I think so too!" says Puri.

"I ask questions through photography," says Daniel. "I take pictures of things and study the photos for answers."

"And what if you don't believe an answer that someone has given you?" says Puri. "Is it okay to ask more questions?"

Daniel pauses. "I've wrestled with that a bit myself lately. Sometimes I'm wary of the answers."

"Do you keep secrets?" asks Puri.

"I have. But I don't like to."

"Me neither. That's why I came to see Ana. She knows all about secrets."

"Does she?"

"Oh yes." Puri nods. "That's why I need her help."

"I'll tell her you want to speak with her," says Daniel.

"You're going to see her?"

"Oh, I just meant that if I happen to see her I'll mention it," he says.

Puri looks at him. She nods with certainty. "You're no good at keeping secrets."

"Yeah, I am."

"No, you're not. You like my cousin," announces Puri.

"You think so, huh?" says Daniel through his side grin.

"Well, I'll ask you the question — do you like Ana?"

Daniel leans in close to Puri. "A lot," he whispers. "Maybe that can be our secret?"

"Trading whispers, Purificación? That's your name, isn't it? You're Ana's cousin. Shouldn't you have a chaperone?"

Lorenza stands on the sidewalk, brows arching.

Puri's hands clench. "Mind your own business," she says.

"*Ay*, fine. Just think it would be a shame if you were issued a yellow card."

Puri's eyes expand with panic. She gives Daniel a bob of farewell and runs away down the sidewalk.

"You scared her," says Daniel.

Lorenza shrugs. "Did I? Oh well. *Ay*, I see you have your camera. Maybe you'd like to take a picture of me, *caballero*?"

He looks at Lorenza. Her uniform is a size too small. Purposely. Her bright red lips and black hair match the flag of the Falange.

"I'm sorry, Lorenza. I'm out of film." Daniel leaves her on the sidewalk and walks back into the hotel.

104

"I'm feeling fine, *cariño.* You needn't worry. I'd love to see your photos."

Daniel shifts to block his parents' view. "If you don't mind, I'd like to wait until I have them all organized."

"They look quite organized." His mother smiles. "But I understand. I'll wait for the full exhibit. Are you sure you can't come to dinner? We haven't had much time together. We're celebrating your father's contract tonight."

"He'd rather be with the young people, María. He's made some friends."

His mother seems surprised. "Really? Who are your friends? Where are you going?"

Daniel struggles to skirt a lie. "They're friends of Nick Van Dorn's. We're having dinner. They mentioned something about a late event."

"Probably a flamenco show," nods his mother.

The note slipped under his door said nothing about a flamenco show. It said:

11:00 p.m.–Tom Collins

"What about breakfast tomorrow?" asks his mother.

"Sounds good." He tries to edge them to the door of his suite.

"Don't wear those denims tonight. You look so nice in your suit."

"Yes, ma'am. See you tomorrow." The heavy door shuts with an answering clasp.

At five minutes past eleven, Ana enters Daniel's room using her passkey.

"Pretty handy key you have there."

"I'm sorry for not knocking. I didn't want to risk being seen in the hall," she explains. "Turndown service has already been here?"

"Yes. But room service hasn't. I'm

starving."

Ana stands with her back against the closed door, clutching her purse to the front of her uniform.

"Come in. You're off duty. You're here for dinner."

She looks about the room as if it's entirely foreign. "I've never been in a guest's room when I'm off duty. I'm breaking the rules."

"No one will find out. I told my parents I was going out with Nick."

"I told the staff downstairs that I was going to Puri's."

"See? No one will ever know." Daniel shrugs and smiles.

105

Ana's stomach tumbles and turns.

"Well, what shall we order?" Daniel holds up a menu.

"Room service mustn't know there are two people in the room. Nothing escapes the employees. They all gossip, you know."

"I know."

He doesn't know. Attendants and domestics have been part of Daniel's life since birth. They fade into his background, like Franco's security guards. They are silent witnesses, seemingly blind and deaf to all conversations and indiscretions. But they are not blind and deaf. Everything is noted. Things in the rooms, in the laundry, within the phone messages, and in the room-service orders.

Daniel's voice is quiet. "Ana, come and

sit down. You can't stand at the door for dinner." He holds out the menu.

Ana accepts the menu and moves to the small sofa. Daniel turns on the radio and the rolling voice of Lola Flores soothes the awkwardness, warming the room.

"I don't know what to order," she says. "You order for us. Something American."

Daniel sits down next to her and takes the menu. "Let's see. What about lobster thermidor and a crab Louie? We'll share a baked Alaska for dessert."

"When you call room service, tell them you want to eat a horse."

Daniel stares at her. "Excuse me?"

"Texans say they're so hungry they want to eat a horse. And then they order everything on the menu. That will sound entirely normal to the room-service operator."

"No, it won't sound normal. Americans say 'I'm so hungry I *could* eat a horse.' It's just an expression, they don't mean it literally."

"Thank goodness," she laughs. "Well, we must hide the fact that I'm here."

Daniel calls in the room-service order. As he hangs up, Ana removes cutlery wrapped in a cloth napkin from her purse.

"You brought your own fork?"

"I borrowed it from downstairs. We can't ask for two sets of flatware. They'll know. I'll use a glass from the bathroom."

Daniel shakes his head, grinning. "Please let me take a picture of you right now."

Ana smiles and laughs, holding up her borrowed knife and fork for the photo. The tension softens amidst the laughter and the radio's clack of Lola's castanets.

"So, I've given it a lot of thought," says Daniel. "Ben has to be the one who took the photos. He mentioned he might use them and I wasn't here to ask."

"But how would he get into your suite?"

"He once commented that he has connections."

While they wait for room service to arrive, Ana asks to see Daniel's portfolio again. They sit side by side on the couch, paging through the album. "This is one of my favorites." Ana points to an enormous tree with thousands of shimmering lights. "What is it?"

"It's the big pecan tree in Highland Park. Each year around Christmas there's a ceremony to decorate it."

They arrive at the photo of the Texas garden party.

"The mansion, this is where you live?"

Daniel nods.

"And that's Laura Beth," says Ana, pointing to the glamorous girl blowing a kiss to the photographer.

Daniel's surprise is audible. "How do you know about Laura Beth?"

"Your mother mentions her a lot. And Laura Beth has sent telegrams to the hotel. Remember, the staff sees every-thing." Ana looks to Daniel for response.

"It's over, but it didn't end well. My mom still doesn't know. Laura Beth couldn't accept me as I am. As soon as she discovered that I wasn't going to change, she started kissing other guys. She broke things off and claimed my family was 'too ethnic.' "

"I don't understand. What does that

mean?"

"My mom is Spanish. It makes our family different."

"But *Señora* Matheson is beautiful."

"Yeah, but she's different from Dallas society women. She raised me differently. We speak only Spanish together. We listen to Spanish records on the hi-fi. Some of her jewelry and clothing are different. She eats dinner late and starts the day late. We celebrate Spanish holidays. Just like Americans seem strange here, I seem strange to Laura Beth and her family. But it's okay. We had nothing to talk about. Everything was difficult. I just didn't realize *how* difficult until I came to Madrid. The first day you took me to Miguel's shop I wanted —"

The knock at the door launches Ana to her feet. She grabs her purse and runs to the bathroom to hide.

Ana stands against the bathroom counter, heart trampolining within her chest. Why did she ever agree to this? She's breaking every rule. She could get fired, or be issued a yellow card. She recognizes the waiter's voice. It's Guillermo, a server from Catalonia. She breathes a sigh of relief. Guillermo is quiet, unconcerned with the business of others. She hears the clink and plink of dishes on the rolling cart being wheeled into the room.

Ana looks in the mirror and adjusts her hair. It's pinned up. Should she have let it down? She pulls one strand loose, letting it spiral against her face. Daniel's shaving kit sits open on the counter. A blue bottle with a white top says, *Arrid Men's Spray. Stops perspiration odor on contact.* Lorenza says American men wear perfume under their arms. Is this what she was referring to? Daniel smells so good it sets her heart fluttering.

She hears the door close but doesn't dare move. Is the waiter still in the room? She stands still, unable to identify the sounds. A few moments pass until Daniel's voice emerges.

"Should I wheel the tray in there?" he asks.

Ana opens the door.

The lights are dimmed. The sheer pearl curtains sway amidst the soft music and quiet breeze from the terrace. The room-service table sits in the middle of the room topped with a pressed white tablecloth, silver cloche domes, and formal serving pieces. Positioned in the center of the table is a single shimmering candle.

Daniel stands next to the elegant table, entirely relaxed in his jeans and dusty boots. He's not looking through a camera lens. He's looking at her, directly at her. He sees her.

"Ready, Ana?"

Her field of vision narrows. Daniel stands at the end of the long tunnel she has so long been walking.

She is not in the hotel.

She is not a maid.

She is on a date with a gorgeous boy.

A boy who likes her.

Threats, yellow cards, war, fear, and silence fall like leaves from a tree abandoning its season. She lets it all flutter away. One night. She will allow herself this one night.

She looks at Daniel and utters the word that sings in her heart.

"Yes."

106

4:00 a.m.

Empty plates. Abandoned table. Thumb of a flickering candle.

Daniel's boots are tossed on different locations of the carpet. Plaid shirt peeled to his white T-shirt. Ana's hair hangs loose around her shoulders.

They sit on the floor in front of the sofa, facing each other.

Daniel trails his fingers along Ana's hand. "That very first day, on the sidewalk."

"The sleeping tourist. We both saw the photo," says Ana.

"Exactly! Then you took me on the Metro. You were standing so close. I was sweating," laughs Daniel.

"Your Arrid wasn't working?"

"Not in the slightest. I kept thinking, holy cow, who is this girl? And then at the dance."

"What about the dance?" she asks.

"What do you mean? You kissed me."

"Are you sure?" says Ana. "Maybe you're mistaken. What did it feel like?"

Daniel leans in toward her neck and ear. "It felt like this."

Knocking sounds at the door. Ana's body pops with fear. Daniel pulls her into him and puts a finger to his lips.

"I know you're in there," calls a voice from behind the door. "I hear the music. Open up." The doorknob rattles.

Ana jumps up in a panic and runs to the bathroom.

Daniel heads to the door. "Go away. I'm sleeping."

"Nice try. Want me to wake your parents?"

He opens the door a crack.

Ben leans against the doorframe, shaking his head. "Did you really think you'd get away with it?" Ben pushes past him and enters the room. "It's one thing if

you want to be stupid, Matheson, but you're on dangerous ground with —"
Ben jerks to a halt as if he's hit a wall. His eyes read the romantic table, the purse on the sofa, and the last of the trembling candle. A grin appears.

"Bad timing?"

"Really bad timing," whispers Daniel. "Why are you here?"

"Because you made off with the press pass!"

"Come back tomorrow. C'mon, Ben, please."

Ben nods, chuckling. "It's Ana. The girl from downstairs. Am I right?"

Daniel pushes him toward the door. Ben grabs a piece of bread from the table on the way. "Your life, Matheson. What I'd give to be you right now." They arrive at the door and Ben puts a hand on Daniel's shoulder. "You realize it, right? Soak it all in, cowboy. You're going to return to this summer for the rest of your life."

"Let me return to this night right now."

Ben exits and turns in the hallway. "By the way, great job today. Your photo —"

Daniel closes the door. He locks it.

Did Ben's interruption ruin the moment? He doesn't want her to leave. They still have two hours. "Ana, he's gone."

She emerges from the bathroom.

"It was just Ben." He walks toward her. "Sorry about that, where were we?"

Ana leans back against the wall. "I think we were here." She pulls Daniel in and kisses him. Her hand reaches for the light switch.

They stand at the door, fighting the pull of the evening and the push of the coming day.

"It's six thirty. They'll expect me downstairs soon," says Ana.

Daniel says nothing. Just nods, staring at her.

"Are you tired?" she asks.

"Not a bit."

"Me neither."

"So don't go."

"I have to," she laughs. "Maybe I can pick up your breakfast dishes." She gives him a kiss and tries to pull away toward the door.

"Wait, I have something for you." Daniel goes to the closet and returns with a book. "I visited the Sorolla Museum like you suggested."

"Isn't it wonderful?"

"It is. I got you this." He hands the book to Ana. "It has pictures of all the paintings, including the ones you love of the seaside. Now you can visit the museum anytime you want."

Ana opens the cover. She sighs, touching a finger to his lips.

For Tom Collins From Robert Capa —
x DM 1957

After much swaying and many long goodbyes, Ana finally leaves, stealing down a staircase to another floor. Daniel leans against the door and pulls a breath, holding close to their unbelievable night together. He feels Ana all around him. And it feels incredible.

He sits on the balcony, watching night retreat to light. The plan falls swiftly into place. He'll attend university in Madrid. He'll work with Miguel. He'll enter the photo competition as planned. If he wins, maybe Ben can get him a job in the Madrid Bureau of the *Tribune.* Or perhaps Mr. Van Dorn can get him a press job at the embassy.

The sun is up. He returns to his room and passes the photos on the wall. He needs ten for the contest. Ana and Miguel will help him choose. He'll think about it later once he learns what Ben needed the photos for.

He's sleeping so soundly he barely hears the noise. How long have they been knocking? Is it Ben? Hoping that it's Ana, he pulls on his jeans and walks shirtless toward the knocking. He yanks open the door with a smile.

His parents, smartly dressed and full of energy, stand smiling in the hall.

"Why, Daniel, did you forget? We agreed to have breakfast."

Daniel runs a hand through his already tousled hair. "Sorry, I'm pretty tired."

"Well," says his father. "We have a surprise that will wake you up." As if on cue, his parents step apart.

Standing behind them in the hallway is

a familiar face.

It's Laura Beth.

107

"Why, Puri, what a surprise to see you here." Julia hugs her young cousin. "Are Aunt and Uncle all right?"

"Yes, they're fine. I'm sorry to visit you at work, Julia. I know you're very busy with the matadors." Puri's voice is soaked with urgency. "But I have nowhere else to go."

"Puri, whatever is the matter? Are you unwell?"

"Very unwell."

"Come in. We can speak in the fitting room."

Julia leads Puri through the workshop.

Puri has spent endless nights thinking of the handsome matadors. She knows her thoughts warrant confession. The visual feast of colors, fabrics, and suits in front of her is what she's dreamed of seeing on, and off, the courageous men. But recent distractions have pushed her interest in matadors aside.

They enter a small room with wood paneling and mirrors. Julia motions for them to sit together on a bench.

"Tell me why you're here, Puri."

Puri looks at her older cousin. "Because you know about secrets."

Julia's eyes dart. Her fingers clutch her skirt. "What are you referring to?"

Puri takes a deep breath. "Julia, when should a secret be kept and what should be kept a secret? If I see something that troubles me, that doesn't feel correct, do I have the right to question it? Should I say something?"

Julia looks at her cousin, evaluating.

"Well, we all have the right to question things in our own minds, Puri. But some things are complex, nuanced. They stand at a cliff of truth. They might appear as fact when in reality we don't have all of the information. So, at the time, it's beyond our comprehension. Speaking of things we don't understand might only complicate things."

"In that case, what do I do?" asks Puri.

"Is this related to your social service work at the orphanage?"

"Yes, and at the clinic."

"Does it pertain to the babies?" whispers Julia.

Puri nods. "And adoption in general."

"Puri, you must give your best self to those children. Whatever they were born of, whatever their circumstance in coming to the Inclusa, they are innocent. Shelter them and show them they are worthy. If you can help them find a loving and stable home," Julia's voice catches, tearful. "Please, Puri. Please do that. Mothers pray for someone like you. Someone who cares enough to hold their children, to love them, to think of their future."

Julia reaches out and takes her hand. "I know it's difficult, Puri, but if you can, try to imagine yourself in the place of those children. What do they deserve?"

A woman enters the fitting room. "Julia, Luis is asking for you."

"I'm so sorry, Puri. I must return to

work." Julia gives her a kiss and guides her out of the fitting room.

Try to imagine yourself in the place of those children.

Was Julia speaking generally of the orphans at the Inclusa or, Puri wonders, was Julia giving her a more direct message? What does she know?

108

Daniel stares at his plate. Laura Beth and his mother have talked nonstop. His mother does that when she's uncomfortable. His father hasn't spoken a single word. He does that when he's uncomfortable.

His father had made a big production of introducing everyone in the lobby to Laura Beth. He referred to her as "my son's sweetheart from Dallas." Daniel feels sick. His sweetheart is somewhere in the hotel and might emerge at any moment. Laura Beth tries to engage him in conversation.

"Your mother showed me the photo with Franco. Front page of the newspaper. Congratulations," says Laura Beth.

Daniel nods. "Thank you."

"Perhaps you can show Laura Beth a

bit of Madrid today," suggests his mother.

"No, ma'am. I have two photo shoots."

"You can take her along."

"The first one is at a slaughterhouse and the second is at a graveyard," says Daniel. "I don't think she'd enjoy it."

"Well, Laura Beth has traveled a very long way. It would be awfully rude not to spend time with her," says his father.

A cloud of tension hangs above the table. Daniel wants to punch something.

"Actually, I'm the one who was rude," says Laura Beth. "That's part of the reason I'm here." Daniel shoots her a pleading look but she continues anyway. "Mrs. Matheson, I'm not sure if Daniel told you, but I broke up with him."

The silence is momentary until Laura Beth continues.

"I felt that our family differences were too difficult to bridge. I've felt badly about the way I handled it. I've missed Daniel so I decided to come to Madrid."

"You came all the way here to tell me that?" says Daniel.

"Well, no. There's a new designer, Oscar de la Renta, who lives here. He designed the debutante gown for the ambassador's daughter and he's designing our dresses for the Ford ball. Mother had the idea. She's here too. No one else will have a gown from Spain," says Laura Beth.

Of course. She didn't come to Spain for him. She came for a dress. "Thank you, Laura Beth," nods Daniel. "It's kind of you to come. I'm seeing someone else."

"You're seeing someone else?" asks his father.

"What do you mean by 'family differences'?" asks his mother.

"Well, ethnicity . . . culture," says Laura Beth.

"I see," says Daniel's mother. She clasps his hand beneath the table and whispers in Spanish. "She doesn't deserve you."

Laura Beth sighs and turns toward Daniel's father. "I'm sorry, Mr. Matheson. I told you this wasn't a good idea. I'm sure my father will reimburse you for the plane fare."

She hands her napkin to Daniel. "You have lipstick on your ear."

109

They stand in line for blood.

June's bright sun shines across a string of women waiting patiently at *el matadero.* Fans snap open and flutter, replying to Madrid's warmth and the scent of open flesh wafting from the slaughterhouse.

The women carry empty jars and cans, bladders for the blood. Daniel lies on the ground, snapping photographs of their well-worn shoes painted with dry dirt and life mileage.

A woman scowls at him until another points to his press badge. *Periodista,* she advises. Upon seeing the government-approved badge, the woman's grimace dissolves. To the rear of the slaughterhouse, young matadors train with their promoters. Daniel snaps a picture.

"*Sí,* that's where El Huérfano will eventually train," announces Rafa.

Daniel takes pictures of empty meat hooks dangling from the ceiling, of Rafa scrubbing and hosing blood from the floor, and tacking his apron at day's end.

"You must return to take training pictures. But for now, let's go to the cemetery."

Rafa flags down a gasping truck. He and Daniel join a dozen men in the back of the vehicle. Their faces are soot stained, labor worn, and hungry. Three men share a clay jug of wine. No one speaks. The violent bouncing upon the pitted road makes Daniel's teeth clack and his tailbone hurt. The man next to him is fast asleep.

He sits on his shins, pulling up to his knees to photograph the men whenever the truck pauses or stops. Daniel has been granted access to a world outside his own. He is inside the photo.

And he loves it.

And then, at an intersection, he sees the shot he has been waiting for.

A group of Guardia Civil stand on the

corner. The Crows.

Patent-leather men with patent-leather souls.

Light hits their faces, and their winged hats throw ominous, bruised shadows on a nearby wall. The men in the truck stare into their laps. Daniel looks through the lens. This is it.

Ben's lecture returns to him. *Be smart about it.* Daniel holds the camera in position but moves his face away from the lens as if he's looking elsewhere. He presses the shutter. He quickly hunches back down in the truck, holding his breath. The vehicle drives on.

Rafa shakes his head. "*Estás loco, Texano.*"

A sense of triumph floods through him. He's not crazy — he's happy.

After several minutes of driving Rafa bangs on the cab of the truck, and it comes to a stop. They jump down and Daniel follows Rafa to a quiet side street that runs along the edge of the cemetery.

"Have you got enough film?" asks Rafa.

"Plenty."

They enter through a small maintenance gate. A corrugated metal shed, the size of a single-car garage, stands at the perimeter. It's dented, rusty, and crooked.

"Welcome, *amigo,* to the house of El Huérfano," says Rafa, opening his arms. "Come inside."

Fuga lies in the corner of the shed, asleep on his straw. Near his sandaled feet are two small coffins made of wood. Daniel crouches, photographing Fuga as he sleeps.

Rafa gives a whistle that awakens Fuga.

"Hola," says Daniel.

Fuga says nothing.

Daniel props open the shed door for light. "I'm here to take some pictures?"

"*Sí.* Fuga believes there is a news story here."

"What kind of story?"

"A confusing one," says Rafa. "These tiny coffins. We receive a couple each month. They are brought by the hospitals or the maternity clinics. Of course it's very sad."

Daniel looks at the coffins, each the size

of a bread box. One has a hand-drawn blue cross on the lid, the other a pink cross.

"Take a picture," commands Fuga.

"Of these?" asks Daniel.

Fuga kneels in front of the coffin. He lifts a small tire iron from the dirt.

"Wait, you're not going to open it, are you?" Daniel's head snaps to Rafa.

"*Tranquilo,* Texano," advises Rafa.

"That's probably illegal," says Daniel.

Fuga pries open the lid.

"Stop!"

Fuga grabs a fistful of muslin from the coffin. He holds up the empty box.

"Wait," says Daniel, exhaling in relief — and confusion. "It's empty?"

"*Sí,*" says Rafa.

"They're asking you to bury empty coffins?" asks Daniel.

Fuga moves to the coffin with the pink cross on top. "*¿Bebita?*" he asks Daniel.

Yes, for a baby girl, thinks Daniel. He focuses his lens.

Fuga wrests the lid off the plywood coffin. Daniel snaps a picture.

Rafa jumps back in horror. He turns around, streams of vomit spilling from his mouth.

The small coffin for a baby girl does not contain a corpse.

It holds an amputated adult hand, black and eaten with gangrene.

110

Fuga stands outside the shed, smoking the dirty stub of a cigarette he found on the ground. Rafa sits in the dirt, head in his hands. *"¿Por qué? ¿Por qué?"*

"How long has this been going on?" asks Daniel.

Fuga shrugs.

"If they're burying empty coffins, where are the babies? Are there funerals?"

Fuga shakes his head. "The clinics deliver and pay."

"They're paying you to bury empty coffins? That makes no sense."

"*Exactamente.* That's why we asked you to come," says Rafa. "It's complicated for us. We must do our job. We work to eat. I work two jobs and still, I'm always hungry. As you know, we finally

have a chance for a better life. El Huérfano will fight again on Sunday. He will
advance, I am sure of it. But this is
something that weighs on Fuga. I pledged
to protect my friend and this is a distraction. Distractions are dangerous for
bullfighters so I'm asking for your help,
Texano. We cannot speak of this." Rafa
pauses, looking at Daniel. "But you can.
Take your photographs home to America.
Show them to people. Ask their opinion.
What is happening to the children of
Spain?"

Rafa takes a breath. "Will you help us?"

Daniel looks at the press badge hanging from his camera. Should he speak to
Ben? Maybe he could talk to Miguel. The
nun with the dead baby, Nick's comment
about children not being orphans, the
photos of the coffins — does it all tell a
story?

Fuga remains by himself. He has replaced the cigarette with a long, dry piece
of grass. He stands tall, practicing his
passes as if in front of a bull.

"Rafa, can I speak to Fuga alone?" says
Daniel. Rafa nods and walks away. The
two young men stand face-to-face, equal

in both height and courage.

"I get the feeling you don't like me," says Daniel.

"I know your kind."

"So, why did you invite me here to take pictures?"

"I didn't. Rafa did. The baby coffins make me angry. He says it's distracting."

"I understand."

Fuga gives a disgusted laugh. His voice drops to a hiss. "You understand? No, you don't. You've never been abandoned, ruined by the hands of adults, seen as trash, so hungry you've eaten grass, so poor that you have to steal. Tell me, have you ever been hungry, Texano?"

Daniel considers his words. "I'm sorry. You're right. What I should have said is, I *want* to understand."

"Why, so you can print sad pictures of poor Spain in your magazines?"

"No," says Daniel. "So I can show the effects of war and a dictatorship."

"You feel powerful because you have money. Your money buys our wine and sunshine, but it doesn't buy the right to our history."

Daniel absorbs his words. If there is a story here, whom does it belong to? He looks at the man standing in front of him. Fuga's face and body are taut, cabled with years of resistance and endurance. He runs from nothing. His truth is his power.

"Is that it?" says Daniel. "No. I think you have something else to say to me."

Fuga bores deep into Daniel's eyes, grabbing the collar of his soul. His words are steeped with threat. *"No le hagas daño."*

Don't hurt her.

Daniel stares back in vow, unwilling to even blink. "I won't."

The glares hold until Fuga concludes with a satisfied nod.

Daniel extends his hand to Fuga. They shake.

Rafa comes running. "*¡Fantástico!* See, it's not so difficult. We can all be friends. But now we must bury these coffins. El Huérfano trains tonight."

111

"Texano! I'm so happy to see you. I was just about to close."

"*Hola,* Miguel. I was hoping I could drop off a few rolls."

"*Sí. Sí.* And I was hoping to congratulate you on this." Miguel reaches beneath the counter and retrieves a newspaper. He points to the photo credit and releases a huge smile. "Front page! *¡Felicidades!* This is sure to win your contest."

"I'm not so sure about that. It's a bit complicated because of the man in the photo."

"The man with Generalísimo Franco?"

"*Sí.* He's my father."

Miguel nods, absorbing the situation.

"The judging committee might find it odd. *¿Nepotismo, no?* But I have some photos on these rolls that could be very strong. I'm also bringing you my negatives. I want you to make duplicate prints of every photo I've taken."

"Every photo?"

"Sí."

Miguel points to the press badge. "An official press badge probably gets you very interesting photos." Miguel reaches to inspect the credential.

"Claro, but I have to give it back. Once the shots are developed, would you help me select some for the contest?"

"I'd be honored. And tell me, how are Rafa and his matador?"

"Very well. El Huérfano has a fight this Sunday in Arganda del Rey."

"Qué bien. And Ana? How is she doing?"

Daniel looks at Miguel, unable to contain his smile. "We're doing very well."

"Ah, I see," says Miguel. "That makes me very happy."

"Me too," says Daniel.

Daniel exits the Metro, thinking of the

first time he rode with Ana. He feels at ease in Madrid now. Perhaps he can rent a car again and surprise Ana with a trip to Valencia. Then he can share his plan about studying in Madrid.

He finds the hotel lobby thrumming with its usual bustle. Carlitos passes Daniel, carrying a suitcase as big as his body.

"*Hola,* Buttons. Have you seen Ana?"

"Wait for me," whispers the boy.

Daniel waits near the elevators. Carlitos sprints back and grabs him by the sleeve. He leads him to the basement staircase, tucked into the wall. They descend two steps and Carlitos stops.

"Is everything okay?" asks Daniel.

Carlitos shakes his head, his eyes full of fear. "*Señor,* Ana was fired."

112

Fired.

"No one knows why," whispers Buttons.

Daniel frantically presses the button for the elevator, hoping Ana is in his room.

Lorenza holds a tray of cigarettes in front of Mr. Van Dorn and Paco Lobo. Standing next to them is Laura Beth. As if on cue, they all turn to him. The walls of Daniel's brain begin to fold, like the sides of a melting candle. He opts for the stairs and takes them in twos until he's reached the seventh floor. He runs down the hall and clatters through the lock and the door.

"Ana?"

His suite is empty.

Don't you hurt our Ana, said the women

in Vallecas.

I love my job, I could not bear to lose it, Ana had said.

And Fuga's threat. *Don't hurt her.*

Daniel paces the room. Someone must have seen Ana in his room last night. Ben wouldn't tell, would he? Did Ana mention their dinner to anyone?

He can help. He can fix this. He'll go to the hotel manager and say it's his fault. He'll beg forgiveness. He'll ask his father to help. He'll pull any and all favors.

Favors.

Shep Van Dorn owes him a favor. He said so, at the hospital, the morning after he defended Nick in the fight. The Hilton is an American hotel. He saw the picture of Mr. Van Dorn with Conrad Hilton himself. A special request from the U.S. Embassy would certainly carry favor. Daniel runs from his room, hoping to catch Van Dorn in the lobby before he leaves.

"Hi there, Dan," greets Van Dorn. "I just met your friend, Laura Beth. What a poised young woman, and quite a looker," he says.

"Yes, sir. Could I speak to you privately for a moment?"

Van Dorn is ever eager. "Certainly. Let's take this table in the corner. Are you okay? You're out of breath."

Shep Van Dorn folds his lean body into a chair. His dress shirt is paper white and perfectly pressed, his suit jacket brushed. With the heat in Madrid, Van Dorn must keep spare clothes in his office for an afternoon change.

Lorenza stops at their table. "Cigars, cigarettes, *señor?*"

"Just matches, baby," replies Van Dorn. He smiles at Lorenza. "And say, send the waiter over with a scotch and soda."

He extends the offer of a beverage but Daniel declines. Van Dorn leans back in the chair, threading his fingers together. His gold cuff links blink from beneath his sleeves. Daniel notes Shep's body language. Nonchalance pleated with power. "So, Dan, what can I do for you?"

Daniel pulls a breath. "At the hospital you mentioned that if I ever needed something I could come to you."

Van Dorn smiles. "Yes, I did."

"Well, a friend of mine who works here at the hotel, she was fired and it's my fault. I have to get her rehired."

"I see," says Van Dorn. "We're speaking of Ana?"

"Oh." Daniel hesitates before replying. "Yes, sir. I know she worked for your family. She said you were very good to her."

Van Dorn gives a low laugh. "Did she now."

Daniel pauses at the sarcasm, confused. "Yes, and since you know her and know her character, I thought you could vouch for her."

Shep Van Dorn leans forward toward Daniel, his expression smug. "Well, you see, Dan, that's not really possible. I'm sorry to be the one to tell you, but Ana is a hustler and a thief. She's a con artist."

The words hit Daniel like a punch.

Van Dorn nods and releases a sigh. "Yes. It's such a shame. She stole a gold bracelet from our villa. By the time I found out it was too late. She melted it down for teeth for both her and her brother. Crafty, eh? With all the tourism coming to Spain, some of these beggars have become talented swindlers. You can't even give them anything. They'll sell it."

Daniel recalls the conversation in Vallecas, about selling the gifts he brought. Has Ana been conning him this entire time? No, it's not true.

"I wanted to alert the authorities but unfortunately Nick took part in some shenanigans with Ana and I didn't want to draw attention to him. They're a duo of sorts. So we transferred her here to the Hilton, hoping that she'd change her ways under the watchful eye of a supervisor. But it seems she's up to her old tricks again. She's a pro."

Daniel stares at Van Dorn, unable to speak.

"I know, terrible. Such a beautiful little thing. What a waste."

Lorenza appears at Van Dorn's side. "The waiter is coming with your scotch, *señor*. He wanted to open a new bottle."

"You don't want to open my bottle,

little mouse?" says Van Dorn with a grin.

Lorenza purses her lips, staring at Van Dorn. She twists a piece of her hair and throws her head back with laughter.

In an instant, Daniel's lens changes. His focus sharpens.

Van Dorn watches Lorenza saunter away before he returns to the conversation. "There are plenty of fish in the sea, Dan. Between you and me, it's fine to try a new swimming hole once in a while, but smarter to fish in your own pond, if you know what I mean," says Van Dorn. "Laura Beth, she's a great girl."

One punch. That's all it would take. And it would feel so good. Assault? No. A gift to the Foreign Service.

Daniel stands to leave, fighting the desperate urge to clench his fists. "Thank you for the information, Mr. Van Dorn. I sure do appreciate it."

"Oh, are we done?" Shep Van Dorn stares at him with a grin.

Daniel smiles back. "Oh yes, sir. We're done."

113

Daniel makes his way to the elevator.

"Texano!" calls Carlitos. "I have your postage stamps." Carlitos gives him a discreet tip of the head and slides a piece of paper into his hand.

Tom Collins. Tomorrow. 10 a.m.
Sorolla.

"Is she still here?"

"They escorted her off the property after she gave me the message."

"Thanks, Buttons." He reaches in his pocket for a tip.

"No, no." Carlitos shakes his head. "This favor is for Ana. I don't understand how this could happen to her." The boy is on the verge of tears. "Texano, can I ask you something? The pretty girl from

Texas — is she really your girlfriend?"

"No, Buttons, she's not."

"*Ay,* I didn't think so." Carlitos releases a satisfied smile.

Daniel knows that Carlitos sees much at the hotel. "Buttons, just between you and me, what do you think of Mr. Van Dorn over there?"

Carlitos leans in to Daniel. "*Ay,* Texano, I know nothing. But my aunts once told me the story of Don Juan, a disguised man who was able to manipulate language and seduce women. Our Spanish flu epidemic many decades ago? It was initially believed harmless but proved deadly. Some still refer to it as *Don Juan.* So you see, I know nothing of Mr. Don Juan over there, except he never tips. The staff prefers his generous son."

And this time, Carlitos does accept a tip from Daniel.

Daniel returns to his room. Should he call Nick? He moves toward the phone.

No. He's calling Ben.

114

To keep his friend sharp and awake for training, Rafa recounts historical details.

"Francisco Romero of Ronda," says Rafa. "Think of him on Sunday when you fight. This is the man they say invented the red *muleta* cape. Remember, for many years bullfighting was used to train knights. Only nobles on horses faced bulls."

Fuga says nothing. He marches ahead as if in a trance.

"Of course red is only a matter of tradition. Bulls are color-blind and —"

Fuga motions for silence. They stand still as statues on the dark dirt road, listening.

Rafa moves his hands in a stepping motion. Fuga nods.

Horses.

They steal to the side of the road, taking cover beneath a line of scrubby bushes. "We're early today," whispers Rafa. "Perhaps the breeders are still in the fields?"

Rafa hopes it's the breeders. The alternative is far worse. The Crows.

Noise is not uncommon. They must wait for others to leave or move to another side of the pasture. Rafa lies on his back, staring at the bright glow of the moon. He glances at his friend, eyes closed, arms folded behind his head. But Fuga's brow is arrowed. He is troubled.

They have spent so many nights sleeping in the dirt of Spain that they feel part of it. But slowly, things are changing. If Fuga performs well on Sunday, he will be granted another fight. He will be allowed to train at the slaughterhouse. A promoter with a fat cigar will drive them from city to city, where Fuga will fight young bulls in the *novilladas.* They will sleep in a nice car instead of the dirt. And once Fuga makes his *alternativa* — his graduation ceremony from novice — he will become a full-fledged matador. Then they will sleep in hotels.

The quiet of night finally descends. Fuga stands from the dirt and begins stretching. Fuga has faced full-grown bulls in the fields for over a year. He became El Huérfano not recently, but the first time he crawled beneath the barbed-wire fence.

There is something special that lives inside Fuga. A sense. A knowing. He fights in the dark, the lamp of the moon his only guide. As part of the *cuadrilla,* Rafa will be by his *amigo*'s side, helping him, learning from him. It will be a big life, better than an education at a university. Ernesto Hemingway, an author whose books are banned by Generalísimo Franco, once wrote, "Nobody ever lives their life all the way up, except bullfighters." Rafa agrees with Don Ernesto.

Fuga sets off alone across the road to the pasture fence. Instead of the rust-soaked blanket, he carries the red *muleta* cape from Julia's suit. Rafa follows patiently behind his friend, knowing Fuga will never leave him behind. He will not cross the margin of the pasture without a prayer.

Rafa kneels in front of the barbed wire

with his friend. "In the name of the
Father, and of the Son, and of the Holy
Ghost, amen," recites Rafa. He makes
the sign of the cross.

They crawl through the fence.

115

The night is thick with the smell of grass. The bulls graze quietly in a herd, fifty yards away. Fuga stands near the grouping, making a single connection. He does not taunt nor jeer the animal toward him. The bull willingly departs the herd and walks to face Fuga. Two meters lie between them. The full-grown bull stands large, head and horns level with Fuga's shoulders. Rafa steps silently away from his friend so he is close enough to aid but far enough to remain separate.

The *muleta* hangs from Fuga's extended left hand in a graceful drape. His left foot slides in lengthened step under the cape, shifting weight to his right hip. Rafa stands, breathless, watching El Huérfano's form emerge, waiting for the subtle movement of the cape. A moment

passes. The cape does not move. El Huérfano remains in magnificent stance, but
unmoving.

Why is he not twirling the cape? Why
does he stand as a statue? The stillness
continues. Rafa does not dare speak, nor
interrupt the exchange between Fuga and
the bull. This is presence. The moment
of complete stillness feels divine. Tran-
scendent.

Bang.

The sound.

No.

No.

No.

The bullet enters Fuga through the
back. The force of the shot propels his
chest forward, pulling his shoulder blades
together. He takes a single step and falls
to his knees, surrendering at the feet of
the bull. Bubbles of blood trail down the
back of Fuga's thin cambric shirt. The
animal runs back to the herd.

Rafa charges to his friend. He slides

across the grass, pulling Fuga onto his lap. He is still breathing. His body trembles. Rafa feels the life and blood of his best friend seeping through his own trousers.

"Amigo," gasps Rafa. "I am here."

Fuga's eyes are open but vacant. His hand extends, searching for Rafa. Their palms clasp. *"Sí,"* says Rafa, cradling his closest friend, unable to stop the oncoming tears.

"Rafa. *Hermano.*"

"*Sí.* Brothers. I am here, brother. I am always here."

"Hermano," stammers Fuga. *"El fin."*

"No." Tears spill down Rafa's face. "You're going to be okay. Please. It's not the end."

Fuga's body shudders. His fingers slowly surrender their grip of Rafa's hand. *"Sí. El fin."* Fuga's lips flutter as they release their final whisper. "Rafa, do not . . . be afraid."

Fuga's body liberates the tension of life force.

"¡Amigo!" wails Rafa. "No. Please. *¡Hermano!*"

Rafa sobs, clutching and rocking the body of his friend so tightly he feels nothing, nothing but Fuga's warm blood pooling in his lap.

Overcome with shock and anguish, Rafa doesn't feel the barrel of the gun — even as it touches the back of his own head.

116

A shift in the weather brings temporary relief to the infernal temperatures. Puri sits on the grass with the older children, enjoying the morning sunshine. Three soccer balls will soon be added to the recreational equipment at the Inclusa. Their impending arrival has caused a flutter of excitement.

"I'm going to be a *futbolista!*" announces one of the boys.

The abandoned boy that Daniel found on the street joins in. "My uncle can bounce a soccer ball on his head."

"Well, your uncle sounds very talented," says Puri.

"He is. I miss him," says the boy, picking at the grass near his shoes.

"*Ay,* I don't miss home," says the boy who wants to be a soccer player. "There was never enough to eat. Here I have food and a nice bed to myself. And soon I'll have a soccer ball! At home I had to share the bed with my four brothers. Their dirty feet were always in my face."

"Ew," grimaces a girl.

"I don't miss home either," says José.

Puri looks to the orphan. José is the boy who lost his tooth, the one whose mother said he could make his own way in the world.

"There were eight kids in our house," says José. "My mother was always tired and angry. She used to yell a lot." José lowers his voice to imitate his mother. *"You miserable brats are going to send me to an asylum!"*

The other children laugh and join in, imitating adults.

A girl jumps to her feet. "Oh, oh, what about this one!" She points a finger and launches a shrill voice. *"You ingrate. Do you know how lucky you are? You don't have a cardboard father."*

The children point their fingers back at her. They howl with laughter and roll in the grass.

"I don't remember my parents," says a boy. "What's a cardboard father?" he asks.

"It's a father who got killed in the war," explains the girl. "His cardboard photo hangs on the wall but they can't talk about him because he's a Red."

Puri stares into her lap. Is there a chance that she too had a cardboard father? The boy who can't remember his parents has circular scars on his legs. Sister Hortensia says that when he came through the *torno* as an infant he had cigarette burns all over his shins. Puri has several odd scars herself. "You were a bit clumsy as a toddler," her mother tells her.

Is that true or just another secret?

"I'm going to be a *futbolista!*" refrains the boy who loves soccer. "Father López says that an orphan once played for Real Madrid. That's going to be me," he says, pointing a thumb to his chest.

The children whoop with delight, talking of jersey numbers and stadium seats, completely forgetting the conversation of parents and cardboard fathers. As Sister Hortensia says, they are well fed, clothed, educated, and safe. They are happy. Puri knows that not all orphanages are as wonderful as the Inclusa. Some children speak of other institutions that sound horrific.

"We want to give children the best chance to thrive, to be raised by those who will devote resources and ensure Catholic values," said Sister Hortensia. "These children are the best chance of protecting our future and all we've worked so hard for."

Protecting the future. That's something Puri hasn't thought of. Generalísimo Franco, Auxilio Social, the Inclusa, and the doctors, nuns, and priests — are they simply protecting the future? With all they've done to make Spain the wonderful country she loves, how could she ever doubt that?

But a quiet part of her does.

Spain protects itself from evil enemies, wanton behavior, and sin.

Lying is a sin. And Puri knows the doctor at the clinic was lying. But questioning is an insult to her leader and her country. It's ugly and disrespectful. A knot rises in her throat. Sometimes she commits sins. Does she search for truths to avoid her own truth? Her eyes well.

The little girl pets her hair. "*Señorita, why are you crying?*" she asks.

Puri shakes her head and forces a smile. *Estamos más guapas con la boca cerrada.*

It's true. We really are prettier with our mouths shut.

117

Daniel sits in the museum garden near the fountain of whispers.

Ana wanted to hide it. Nick wanted to hide it. The comments in the car between his father and Mr. Van Dorn were not incidental. In saying that Daniel was a gentleman, his father announced that Mr. Van Dorn wasn't.

And he was right.

Despite their circumstances, Daniel knows he and Ana are more alike than different.

He called Ben and Ben agreed, grumbling and lecturing over the phone.

"No, I didn't take your photos and, oh yeah, news flash: Shep Van Dorn's a louse. He's notorious. That's why his wife is never in Madrid and poor Nicky's so messed up. Nick came to me when he was trying to help Ana. Yeah, the gold teeth are from a bracelet, but Ana didn't steal it. The family gave it to her for Christmas. Shep toyed with her, insisted she call him by his first name, told her he'd bring her on at the embassy as a secretary or something. Ana was too sweet to realize he expected something in return."

"He can't get away with this," says Daniel.

"Oh, he'll get away with it and more. C'mon, Dan. Politicians and businessmen, they get what they want. When Van Dorn didn't, well, he got mean, tried to intimidate her. I could share tales, both hilarious and terrifying, about these guys on overseas posts. I pray the stories make it into the D.C. archives. This one guy, he roared into a village —"

"I don't want to hear stories. We have to do something."

Daniel hears Ben slap his desk. "I love your energy, Matheson! What are you going to do?"

"I'm going to write to the ambassador." Daniel pauses. "And I'm going to write to the State Department and let them know who they've got representing our country."

Daniel hears Ben exhale a double lung of smoke and light another cigarette.

"Sure, you can do that. Your sense of justice, it's refreshing. But listen, cowboy, if I were you — and believe me, I wish I was — I wouldn't waste this time. You're nineteen in Madrid, and you're in love, for Christ's sake. Don't blow your breath on a horse's ass like Van Dorn. This is your golden hour. Rent the Buick and whisk her off to the Costa Brava. Roll the windows down and feel the sun on your face. Walk along the beach together. Take pictures. Stay up late and sleep in later. Wake up with sand in your hair, sand in your pants. Don't come back until you run out of money. This is your time, Dan. Grab it and run. Do the stuff you see in the movies. It's the stuff no one gets to do. But you can do it, Matheson. I don't want you calling me in ten years whining that you should have done this and should have done that. As the saying goes, it's later than you think."

Daniel stares at the numbers on the telephone in front of him. "Did you do all this stuff?"

"Hell, no. Why do you think I'm telling you to do it? So you don't end up like me, alone in the movie theater at four in the afternoon, smoking fistfuls of cigs and watching couples stroll along the beach in Costa Brava."

Daniel smiles.

"Listen, Matheson, I like you. You're a heck of a photographer and you throw a punch like Joe Louis. I have no idea what else you do. But whatever it is, now's the time to do it."

118

"Hola."

Ana appears at the bench. She wears the faded dress she wore to the dance.

Daniel's rehearsed the speech so many times. He's going to write letters. They'll go on a trip, like Ben suggests. They'll walk along the beach. But now that she's standing in front of him, beautiful and defeated, all he can say is, "Ana, I'm so sorry."

She sits down close, but the ease of their night together is lost. "It's not your fault."

"Of course it is. I'm the one who convinced you to come to my room."

"That's not why they fired me."

"It's not?"

"No. They found the Sorolla book with

your inscription to Tom Collins. They accused me of being a thief."

"Ana, you're not a thief. This is all just a misunderstanding. I'll speak to your manager."

"No. People can't know about us."

"We had dinner. That's all."

"That's not all." Ana looks at him. "The photos, the dancing," she lowers her voice, "the kissing. I broke so many rules being with you. It was foolish."

"I thought you wanted to be there."

Ana's voice drops to a whisper. "Of course I wanted to be there. I want a lot of things I can't have. For you this is a vacation, but for me it's real life. I'm the daughter of Republicans. Do you understand what that means in this country? This is not America. I know it's hard for you to understand because you live more like them."

Daniel recoils in shock. "Wait, are you saying I'm a fascist?"

"I'm saying that you're not shackled by poverty and silence. You could never understand what it's like for me."

"I want to learn. You can help me. I

have a plan. I'll attend university in Madrid. We'll go to Valencia."

"You could have many plans. But don't you see? I've lost the only chance I have."

"That's not true."

Ana looks at him. Her eyes fill with tears that spring and trail down her cheeks.

Her tears grip, pulling his heart. "Don't cry," whispers Daniel. "We can be together."

"No, we can't." A flush of tears spills down Ana's face. "I have to go."

Daniel stands with her. "Don't leave. Let's go somewhere private to talk."

"No!" she cries. "Julia needs my help. Lali is fussy and Rafa didn't return home last night."

"Ana, please," he whispers. He reaches gently for her hand. "At least let me take you back to Vallecas."

Ana looks at their clasped hands, her eyes swollen with tears. "I'm begging you," she says. "Please, stop. You're making this harder and it's hurting me."

Daniel releases her hand.

"Thank you." She reaches out and touches his cheek. Her words are spoken between sobs. "You are wonderful. Truly." She looks up at him, lips quivering. "But you can't love me. You don't understand me. Goodbye."

Ana kisses him and runs from the garden.

119

They stand in line for blood.

One following the other, the Crows march to the crowded jail cell. They ask Rafa questions. They ask the same questions again. And again.

"What was your friend's full name?"

"I don't know."

"How old is he?"

"I don't know."

They don't believe him. They hold up a picture of Fuga. Where did they get it?

"How could a man who is weeping, leaking loss from the depths of his soul not know his *amigo*'s name? You're a liar."

Rafa reaches through the bars of the cell for the photo. They snap it away. *"Él quería ser torero,"* Rafa tells them. He wanted to be a bullfighter. That's all. He tells them over and over.

"And you?" they demand.

Rafa hangs his head. I pledged to protect him, he should say. But he won't. The Crows don't deserve the satisfaction.

When the Crows step away, a prisoner next to him whispers, "Don't tell them anything. Say you're from Andalucía, that you'll leave Madrid and never come back."

A man from Vallecas is also in the jail cell. He moves toward Rafa. "He's right, Rafa. Tell them nothing. You've never been arrested. They don't know you like they know us. Come to the back of the cell where you can't be seen. They'll keep you for a few weeks. When you leave, walk the road south out of Madrid. They'll follow you for a while. Just keep walking. Eventually, Father Fernández will come for you. He always does. He'll take you back to Vallecas. That's how this works."

Rafa won't listen. He grabs the bars of the cell, trying to shake them loose as he screams. "Where is he? Please, let me bury his body!"

The man from Vallecas puts a comforting hand on his back.

Rafa can't bear the thought of Fuga being dumped in a common trench, his limp body salted with the dirt of his own shovel.

"Who is your family?" demand the Crows.

The question drills into Rafa. His family. If they discover who he is, could Julia, Antonio, and Ana all be punished? Will their years of hard-won anonymity in Madrid be ruined?

You know my family, he wants to say. When I was a tiny boy, I watched you murder my father. My parents were respected teachers. You arrested our mother for sewing flags.

And don't forget the children.

Rafa's head snaps like a whip. The voice is Fuga's. It's clear and close.

This reminds me of our time in the detention hole in the boys' home. Remember?

Rafa looks behind him. He looks out from the bars.

Not out there, amigo. *In here.*

120

Puri dashes from cabinet to cabinet, opening and closing the drawers.

Where is 1940, the year of her birth? Her parents met and married in Madrid. If they adopted her, it would have been from the Inclusa. Her pulse beats. Her neck is chilled with sweat. How long has she been in the basement? Has Sister noticed the keys are no longer on her desk?

She pulls a file. Year: 1940.

Assigned orphan numbers mean nothing to her. She must look for her parents' names.

It's taking too long. She slams the file drawer.

She heads to the next row of cabinets. *Faster, Puri. Faster!* She rounds the corner and hits a wall. As she falls to the cement floor, the iron keys tumble from her hand and clatter to the ground.

Puri looks up. It's not a wall. It's the stark white robes.

Of Sister Hortensia.

She stares at Puri. Silent.

"Sister . . ." Puri scrambles to rise.

"No, stay there. I've been standing here, listening to you rifle through each cabinet. I knew you were up to something. Don't compound your filthy sins with lies. What are you looking for, Purificación? Tell me."

The slap of condescension and the words *filthy sins* spark a familiar anger in Puri. "I'm looking . . . for answers," she says flatly.

Sister Hortensia opens her arms. "Ah . . . and what would you like to know?"

Sister looms over her, eyebrows raised, waiting. Her expression suddenly softens. She releases a deep sigh and drops her arms.

"Just tell me, child."

Puri notes the retreat of her grimace,

her look of concern. She makes the decision.

"Am I adopted, Sister? And if so, did my parents have to pay a ridiculous sum of money for me?"

Sister Hortensia's mouth pulls into a tight smile as she nods slowly. "Ridiculous. I see. You are looking for your story, Purificación? Why didn't you just say so? Well, let us begin. Once upon a time there was a pair of filthy Reds who created a degenerate child. The Reds cared more for themselves than for the baby so they abandoned her. The girl was blessed to be adopted by a wonderful, loving couple. But despite many years of efforts, and even the girl's own best intentions, she remained rotten on the inside. You see, like her Red parents, she cared more for herself than others — so much that she stole keys to a private file library, trespassed, violated privacy laws, and committed crimes against the country of Spain. Oh dear, how shall the story end? Perhaps I should find the police and let them decide."

"No. Please," cries Puri.

"*Sí.*" Sister Hortensia nods. "The police

607

or the Guardia Civil will best know how to handle this." Her voice deepens and she speaks through gritted teeth. "Hand me the keys."

Puri reaches for the keys and throws herself at the feet of Sister Hortensia.

121

You don't understand me. You're making this harder and it's hurting me. How could she say those things? He's equal parts upset and angry.

Daniel returns to the hotel and Carlitos rushes to his side. "Will she be coming back? Can anything be done?"

Daniel shakes his head. "I don't think so, Buttons."

Carlitos balls his small fists. "Lorenza says that Ana is in trouble because she stole something. But I know that can't be true."

"Don't believe Lorenza."

"*Ay,* of course not! Lorenza and the man from the embassy are making trouble together."

Daniel stops to face Carlitos.

"Which man from the embassy?"

Carlitos hesitates.

"C'mon, Buttons. I need your help. Which man from the embassy?"

Carlitos leans toward Daniel and points up to the lobby where Nick is sitting. "The one we spoke of, his father. Don Juan. But, *señor,* don't bother yourself with this. It's just gossip and whispers from the basement."

"What else have you heard in the basement?"

Carlitos looks around quickly. He takes a breath. "They say Lorenza flatters Don Juan so he'll give her American dollars and information. She wants the attention of all the men. Lorenza dated Rafa, but only because Fuga rejected her. Rafa broke up with Lorenza and now she's angry. They say Lorenza is jealous of Ana and writes secret notes to scare her. Sweet Ana has no idea it's Lorenza."

Carlitos shakes his head dramatically. "So much silliness. But I know something about Lorenza that no one knows." He nods, beckoning Daniel closer. "Lorenza's father," he whispers. "He wears a cape. He's a Guardia Civil. Of course Rafa doesn't know. I'd bet a pail of *pesetas* that Ana doesn't know either."

Daniel stares at the bellboy, trying to process the information:

Lorenza has been writing notes to Ana?

Rafa was dating Lorenza?

Lorenza's father is a Crow. Ben's words return to him:

Steer clear of those fire engine lips. You don't know who she's flapping them to.

"Thanks, Buttons. Your help is worth more than a pail of *pesetas.*" He removes a large bill from his wallet and gives it to Carlitos.

His attempts at maturity thin and Carlitos bounces with excitement. He pistols his fingers at Daniel. "Tex-has. Pow! Pow!"

Daniel walks through the lobby to Nick, whose face is still mottled with remnants of the alley incident.

"*Hola,* cowboy," says Nick. "Rough days, eh?"

Daniel sits to face him. "I spoke to your dad. After your fight he said he owed me a favor. So I asked him to get Ana re-hired."

Truth and regret rise to Nick's face. "Oh, Dan, I —"

"Don't worry. I figured it out on my own. Ben filled in the rest."

"It's just — Ana and I — we made a promise." Nick looks around before speaking. "It's so complicated. The embassy, my mom, it's embarrassing for both of us."

"I understand."

"No, I don't think you do," says Nick. His tone softens. "I see your parents together. Your father's a steady guy, an honorable guy. My dad? Shep's a lech. I can't even bring a girl home. He's awful and humiliating. It's a game for him. And sometimes people get hurt. Me. My mother. Ana. Have you spoken to her?"

"Just did."

"And?"

Daniel shakes his head, struggling to hold his emotions in place. "Nick, talk to her for me. Please. I can't let things end like this."

"Sure. I can try," says Nick earnestly.

"I want to help. What do you want me to tell her?"

"Tell her to meet me for dinner. A real dinner. Have her meet me at Lhardy at nine tomorrow. Will you do that? I just need a few hours with her, to talk things through."

"Okay, I'll do it."

Daniel stares at Nick. Can he trust him? "Nick, promise me you'll get Ana there."

"I will. I owe you that and more."

Nick Van Dorn does owe him. But he just told Daniel that he doesn't understand. Nick, Fuga, Ana. They all say he doesn't understand. But he's sure he does. What is he missing?

"Say . . . Dan," stammers Nick. "There's something I want to run by you."

Laura Beth appears in the lobby. She strides toward them in an emerald-green dress and white gloves. "Well, hello there. Daniel, I've asked Nick to show me around Madrid."

Nick looks to Daniel and shrugs sheepishly.

122

"What do you mean, we're leaving?"

"The deal is done, Dan. It was quicker than I thought. Franco wanted to finish things before his fishing trip. We're anxious to get home now. We've booked a flight for the day after tomorrow."

"Well, I'm sorry. I need to stay. Just for a few more weeks. That was the plan."

His mother comes to him on the sofa. "The plan has changed a bit. We'll need you at home, *tesoro.*"

"Are you not feeling well?"

"On the contrary. I'm feeling wonderful."

"We'll need you, well, because we have some news," says his father. "It's mighty exciting."

His mother gently takes his hands in

hers. "Daniel, my love," her face fills with light, "it *is* exciting news. Your father tells me that you knew of our communication with the orphanage, but now it's confirmed. We've adopted a baby."

123

Ana cries at the table. Lali cries in her box.

"Padre," gasps Julia, staring at the priest. "Rafa. Fuga. Please, tell me it's not true."

"I'm sorry, my child." The priest leaves their shack, a small man freighted with duty.

Julia turns pale as paper. She reaches for the table to steady herself. Small movements travel through her limbs until her entire body is quaking.

"Julia," sobs Ana. "I'm so sorry."

"Don't cry. I'm here," whispers her sister, staring into nothingness. "Father Fernández says they will release Rafa in a few weeks."

Despite her sister's pleadings, Ana and

Rafa have failed her. It's not fair of life to ask so much of Julia, to sacrifice so much. The words return to Ana, haunting her heart:

We have five mouths at the table now. No one can lose their job.

The world at the hotel is a fairy tale. That is not our world.

Julia warned her. Repeatedly. But despite the warnings, Ana began to dream from the deepest part of her heart. A trustworthy, honorable young man treated her with kindness and respect. She finally felt safe. She allowed herself to love him. But that was selfish. She put her own hopes and dreams before her family and now they will all suffer because of it.

Ana wipes her tears and lifts her niece from the orange crate, kissing her head and soothing her cries. She must help her sister. She must distract herself from the searing pain of losing her job, of losing Daniel.

The gravity of the situation pushes Julia into a chair.

"I'll ask Luis if you can help at the shop

or clean his home," murmurs Julia. "Father Fernández says the men are taking up a collection for Rafa. We'll have to use the money I saved for the apartment." Julia speaks to the air, making plans aloud.

"Julia," says Ana.

"Yes, we'll use the apartment money."

"Julia," Ana repeats. But her sister ignores her.

"Aunt Teresa. Yes, Aunt Teresa will help."

"Julia!"

Her sister's gaze finally floats to her.

"Lali," Ana says, touching the infant's flushed cheeks. "She has a fever."

124

Rafa leans against the grimy stone wall in the back of the jail cell. Rats gnaw and claw at the soles of his shoes. He wants to go to confession, to be in the sole presence of his dear and trusted priest. Father Fernández understands him. He always listens. He is always interested, always fair.

Rafa closes his eyes. He parts the drapes of the imagined confessional and sits on the smooth wooden bench. He begins his silent confession.

"Hail Mary the Purest," says Rafa.

"Conceived without sin," replies the priest.

"*Padre,* you have supported and guided me since I arrived in Vallecas. I stand now at a crossroads of conscience."

"What troubles you, my child?" asks

Father Fernández gently.

"The concept of sacrifice. You see, I thought sacrifice was doing something reluctantly. But now I question that. My father and mother sacrificed their lives in defense of education. They did it willingly. You have probably heard about my friend Fuga, El Huérfano. He has been promoted to heaven because he made such a grand sacrifice. And, *Padre,* he knew exactly what he was doing.

"Fuga had . . . a knowing. He sensed lies around the infants and threats around Ana. Even in that final moment, he was aware. I stood there in the field, waiting for El Huérfano to twirl the cape, but he did not. I became confused. I had no idea what was transpiring. But Fuga, he knew. He knew a man stood behind us. He knew the man had a gun. But he did not turn.

"At first, I could not abide this. You see, this was not Fuga, *Padre.* He would not turn his back to anyone or anything, not fear, not death. So I've wondered, why did he not face his opponent?

"I've sat in this cell among the rats, *Padre,* asking questions. I realize this sounds crazed, but when I still my mind, I've discovered I can hear Fuga. He brings me thoughts in the dark. And here's what I've discovered.

"Fuga knew that if he turned and ran, multiple shots would be fired. He knew that they might hit the animals or me. So he stood, in majestic stance, his final fight of life, and do you know what?" Rafa's voice quivers with emotion. "He was not afraid.

"And so I confess, dear *Padre,* that I feel confused. Fuga is gone. Taken by a bullet. I should feel guilty and full of fear. But somehow, I feel more connected to my friend and more proud of him than ever. Fuga never compromised. He never apologized for who or what he was. His difficult past was not a burden to him but an inspiration.

"My feelings and this communication with Fuga, it leaves me peaceful but also doubting the balance of my own mind. Yet I feel certain that Fuga has been promoted. I can feel him. He is an angel in a heavenly suit of lights. And do you know what he is doing? He is taking care of the children. All the poor children, the forgotten children, the stolen children.

"El Huérfano is taking care of his own."

125

Daniel lies on the hotel bed, staring at the ceiling. A light knock sounds at the door. He jumps from the mattress, hoping that somehow it might be Ana.

Carlitos walks into the room and closes the door.

All bravado and mischief have fled from his face. He is no longer an errand broker or bellboy. His bottom lip quivers and his hands shake.

"What is it, Buttons? What's wrong?"

Carlitos hides his face in the crook of his arm. He begins to cry.

Daniel kneels. "Hey, it's okay."

"It's not okay," cries Carlitos. "Fuga — El Huérfano — they shot him in the pasture. They've put Rafa in jail."

"Where did you hear this?"

"From Lorenza," sniffs Carlitos. "El Huérfano is dead."

"What? Does Ana know?" he asks.

"Lorenza said she does," nods Carlitos. "*Ay*, I hate Lorenza. This is probably all her fault." Carlitos stamps his foot and trembles with tears.

Daniel soothes Carlitos as best he can, trying to navigate his own emotions and the impulse to run to Vallecas.

The telephone rings. It's Nick.

"Is it true?" asks Daniel.

"Unfortunately. A man from Vallecas was in jail with Rafa and heard the story. They shot Fuga through the back."

Daniel sits with his ear to the receiver, stunned. "Where is Rafa? We need to go to Vallecas."

"Dan, you're not thinking straight. Fuga and Rafa are considered criminals. Rafa doesn't want the authorities to know who he is or that he lives in Madrid. That could endanger his entire family. Once he's released, he'll probably disappear for a while. And Fuga, he was considered a vagabond. They've probably dumped his body in a ditch somewhere with the Protestants."

Daniel recalls his last exchange with Fuga. The promise he made. Their handshake.

"Nick, are you sure they shot Fuga because he was trespassing in the pasture?"

"Of course, why else would they shoot the guy?"

Daniel thinks of the empty coffins in the graveyard. He thinks of the Guardia Civil.

Lorenza. *This is probably all her fault.*

Is Carlitos right? Could Lorenza have given information to her father?

Fear creeps toward him from the vacant spots on the wall that once held his missing photos.

126

The confrontation with Sister Hortensia remains trembling inside of Puri. Her stomach rolls, dread pounds at her temples. The threats. What should she do?

"What's wrong with you, Puri?"

"It's late and I'm very tired. I want to go to bed."

"It's an emergency," scolds Puri's mother, clutching the large bag to her chest. "Julia wouldn't ask unless it was dire."

Puri exits the taxi in the dark and follows her mother through the pitted road into the village of Vallecas. They pass a shawled woman sitting outside a shack who gives them a prickled stare.

"Do you know where you're going?" whispers Puri.

Her mother nods.

"You've been here before?"

Her mother doesn't reply. More secrets.

Puri has never visited Ana's house. Generally, the family meets in a café.

Doors to the shacks stand open, allowing the heat of summer to escape. Puri eyes the crumbling, huddled structures and the people inside. A sewage trench carves its way through the side of the road. This is where they live? How could her parents allow it? Why haven't her parents brought them to live at the apartment? It would be crowded but certainly better than this.

Puri follows her mother and darts through an open door.

"Aunt Teresa," gasps Julia. "Thank you for coming."

"Is she any better?"

"No. She seems to be getting worse," says Julia.

Puri stands in the doorway of the shack, hesitant to enter. Ana approaches and gives her a kiss on both cheeks. "*Hola,* Puri."

Ana's beautiful face is forlorn. "Are you

not feeling well either?" asks Puri.

Ana gives a sweet smile and shakes her head. "Our spirits are a bit low."

"Where is Julia's husband? Where is Rafa?" asks Puri.

"Antonio is at work. Rafa . . . he's at work too," says Ana.

"I don't have any ice or rubbing alcohol," says Julia.

Puri snaps to attention. "You mustn't use either of those with an infant. Alcohol can seep into the bloodstream and lead to poisoning. If her fever is high, we must take her to the hospital."

"No!" The response comes from Ana and Julia, in unison.

"No hospitals," pleads Julia. "Please, Aunt Teresa."

"I understand, dear," she replies.

Have they all gone mad? Of course they should take the infant to the hospital. A fever indicates infection. If left untreated, the child could have a seizure or convulsions. While her mother digs through the bag she brought, Puri rushes to look at the baby.

"Remove the bundling and blanket," instructs Puri. "It's trapping the heat."

Puri holds Lali while Julia pulls off the blanket. Lali cries of discomfort and fever. Once the blanket is removed, Puri dips it in a nearby bucket of water and begins to sponge the child. She looks down at Lali. Her heart goes still. A shiver rises to her skin.

Puri's eyes dart to Julia. "What . . . what is this?" asks Puri.

"What do you mean?" asks Julia. "It's my baby. She has a fever. Help me!"

Puri stares at the baby. She closes her eyes.

¡Virgen Santa! What have I done?

127

Daniel sits at the table, staring into the flickering flame of the candle. He runs his finger across the blue cursive, arched across the bottom of the plate. *Lhardy.*

Nick said he told Ana about the dinner. Did he? Or did he drink too much and forget?

His mother has been shopping for baby clothes, his father arranging immigration paperwork. He spent the day by himself.

Daniel walked through the entire cemetery. He stood alone in the empty metal shed thinking of Rafa and Fuga and the width between their lives and his own. He photographed the soft depression in the bed of straw that used to hold Fuga. He gathered what appeared to be Fuga's sole possessions: a magazine clipping of a Miura bull and a small gold pendant with a crackled enamel image of Blessed Mother Mary. Carlitos will get them to Ana.

He picked up his last rolls of film from Miguel and had lunch with Ben to return the press pass.

"These are some of the pictures Miguel and I chose for the contest. Miguel reprinted the missing photos."

Ben scans the line of images:

General Franco with his father — Shoeless children in Vallecas — Women in line for blood — Fuga in his suit of lights — Children saluting the photo of Franco — Champagne glasses on the Van Dorns' dinner table — The nun with the dead baby — The empty infant coffins — The wicked silhouettes of the Guardia Civil.

Ben rustles with excitement. "Jiminy Christmas. These shots, they're downright provocative, Matheson. *Provocative,* that's the word." Ben exhales a snake of smoke. "That shot of the Guardia Civil — holy Moses."

"Thanks. I need a title for the essay submission. I was thinking . . . 'War After War.' "

"YES!" bellows Ben. "Quick, write that down!" He waves his cigarette enthusiastically, decorating his tie with flakes of burning confetti.

"But the ending," says Ben, "add the bloody self-portrait that you took in the elevator mirror, the one after Nick's fight. That shot, it shows rite of passage."

"You think so?"

"I know so. Your photos have the grit of Capa with the thirst of Dorothea Lange. And seeing a bloody young photographer? That tells a story in itself."

Daniel nods, silent. He flips through the stack of photos and retrieves the print Ben speaks of. He tosses it on the table without looking at it.

Ben eyes Daniel and his enthusiasm retreats. "It's not your fault, Dan. Entering a breeder's pasture is highly illegal. Lorenza's to blame. She felt jilted and became vengeful. She stole the photos from your room. It was Lorenza, not your photos, that led them to Rafa and his friend."

"How can you know that for sure?"

"I don't. But what I do know is that

you're the real deal. You're going to win this blasted photography contest, you'll go to J-School, and you'll come back and get your girl."

"I love your optimism."

"It's undeniable. The world is full of Lorenzas: jealous, deceitful people. But you guys?" Ben grabs the stack of pictures, pulls two from the pile, and sets them side by side. It's the shy picture of Daniel at La Violeta and the picture of Ana, sweetly holding up her knife and fork. "Look at you two. That — is the truth."

Daniel stares at the empty chair across from him. The waiters refill his water glass. He replays the room-service dinner with Ana in his head. They're sitting on the floor, talking, laughing, so comfortable together. He can feel her fingers in his hair, grazing the back of his neck.

No. It's not over.

An hour passes. Two. Three. The restaurant empties and quiet descends. Daniel sits alone amidst a room of vacant tables. The candle is nothing but a flicker of wick in a tiny well of wax. And suddenly, a figure appears, walking toward the table.

Declining offers from the waiters, Nick takes a seat.

They remain silent, one across from the other.

"You spoke to her?" Daniel finally says.

"In person. I went out to Vallecas."

The hush of quiet speaks loudly. The pained look on Nick's face is genuine.

"Her niece is sick. Rafa's in jail. I told her she's not thinking straight and —"

"Just tell me what she said."

Nick takes a breath. "Dan, she says that if you truly do care about her . . . you won't contact her."

Daniel remains motionless, absorbing the painful remark while trying to fight the heartache rising quickly to his throat. He thinks of Fuga. *Don't hurt her.* He vowed he wouldn't. If he truly cares about her, he won't contact her. That's what she said.

"I'm sorry. Maybe —"

Daniel raises a hand to stop Nick, barely managing a whisper. "Got it."

128

The plane ascends. Daniel stares out the window. The landscape, baked brown, fans out beneath him. He sees downtown Madrid, the cemetery, the hotel, Vallecas, and the road to Talavera de la Reina. He watches as Spain shrinks smaller and smaller. He watches until Ana vanishes beneath layers of cloud.

Has Carlitos discovered the box yet? He left it at the front desk. A letter to deliver to the ambassador. A letter to mail to Washington. Five silver dollars and his belt buckle.

Tex-has. Pow. Pow.

His eyes close, defending his masculinity against the rising tears. He is angry, gutted hollow, and so impossibly sad.

He wakes to the sound of a meal being

served. He has no appetite.

"Oh, good, you're awake," says his mother. "Hold your sister please while I use the restroom." His mother hands the baby to Daniel.

His sister.

They came to Madrid for oil business. He's leaving with a shattered heart and his parents are leaving with another child. Had they planned this all along? Did they adopt the child from the Inclusa? Daniel looks down at the infant.

She smiles at him, her face alive with joy and wonder. She quiets his pain.

"You're happy," he says. "Did your ears finally pop?"

She bats her tiny feet and in the process one of her socks falls off. Daniel takes her foot in his hand. The baby's smallest toe is nearly nonexistent. "You barely have a fifth toe," he whispers. "Your foot looks like a four-leaf clover."

The baby smiles and a dimple appears on her left cheek. Her eyes bind to his. They stare at each other.

"Thank you, dear," says his mother upon her return.

"I'll hold her for a while. She's so happy. I like her," says Daniel.

"Well, I hope so. She's your sister now."

"Did you see her foot?"

"There's nothing wrong with her foot. She just has small toes. Don't let your father hear you. He's already groused about the cost of the adoption. She's perfect." His mother kisses the baby's downy hair. "Aren't you just the sweetest girl, Cristina? Isn't everything just perfect?"

He hopes his mother feels that way when she returns to Dallas. She'll have to cope with the questions. Adopting a child from a foreign country will set her even further apart from society. And Daniel has questions of his own. How much does it cost to adopt a child? Where did the empty coffins really come from? Who are the baby's birth parents? As the girl grows up, will she wonder about them? And —

Will she long for Spain as he already does?

129

Rafa walks alone down the two-lane road that winds away from Madrid. As expected, the Crows follow him for a few miles until they're convinced he truly is departing. Once they're gone, Rafa slows his pace.

"Don't worry. Someone from Vallecas will come for you. They always do," whispered the man in jail.

He stands alongside the road. Day turns to afternoon and folds into evening. He thinks of Fuga, his traveling partner for over ten years. He sees them walking the roads from Barcelona, sleeping under the olive trees, and punching the memories from each other. He feels his *amigo.* Close.

It was supposed to be three weeks. Three months in jail have left him shades paler and thinned. But somehow, he is stronger. Clearer. *Sí,* life is struggle. But he will commit wholly to the struggle and find meaning in it, rather than trying to silence it. Fear is an unholy ghost, but it is the one thing that Franco and the Crows can never take from him — his freedom to fight fear. The realization fills him with confidence. On the floor of the jail cell he scratched a proverb for future inmates:

Just when the caterpillar thought the world was over, it became a butterfly.

As the sky loses its light and his legs begin to ache, a car pulls to the side of the road.

The smiling face of Father Fernández greets him through the open passenger window. Rafa does not recognize the driver or the car, but doesn't care. Father Fernández has come for him. He is going to Vallecas. He is going home.

Rafa climbs into the vinyl back seat. It's hot, holding tight to the temperature of the day. "How is my family?" he asks.

"Some changes but they are well,"

replies the priest. "Antonio was given a night job at the Pegaso Truck Factory. More money and much better than garbage collection. Ana has a new job too. Lali was quite sick for a while but seems to have recovered. We'll catch up on everything soon enough." He hands Rafa a bundled cloth. Inside are an orange, olives, and a clutch of black bread.

A newspaper sits on the seat next to Rafa. A picture of Generalísimo Franco stares silently at him. Rafa looks at the picture and smiles. He leans back on the warm seat and closes his eyes.

You don't know me, Generalísimo, but I know you.

I am Rafael Torres Moreno and today, I am not afraid.

At 68, General Franco shows no signs of wearing out or wishing to retire. He gives no indication of sharing his power to any significant degree with anyone as long as he maintains his physical and mental health. Thus he is expected to continue to rule for the foreseeable future as he has in the past.

"Contingency Paper — 1961: Succession Problem in Post-Franco Spain"
John F. Kennedy Presidential Library and Museum
November 1, 1961

January 20, 1961

Mr. President [Kennedy],

On behalf of various Spanish democratic groups, we are addressing this letter to you on this date, which symbolizes an end and a beginning, because we understand that when you take the oath of office today as President of the United States of America, you will assume, together with the obligation of preserving, protecting, and defending your country's Constitution, that of ensuring the survival and triumph of freedom throughout the world and maintaining and strengthening the unity of the Western World.

. . . Lastly, Mr. President, we Spanish democrats hope that, with your skill and your help, we can very soon fully obtain for Spain what the great Abraham Lincoln desired and obtained for his country: ". . . that this nation, Under God, shall have a new birth of freedom, and that government of the people, by the people, and for the people shall not perish from the earth."

We sincerely extend to you again our best

wishes for a successful administration. Very respectfully yours, [Personal signatures representing] The Christian Democrat Left, The Spanish Workers' Socialist Party and the General Labor Union, Democratic Action, Democratic Republican Action

from declassified letter to President John F. Kennedy (delivered to the U.S. Embassy in Madrid on January 20, 1961) John F. Kennedy Presidential Library and Museum

"We in the United States feel grateful to Spain and Spanish culture, which contributed so much to American life," Nixon said in brief remarks interrupted by screaming jetliners moving into position at Madrid's Barajas Airport.

"Particularly in the past 10 years," he continued, "we have seen increased cooperation between the United States and Spain."

He pledged to continue working with Spain's leader, Generalissimo Francisco

Franco, and the Spanish cabinet for peace and for the economic improvement of the two nations.

— HERB SCOTT
from "1.5 Million Cheer Nixon in Madrid,"
Stars and Stripes,
October 3, 1970

Spaniards of all walks of life could see the Americans with all kinds of special privileges — special stores they could shop in, goods that were not available for the Spaniards, cheap gas, all kinds of things, so that they could drive their big gas guzzlers along the small Spanish roads. These were all things that were very irritating to the average person in Spain. The Spaniards were very definitely pushing. What they would have liked on the Foreign Ministry side was to close down Torrejon and to limit severely these extraterritorial rights that the American servicemen had. But, as I say, they were overridden by the military. Franco went along with the military, so that we got our way on almost every issue.

— CURTIS C. CUTTER, U.S. political officer,
Madrid (1970–1972)
Oral History Interview Excerpt,

February 1992
Foreign Affairs Oral History Collection
Association for Diplomatic Studies
and Training
Arlington, VA www.adst.org

■ ■ ■ ■

PART TWO

■ ■ ■ ■

1975
Dallas, Texas

1976
Madrid, Spain

130

Born in Valencia in 1863, Sorolla was orphaned at two years old. He met his wife and lifelong muse, Clotilde, when he was just a teenager. Together in Madrid they —

The museum director appears, pulling Daniel's gaze from the plaque on the wall. "Thanks for coming, Dan. The family appreciates your support."

"My pleasure."

"How's your sister?"

"She's well. Nearly eighteen," he replies. "Hard to believe."

Daniel stands amidst a charity reception in the Spanish gallery of the Meadows Museum. "Quite a collection of Spanish art to have here in Dallas," he comments.

"Yes." The director nods. "I know your

mother was Spanish. Didn't you spend some time in Spain?"

Daniel stares at the painting on the wall. "Yes," he says softly. "Like the Meadows family, we had oil business in Madrid. My sister was born there."

The museum director notes Daniel's enchantment with the painting. "You're a fan of Sorolla?"

Daniel sees Ana's glowing face shining with excitement over the Sorolla book he bought her. He sees her walk into the flowered garden of the museum toward the fountain.

"Dan?"

"Sorry. Yes, a fan of Sorolla," he replies.

"I'd like a Tom Collins, please."

Daniel turns toward the voice. A gray-haired woman stands at the bar. She puts an affected hand to her pearls, greeting a friend. "Bless your heart. You've lost more weight than Patty Hearst. Have a drink."

"Excuse me," says Daniel to the museum director.

He walks through the gallery, exchanging quick pleasantries with those who recognize him.

"Great year for your company," says a man in a turtleneck with thick sideburns. "Your father must be proud to have you on board."

"Thank you," nods Daniel.

"But still the elusive bachelor," says the man's wife disapprovingly. "I hear Laura Beth is divorced. Didn't you two date in high school?"

"What a strong memory you have. Excuse me, ma'am."

He can't exit the museum fast enough. Thunder rumbles in the distance as he jogs to his truck. The angry clouds are the stock of childhood nightmares, like villains descending from the sky. He grabs his camera from the floorboard and looks at the smoky, churning formations. Uninspired, he doesn't press the shutter.

Drops fall against his windshield as he heads toward Preston Hollow. He turns on the radio, hoping to catch a forecast and hoping the horses are in the stable. Instead of a weather bulletin, the station offers a promotion for Foster Grant sunglasses. He turns it off.

Eighteen years. It's been eighteen years and seeing a Sorolla painting or hearing the words *Tom Collins* still throws him into a spiral of memory.

Pathetic.

The storm swells past midnight with threats of tornadoes. Daniel spends the night in the stable with the horses, trying to calm the animals and stay on top of the weather. At 3:00 a.m. the breaking news tone sounds from the radio. He turns the volume dial, listening for the storm bulletin.

"CBS News reports that Generalísimo Francisco Franco, dictator of Spain, has died in Madrid. Despite his team of thirty-two doctors, the end was a struggle for Franco. The dictator came to power thirty-six years ago during the Spanish Civil War, with support from Hitler and Mussolini. Franco ruled his country with an iron hand. Recently, Spain has enjoyed relative stability, especially after reforms introduced in 1959. Leaders of European countries have been guarded in their re-action to the dictator's death and express hope for modern democracy in Spain.

No Western nations will be sending a head of state to the funeral apart from Monaco. Flags around Spain are at half-mast and the general's body is now lying in state at El Pardo Palace. Franco will be buried next week at the Valley of the Fallen. Official mourning will last thirty days."

A haggard and grief-stricken Carlos Arias Navarro, the Prime Minister, speaking to the nation at 10:00 a.m., said in a breaking voice:

"Spaniards. Franco has died. The exceptional man who before God and history assumed the immense responsibility of demanding and sacrificial service to Spain, has given up his life, burned up day by day, hour by hour, in the fulfillment of a transcendental mission."

Then with tears welling up, he read the message General Franco is believed to have written a few days after he fell ill on Oct. 14. The general spoke of his love for Spain and implored his countrymen "to continue in peace and unity" and to "extend the same affection and support you have given me to the future King of Spain, Don Juan Carlos de Borbón."

"Do not forget that the enemies of Spain

and Christian civilization are watching," he added.

At another point he said: "I ask forgiveness from all, as I give my most heartfelt forgiveness to those who declared themselves my enemies. I believe and hope that I had no enemies other than those who were enemies of Spain — Spain, which I will love until the last moment and which I promised to serve until my dying breath, which is near."

Many Spaniards shared the Prime Minister's grief and genuinely felt affection, or at least respect, for the only leader most of the country had known. There was official mourning in the form of black armbands on policemen, and many men wore black ties today. When the hearse with the highly polished wooden coffin went through the gate of the palace a small knot of people applauded and old women wept.

Others were glad to see what they considered a hateful period of Spanish history close and were impatient to get on with the task of forging a more liberal regime.

from "Franco Urged Spain in a Final Message to Maintain Unity"
The New York Times
November 21, 1975

It was with sorrow that I learned of the death of Generalissimo Francisco Franco, who led his country for almost four decades through a significant era in Spanish history. With his passing, I express deepest sympathy to his wife and family on behalf of the Government and people of the United States.

We wish the Spanish people and the Government of Spain well in the period ahead. The United States for its part will continue to pursue the policy of friendship and cooperation which has formed the touchstone for the excellent relations existing between our two countries.

— GERALD FORD, 38th president of the United States (1974–1977)

Statement on the Death of Generalissimo Francisco Franco of Spain
November 20, 1975
National Archives, Collection GRF-0248
White House Press Releases (Ford Administration) 1974–1977

131

Daniel slides the metal box from the closet. He opens it once every few years. Is it good or bad that the defining items of his life can fit into one small box?

His mother's death notice. It mentions that she was a member of the garden club and supported the symphony. It mentions nothing of her vicious battle with cancer.

His Magnum photography prize certificate.

His acceptance letter and J-School diploma from Missouri School of Journalism.

A copy of Ben's recommendation to *National Geographic.*

State Department credentials as a news service photographer.

The memorial card from Ben's funeral.

And as he digs deeper into the box —

The newspaper photo with Ana and Nick at the embassy fashion show.

His photo negatives from Spain and Ana's handwritten captions.

At the very bottom is the stack of envelopes. Seventeen of them, held together by an old rubber band. The eighteenth will arrive next month. They're all from Nick Van Dorn. Every December, without fail, an envelope arrives from Nick. Each contains a photo with a brief message on the back, but never a return address.

He opens one. Nick lies in a hospital bed, his arm in traction.

1959. Skiing in St. Moritz. Tough break. Aren't I punny?

He opens another. It's a wedding picture in the South Pacific but the woman's face is crossed out.

1965. Beach blanket bomb. Married and annulled in three weeks.

He opens the most recent envelope. It's

postmarked last December. Nearly a year ago. From Madrid.

1974. Look where I am. Embassy job. Come back to Madrid!

Daniel looks at the photo. Nick has aged hard. He's not sure he would recognize him on the street. But the woman in the photo has not aged. She's beautiful.

She is Ana.

When Daniel first received the card, he spent weeks staring at the photo. Of course she must be married. Of course Nick mentioned nothing of it. Of course he'd be an idiot to fly to Spain to find out.

What would they even talk about? How after a decade as a photojournalist he succumbed to his father's pleas and joined the business to provide stability for his sister? How he and his father struggled to raise a teen girl in an era of upheaval and free love? How he floundered through Hockadaisy sleepovers, David Cassidy concerts, Kotex errands, and a dreaded debutante ball? Or maybe they could discuss his father's new marriage. No. None of it is interesting.

He looks at the photo. For eighteen years he's carried a torch for a girl he spent a month with in Spain. It used to be an angry, flaming torch.

He and Ben argued about it one night during an assignment in Australia.

"You're disappointed, I get it, but don't play the blame game."

Daniel certainly didn't blame Ana. He didn't blame himself. He blamed Franco.

"Blame's a cop-out, Dan, and you're better than that. It's easier to blame someone or something than do the work. You gotta do the work," said Ben.

"What are you talking about? I've been working my tail off for years."

"Mileage doesn't make the man. You've been working your tail off and you've been pissed off, but you're avoiding the work. The work's in here." Ben tapped his chest. "You don't think I'm disappointed? My parents died in a car accident when I was nine. It messed me up. I clung to books and words because, unlike people, they'd never abandon me. I'm so bad at relationships that no one's ever loved me enough to marry me — or hell, even date me. But I'm not running around blaming anybody. I'm doing the work."

"Which is what, exactly?"

"Letting it hurt. Scraping the rust off my heart. Sitting around this tent fire in the godforsaken bush, freezing my can off, and pondering life's mysteries with my sad-sack cowboy pal, creating memories that will make me laugh."

It made Daniel laugh too. "I can't believe you're actually sleeping in a tent."

"Neither can my bulging disc. But I wanted to see the stars on this side of the earth. Thought if I put myself out here something might come of it. I'm doing the work."

Many years later, he still thinks of Ben's words. What good did anger and blame bring? It polluted him. It didn't empower him. It didn't bring him peace.

It didn't bring him Ana.

Almost any bigtime Dallas socialite is likely to hire Draper's Party Service to handle invitations. That means providing the printed invitations of course, as well as addressing them (you can always tell a Draper envelope — the handwritten lines are flush right), mailing the invitations and keeping track of RSVPs. Draper might also consult with a hostess on whom she's inviting to the party. . . . If necessary, she might even do some matchmaking. Draper has lists of acceptable young men and women who want to attend the fall social events, and will match dates from her list, notifying a young man of his date for a given evening.

"Party Power: Why Society Loves
Ann Draper"
D Magazine, *October 1976*

132

Daniel parks outside of the estate. He pushes the Eagles 8-track into the player and stares out the windshield. He'll sneak in late and slip out early. The grand gala, organized by a professional party planner, is a birthday celebration for his father's new wife. Sissy is a lifelong Dallas socialite. She's thoughtful, patient, and very kind. But she's nothing like his mother.

Prior to the second marriage, the house held tight to the essence of his mom. The spirit of María Alonso Moya Matheson walked barefoot through the expansive rooms. She hummed her favorite melodies and hovered nearby during late paella dinners. He felt her. But over the past months Spanish food, music, and art have all slowly disappeared from his childhood home. Mealtimes have been altered. It's not her fault, but Sissy's presence seems to amplify his mother's absence. It stings.

Today Spain has an absence — their dictator who ruled for thirty-six years. What is Ana's reaction? What is the country feeling? If Ben were alive, they'd be on the phone. Daniel puts his hand on the steering wheel and closes his eyes, listening to the song, letting it hurt. He'll do the work.

A knock sounds on the glass. A clean-cut valet gives him a wave. He rolls down the window.

"Good evening, Mr. Matheson. Your sister thought you might be out here. She said your father will be asking about you."

"Thanks, Buck. You can take it from here. I'll walk up."

Daniel heads down the road. He runs a hand through his hair and steps through the high, pillared gates of the family property. A trail of expensive cars lines the long ribbon lane leading to the fountain and circular drive in front of their Preston Hollow estate. The trees bordering the drive twinkle with tiny gold lights.

The party swings. Tuxedoed waitstaff circulate with champagne and hors d'oeuvres while a jazz singer croons from an interior Juliet balcony. His sister stands with a group of classmates from Hockaday. When she sees Daniel, she darts toward him.

"¡Hola!" She throws her arms around his neck. "No fair hiding in your truck, unless you take me with you," she whispers in Spanish.

"Hola," he laughs. "Thanks for sending Buck with the two-minute warning."

"De nada." She tugs at his sleeve. "Oh my, letting your rebel run? Most men are in suits and you're wearing a blazer and boots. Mrs. Draper will not be pleased. You're sabotaging her matchmaking efforts." Daniel rolls his eyes.

His sister steps back to display her dress. "The new wife bought it for me. It's pretty, don't you think?"

"Very pretty, but don't call her that. Her name is Sissy. And remember, no Spanish. It's unfair. She doesn't understand."

Cristina sighs. "Mom would hate that the house staff speaks English now. It's weird."

It is weird, but he doesn't comment.

"And . . . do not go upstairs. Sissy redecorated. Everything is chintz charming. Dad doesn't like it but won't say anything. Last weekend I found him long-faced, rooting around in the attic. He claims things are missing. Did you steal some of Mom's stuff?"

"I didn't steal it, I rescued it." He smiles.

Cristina grabs his arm. "Oh, Danny, please let me come live with you. My friends, they all love you."

"Shh," he says. "Here they come. Remember, no Spanish."

Daniel's father and his wife circulate toward them through the crowd.

"Happy birthday, Sissy," says Daniel.

"Thank you, Daniel, darling. And thank you for the beautiful flowers!"

"Well done, Dan. You're showing me up," jokes his father. Mrs. Draper, the party sovereign, appears.

"Good evening, Daniel." She surveys his attire and pinches a smile. "So handsome and . . . individual. Funny, I know you were born here but sometimes you seem more Spanish than your sister."

"Thank you, ma'am," he replies, sliding a grin to Cristina.

Ann Draper takes Sissy by the elbow, pulling her toward a newly arrived guest.

"*¡Ay, por favor! No me vengas con tonterías,*" whispers Cristina. "You are not more Spanish than me."

"It's not a competition," laughs their father. "All well at the office today, Dan?"

"Yes. Delta Drilling sent numbers over." Daniel accepts a glass from a waiter and tries to sound casual. "Say, Dad, did you hear? General Franco died."

"I heard it on the news. Must be quite the shock in Spain."

"What do you think Mom would say?" asks Cristina.

Daniel has wondered the very same thing.

Their father pauses, enjoying the memory of his wife. "Honestly, I think María would be very sad."

"Really? Was Mom a fascist?" asks Cristina.

"No," says their father quickly. "Your mother was romantically old-fashioned about Spain. That doesn't mean she was a fascist. I don't think you'd understand. It's difficult." He sighs and leaves to join Sissy.

Cristina stares at the floor.

Daniel slings an arm around her. "As if being adopted from a foreign country and losing your mom isn't difficult," he says.

His sister nods, grateful. "Exactly. Just because I've never been to Spain doesn't mean I won't understand. Don't forget. You promised, Daniel."

"I know."

"We better start planning now. I'll be eighteen before you know it. Adventure in Madrid!" Cristina hugs him and sashays off to rejoin her friends.

Of course Cristina wants to visit her birthplace, that's natural. His mother's adamant refusal to take her to Spain always puzzled him. Perhaps her health was a factor. She felt so compelled to hide her illness.

Jorge, his father's elderly butler, approaches. He's well past retirement age but refuses to consider it. "*Hola,* Jorge."

"*Buenas tardes, señor.* You received a phone call very early this morning. It was an international call and the connection was quite poor. Or perhaps the caller was inebriated. He kept repeating, 'Tell Danny boy, *Franco ha muerto.*' "

"Did the caller give his name?"

"Indeed. It was Dick. Or Nick. Or maybe Rick. *Lo siento,* I can't remember."

Jorge has worked with the family for decades. He left Spain just before the Civil War. Daniel wonders what he thinks of the news. "Jorge, *Franco ha muerto. ¿Qué piensas?*"

Jorge releases a slow, content smile. "Every opportunity lies ahead, *señor.*"

133

"Your sister runs a mile a minute. I'd never keep up with her. You're sure you don't mind this?" asks his father.

"Not at all. Just a bunch of sightseeing. It'll give me a chance to use my camera."

"Sissy wants to take a vacation too. But of course Spain isn't appropriate for us. I think I'll whisk her away for a weekend." Daniel's father appraises him. "It's been a long time since our trip to Madrid. Think it will all come back to you?"

"Maybe," he lies. It's never left him.

"Have a good trip, son. Give a call if you need anything. Do you have enough travelers checks?"

"Plenty. We'll be fine, Dad. I traveled for the magazine with just a backpack."

"I know. But Cristina's hardly a backpacker."

His father is uncharacteristically attentive. There's a quiet sadness in his eyes. "I hope this won't be too emotional for her," he says.

I hope this won't be too emotional for *you,* thinks Daniel.

His father gives a defeated sigh. "I know you didn't want to leave *National Geographic,* Dan. But having you here these past years, well, I couldn't have done it on my own." His gaze turns to his daughter. "And I think we did a mighty fine job."

Cristina stands near the TWA gate in red culottes and large sunglasses. She's speaking Spanish to the gate agents. Cristina has the strength of their mother but a warmth and sense of humor all her own. She comes bubbling over to them.

"Dad, don't look so serious. It's only two weeks. I'll be back before you know it. I just learned that our hotel, the Inter-Continental, used to be the Castellana Hilton. Isn't that where you stayed? The gate agent said it was quite a scene back in the day. Do you remember much about it?"

"Of course I do." Their father's eyes become misty. "Your mother loved it. She loved everything about Spain. It was her true home."

Daniel's eyes begin to well.

"Good grief. You two are worse than a pair of debutantes. Enough of that or I'll start crying and we'll all be a puddle. Mom wouldn't like it."

She's right.

His father hugs Cristina to him as if she might blow away. Without making eye contact with Daniel, he gives an extended handshake and pats him on the shoulder as they board the plane.

"You take the window now," says Cristina, "and I'll take it when we land."

Daniel accepts her plan and takes his place at the window.

Eighteen years. He could have returned to Spain. But he didn't. He could have accepted magazine assignments in Madrid. But didn't. Instead, he remained miles away, both in geography and relationships. Photography kept him on the road, making it easy to be alone. He hopped from assignment to assignment, continent to continent. He developed film in the sea, broke his leg jumping from a helicopter, and worked through two bouts of dengue fever. Fellow Texans referred to him as intrepid, venturous, mysterious. When he returned home to Preston Hollow, people whispered.

Poor Daniel. No wife. He lost his mother to cancer. What did he see covering Vietnam? Had he been jilted by a fiancée along the way? So eligible, especially since he cut his long hair. The casserole committee came out in force.

"My daughter, Fern, made this Stroganoff for you. She isn't married either."

"You remember Alice. She's quite recovered from her episodes."

"Call me sometime. We could have a drink," said Laura Beth.

"The sweet girl in Madrid," his mother commented quietly one Christmas. "It probably wouldn't have worked. The divide was too wide. Memories are hungry, *tesoro.* You mustn't feed them. I'd hate to think that a teenage fling might leave you alone for the rest of your life."

Ben never called it a fling. He understood. He scheduled intersections with Daniel's assignments whenever he could to reminisce.

"Our summer in Madrid, Dan. That summer in Madrid! I'm counting down to the 'I told you so.' "

The card from Nick gave him hope. Cristina's interest gave him courage. Nick was elated to learn of their visit.

Daniel releases a breath, trying to loosen the tightness that's lived in his chest for eighteen years. He looks out the oval window of the plane.

Behind the tall glass terminal window waits his father. He stands, staring at the jet, Stetson clutched in his hands. Daniel squints to sharpen his view.

Despite their many differences, he and his father do have one thing in common.

They love their family.

Daniel buckles his seat belt. He's really doing it. He's returning to Madrid.

134

"There he is! Over here, cowboy."

Nick Van Dorn stands in the arrivals hall of the airport with a young woman. He's older and journey-weathered, but has the same darting eyes and mischievous exuberance. He slaps Daniel into a hug.

"Not fair. You haven't even aged!" says Nick. "I expected you to look mealy and road-torn like the people you photograph. Or maybe my ego hoped the Marlboro Man would pickle a bit." He laughs. "This is my secretary, Ruth."

"Nice to meet you, ma'am," nods Daniel.

"Texas. Nothing but 'yes ma'am' and 'no sir' from this guy," says Nick to Ruth. "So, where's the baby sister? Did she get fed up with you already?"

Daniel waves to Cristina who approaches. "There she is."

Nick's face loses animation. "That's not your little sister," whispers Nick.

"Yes, that's Cristina. And hey, eyes off. She's eighteen, but barely."

"No, I didn't mean —"

"I know exactly what you meant." Daniel laughs. "You haven't changed at all, Nick."

"*Buenas tardes, Señor* Van Dorn! I'm so happy to finally meet you!" says Cristina. Her extended hand hovers, ungrasped, while Nick just stares. "Oh, forgive me, we're in Spain!" she says. "We'll kiss on the cheek, of course."

She turns to greet Ruth. "*Buenas tardes,* I'm Cristina Matheson. Daniel's sister."

"Such a pleasure to meet you, *Señorita* Matheson," says Ruth. "I work for Mr. Van Dorn. On behalf of the embassy, welcome to Madrid." Ruth retrieves a massive bouquet of flowers from the chair.

"*¡Qué bonito! Gracias!*" says Cristina.

While the women chat about the flowers, Nick's brow twists in confusion.

"What is it?" asks Daniel.

"Nothing." Nick looks from Cristina to Daniel. "I guess I'm . . . just surprised that so much time has passed and we're all adults."

Daniel takes in the scenery as Nick drives them to the hotel. Things have changed. Women wear pants and sleeveless tops on the street. There are cars of every color. Foreign magazines appear on corner newsstands.

"You still fighting?" asks Nick.

"Fighting?" calls Cristina from the back seat.

"He means boxing," replies Daniel.

"You didn't know, Cristina? Your brother's a brawler. He hits harder than any drink," laughs Nick. "Don't tell me you never threw a punch while on assignment, Dan. You had to protect your camera gear, right?"

"Well, maybe once or twice. What about you, Nick? Are you still fighting?" Daniel laughs.

"Of course I am. Life's a fight. Speaking of, I'm sure you read about Shep and the New York campaign scandal. What a doozy. But somehow the guy always lands on his feet."

Daniel thinks of the letters he wrote to the embassy and the State Department about Shep Van Dorn. Nothing came of them. Nick is right. Guys like Shep always seem to land on their feet. He should have decked him when he had the chance.

"My parents are finally divorced," says Nick. "Mom is dating a college rowing coach. Great guy. Ben told us about your mom. I'm very sorry. I should have sent a card. But I bet your dad is happy to have you back in Dallas. Try as we might, we both ended up in the same professions as our fathers. Isn't that crazy, Dan?"

"Yeah," says Daniel, staring out the window. "Crazy."

135

The arrival at the hotel takes on a sur-real, dreamlike dimension. The crescent apron drive, the marbled chessboard foyer with steps up to the circular lobby. It's completely the same, yet different. An old film ghosts through Daniel's head and heart. He expects Carlitos to pop out at any moment or Lorenza to stroll by selling cigars and cigarettes. He looks to the corner of the lobby where Ben and Paco Lobo sat for hours. He tries to swallow past the lump in his throat.

Ruth handles check-in while a porter takes their luggage. "Is any of the old staff still here?" asks Daniel.

"I doubt it. Maybe one or two." Nick sighs. "Life's a river, Dan. It moves and it flows. So, is there anything specific Cristina would like to do?"

Daniel follows Nick's gaze to his sister, chattering away to the porter handling her towers of luggage. "Well, think of us when we were eighteen. I'm sure Cristina wants to see as much as possible."

"And what about you?" Nick studies his face. "As much as possible?"

Daniel scans the lobby. The opening to the staircase and the double basements is still there. Dinner with Ana in the staff cafeteria flashes before him. The same narrow elevators are still there. Her reflection in the mirrors blinks through his mind.

"I know you won't ask, so I will," says Nick. "I've reconnected with Ana since I've returned to Madrid. Do you want to see her?"

The question has such an easy answer, yet Daniel stands, frozen. He thinks of his mother's words, that feeding memories is dangerous.

"Let me rephrase," says Nick. "I've reconnected with Ana since I've returned to Madrid. We're friends. She's single. Are you single?"

Daniel nods.

"Okay, then. I'll speak to her."

"Wait, when?"

"Probably today."

"Today? That's so soon," says Daniel.

"Don't worry, I'll give you plenty of notice. I have to speak to her anyway."

"How is she?" asks Daniel. "How's her family?"

Cristina comes running, waving a key. "We're in suite 760!"

Daniel looks to Nick. He shrugs. "A little bird reminded me."

"We stayed on the seventh floor when we were here," he tells his sister.

"Ruth says Ava Gardner used to stay on the seventh floor and that she held wild parties. I'm so excited, I could just burst!" says Cristina, hugging Daniel.

Excited. Is that what he's feeling? No. It feels more like the old unholy ghost of Spain.

Fear.

136

Cristina unpacks her luggage and chatters nonstop. "Your bag is so small. You did bring shoes other than boots, didn't you?"

Daniel assures his sister that he brought clothes and won't embarrass her. He also brought his camera, and for the first time in years he feels an incredible desire to use it.

The layout of the suite is exactly the same. Only the furnishings are different. Two beds are situated in the bedroom. In addition to a radio, there is now a television in the suite and a modern rotary dial phone. The Castellana Hilton crest is gone, replaced by the InterContinental logo.

Eighteen years ago he stood in this exact room, taping photos to the wall.

He looks to the floor in front of the sofa, where he and Ana sat for hours after their room-service dinner. He sees the wall where Ana pulled him in for the kiss that never let go. He thinks of the knife and fork she smuggled to the room. It makes him laugh.

"What's so funny?" says Cristina.

"The amount of luggage you brought," he replies.

Daniel takes a seat on the terrace. Madrid's heat wraps him in its arms, stirring anticipation from ash. He's excited, scared, and nervous. He's never felt this way, not even during a dangerous photo assignment. Nick seems exactly the same, just a bit more mature. Is his unpredictable nature the same? Will he show up tipsy at the hotel room door with Ana in tow? He hopes not. Should he shower and shave just in case?

Cristina joins him on the balcony. She reclines, lifting her long, dark hair and dropping it to hang off the back of the chair. She closes her eyes.

"It's so odd," she says. "I only spent a few months of my life here. But as we drove from the airport, I felt this magnetic tug toward the city. I felt . . . emotional. Do you think I'm having a midlife-adoption-identity crisis?"

Daniel looks at his sister. She doesn't resemble him nor their parents, but doesn't stand out in Dallas as different, either. "Well, I think you're a ways from midlife, Cris. But identity, sure. Roots and heritage, they're powerful. I'm glad you feel a connection here."

"It's more than a connection. I can't describe it. Maybe I'm just excited to be here. Or excited to be out of Texas. Or maybe I'm creating emotions to fill the gap of Mom."

At times his sister displays surprising insight for her age. Sometimes it's as if she's observing and commenting on her life from above, rather than living inside it as an eighteen-year-old girl. He raises his camera and takes her picture.

Nick calls and insists on taking them for a late dinner and a brief walking tour. He says nothing of Ana. Daniel feels too awkward to ask. When they return to the hotel, it's after midnight. They're exhausted but Madrid is just beginning to rouse. Nick and Ruth suggest an outing the following day for Cristina.

"Ruth and I will take you to the Prado Museum and for tea at the Ritz."

"And what about Daniel?"

"I've imposed on Dan to take a meeting tomorrow afternoon," says Nick. "He'll join us for dinner." Nick looks to Daniel, his face completely sincere.

"Tom Collins will meet you at the Sorolla garden tomorrow at three," says Nick.

137

Daniel arrives an hour early, telling himself that he wants to photograph the gardens and fountain. He also tells himself he's not nervous, he's not sweating, and he's not hopeful. So much can happen in eighteen years. She's probably an entirely different person. Maybe he's an entirely different person. That's normal, isn't it? Ana told him that he couldn't understand her. How could he understand her now, with nearly two decades between them?

Visitors stroll and linger amidst the lush, richly scented gardens of the museum. The trickling sound of the fountain is familiar, the figures still whisper, but the courtyard has been slightly altered. The bench they sat upon is no longer there. New benches have been added. He momentarily worries, unsure where they're supposed to meet. The feeling resembles an anxious dream, but one you're able to wake yourself from. They no longer have to hide, he reminds himself. They can be friends openly. Yes, they'll be friends.

He chooses a bench that allows him to remain slightly concealed while still having a view of the entrance. This way, he'll see Ana before she sees him.

The hour approaches. He feels nauseous.

His mother's words return and issue warning. *The divide was too wide,* tesoro. *I'd hate to think that a teenage fling might leave you alone for the rest of your life.*

He sets his camera on a ledge and wipes his palms down the sides of his jeans. This is crazy. He should leave.

He doesn't want to.

They'll say hello, speak awkwardly for a few minutes, and then properly close a door that's been open way too long.

Ana. He feels her before he sees her.

Daniel stands, locking his eyes to the archway draped with ivy and blooms. She walks through the entrance, aglow. Her dark hair swings and lifts in waves as she turns, looking toward their fountain. The skirt of her flowered dress sways about her legs, dancing above her high heels. And then, as if in slow motion, she turns toward him.

They stand, suspended within the eighteen years between them. The moment is a fraction. An instant. Ana's face flares with an enormous smile. She takes a step toward him. Then another. Her stride is suddenly longer, quicker. She's running. His heart vaults as Ana jumps into his arms. His face is in her hair. Her arms are around his neck. She's kissing him. She's crying. He feels her drawing deep breaths against his chest. He pulls her closer, spiraling her small hips beneath his arms.

She looks up at him, her face awash with joy and tears.

"*Hola,* Daniel."

He gently takes her face in his hands.

"*Hola,* Ana."

138

"It's crowded here. Let's go to *El Retiro*," she whispers, threading her fingers through his.

They head down the stairs to the Metro. The platform is clogged with passengers.

Women look twice at Daniel and Ana knows why. He's more handsome than ever. Same lean build with jeans and boots, but an older, more alluring version of his rugged teenage self. Some men soften and stretch with years. Daniel's jawline and cheekbones are more defined. His shoulders and arms cut broader. His disobedient hair is now fashionable.

He catches her staring and laughs. "Do you approve?"

"Definitely," she breathes. "Quick, let's

catch this train before it departs." Ana pulls Daniel by the hand into a throng of people boarding a car. The door closes, sandwiching the passengers together.

Instead of grasping the metal handrail, Ana grasps Daniel. The air inside the car is heavy with heat. A trickle of sweat make its way from Daniel's hairline down to his ear. They stand so close a sheet of paper could not slide between them.

"Is it too hot for you?" whispers Ana.

He leans down to her. She feels the wisp of his breath on her ear. "No. It's perfect."

Ana gazes at him with an elated smile. "I'm so happy you brought your camera. I've been a faithful reader of *National Geographic,* you know."

"Really?"

"*Sí.* The librarians must have thought I was obsessed with travel or that I was some sort of detective. In one of your photos from Buenos Aires there was a faint reflection of you in the glass."

"You saw that?"

"I not only saw it, I asked the librarians for a magnifying glass. I sat there with the magnifier trying to pull you out of that photo." She runs her hand along the seam of Daniel's shirt. "I researched photography to decipher your thoughts. In the beginning, your shots were aggressive, pushing so far into life that it scared me. The aerial photos."

"Sitting on a helicopter skid. Stupid. Early on I pushed boundaries and always tipped toward ten. Felt like I had something to prove, I guess."

"If your photos had horizon lines I learned that meant hope and possibility. A quiet photo meant you were sitting, contemplative, waiting for the moment to come to you."

"Kinda like I've been waiting for this moment?"

She runs her finger down his nose and lips to his chin. "I can't believe it. You're really here. I haven't slept. I've been too excited."

"Me neither. I was so nervous at the museum I felt sick."

"How do you feel now?" she asks.

Daniel takes her hand and presses it flat against his chest. Ana's eyes expand.

"Exactly. If my heart beats any harder or faster, we're in trouble," laughs Daniel.

139

Daniel watches Ana's graceful steps and bright smile. He would follow her to Retiro Park or through a seam in space. He feels like he already has. And suddenly, it all feels worth it.

By the time they arrive at the park, their conversational ease is reestablished. They hold hands as if they never parted.

"Since Nick and Ruth are at the Prado with your sister, I thought this would be convenient. It's very close."

"Yes, I want you to meet Cristina."

Ana's lips give a small smile. "Let's find a quiet spot to talk. It's such a beautiful afternoon."

The sun shines amidst a clear blue sky. Ana leads him to the El Parterre section of the park and chooses a bench under a bouquet of sculpted cypress trees.

"I'm sorry. I can't stop looking at you." She laughs, putting her hand on the side of his face. "Yes, you're older, but you look the same." She weaves her fingers up the back of his neck. "Your hair's a bit longer."

Her hand on his neck is silent yet breaking. "You look the same too. Better."

"No more gold tooth. That was a happy day," she says.

"Have you had a lot of happy days?"

"Some. I'm lucky for the ones I have. After you left, I got a job. Do you remember Paco Lobo?"

"The quiet man who lived at the hotel and adopted a village?"

"Lives at the hotel," corrects Ana.

"Still?"

"Yes. Paco needed a bilingual assistant for a project team. He hired me and put me through business school."

"That's fantastic! That guy was a mystery to me. I couldn't figure out if he was retired or what business he was in."

"Ben didn't tell you?" Ana's voice

drops to a whisper. "Paco hunted Nazis."

"What?"

"After the war, some Nazis received new identities in Spain. Paco came to track them down and report their locations. He reported to Ben and Ben reported to someone in New York. Speaking of Ben, I was so sad to hear of his passing."

The mention of Ben calls emotion to the surface. "Yes. It was so unexpected, just knocked me to my knees. We'd grown close over the years and he was a great mentor. He even visited me on overseas assignments. I had just seen him the month prior."

Ana nods. "I've always wondered if Ben was responsible for Paco hiring me."

They sit, silent in the memory of Ben. Ana softly traces her finger across a large, angry scar on Daniel's forearm. "That's new."

"Not recent, but new since we last saw each other. I don't mind admitting, that one hurt. It cut straight through to the bone. Twenty-two stitches and two infections."

Ana lifts his arm and kisses it. She then takes both of his hands. "Daniel, your mother. I'm so sorry."

He nods, the electricity of Ana lingering on his arm. "Thank you. Mom's death wasn't a surprise, like Ben's. I was able to spend time with her. She was sick for several years, in and out of treatment, always trying to hide it. Cristina was just twelve when Mom died. My father was completely lost. I stayed home after the funeral to pitch in. He begged me to move back to Dallas to help with my sister."

"Did you want to move back?" asks Ana.

"Initially no. But I knew it's what my mom would have wanted. So, I left the magazine, became second father to a teenage girl, and now work with Dad in oil. It sounds crazy, even as I hear myself describe it."

She holds both his hands and heart, full of compassion.

"But, Ana, what about you?"

"Ask me anything. I think we've waited long enough. And just in case you're

697

curious, no, I've never dated Nick," she laughs. "Admit it, you were wondering."

"Well, maybe." He smiles. She knows him so completely and he loves it. "Do you still live in Vallecas?"

"No, I live in the city now. But I still live with Julia's family. Do you live with your dad on the estate?"

Daniel shakes his head. "I have a place of my own nearby."

He looks at her face, so open and eager to talk. "Rafa?" he asks.

She takes a breath, smiling. "Rafa works for the Las Ventas arena. He loves his job. He married the sister of a bull-fighter and they have three beautiful children. Rafa still lives in Vallecas. It's changed quite a bit but Rafa would never leave. He helped build a new church there."

"And your cousin? What was her name?"

Ana gives an awkward chuckle. "Puri. Yes, Purificación is well."

She adjusts her posture and again takes his hands. A bird chirps from the tree above. "We've been apart for so long.

Much has changed in Spain over the years. Since the 1940s each decade has been different. Now that Franco's dead I don't know if anyone outside of Spain could ever understand what it was like. It's so complicated."

She looks into his eyes. "Daniel, I was so foolish. I pushed you away. I said that you could never understand me, yet years have passed and I think you're the only person I can truly feel myself with. You saw my life. You saw my fear. You do understand me. I've imagined and dreamed of being able to speak to you. To apologize and set things right."

"Trust me," he says, brushing a lock of hair from her eyes. "At this moment everything feels really right."

She shakes her head. "Not exactly. There's something you don't know."

Certainly, there is an argument to be made that, because of our close association with Franco, the kinds of economic and financial support that we'd given Spain, in return for the bases, we had prolonged the Franco period. It might have died a more natural death, in the minds of many people in Spain, if we'd not been there to support that structure. But you had the whole spectrum of views on the U.S. role.

— CURTIS C. CUTTER, U.S. political officer, Madrid (1970–1972)

Oral History Interview Excerpt, February 1992
Foreign Affairs Oral History Collection
Association for Diplomatic Studies and Training
Arlington, VA www.adst.org

140

Ana shakes her hands out in front of her. "I'm so nervous."

"Don't be nervous. Just tell me."

She takes a breath, gathering strength, and begins to whisper. "This was many years ago and I'm not sure you'll even remember. But Rafa told me that you took photos at the cemetery."

Daniel nods, remembering his pictures. The picture of the nun with the dead baby anchored his winning contest entry for the Magnum. He tried to share the story of the empty baby coffins with news outlets in the U.S. but no one seemed interested.

"Fuga convinced Rafa that children of Spanish Republicans were being stolen from maternity clinics around Spain. They suspected children were sold to fascist families."

Ana looks over each shoulder, making certain no one is nearby. "But what they didn't know is that it involved my sister, Julia."

"I don't understand."

"Julia was pregnant," begins Ana.

"What do you mean? I took pictures of her baby," says Daniel.

"You took pictures of one of her babies," whispers Ana, trying to bind her emotion. "Julia had twins. The birth was premature. Both infants were small, but one was stronger than the other. The doctors told Julia and Antonio that one of the babies had died. They both had deep suspicions but were too frightened to speak of it. The nuns and doctors were so adamant, and given that our parents were considered Reds, Julia was fearful to say anything."

"Are you saying they stole Julia's baby?"

Ana nods.

"Jeez," breathes Daniel, pulling Ana into his arms. "And how is Julia's daughter now?"

"Lali, she's okay. When she was little, she had a terrible phobia of being separated from Julia. Growing up in Vallecas had its challenges. I have a recent photo of her . . . but I'm not sure I should show it to you."

"I'd like to see it."

Ana opens her mouth to speak but then shakes her head. She leans in to Daniel and kisses him. "I've missed you so much, you could never imagine how I've felt."

"Believe me, I can."

"I don't want to ruin things." A tear falls across her face. "But there can't be any secrets between us."

"Ana, why are you crying? You won't ruin things."

"Promise?"

"I promise," he assures her.

She nods, choking back tears, and reaches in her purse. She hands a photograph to Daniel. "This is Lali."

Daniel looks at the photo. It's not Lali. It's his sister, Cristina.

141

Daniel stares at the photo. "I don't understand. This is my sister."

"No, that's Lali. Your sister is Lali's twin."

Daniel leans back against the bench, trying to absorb what Ana's telling him. Cristina is a twin. Cristina is Julia's daughter. His parents adopted Julia and Antonio's daughter? He's in love with his sister's aunt?

"Daniel?"

"I'm sorry." He pauses. "I'm completely thrown for a loop. Of course I knew she was adopted, and I figured one day she might wonder about her birth parents."

"No, you can't tell her. Please, not yet. This is complicated. I've known of Julia's suspicions for years — that she thought

Lali's twin was alive — but Rafa doesn't know."

He stares at the photo.

"Daniel, please think carefully. No one knows how Spain will transition, if things will change or stay the same. Julia and Antonio have endured a lot over the past eighteen years. Cristina is their daughter. They've had two more children so Cristina is a twin but she also has two other siblings. Think of the difficulty in explaining to Lali and her siblings that there's a twin sister in America. The whys, the hows. Please, promise me you won't say anything. Not yet. Julia must take the lead here."

Daniel nods and hands the photo back to Ana, struggling to make sense of it all. How did this happen? "If it's okay with you, I'd like to speak to my father, to see what he knows."

"*Sí,* I understand."

There's a part of Daniel that wishes she hadn't told him, not yet, that they could have vanished inside their reunion and enjoyed one blissful day together. But there's another part of him that feels overjoyed to share this connection with her. He'd tried so hard to manage his expectations, but the moment he saw Ana in the Sorolla courtyard, his heart exploded.

Ana bites her lip. "Your mind is racing. Are you angry?" she asks.

"No, I'm not angry. I'm just shocked. And selfishly, I'm worried this might be the only reason you wanted to see me."

Ana takes his face in her hands. "No. As I said, I've wanted you for years. I didn't know the truth until yesterday. Nick phoned after seeing Cristina at the airport. He was rattled and said he had seen a ghost. He felt certain you knew something was awry, that you could tell his behavior was odd."

"Nick's behavior has always been odd."

"Only because we tried to stay silent. Silence warps everything. I can accept if there's silence around us, but not between us. Not anymore, Daniel. So I had to tell you right away. But I promise, this is not why I wanted to see you. I wanted to see you" — she leans in close — "because I want to be with you and I hope you might feel the same."

She wants to be with him. Ana runs her

fingers across his back. Her touch is both soothing and stirring. It pulls things into focus. He thinks of Fuga and their hand-shake in the cemetery.

If someone had told him that he could have Ana but it would be complicated — he wouldn't have cared. The endless days and nights on assignment, looking into the sky for her. And now she's right beside him. Her head is on his shoulder. Her hand is washing across his back. Who cares if it's complicated. Life is complicated. He lost his mom, he lost his career, he lost Ben, and for eighteen years he lost the woman he loved. But being with her now has brought every-thing close again. He hears Ben strike a match.

This is your time, Dan. Grab it and run. Do the stuff you see in the movies. It's the stuff no one gets to do. But you can do it, Matheson. I don't want you calling me in ten years whining that you should have done this and should have done that. As the saying goes, it's later than you think.

He turns to face Ana. He kisses her. He kisses her again, holding her close and summoning his every strand of strength to remain decent in public.

"Do you want to meet her?" he finally whispers. "She's a beautiful, strong woman." He smiles. "Like you."

142

Ana and Daniel wait outside the Prado.

"Let's try to remain casual. Nick told her I was meeting Tom Collins."

"The man with lots of ice," laughs Ana.

"I'm glad you're laughing. My stomach is in knots. Maybe we shouldn't hold hands. Cristina will be confused." Their hands reluctantly separate. Ana steps slightly apart.

"There she is," gasps Ana, her voice catching. "*Dios Mío,* she's beautiful!"

Cristina appears on the stairs of the Prado with Nick and Ruth. She wears a green halter dress with leather platform sandals. Nick spots Daniel in the crowd and gives a wave.

Cristina bounds directly for her brother. Alight with excitement, she begins chattering in Spanish.

"Oh, Danny, it's the most incredible museum ever! *The Lovers of Teruel,* have you ever seen it? I bought a postcard to show you, just in case."

"Did you see the Bosch pieces? They were always my favorite."

"*El Bosco,* yes." Cristina nods, serious. "Very confusing. Very you."

Nick greets Ana and pulls her toward the others.

"Cristina, this is our friend Ana. Ana, this is Daniel's sister."

Without hesitation, Cristina greets Ana enthusiastically with a kiss on both cheeks.

"Do you know the story behind *The Lovers of Teruel*?" asks Ana. "It's tragically romantic."

Cristina links her arm through Ana's. "You must tell me everything!"

"Diego and Isabel were desperately in love, but her father did not approve of the match. Diego promised that within five years he would make something of himself and return for Isabel's hand."

"Five years!" gasps Cristina. "That's a long time."

"Five years? That's nothing," laughs Daniel.

While Ana recounts the legend of the lovers, Nick pulls Daniel aside. "You okay?" he asks.

"Spinning. My head is spinning."

Nick appraises him. "But hopefully part of the spinning is good? Seeing Ana?"

"Sorry, yes. It's indescribable. Best day of my life. But now . . . this?"

"Maybe you noticed my shock at the airport. Ana showed you the photo, right? She swore me to secrecy. You have to see Lali. There's no doubt. What are you gonna do?"

"I have to call my father."

"Let's get you back to the hotel. Clear your head. Call your dad and we'll meet for dinner later."

"Ana too?"

Nick laughs. "Dan, wake up. Ana's spent eighteen years dreaming of you. I bet she applied for a passport the day Franco died. I won't be able to pry her off you as long as you're here."

Daniel looks to Ana and his sister. While Cristina chatters, Ana's eyes slide to his. She smiles. Her smile floods him with a sense of hope that pulls all strings of lost time.

143

Cristina lies on the hotel bed, eyes closed. "You're acting weird," she announces.

"No, I'm not."

"Yes, you are. And I can hear it in your voice."

"It's jet lag."

"Liar."

He's never lied to his sister. She understands him better than even his mother did. She truly can hear things in his voice. That means she also sees it on his face. He has to tell her something. He remains quiet for several minutes, hoping she'll fall asleep.

"Remember Ana, the woman you met today?" he asks softly. Maybe she's dozed off.

Cristina snaps upright in bed. "Yes! *The*

Lovers of Teruel. Tell me everything this instant."

His sister's dramatics make him laugh. "Well, you see . . . I've liked Ana for a really long time. She's a wonderful person."

Cristina rolls her eyes. "Oh, please, Danny. We've liked our postman for a long time. *He's* a wonderful person. Fess up."

The vision of Ana running into his arms in the Sorolla courtyard plays back to him.

"Wait, are you blushing? Look at you! Daniel Matheson, what's happened?"

His feelings overtake him. He's so excited and he's dying to tell her. "Cris, I'm still single because . . ." He exhales the words, "I've been totally, completely in love with Ana."

"For how long?"

"For eighteen years. Since I was last in Madrid. She used to work here at the hotel."

Cristina launches from the bed to her brother's side. "WHAT? Does Dad know? Is that why you became such a sad lone wolf? You were traversing the world, trying to forget about your one true love? Oh my gosh, this is fabulous!"

"I'm glad you think so."

"I do think so!" Cristina's eyes begin to pool. "For the longest time I've felt so guilty. People in Dallas imply that you sacrificed your own personal happiness to take care of me."

"That's not true."

"Well, now I know! You weren't saddled with me. Your loneliness was your own fault. You were pining pathetically for a woman thousands of miles away!"

Daniel smiles. "Well, maybe not pathetically."

"Have you kissed her yet? Does she know that you chucked photography for oil? When will she come to Dallas? Wait, are you going to move to Madrid? Can I come with you?"

He laughs. "Get some rest. You'll see Ana tonight at dinner. I'm going down to the hotel's business office for a bit."

Cristina flings herself onto the bed, sweeping her arms open. "Business? Who can think of business? My brother's in

716

love! It's the happy-ending version of *The Lovers of Teruel*!"

144

Daniel pictures his father, alone in his study. His colossal mahogany desk stands before a wall of bookcases. The photos of his mother that lived in the study now live at Daniel's. A sterling frame with a photo of Sissy sits on the desk between his father's Com Key multiline telephone and a crystal decanter of whiskey.

"Of course we paid. Adoption isn't free. But everything was entirely legal and appropriate," his father assures him. "I'm certain our attorneys still have the paperwork. Have you seen the girl? Many people bear a strong resemblance but that doesn't mean they're related."

"I've seen a recent picture. I thought it was Cristina. They're identical. Nick saw Cristina and nearly passed out. Do you remember the name of the person you worked with at the Inclusa?"

"It was eighteen years ago, Dan. I don't remember. Of course your mom would."

"Dad, do you think Mom knew?"

His father is silent. "Hard to say. Again, everything was processed appropriately through the embassy. I do remember . . ." He pauses. "Your mother wondered about the parentage and the family line. The nun told us that Cristina was *sin datos*. I remember I had to ask your mother what that meant. We were told that she was simply dropped off at the orphanage with no note. They had no information on the child and told us that her birth date was an estimate. They also mentioned that some Catholic American couples on the military base had adopted children too. I don't know if that's true but that's what they told us."

"Well, you were doing direct business with Franco, Dad. I'm sure you had privileges."

"C'mon, Dan. Be fair. I've only been to Spain a few times in my life."

"Well, now Franco's dead. If this is true and babies were taken from families, all of this will become public. Everything will have to be acknowledged and set right."

His father releases a heavy exhale. "I'm not so sure, Dan. It depends how the country of Spain moves forward. One of the contractors said they heard Spain is heading toward democracy and amnesty was mentioned."

"Amnesty? Meaning crimes of the past will simply be erased? Surely that won't work."

"It's hard to go back and prosecute three decades of old offenses. The Spanish people have endured so much. They may want to move forward and shed all shackles of the dictatorship." His father clears his throat. "Dan, this friend of yours, is her family angling for anything here? Are they making claims or allegations of any sort?"

"Dad, no. The only claim they're making is for truth between us. They're not even suggesting I tell Cristina yet."

"That's wise. It could open a box of problems prematurely." His father falls quiet. Daniel hears the ring of the decanter's crystal stopper and liquid being poured into a glass. "Son, you've been a devoted guardian. What do you think?"

His father is a proud man. Asking Daniel's opinion indicates enormous respect.

"If we can confirm it, I want to tell her. Cristina knows she's adopted. She's a legal adult and one day she'll want to track down her birth parents. She's also compassionate and resilient. She's helped us through losing Mom, more than we helped her."

"That's certainly true. But we can't rush. We have to do this right, for everyone involved. And we should keep it silent. Your mom would want that. I know a scientist at Texas Medical Center in Houston. Last time we played golf he told us about something called a paternity test. Let me speak to him. If the parents in Madrid agree, we can do the testing, but it must be done here in Texas. I don't want Cristina to hear anything unless we get confirmed results."

"Yeah, it's probably wise to get confirmation first."

"Explain it to your friend and maybe you can speak to her sister. I'll have a private meeting with the attorneys."

His "friend." That's how his father refers to Ana. He has no idea what he's feeling, or has felt, for so many years.

"Well, this is mighty unexpected. Does Cristina suspect something?"

"Not at all. She's having a great time."

"Good. Well, this is an international call so I'll let you go. As you can imagine, I've got a lot to process."

"You and me both," says Daniel.

<u>145</u>

"Ruth, come sit by me. Daniel, you sit next to Ana," says Cristina, playing Cupid. She eyes the new couple with a knowing smile throughout dinner.

"She has no idea that we're talking about her," says Daniel.

"She's adorable. And I think your father's suggestion is wise," says Ana. "I don't know how a test could be conducted in Texas with Antonio here, but perhaps Nick could help? I think Julia would feel more comfortable with testing abroad. It will give her a bit of time. She's terrified that a family member or friend might see Cristina in Madrid. She fears they'll think she gave up the child. Or worse, that she could be punished somehow."

"She's not the one who should be

punished. Madrid's a big city, but I don't want her to be uncomfortable. We could do some sightseeing in other towns. But will she and Antonio agree to meet with me?"

"Yes. And of course they'll want to see Cristina somehow. Nick had an idea and said he'd put something together. Julia and Antonio will be present, but Cristina won't know anything."

Daniel nods, trying to sift through it all yet remain casual at the table. "This is all so crazy."

"I know. It doesn't feel real. But guess what," whispers Ana.

"What?"

She leans in close. "We're in a restaurant together." Her eyes sparkle with excitement.

Daniel looks at Ana's dark eyes and soft hair, her full lips and delicate hands. Each feature is a frame of its own. The light above accents the soft angle of her neck. She wears a maroon dress that clings and drapes to distraction.

She's right. They're finally in a restaurant together. He wishes they could be alone for the evening. He wants to order room service and sit on the floor, with Lola Flores singing through the radio. He wants to stay awake all night, catching up. He wants to kiss her.

Ana reaches beneath the table and takes his hand. "I know," she whispers. "Me too."

146

Daniel waits in the lobby of the hotel. He orders coffee, hoping to revive for the afternoon. He probably looks like Ben, disheveled and untied by the snapping fingers of Madrid. For two nights he's stayed awake with Ana in the lobby long after Cristina says she's jet-lagged and heads to the room.

Last night Ana convinced him they should steal down to the basement.

"No one will see us. We can sit in the cafeteria at our corner table. It will be quiet."

They sat at their corner table, they talked at their corner table, they held hands at their corner table until the sparks between them were so fierce that he pulled Ana onto his lap. A flustered employee discovered them and called a supervisor.

The thought of it makes him smile.

Daniel stands as Ana enters the lobby with Julia and Antonio. The shape of Julia's face, her eyes, they're the same as the little girl who used to hide in his truck, the same as the young woman who offered him the window seat on the plane.

"Bienvenido, caballero," says Antonio.

Their greetings are genuine and warm, but Julia's face carries the ceaseless weight of secrets. Her eyes snap like a camera shutter across the lobby.

"I wasn't certain we should come," says Julia.

"I chose a private table in the back," says Daniel.

"Gracias," replies Antonio, taking a seat. "I told her we must come. What Ana has told us is what our hearts have told us for years."

Daniel removes a photograph from his wallet. Heart pounding, he passes it to Julia.

"¡Ay, Dios Mío!" Julia's hands tremble. She begins to cry.

"Virgen Santa," breathes Antonio. "Rafa's matador, he was right all along." They stare at the image, nodding.

"You call her Cristina," says Antonio.

"Sí. Cristina María Alonso Moya Matheson."

"Muy guapa," sighs Julia.

"My father said Cristina's file at the Inclusa claimed she was *sin datos,"* says Daniel. "The Inclusa told my parents that Cristina's birthday is estimated around March twenty-second but Ana tells me that Lali's birthday is February twentieth."

"The twins were premature. They were so tiny," says Ana. "Daniel and I now wonder if they intentionally separated the birth dates? Maybe the Inclusa wanted people to think they were adopting a child closer to a newborn?"

"And maybe they wanted to put physical distance between twins," says Daniel.

Julia wrings her hands in her lap. *"Señor* Matheson —"

"Please, I'd prefer if you both call me Daniel."

"Daniel," begins Julia. "Please know

that we accuse you of nothing. So many years have passed. You were just a boy. But your sister and my daughter look to be identical. I held the girls in my arms shortly after they were born. I kissed them both, as a new mother does, from head . . . *to toe*," she emphasizes. "Do you understand what I'm saying?"

He nods. "Of course." His nod halts and his eyes expand. "Wait. I do understand."

"*¿Sí?*" asks Julia. Her hands clasp with attendant hope.

"*Sí,* her baby toe."

"Which foot?" asks Antonio.

"Her left foot. I call it the little clover," says Daniel.

Antonio claps his hands to his knees. Ana wraps an arm around Julia.

"Is that correct?" asks Daniel.

"*Sí,*" says Antonio. "Years ago, when Rafa and Fuga believed something was happening, they thought it might involve hundreds of children."

"Once Spain transitions maybe the adoptions will be acknowledged in some way," says Daniel.

Julia smiles. "You're an optimist. For now the acknowledgment will be between us. Please, let's proceed carefully," says Julia.

"I think my father would like that too. But there's a complication. I'm not sure if you know, but when I met Ana eighteen years ago —" Daniel takes her hand.

"Amigo," says Antonio, laughing. "Trust me, we know. We know!"

"They know," agrees Ana. "They've put up with my crying for years."

"Ay, how she lamented. 'Daniel, her Daniel,' like *The Lovers of Teruel!"* says Julia with a flap of her hand. She pauses, then releases a genuine smile. "But truly, I'm so happy for my sister."

"So, you see, I don't want to keep our families apart," says Daniel.

"We appreciate your patience. Julia and I will certainly discuss it," nods Antonio.

"Nick says there's a reception in the Toledo Room of the hotel this afternoon," says Ana. "Apparently, many people will be mingling so you can see her and it won't feel forced." She turns to Julia. "Cristina's stunning and speaks lovely Spanish. But you must brace yourself. She's quite American."

"I don't care what she is," whispers Julia. "She's my daughter."

This was a fascinating period to be there because to watch a country that has been almost 40 years under a dictatorship gradually turn itself into basically a very successful democracy is, from a professional point of view, a fascinating thing to watch.

— WELLS STABLER, U.S. ambassador to Spain (1975–1978)

Oral History Interview Excerpt, February 1991
Foreign Affairs Oral History Collection
Association for Diplomatic Studies and Training
Arlington, VA www.adst.org

147

"I don't think I ever saw this part of the hotel," says Daniel.

"Like the *Placita,* the Toledo Room is preserved from the original palace," Ana explains.

"You were going to give me a full tour years ago but we became distracted with other things."

"Which I'm hoping happens again soon." She smiles.

"*Hola,* buddy!" bellows Nick from the hallway. "Come with me." He corrals Daniel down the corridor to the Toledo Room and throws open the door.

"*¡Bienvenido!*" cheers a small group of people.

Daniel looks around. Who are they welcoming? Wait — him? The reception is for him?

A Spanish guitar begins to play. Cristina runs to him with excitement.

"Please don't be mad. I know you hate being the center of attention, but when Nick suggested a little welcome-back gathering, I thought it was a fun idea!"

A round table with food and drinks sits in the center of the lavish blue room. Nick greets fellow diplomats from the embassy. Daniel cringes, hating parties, but he knows why Nick organized this one. Near the door stand Julia and Antonio.

"Got a little surprise for you," says Nick, pulling him across the room. Carefully displayed on the wall is a selection of his photos from 1957. The hotel. The exotic streets of Madrid. The Van Dorns' dinner party. Rafa. Fuga. Vallecas. Nick. Ana. Standing proudly next to the photographs is an elderly man with bushy gray eyebrows.

"Miguel?" asks Daniel. "Miguel, is that you?"

The man opens his arms and the two photographers reunite with an embrace.

"Miguel, it's so good to see you! I've

thought of you so often. I can't believe it, you kept my duplicate photos, after all these years?"

"*Sí.* A promise is a promise. I also have these photos." Miguel lifts a copy of *National Geographic* from the table. "We followed you through the years, Texano. Ana would run to the shop and ask questions about your photos. Together we dissected every detail and made markings on a map to follow you. *Caramba,* we worried." Miguel puts his hands on Daniel's shoulders. His voice rolls low with emotion. "What a journey you've been on. I am so proud of you, *amigo.* Capa would be proud too."

Daniel doesn't care that his eyes are welling for all to see. Like Ben, the man in front of him believed when others didn't. He gives Miguel another hug and in the process spots Julia and Antonio speaking to Cristina. The conversation appears light and happy. Cristina, ever affectionate, reaches out and touches Julia before she leaves and heads toward the photos. Julia's joy is radiant, even from afar. Ana smiles and squeezes his arm.

Nick regales a press attaché with stories about the photos.

"Look at my busted face!" says Nick. "I had two sinus surgeries after that beating. But you should have seen what Danny boy did to the other guys. He took that picture from the front seat of a taxi on the way to the hospital."

Daniel looks at his self-portrait, taken after the fight, in the mirrored elevator. Staring back at him is an eighteen-year-old kid, standing tall, bloody, and unapologetic, ready to charge against the wind.

Miguel's hand touches his back. "*Ay,* still the same," he says quietly.

Cristina approaches the group. "Who's the smoking man in so many of the pictures?" asks Cristina. "Is that Ben? Your Ben?"

The smoking man. Daniel looks at a photo of Ben, alone on the dance floor. He moves to a beat entirely his own, life pouring in and out of him. He lived hard and played harder. He did the work.

"Yep, that's Ben. You met him once when you were little. He's the one who got me in at the magazine. They needed a bilingual photographer for some projects in South America."

Cristina points to the photo of Fuga. "And who's the bullfighter?"

Fuga sits in the back seat of the car before the *capea*. Hordes of smiling children from Vallecas press against the window. Fuga's hand touches the glass, returning their love and respect.

"Oh, man, that guy was mythic," says Nick. "He ate fire for breakfast. So angry and mean."

"No," says Daniel. "Not at all. He was much more than that. He was special." He reaches out and touches the photo of Fuga, recalling the matador's concern for Ana and his belief about the stolen children.

"Come." Ana gently leads Daniel toward the corner. An elderly and shrunken Paco Lobo sits, his cane resting against the table. His suit jacket, once a perfect fit, now hangs large on his reduced frame. "Here he is, Paco."

The man's hand trembles as he reaches up to adjust his glasses. He peers at Daniel through impossibly thick cataracts that milk his eyes. "Welcome home, Matheson. You certainly kept her waiting long enough."

"Am I a stupid man, or what?" says Daniel.

"Very stupid, I think. But Ben disagreed. He always told me, 'Don't let her marry anyone, Paco. He'll be back.' Ben was your biggest fan, you know."

"And I his."

"Of course, who else would let you steal press badges?" says Paco Lobo.

Daniel feels a tap at his shoulder. He turns to find Cristina, holding hands with a young man in a suit.

"Daniel, this is Jaime," says Cristina.

"*Hola,* Jaime," says Daniel slowly, looking to Ana for answers.

The young man is polite, well-spoken, and clearly nervous. He clings to Cristina's hand tightly.

"Where did you two meet?" asks Ana.

"Jaime is working at the hotel for the summer. He brought my mountains of luggage to the room on the very first day and we just clicked. I've told him all about Texas. He'll be starting university here in the fall. Jaime would like to take me to dinner tonight and sightseeing this week, but of course I told him we'd need your permission."

Daniel looks at his sister. When did this happen and what is she thinking? Their father would object.

He feels Ana's hand in his.

"Oh, I guess that's . . . okay. Actually, I was thinking of taking Ana to Valencia for the weekend. Maybe you'd both like to join us."

"Really?" says Jaime.

"That is, if your parents approve."

"I told you," says Cristina. "He's the best brother."

"Enjoy dinner. Be back by midnight, please," says Daniel.

"Midnight?" says Jaime, confused.

"*Mi amor,* this is Madrid," whispers Ana.

Daniel grants a later curfew and his sister exits with Jaime. "Have we been duped?" he asks. "These past few nights, do you think she was really upstairs, jet-lagged?"

"She may have been upstairs, but she wasn't lonely or jet-lagged," laughs Ana. She smiles. "Speaking of upstairs, we're finally on our own for the evening." She looks up at Daniel, running her fingers along his arm.

He's suddenly desperate to leave the party. Daniel leans down and whispers in her ear. "Room service or Lhardy?"

"Room service. I'll bring my knife and fork."

148

"Don't worry," Ana had assured him the next morning. "They won't give Cristina any information. Believe me, they'll stick to *sin datos.* But maybe you'll learn something."

Daniel leads Cristina through the gates of the Inclusa. He recounts the story of finding the little boy on the street and bringing him into the office.

"How heartbreaking. Was I just left on the street like that, like *Oliver Twist?*"

"You were in fine form when Mom and Dad adopted you. You weren't roaming the street."

Cristina looks up at the imposing building. "It's so . . . austere. I can't imagine our mother coming here," she says. "But thank God she did."

The inside of the Inclusa stands quiet,

more solemn than Daniel remembers. Their footsteps echo across the weary gray tile to the receiving office. After a few moments a nun enters. "*Buenos días.* May I help you?"

"We're here to see Sister Purificación, please."

"Is she expecting you?"

"I don't think so. Please tell her that an old friend would like to say hello."

The nun looks at them appraisingly. "Have a seat in the library. It's the second door on the right."

Cristina slips her hand into Daniel's as they walk down the hall. The hush of the Inclusa inspires whispering. "This is it. My very first home."

"You okay?"

She nods.

They sit at a table in the stark and lonely library. Cristina's orange-and-yellow minidress screams with color amidst the drab books clinging to decades of silence. After an extended period a nun appears in the doorway. She does not enter, but stands, peering into the room. She is of medium height, thickset, and plain of face. Her lips purse, as if holding a button within them.

Daniel stands. "Sister Purificación, so good to see you."

"Hello." The word is spoken so softly it's barely audible.

The nun takes a cautious step forward, peering at them.

"It's been many years, Sister. I'm Daniel Matheson from Texas. We met one summer long ago when I was visiting Madrid. I stayed at the Castellana Hilton. I'm a friend of your cousin Ana."

Puri looks at Daniel and a nerve near her mouth twitches. Her eyes move to Cristina. She stares, unblinking.

"Do you remember me, by chance?" he asks.

Puri breaks her gaze and turns to Daniel. She does not meet his eyes. "I'm sorry. I'm not sure I do." The fingers on both of her hands extend like a starfish and then ball tightly closed.

"Please, have a seat. This is my sister, Cristina."

Puri sits down at the table carefully, as

if the chair might explode.

Daniel looks to Cristina and nods.

"Good day, Sister. It's so lovely to meet you. Thank you for taking the time. I'm on a trip down memory lane, you see. Well, I don't actually have memories, only what I was told by our parents. I came to the Inclusa sometime around spring of 1957. I was *sin datos.* My parents came to Spain from Texas and Mother desperately wanted another child and — well, that's too much detail. My parents came here to the Inclusa and you persuaded them to adopt me."

Puri's eyes widen. "No, no, I didn't."

"Oh, forgive me. Mother always said a young girl spoke very kindly of me. She convinced them that I was worthy and suited for the family. I thought perhaps it was you? If so, you were instrumental in my good fortune."

"Forgive me if I . . . don't recall the situation," says Puri. Her eyes shift to Daniel momentarily and then back to Cristina. "Tell me. Are you happy, child?"

"Yes, Sister."

"You were raised speaking Spanish in

Texas?"

"Yes, Mother was from Galicia and insisted that we speak Spanish."

"And you've been raised in the Catholic Church?"

"Yes, Sister."

"And how are your parents?"

"Mother died six years ago."

"Oh, dear girl." Puri's face pinches with distress.

"My brother and father have done a wonderful job, though."

"Is your father still working in oil?" she asks.

"Oh, you remember our father?" asks Daniel.

Puri pauses, then shakes her head quickly. "Many oil men were in Madrid at the time."

"Yes, our father is still very successful in oil," says Cristina. "Daniel works with him . . . well, he was a great photographer but quit when Mom died. He came home to help raise me."

Puri nods carefully. "I'm very sorry for your loss."

"Thank you. I graduated in May with high honors, Sister, and I've been accepted to Vanderbilt University. I had my debutante ball last year."

Puri's face brightens. "My, how wonderful. What a blessed child you are. Such a lovely young lady with a caring and successful family. Your future sounds plentiful with opportunity."

Daniel watches Puri. She's sincere but solemn. Detached. He vaguely remembers her as a giddy girl, someone who asked a lot of questions. But something has stolen the light from her eyes. Puri must favor her father's side. She's Ana's cousin, but looks nothing like her. Puri must see the resemblance between Cristina and Lali. Does she pretend not to? Is that why she seems so unnerved by their conversation? Of course she has no idea that he has reunited with Ana.

"If my birth parents ever came to inquire about me, would there be record of it?" asks Cristina.

Her question pains Daniel. He has to tell his sister.

Puri shakes her head. "As you said, you were *sin datos*. You arrived with no name, no information. You were likely issued a number. Upon your adoption, a birth certificate was created. In Spain, the adoptive parents are listed as the birth parents."

Cristina nods acceptingly. "Would it be possible to take a tour of the Inclusa? I'd like to see where I slept and played."

"There's not much to see. Our Inclusa is much quieter these days. We don't have nearly as many children. If you were here for a short time as an infant, you would have been in the nursery," says Puri. "But if you'd like, I can ask someone to guide you through."

Puri enlists the help of a young aide to assist Cristina.

"I'll wait here for you," he tells his sister.

Puri rises to leave.

"Sister Purificación. Please, stay a moment?"

149

Puri sits, staring at Daniel. He's relaxed. Quietly confident. So handsome. And so unaware.

"It's nice to see you again," he says.

Puri manages a smile.

"I'm wondering, Sister. Are there many adoptive families who come from outside of Spain?"

"I'm sorry, I don't know," shrugs Puri. She carefully rests her clasped hands on the table. "*Señor* Matheson, what a beautiful life your sister has. Clearly, she wants for nothing and every opportunity lies before her. It brings me indescribable joy to see how profoundly she has benefitted from adoption. That's not always the case."

Daniel looks at her and Puri's nerves begin to tingle. Why does he stare like that? Could he know something? She feels compelled to fill the space.

"You mentioned you were here before. Do you remember our former director, Sister Hortensia? Sister has gone with God, but was responsible for most of the adoptions."

"Yes, I vaguely remember her," says Daniel.

"She would have placed your sister. She placed so many. Plenty have returned looking for her" — she clears her throat — "and I imagine many more will come."

Daniel says nothing, just nods. Silence continues to tick between them.

The look on his face. Discomfort. "Are you unwell, *Señor* Matheson?"

"Forgive me, Sister. I'm very well, just a bit disappointed that you don't remember me. I came here with a lot of questions. I still remember the day we spoke in front of the hotel. You told me I was terrible with secrets and that I liked your cousin Ana. You were right. I did like Ana. And you were also right — I'm terrible with secrets. I don't like them."

But he has no real intimacy with secrets, thinks Puri. His genes are true to his name.

"Sister, could you have known who Cristina's birth parents were?"

Puri's face fills with sadness. She still does not know who her own birth parents are. "You speak of knowing, *Señor* Matheson. The time you speak of, I would have been a teenager, a frightened teenager, at that. My 'knowing' was probably quite limited. Through my own struggles I've learned that knowing is something that evolves. What we think we know can be quite far from the truth. If we continue to seek and ask questions, we may one day find our way into the answers. But sometimes the answers only lead to more questions."

Daniel sits, absorbing her words. "Speaking of questions, what if one day I was to reunite with Ana . . . permanently."

Puri smiles wide. Her face is completely transformed by authentic joy. "Oh, that would be wonderful! Ana is a beautiful human being. She deserves every happiness."

"I agree. Of course I have no way of

knowing how things will progress. But I'm hopeful." Daniel shrugs and smiles. "I'm just trying to imagine the blending of our families — Julia, Antonio, Rafa, my father" — he pauses — "Julia's daughter, Lali, together with my sister, Cristina. I'm told they're the same age." He gives a questioning look. "Perhaps they'll have things in common and become friends?"

Is Daniel speaking hypothetically or does he really know something? He's treading suspicion, searching for air between a break in the waves. She knows exactly what it feels like and she feels badly for him. He has the desire to search and turn over rocks, but also the fear of what might lie beneath. Fear. It's kept her mute and alone for many years.

"Friends," says Puri quietly. "Yes, maybe they could be friends. Maybe one day we could all be friends."

Daniel pauses. "Forgive me for saying so, Sister Purificación, but your path to the religious order has surprised me. But I'm happy you have found contentment," he says.

The familiar twinge appears inside

Puri. He speaks of contentment. He is probably well acquainted with it. He pursues his questions with a rigor of authority. He is never chastised, threatened, or laughed at for seeking explanation. Puri hears the threatening words of Sister Hortensia.

God is calling to you through these questions, Purificación. Rather than sharing your sinful queries aloud, you will devote yourself to contemplation and prayer. You will.

Puri rises to leave. Yes, she sees it all around him. Handsome and kind Daniel Matheson knows contentment, so he assumes she does as well.

"It's not contentment," says Puri, walking to the door. "It's a vocation, from the Latin *vocare,* 'to call.' It's a calling — to love and serve. We all choose to live out our vocations in different ways. Your father has a calling to oil. Your sister mentioned your calling to photography. Our former director, Sister Hortensia, she had a calling to orphans and placed so many of us."

Daniel's brow lifts in surprise.

"Yes. Any life choice involves sacrifice.

Perhaps you've discovered that? I chose to enter this order seeking God, not explanations. So, you see, *Señor* Matheson, after many years of questions and prayer, I finally felt a calling of my own. And my calling was to silence."

"But, something you said," begins Daniel. "It resonates with me. You said that knowing is something that evolves, that what we think we know can be quite far from the truth."

"Yes."

"But what if we actually *do* arrive at certainty? In your opinion, Sister, once we discover the truth" — he stares at her — "what should we do?"

A note of hope rings through Puri's heart.

He knows.

She walks back to the table.

"When you discover the truth, you must speak it aloud and help others to do the same, *Señor* Matheson. Truth breaks the chains of silence." Puri puts a trembling hand to her chest. Her voice drops to a whisper.

"It sets us all free."

Thousands of babies were stolen from their parents during the Franco dictatorship in Spain, but the story was suppressed for decades. Now, the first stolen-baby case has gone to court. The trial is expected to last months. As Lucía Benavides reports from Spain, it's a dark part of Spanish history that is finally getting more recognition.

Between 1939 and the late 1980s, it is alleged that over 300,000 babies were stolen from their birth mothers and sold into adoption.

— LUCÍA BENAVIDES

from "First Stolen-Baby Case from Franco Dictatorship Goes to Court in Spain"
NPR
August 14, 2018

Spaniards after Franco's death and during the transition to democracy entered into what has long been called here a pact of silence, which the new law clearly aims to undo. As the historian Hugh Trevor-Roper put it 40 years ago, about a different regime, "A single personal despot can prolong obsolete ideas beyond their natural term, but the change of generations must ultimately carry them away."

— MICHAEL KIMMELMAN

from "In Spain, a Monumental Silence"
The New York Times
January 13, 2008

AUTHOR'S NOTE

The Fountains of Silence is a work of historical fiction.

The Spanish Civil War and the ensuing thirty-six-year dictatorship of Francisco Franco are, of course, very real. If this novel intrigues you, please research the history of Spain, the Spanish Civil War, and the dictatorship.

I am indebted to the many incredible writers, historians, scholars, diplomats, artists, photographers, and journalists who have chronicled both the dictatorship and the Spanish Civil War. If historical novels stir your interest, I encourage you to pursue the facts, nonfiction, memoirs, and personal testimony available. These are the shoulders that historical fiction sits upon.

I first explored Spain while on tour for

my debut novel. I fell in love not only with the country, I fell in love with its people. From Bilbao to Barcelona, through Madrid to Valencia, Tarragona and beyond, I met readers from varied family backgrounds who displayed deep empathy for hidden history. They welcomed me with open arms and shared insight on conflict, human suffering, and resilience. I discovered that Spain is a classroom for the human spirit.

In 2011, Tamra Tuller and Michael Green at Philomel sent me an article by Raphael Minder from the *New York Times* entitled "Spain Confronts Decades of Pain over Lost Babies." I began to research the Spanish Civil War and the postwar period — from 1936 to Franco's death in 1975, through the transition to democracy. I studied birthright, the many definitions of *fortune,* and the lines that divide. I embarked on research trips to Spain, meeting witnesses who brought the country's history and hardship to life. During my trips I heard common refrains:

It's very difficult to explain.

It's nuanced and complex for an outsider.

You just can't understand.

Like the character of Daniel, I wanted to understand. I wanted to reciprocate the affection, comprehension, and compassion that the people in Spain had shown toward me and the history within my books. As my research progressed, I realized that the refrains were accurate. Not only is it difficult for an outsider to understand, I often found myself asking, "What right do we have to history other than our own?"

My previous projects have contained threads of my own personal family history, so I was able to write those stories from the inside out. When I began my research for what became *The Fountains of Silence,* I realized that if I wanted to write about Spain I'd have to write from the outside in.

So I studied the postwar intersections between the United States and Spain, examining the difficulties between two very different nations attempting to interact and cooperate while also pursuing individual goals.

*How can they bridge the width to under-
standing?*

I then pulled the focus tighter — hopeful young people from different backgrounds, desperate to cooperate, express
love, and pursue truth, but fenced by
culture and circumstance.

*How can they bridge the width to under-
standing?*

During my study and examination, the
fragile tension between history and memory emerged. Some were desperate to
remember and others were desperate to
forget. I was haunted by the descriptions
of the war — and also war after war.
Hunger, isolation, fear, and the socializa-
tion of silence. Suffering emerged the
victor in Spain, touching all sides and
breaking many hearts.

History reveals that, amidst war, the
highest tolls are often paid by the youngest. Helpless children and teenagers
become innocent victims of wretched
violence and ideological pressure. Some
in Spain were orphaned or separated
from their families. Others, like Rafa and
Fuga, were sent to social aid "homes,"
where they were fed a steady diet of

torture. During the postwar period and dictatorship in Spain, young people were left amidst the wreckage to navigate an inheritance of heartache and responsibility for events they had no role in causing. The young adult narrative is what I chose to represent in the story — innocent youths who, instead of pursuing hopes and dreams, became fountains of silence.

Following Franco's death in 1975, Spain began the herculean task of transitioning to democracy. In hopes of pursuing peaceful progress, an amnesty law was passed in 1977 that freed political prisoners and allowed those in exile to return to Spain. The law also granted impunity to those who may have committed or participated in crimes during the war and the dictatorship. The law paved the way for *El pacto del olvido* in Spain, the Pact of Forgetting.

Some historians have described the Pact of Forgetting as necessary for a smooth and peaceful transition. Others question the long-term effects of silence on historical memory, identity construction, and human dignity. Scholars question whether the absence of a common historical narrative creates painful obstructions of justice and trust.

Studies estimate that over three hundred thousand children in Spain were possibly stolen from their birth parents and transferred or sold to families deemed "less degenerate." The adoptions and thefts began in 1939 and lasted into the 1980s. During and after the Civil War, some infants were taken as punishment to those who opposed Franco. In the postwar period, the thefts were seen as a way to "rehabilitate" children who had parents or grandparents with the "Red gene." In later years, the stolen children were said to be part of a continued trafficking operation involving doctors and the Church.

Today, there are many wonderful groups in Spain advocating tirelessly for stolen children. The United Nations has urged human rights investigations. Some have suggested the creation of a special DNA database (as was done in Argentina for stolen children) to pursue truth and reunification. Although this is incredibly complex, I am confident that progress is possible. I am also confident that readers can be part of that progress — particularly young readers.

I am considered a "crossover" author because my books are read worldwide by both teens and adults. It will be the young readers who carry our fading stories, their associated challenges, and necessary dialogue into the future. I have every confidence that the young generation — a generation of empathy — will gently clean the wounds and work together toward strength and healing.

Every nation has scars and hidden history. When stories of historical conflict are read and discussed, we have an opportunity to be united in study and remembrance. In that way, books join us together as a global reading community, but also a global human community striving to learn from the past.

I extend my heartfelt gratitude to the people of Spain and the regions within its borders. Thank you for allowing me to study your history. My hope is that this novel might inspire others to conduct their own research in an effort to learn, grow, and build bridges that will endure the tests of time and historical memory.

When that happens, history will no longer stand between us, it will flow through us.

— Ruta Sepetys

RESEARCH AND SOURCES

The research process for this novel was a global, collaborative effort that spanned eight years. That said, any errors found herein are my own.

My Spanish publisher, Maeva, connected me with people, places, and experiences to bring this story to life. Laura Russo simply went above and beyond. I am forever grateful to Maite Cuadros, Mathilde Sommeregger, Eva Cuadros, Rocio de Isasa, Sara Fernandez, Montse Vintró, and the entire Maeva and SGEL team.

Translator and screenwriter Marta Armengol Royo in Barcelona is often my interpreter for events in Spain. Marta served as a consultant and partner for this project, read multiple drafts, passionately guided my efforts and research, and gently corrected my terrible Spanish. My longtime friend Claus Pedersen is a teacher of history and Spanish in Denmark. Claus worked with me for years, helped me find research materials, advised on many topics, and provided much-needed encouragement. Dr. Almudena Cros is a history professor in Madrid and helped plan and complete my research. Almudena accompanied me for many long days in Spain and for years after, exploring history and the myriad emotions it brings with it. Jon Galdos devoted much time and patience guiding me through Bilbao, Guernica, Getaria, Hendaye, Irún, San Sebastián, and the stunning Basque countryside.

Professor Soledad Luque Delgado is the president of the organization *Todos los niños robados son también mis niños,* which she formed to mobilize and educate people about the disappearance of children during the Franco dictatorship and in subsequent transition years. Soledad believes her twin brother was stolen and has spent many years speaking on the topic and tirelessly advocating for others. Soledad spent time with me in

Madrid and was an enormous help with my research.

Ángel Casero, president of the organization *Adelante Niños Robados,* met with me and explained the history behind the thefts of children, the adoptions, as well as the treatment of women during the time period. Ángel's baby brother disappeared from a medical facility in the sixties and his older brothers were shown the frozen corpse of a child, purported to be their deceased sibling.

Soledad and Ángel invited me to attend a panel presentation and meeting in Madrid devoted to stolen children. The sweltering room was over capacity with attendees. The stories shared were both heartbreaking — such as quests for true identity — and horrific — an exhumed coffin of an infant that did not contain the remains of a child, but instead held the bones of an adult arm. I'm grateful to all of the attendees who shared their personal stories, photos, and hopes for the future. You are constantly on my mind.

During my research I discovered Carlos Giménez's award-winning graphic memoir *Paracuellos: Children of the Defeated in Franco's Fascist Spain*. The heartbreaking stories tinged with humor depicted in the art made a profound impression and informed the characters and journey of Rafa and Fuga.

Father Fernando Cerracedo, a priest in Vallecas for over forty years, generously shared both heart and historical detail of the district that helped me bring the beauty of Vallecas to the story and those in it.

Dr. José Ignacio de Arana served as a physician at the Inclusa in Madrid for over forty years. He explained the structure and daily workings of the Inclusa, which underscored the love and dedication that most doctors and staff had for the children at the orphanage.

Mariluz Antolín and Elena Nieto welcomed me for extended stays at the InterContinental in Madrid, formerly the Castellana Hilton. Mariluz shared archival materials, provided space for research meetings, and allowed me to explore every last corner of the hotel during my stay to create Ana's and Daniel's world depicted in the book.

Antonio López Fuentes, master tailor at Fermín in Madrid, answered my endless questions and allowed me to spend time in the shop with his team to explore the creation and traditions surrounding a suit of lights.

Eduardo Fernández and his father, Antonio Fernández, generously shared their family's story and memories with me. Antonio survived Asilo Durán, a "home" for boys in Barcelona, and became a waiter at the Castellana Hilton.

Efraín Royo Lascorz patiently recounted details and memories of working at the slaughterhouse, contributing information and dimension to the character of Rafa.

Special thanks to Adelaida Caro at the National Library of Spain who welcomed me and assisted me with research.

Javier Pagola and the staff at Lhardy made each research visit magical.

I am very grateful to curator Luis Alberto Pérez Velarde and Blanca Pons-Sorolla Ruiz de la Prada at the Sorolla Museum for their continued help, generosity, and patience with my frequent visits.

771

J. Edgar Williams was consular officer at the U.S. Embassy in Madrid between 1956–1960 and worked with U.S. Ambassador John Lodge. Mr. Williams answered my many questions about foreign relations and shared his memories of Spain during the time period.

Mr. Pierce Allman, former journalist and a lifelong resident of Highland Park in Dallas, shared information that helped me build and understand the character of Daniel Matheson.

Writer and journalist Karen Blumenthal directed and connected me to many resources and toured me around Preston Hollow so I could conceptualize Daniel's home.

While writing and researching, I returned constantly to reference the invaluable works of Robert Capa, Gerda Taro, Paul Preston, Helen Graham, Adam Hochschild, Neil M. Rosendorf, Ángela Cenarro, Larry Collins, and Dominique Lapierre.

I also thank the following for their generous assistance and inspiration:

Anadir, The Association for Diplomatic Studies and Training, American Foreign

Service Association, The Association for the Recovery of Historical Memory, Mary Ann Campbell, the City of Vallecas, Niki Coffman, Corral de la Moreria, *D Magazine,* The Dwight D. Eisenhower Presidential Library, Hilda Farfante, The Foreign Service Journal Archives, The Gerald R. Ford Presidential Library, Hargrett Rare Book & Manuscript Library at the University of Georgia, The Hockaday School, The Hospitality Industry Archives at the Conrad N. Hilton College of Hotel & Restaurant Management at the University of Houston, International Center of Photography, Juan de Isasa, The John F. Kennedy Presidential Library, La Venencia, La Violeta, Lucía Lijtmaer, Low Media, Magnum Photos, Andrew Maraniss, Gerard Solé Martinez, The Meadows Museum at SMU, The National Archives in Washington, D.C., *National Geographic,* Dr. Ann Neely, *The New York Times,* the Ordóñez family, Manuel Benítez Pérez, The Prado Museum, Restaurante Botín, The Rockefeller Foundation Bellagio Center, Sim Smiley, S.O.S. de Bebés Robados, St. Mark's School of Texas, Steve Norris-Tari, Carol

Stoltz, Taberna de Antonio Sánchez, the Harry S. Truman Presidential Library Archives, Dr. Mark E. Young, Patty Young.

The Fountains of Silence was built with bricks from the following books, academic papers, articles, films, and resources:

An American Diplomat in Franco Spain by Michael Aaron Rockland

El año que tú naciste: 1953, 1954, 1955, 1956, 1957, 1958, 1959, 1960

Aquel Madrid que se nos fue . . . 1957–1967 by Antonio Alcoba López

The Basque History of the World: The Story of a Nation by Mark Kurlansky

Be My Guest by Conrad Hilton

Big D: Triumphs and Troubles of an American Supercity in the 20th Century by Darwin Payne

The Big Rich: The Rise and Fall of the Greatest Texas Oil Fortunes by Bryan Burrough

Castellana Magazine: Castellana Hilton Hotel Monthly, 1957–1959

Child of Our Time by Michel del Castillo

Colores del toreo by Paco Delgado

Dances and Cooking Specialties of Spain by the American Women's Club of Madrid

The Dangerous Summer by Ernest Hemingway

Death in the Afternoon by Ernest Hemingway

The Death of Manolete by Barnaby Conrad

Exhuming Loss: Memory, Materiality and Mass Graves of the Spanish Civil War by Layla Renshaw

"Facing up to Franco: Spain 40 Years On" by Tobias Buck, *Financial Times*

"Families of Spain's 'Stolen Babies' Seek Answers — And Reunions" by Sylvia Poggioli, *Morning Edition,* NPR, December 14, 2012

For Whom the Bell Tolls by Ernest Hemingway

Franco by Paul Preston

"Francoist Crimes: Denial and Invisibility, 1936–2017" by Jorge Marco

"The Francoist Repression in the Catalan Countries" by Conxita Mir y Curcó

Franco Sells Spain to America: Hollywood, Tourism and Public Relations as Postwar Spanish Soft Power by Neal M. Rosendorf

Franco's Forgotten Children, documentary film directed by Montse Armengou and Ricard Belis, TV3

Freedom and Catholic Power in Spain and Portugal: An American Interpretation by Paul Blanshard

From Bullfights to Bikinis: Tourism and Spain's Transition to Modernity Under the Franco Regime by Alexandra Lawrence

Ghosts of Spain: Travels Through Spain and Its Silent Past by Giles Tremlett

Give Me Back My Child!, documentary film directed by Montse Armengou and Ricard Belis, TV3

Guide Museo Sorolla

"Haute Couture, High Fashion in the 50s" by Dr. Mercedes Pasalodos Salgado

Hidden Madrid by Mark Besas and Peter Besas

The Hiltons: The True Story of an American Dynasty by J. Randy Taraborrelli

Iberia by James A. Michener

La inclusa que yo viví: 1945–1990 by Dr. Javier Matos Aguilar

Interrogating Francoism: History and Dictatorship in Twentieth-Century Spain edited by Helen Graham

Lavapiés y el rastro by Carlos Osorio

"*LIFE* Goes to a Fancy Madrid Hotel Opening, U.S. Guests Launch Hilton's Latest," *LIFE,* August 3, 1953

"Lorca's Bones: Can Spain Finally Confront Its Civil War Past?" by Jon Lee Anderson, *The New Yorker*

Madrid a pie de calle: fotografías de Manuel Urech by Miguel Á. Urech Ribera

"Memories of Repression and Resistance: Narratives of Children Institutionalized by Auxilio Social in Postwar Spain" by Ángela Cenarro

The Mexican Suitcase, documentary film directed by Trisha Ziff

Nada by Carmen Laforet

National Geographic Live! photography interview series

Never in Doubt: A History of the Delta Drilling Company by James Presley

New Guide to the Prado Gallery, 1957

Niños robados by María José Esteso Poves

"El niño y los pediatras en la Guerra Civil Española," *Cuadernos de Historia de la Pediatría Española, No. 10*

Nos encargamos de todo: Robo y tráfico de niños en España by Francisco González de Tena

Nosotros, los niños de los años 50 by Margarita Gómez Borrás and Lucía Molina Zamora

Of Hearts and Mind: The Hockaday Experience, 1913–1988 edited by Camille R. Kraeplin

The Oral History Reader: Spain 1931–1995, Foreign Affairs Oral History Collection, Association for Diplomatic Studies and Training, Arlington, VA; www.adst.org

Or I'll Dress You in Mourning by Larry Collins and Dominique Lapierre

Paracuellos: Children of the Defeated in Franco's Fascist Spain by Carlos Giménez

"Petroleum in the Spanish Iberian Peninsula" by Octavio Puche Riart, Luis F. Mazadiego Martínez, and José E. Ortiz Menéndez

Practical Guide for the Diplomatic Corps

Accredited in Spain

The Prado Guide: Museo Nacional Del Prado

Proof: The Photographers on Photography, National Geographic series

A Saga of Wealth: The Rise of the Texas Oilmen by James Presley

St. Mark's School of Texas: The First 100 Years by William R. Simon

La Sección Femenina by Luis Otero

"La Sección Femenina: Women's Role in Francoist Spain" by Lara Pugh

The Silence of Others, documentary film by Almudena Carracedo and Robert Bahar

Silk Hats and No Breakfast: Notes on a Spanish Journey by Honor Tracy

The Sleeping Voice by Dulce Chacón

Slightly out of Focus by Robert Capa

Social Register of Dallas, 1953

The Society of Timid Souls: or, How To Be Brave by Polly Morland

Spain and the United States: Since World War II by R. Richard Rubottom and J. Carter Murphy

"Spain Confronts Decades of Pain Over

Lost Babies" by Raphael Minder, *The New York Times,* July 6, 2011

Spain in Our Hearts: Americans in the Spanish Civil War, 1936–1939 by Adam Hochschild

Spain in Your Pocket by Peggy Donovan

The Spanish Civil War: A Very Short Introduction by Helen Graham

The Spanish Cockpit: An Eye-Witness Account of the Political and Social Conflicts of the Spanish Civil War by Franz Borkenau

The Spanish Holocaust: Inquisition and Extermination in Twentieth-Century Spain by Paul Preston

Spanish Leaves by Honor Tracy

"A Spanish Rose for Beatrice. Madrid Applauds U.S. Ambassador's Popular Daughter on Her Debut," *LIFE,* July 9, 1956

"Spanish Village. A Photo Essay" by Eugene Smith, *LIFE,* April 9, 1951

"Spain's First 'Re-Branding Effort' in the Postwar Franco Era" by Neal M. Rosendorf

"Spain's Stolen Babies," *This World —* BBC documentary, October 18, 2011

"Spain's 'Stolen Babies' Attempt to Blow Lid Off Scandal" by Giles Tremlett, *The Guardian,* January 5, 2012

"Spain's Stolen-Babies Scandal: Empty Graves and a Silent Nun" by Lisa Abend, *Time,* April 13, 2012

Stolen Babies in Spain: Human Rights Abuses and Post-Transitional Justice by Kimberly Josephson

"Stolen Babies Scandal Haunts Spain" by Atika Shubert, CNN, April 26, 2012

"The Story of a Boy Who Went Forth to Learn Fear" by the Brothers Grimm

The Sun Also Rises by Ernest Hemingway

Texas Rich: The Hunt Dynasty from the Early Oil Days Through the Silver Crash by Harry Hurt III

The Time of the Doves by Mercè Rodoreda

Transition in Spain: From Franco to Democracy by Víctor Alba

"The Untold Story of the Texaco Oil Tycoon Who Loved Fascism" by Adam Hochschild, *The Nation*

Vallecas: Fotos Antiguas by Sixto Rodríguez Leal

Wind in the Olive Trees: Spain from the Inside by Abel Plenn

Writers in Arms: The Literary Impact of the Spanish Civil War by Frederick R. Benson

A Young Mother in Franco's Prisons: Señora Pilar Fidalgo's Story by Pilar Fidalgo

ACKNOWLEDGMENTS

I am amazed by writers who create and succeed on their own. I am not one of them.

My incredible agent, Steven Malk, guides my steps. I could not dream of a better mentor and friend. Kacie Wheeler manages my days and does so with incredible love and care. She is the epitome of grace.

Liza Kaplan, my brilliant and tireless editor, devoted years to this novel and the associated journey. Liza's talent, creativity, and inspiration keep me going. I am so grateful to Michael Green, who believed in me from the very start. Heartfelt thanks to Ken Wright, Jill Santopolo, Talia Benamy, Shanta Newlin, Kim Ryan, Jen Loja, Felicia Frazier, Emily Romero, Erin Berger, Carmela Iaria, Trevor Ingerson, Theresa Evangelista, Ellice Lee, and my Philomel family for giving history a voice and my stories a home.

None of this would be possible without the beautiful people at Philomel, Penguin Young Readers Group, all of the Penguin field reps, Penguin Subsidiary Rights, Writers House, UTA, Penguin Audio, Penguin Random House Speakers Bureau, and SCBWI. Sincere gratitude to my wonderful foreign publishers, subagents, and translators for sharing my words with the world.

The hands and heart of Court Stevens have touched every page of this novel. Together we walked hundreds of miles (literally) discussing story, history, and memory.

My writing group sees everything first: Sharon Cameron, Amy Eytchison, Howard Shirley, and Angelika Stegmann. Thank you for over a decade of dedication and friendship. I couldn't do it without you and would never want to.

Pam Aanenson, Ruta Allen, Genetta Adair, the Baysons, Mike Cortese, the Faber boys, Brian Geffen, Beth Kephart, the Lithuanian community, Hannah

Mann, Marius Markevicius, Andrea Morrison, the Myers, Niels Bye Nielsen, the Peales, Claus Pedersen, the Reids, Jason Richman, the Rockets, Emmett Russell, JW Scott, Yvonne Seivertson, the Sepetys family, the Smiths, team Schefsky, Mary Tucker, and Steve Vai all contribute to my writing efforts.

Deepest gratitude to my biggest supporters: the teachers, librarians, and booksellers. And most of all — the readers. I appreciate each and every one of you.

Mom and Dad taught me to dream big and love even bigger.

John and Kristina are my heroes and the best friends a little sis could ask for.

And Michael, whose love gives me the courage and the wings. He is my everything.

GLOSSARY

Adelante Come in (when used at an entry)

¿Ah, sí? Oh yeah?

¡Ahí no! Not there!

Alternativa Graduation ceremony from amateur bullfighter to matador

Americano American

Amigo Friend

El Auxilio Social Spain's social aid organization during Franco's dictatorship

Ave María Purísima The Virgin Mary

¡Ay, no! ¡Ay, no! Oh no, oh no

"¡Ay, por favor! No me vengas con tonterías. Oh please. Give me a break.

Basta Enough

El bebé The baby

Bien hecho Well done/Good job

Bienvenido Welcome

El Bosco Dutch painter Hieronymus Bosch

Botones Buttons/Bellboy
Braceros Manual laborers
Bueno Good
Buenos días Good morning
Buenas noches Good night/evening
Buenas tardes Good afternoon
Caballero Gentleman/Sir
Cálmate Take it easy/Calm down
Capea Caping
Caramba Wow
Caray Wow
Cariño Darling
El Caudillo Leader/Leader of armies (in reference to Franco)
Cava Sparkling wine
Chabolas Shanties
Chaquetilla Short jacket worn by bullfighters
Chico Boy
Churros Fried dough dusted with sugar
Claro Clear, understood/Of course
Cocido a la madrileña Stew of chickpeas, meat, and vegetables
Corrida Bullfighting
Cuadrilla The matador's team
¡Cúcú! Cuckoo/Peekaboo
Culón To have a big bottom
De nada You are welcome
¡Dios Mío! Oh my God!

Entonces So/Then

España Spain

¡Espere! Wait!

Estamos más guapas con la boca cerrada We (women) are prettier with our mouths shut

¿Estás ahí? Are you here?

¿Estás bien? Are you okay?

Estás loco You're crazy

Exactamente Exactly

Excelentes Excellent

Fabulosa Fabulous

La Falange Fascist movement founded in Spain in 1933

¡Qué fantástico! How fantastic!

Felicidades Congratulations

El fin The end

Flamenco A genre of Spanish music and dance from Andalusia

Franco ha muerto Franco has died

Fuga Escape

Futbolista Soccer player

Generalísimo General (in reference to Francisco Franco)

González Byass A well-known Spanish sherry producer

Goya Francisco Goya — Spanish painter and printmaker

Gracias Thank you

Los grises The grays. Slang term for police in gray uniforms.

Hermano Brother

Hola Hi

Huérfano Orphan

Inclusa Orphanage

Jerez Sherry

Federico García Lorca Spanish poet, playwright, and theater director

Lo siento I'm sorry

Madre Mother

Maletilla Untrained, amateur bullfighter — a novice

Manzanilla Chamomile; also a type of sherry

Maravilloso Marvelous

El matadero Slaughterhouse

Matador During a bullfight, the one who kills the bull

Mentirosos Liars

Mi amor My love

Ay, mi madre Oh, my mother/Oh, my goodness

Miedo Fear

El momento The moment

Morcilla Blood sausage

Mucho gusto Nice to meet you

Muleta In bullfighting, a stick with a red cloth that is used in the final third of a bullfight

Muy bonito Very beautiful

Muy guapa Very pretty

Nenaza Sissy

Nepotismo Nepotism

Niño Child

No era mi intención asustarte I didn't mean to scare you

No le hagas daño Don't hurt her

Novilladas An event with younger bull-fighters who have not yet achieved the rank of matador

No, soy yo el que lo lamenta No, I'm the one who's sorry

Novillero Junior bullfighter

Oh, qué chiquitita Oh, she's so tiny

Olé Exclamation of approval at a bullfight

Padre Father

Papá Papa

Pasodoble Musical Spanish military march

Pequeñines Little ones

Perdón Excuse me

Periodista Journalist

Permiso marital A set of laws that prohibited a wife from employment, owning property, and traveling away from home without her husband's approval, and in most cases, written marital permission

Pesetas Monetary unit, currency in Spain until 2002

Placita Plazita, plaza

Por favor Please

¿Por qué? Why?

Portales Entrance gates to apartment buildings

Qué bien How good, that's great

Qué bonito How beautiful

Qué duro How difficult/tough

¿Qué haces aquí? What are you doing here?

¿Qué hay, amigo? What's up, friend?

¿Qué pasa? What's the matter?

¿Qué piensas? What do you think?

Él quería ser torero He wanted to be a bullfighter

Querida My dear

Rioja Spanish wine, region in Spain

Rojilla A derogatory term for a woman who aligns with the political left

Sección Femenina Women's section of the Falange political movement in Spain

Señor Sir or Mr.

Señora Madam or Mrs.

Sensacional Sensational

Sentido Bullfighting term describing the bull's realization that the man is the challenger, not the cape.

El Sereno Night watchman

Sí Yes

Siesta Break period in the afternoon when the heat is most intense

Sin datos Without data or information

Sí, tú Yes, you

Sorolla Joaquín Sorolla, Spanish painter

Suerte Luck/Good luck

Tandas Bullfighting term describing a series of passes with the bull

Tesoro Treasure

Texano Texan

Tío Pepe A brand of Spanish sherry produced by González Byass

El torero Bullfighter

El torno The lathe or wheel

Toro Bull

Tortilla de patata Potato (and often onion) omelette

Traje de luces Suit of lights

Tranquilo Calm/Calm down

Uy Oops

El Valle de los Caídos The Valley of the Fallen

Virgen Santa Holy virgin

¡Viva España! Long live Spain!

Voy a ser torero I'm going to be a bullfighter

¿Y qué? And so?
Ya lo veo I can see that
Yo I
Yo hablo español I speak Spanish

General Francisco Franco.

*Francisco Franco waving to the Spanish people
from the balcony of the Royal Palace.*

Children in Spain salute an image of
Francisco Franco on the street.

Maternity ward in Madrid.

Auxilio Social home for boys.

Original ad for the Castellana Hilton in Madrid.

The Guardia Civil.

The Valley of the Fallen, which contains the remains of forty thousand people who fought in the Spanish Civil War. The site remains controversial in Spain.

Nationalist painting on a building in Bilbao, containing symbols of the Falange.

ABOUT THE AUTHOR

Ruta Sepetys (www.rutasepetys.com) is an internationally acclaimed, #1 *New York Times* bestselling author of historical fiction published in more than sixty countries and forty languages. Sepetys is considered a "crossover" novelist, as her books are read by both teens and adults worldwide. Her novels *Between Shades of Gray, Out of the Easy,* and *Salt to the Sea* have won or been shortlisted for more than forty book prizes and are included on more than sixty state award lists. *Between Shades of Gray* was adapted into the film *Ashes in the Snow,* and her other novels are currently in development for television and film. Winner of the Carnegie Medal, Ruta is passionate about the power of history and literature to foster global awareness and connectivity. She has presented to NATO, to the European Parliament, in the United States Capitol, and at embassies worldwide. Ruta was born and raised in Michigan and now lives with her family in Nashville, Tennessee. Follow her on Twitter and Instagram @RutaSepetys.

The employees of Thorndike Press hope you have enjoyed this Large Print book. All our Thorndike, Wheeler, and Kennebec Large Print titles are designed for easy reading, and all our books are made to last. Other Thorndike Press Large Print books are available at your library, through selected bookstores, or directly from us.

For information about titles, please call:
(800) 223-1244

or visit our website at:
gale.com/thorndike

To share your comments, please write:
Publisher
Thorndike Press
10 Water St., Suite 310
Waterville, ME 04901